# Praise for the novels of Maisey Yates

"[A] surefire winner not to be missed."
—*Publishers Weekly* on *Slow Burn Cowboy*
(starred review)

"This fast-paced, sensual novel will leave readers
believing in the healing power of love."
—*Publishers Weekly* on *Down Home Cowboy*

"Yates' new Gold Valley series begins with a sassy,
romantic and sexy story about two characters whose
chemistry is off the charts."
—*RT Book Reviews* on *Smooth-Talking Cowboy*
(Top Pick)

"Multidimensional and genuine characters are the
highlight of this alluring novel, and sensual love scenes
complete it. Yates's fans...will savor this delectable story."
—*Publishers Weekly* on *Unbroken Cowboy*
(starred review)

"Fast-paced and intensely emotional.... This is one of
the most heartfelt installments in this series, and Yates's
fans will love it."
—*Publishers Weekly* on *Cowboy to the Core*
(starred review)

"Yates's outstanding eighth Gold Valley contemporary...
will delight newcomers and fans alike.... This charming
and very sensual contemporary is a must for fans of
passion."
—*Publishers Weekly* on *Cowboy Christmas Redemption*
(starred review)

For more books by Maisey Yates,
visit www.maiseyyates.com.

# MAISEY YATES

## The True Cowboy of Sunset Ridge

HQN

ISBN-13: 978-1-335-62096-5

Recycling programs
for this product may
not exist in your area.

The True Cowboy of Sunset Ridge
Copyright © 2021 by Maisey Yates

The Cowboy She Loves to Hate
Copyright © 2021 by Maisey Yates

This edition published by arrangement with Harlequin Books S.A.

For questions and comments about the quality of this book,
please contact us at CustomerService@Harlequin.com.

HQN
22 Adelaide St. West, 41st Floor
Toronto, Ontario M5H 4E3, Canada
www.Harlequin.com

**Printed and bound in Barcelona, Spain by CPI Black Print**

# CONTENTS

To everyone who doesn't know—you're worthy of love.
You are.

# THE TRUE COWBOY OF SUNSET RIDGE

# *CHAPTER ONE*

IT WAS HIM. The man. The fantasy man. The one who had haunted her dreams for the past six months.

And he was just like Mallory Chance remembered him.

Tall, broad shoulders, broad chest. Tight black T-shirt and black cowboy hat. His midsection looked hard and solid, and so did his thighs.

He was the sort of man who would have terrified her when she was a teenager. Far too much masculinity to cope with—and why bother?—when there were soft, gentle boy band members to fantasize about from the safe distance of a bedroom wall poster.

The sort of man she'd never had the chance to lust after because she'd made her choices about men at fifteen—again, when she'd been more into boy bands than bad boys and had proclaimed chest hair "gross"—and had therefore been stuck with her teenage sensibilities even as she'd transitioned into adulthood.

He looked like danger. The kind you ran from when you were a girl and wanted to run to when you were a woman.

The hardest-looking man in the room.

The one who would win the bar fight.

The one whose muscles looked like they could carry the weight of the whole world. Or possibly just handily beat up her trifling ex.

But it wasn't enough that the man had the most incredible body she'd ever seen.

He had dark blond hair, dark stubble covering a square jaw. His mouth was perfectly formed, and while she'd never given much thought to what constituted a perfectly formed mouth, it turned out she knew it when she saw it.

But his eyes...

That night in the Gold Valley Saloon, six months ago, while she'd been seated next to her boyfriend, they'd locked eyes.

And she'd felt it all the way down to her core.

Like a bolt of lightning.

An electric current that had run beneath her skin and down to her bones and had left her feeling changed.

It had been a moment. A brief moment. But she hadn't been sure how she would breathe through it, let alone carry on like it hadn't happened.

She'd never experienced anything like it before.

Like she was staring down fate in cowboy boots.

But that had to be ridiculous because she didn't believe in things like that, and if she did, she'd have to claim Jared as her fate, not some random guy in a bar.

Jared, the man she'd been with since she was fifteen years old.

What was *that* if not fate?

At least, that was what she told herself. For a long time. Too long.

*Fate.*

The word whispered over her skin, the concept like firecrackers going off in her stomach.

It was why she had come here tonight, and she would be lying if she said that wasn't true.

All the whole way from San Francisco she had played the

music as loud as she could, had rolled the windows down and shouted Taylor Swift lyrics into the wind. Because her world had been broken open, and because Jared had hated that music.

And it didn't matter what he liked or didn't like.

Not anymore.

So she'd done it, because she could. And she had ignored the ten times her cell phone had rung with his number flashing across the screen.

She wasn't taking him back. Not this time. Not ever again.

In the past he'd left her, and she was the one who felt lost. And every time, she'd just get used to him being gone, he'd call and she'd pick up. She'd tell him to come home. Because she needed him.

She hadn't known how not to need him. And she'd done her best to make sure he needed her. Because it was in that space where she felt right. Like she was doing the right thing, and like she mattered.

That sweet spot of contentedness and a little bit of penance.

Not this time. This time she'd done the leaving.

With very little forethought, and nothing more than a couple of haphazard emails, she had decided to uproot her entire life and go to the town of Gold Valley.

Mallory had been enchanted by Gold Valley from the first time she had come to visit her brother, Griffin.

She and her parents had come six months ago, along with Jared. It had been wonderful. And *he* had been horrible. And all of the doubts that bubbled up on occasion had come roaring to the surface during that week.

He'd been bored at dinner; he'd been completely uninterested in all of the quaint brick buildings in town. He'd overslept and missed family breakfasts.

In general, every single one of his bad qualities, every single thing that Griffin hated about him had been on full display.

*Your brother already hates me. I'm not going to perform.*

He'd said that while lounging in the passenger seat of her car, his sunglasses on, holding his phone up, paying it more attention than he did her, as usual. In the years since they'd started dating, his blond hair had transitioned from floppy boy band to man bun, which was the only way he'd transitioned from boy to man, really. He was still handsome in that smooth way, slim and… Well she'd always found him… Cute.

But he was much less cute when bored and slumped in her car, texting on a phone she'd paid for while he acted aggrieved by the vacation she'd also paid for.

He'd said that her brother hated him. And it was true. Griffin *did* hate him. But it was based on things like that, not on nothing.

Griffin had never been shy about his feelings for Jared, and it had always hurt Mallory.

She'd idolized Griffin all her life. Her older brother was her hero and always had been. A shining beacon of everything good and successful. Her parents had always been so proud of him. And so had she.

Eight years older than her, she'd been ten when Griffin had moved out, and it had devastated her. Even though it was the natural order of things. It had changed her world, and she felt unspeakably lonely with him gone.

He'd gone off and gotten his own life. Fallen in love, gotten married.

And then he lost his wife and little girl, and Mallory had lost her beloved sister-in-law and cherished niece.

Even though Griffin had survived, in many ways she'd felt like she'd lost him too.

It was only since he'd met Iris that Mallory felt like she really had them back.

Which, other than the natural pull she felt to the town, had been the reason that she'd come to Gold Valley.

She wanted to be near her brother.

And she needed, desperately, to be very far away from Jared.

Her rental wouldn't be ready for a couple of days, but she just… She hadn't been able to stay. Not anymore.

And there were a whole lot of conversations that she was due to have. Mostly because Griffin didn't even know that she was moving to Gold Valley.

Her *parents* didn't even know what she was doing.

*Par for the course, isn't it?*

Maybe. But there were just… There were some things she just wanted to keep to herself. So she didn't have to feel the sting of their disappointment. Her own failures mixed together with disapproval from the two people who mattered so much to her.

She'd always tried to cover for Jared too. Every time he'd left and hurt her, she'd tried to minimize it. Every time he'd spent three weeks or a month apart sleeping at another woman's house, only to come home, she'd tried to hide that.

And she'd tried to forget it.

Her relationship with Jared was fifteen years long. They'd grown up together. Well, he'd grown up less, she'd grown up more. But they'd shaped their lives around each other and she'd felt like…

Like he was the only person who knew everything about her. Things she'd never shared with her parents, never with her brother… He'd been there for.

And in the darkest time, he *had* been there. And she'd clung to that through every bump in their road.

But this time, he'd cheated. They hadn't been separated before he'd found his way into another woman's bed. She'd thought everything was fine. Great. Better than it had been for a long while, in fact.

And that was what hurt the most.

She gritted her teeth. Feeling angry. And she looked back over at her mystery cowboy.

Yeah, the thing was, he had probably cheated on her before. He had probably been cheating for their entire relationship, and she had just believed him every time he ever said that the only times he'd touched another person had been when they were on a break.

That had hurt. It always had. Because she had never...

He was her one and only.

And of all the silly things that had enraged her, the one that had fueled her down I-5 the whole way here, was... That.

Was the fact that she had seen a man that had made her feel things just with one look that no one, not even Jared, had ever made her feel before.

She'd felt that deep connection back then. Sitting there with a man who was tipsy off his sixth beer, which *she'd* paid for, while she looked at another man who incited some kind of fire in her stomach—it felt unfair. And in that period of time when she'd been in that house she used to share with Jared in a town that she wanted to leave desperately, she just decided she needed to... Go.

And she could stay in a motel until the rental date.

But she needed to be gone. And she had told herself that it wasn't the vision of that man's eyes that had propelled her. She had told herself that it wasn't why, after she checked into the little Wine Country Motel on the edge of Gold Valley, she'd taken a shower and freshened up, put on some makeup for the first time in three weeks and a light, summer dress.

No, she had told herself that none of those things had anything to do with her mystery man.

And then, when she was bored and hungry and had bypassed any number of actual restaurants on the main street of town, walking to the Gold Valley Saloon, she had decided that there was no way she had any hope of seeing that man. Because what were the chances?

But then, in the back of her mind it was there. How people did like their regular bars. How it was possible.

But so not likely that, six months from the first time she had seen him, he would be there. Just happened to be there.

When she was free and unattached, *angry* and needing desperately to reclaim something… Or rather, claim it for the first time.

But there he was. There he was. And she was frozen to the spot in that Western bar, her feet grounded to the rustic wood floor. People were talking and laughing and dancing all around her. Country music was playing over the jukebox, and there was tension filling the air. Couples were everywhere. New and old, she imagined. Some who had forever. Some who were looking for a night.

But he was alone. Standing there at the back of the bar with the neon light from a beer sign shining over him like an unholy sign from the heavens. She knew it was him. Because she could never have confused him with anyone else. Sure, there were other handsome men in the room. But none of them made her feel like fire.

None of them made her feel like everything she'd ever known before was a pale, cardboard construct, and he might be the only thing that was real.

The only thing that could make her real.

She swallowed hard, walking over to the bar. The bartender was a handsome man, broad chested with a quick smile, tattoos up his brown forearms, a bright gold wedding band and a twinkle in his eye. "Can I help you?"

"Yeah. I… Whiskey. Please."

"All right. Any particular kind?"

She didn't know anything about whiskey. "Do you have a special kind that makes you brave?"

He grinned. "Even cheap stuff will do that. Just comes with a headache."

"It's my experience that just about everything in life comes with the headache," she said, trying to smile. And then she felt the hair on the back of her neck stand up. Goose bumps broke out over her arms.

And the fire inside her flared.

That happened a split second before she heard a low, husky voice just behind her.

"It's you, isn't it?"

She turned, and there he was.

So close.

Impossibly close.

And she didn't know if she could survive it.

Because those electric blue eyes were looking right into hers. But this time, it wasn't from across a crowded bar. It was right there.

*Right there.*

And she didn't have a deadweight clinging to her side that kept her from going where she wanted to go, doing what she wanted to do. She was free. Unencumbered, for the first time in fifteen years. For the first damn time.

She was standing there, and she was just Mallory.

Jared wasn't there. Griffin wasn't there. Her parents weren't there.

She was standing on her own, standing there with no one and nothing to tell her what to do, no one and nothing to make her feel a certain thing.

So it was all just him. Blinding electric blue, brilliant and scalding.

Perfect.

"I… I think so. Unless… Unless you think I'm someone else." It was much less confident and witty than she'd intended. But she didn't feel capable of witty just now.

"You were here once. About six months ago."

He remembered her. He remembered her. This man who had haunted her dreams—no, not haunted, created them. Had filled her mind with erotic imagery that had never existed there before, was… Talking about her. He was.

He thought of her. He remembered her.

"I was," she said.

He looked behind her, then back at her. "Where's the boyfriend?"

He asked the question with an edge of hostility. It made her shiver.

"Not here."

"Good." His lips tipped upward into a smile.

"I…" She didn't know what to say. She didn't know what to say, because this shimmering feeling inside of her was clearly, clearly shared and…

Suddenly her freedom felt terrifying. That freedom that had felt—only a moment before—exhilarating suddenly felt like too much. She wanted to hide. Wanted to scamper under the bar and get behind the barstool so that she could put something between herself and the electric man. She wondered if she was ready for this.

Because there was no question what this was.

*One night.*

With nothing at all between them. Nothing but unfamiliar motel bedsheets. A bed she'd never sleep in again and a man she would never sleep *with* again.

She understood that.

Any number of her friends had had those sort of experiences. And she never had.

It was such a funny thing. Because she had felt...

She'd felt lonely and *wrong* a lot of the time in her life. Not quite the golden boy her brother was, though her parents loved her, and she knew it. But she'd had to work to reach even a minimal standard. She hadn't been popular at school. Hadn't excelled at anything in particular.

She wasn't conventionally pretty. Her hair was frizzy and a mousy brown color, her curves unremarkable as far as she was concerned. She had never been popular, but she had never been particularly alternative either.

She hadn't had a big group of friends, until she'd started dating Jared at fifteen. And then suddenly it had changed. He had been fun and funny. He had a whole group of people who surrounded him.

And she'd been one of her first friends to lose her virginity.

She'd felt worldly and sophisticated. Special. Because she knew all about those things that transpired between men and women. It had caused a sort of rift between the old friends she'd had before beginning to date Jared, who were convinced that she was losing herself and her perspective.

She'd felt like she had *gained* perspective. She was in love and they didn't understand. She was ready for deeper, more mature things than they were.

She'd kept it all a secret from her family. Carving out a division between her social life and the life she had at home. Trying to be perfect in every arena. Sexually experienced, confident Mallory at school. Studious and well-behaved Mallory at home, who might not be quite the all-star Griffin was, but who was self-sufficient, didn't cause trouble and didn't give her parents grief.

And then her world had caved in around her. And she'd still tried to keep everything separate.

The impending changes, the fear, then the overwhelming grief.

Only Jared knew. Only he had walked her through it. The course of her whole life had changed—her grades had suffered and her parents had been so disappointed when she'd missed getting into the school she'd wanted to get into.

Because her grades had slipped so much in her sophomore year of high school and had never recovered. And she'd never told them why.

But their disappointment over her not getting into the university she'd wanted, into deciding not to do medical school at all, had only confirmed her decision to keep her other transgressions from them.

But she'd found a purpose in training to be a midwife; she'd gotten a good position, earned good money. And Jared came along for the ride.

It was like everything had stalled out. Like she was still dating Jared in high school.

And her friends had gone on to have all these experiences that she'd never had. They'd left their hometown. They'd dated multiple men. Had one-night stands. Brief flings. Lived alone, lived with roommates, lived with boyfriends.

She'd lived with Jared.

In a house that she'd paid for.

And the sheets on that bed had been paid for by her.

And that was her experience. Her one and only experience.

This was an unknown. And it felt… Dangerous.

But then a surge of defiance shot through her. He didn't know anything about her. And he didn't have to. She never had to see this man again.

*Apparently, you found him in this bar.* And she didn't need to go to it. Ever again.

She was here to start fresh. He didn't know about her experience or her lack of it. Didn't know that she wasn't actually a sex goddess.

For whatever reason, he felt *this*. The chemistry. This pull between them. Because she knew it wasn't about her being... The most beautiful woman in the room.

Not by half.

There were women in here that looked like they belonged between the pages of men's magazines, and they hadn't put on summer dresses to come out and have a drink. They were in painted-on jeans and skintight red dresses. Not flowing, sweet yellow frocks that fell down to their knees.

Some of them had big hair, but it was intentional. Not expanded from humidity and a general lack of knowledge on what to do with it, in spite of it having been on her head for the last thirty years. Their makeup was applied expertly, and not in the sparing manner that she'd used. Some sheer lip gloss, and a little bit of shiny stuff on her eyelids, because she just didn't really know how to handle makeup, and it always made her feel like an imposter. And the one time she tried really hard to follow some kind of a tutorial, Jared had asked her what had happened to her face.

This man didn't know any of that. And for whatever reason, he didn't seem to *see* it. With Jared she'd always felt uncertain. Never sure if she felt more than he did. If she cared more. If the excitement that she felt when they'd kiss had been mostly weighted toward her. If the strongest feelings that existed were on her end. She was confident that he was feeling the same thing, this stranger. And she had never felt that kind of connection with another human being before. That kind of certainty.

The fire was in his belly too.

It was reflected there in those blue eyes.

And she *knew*.

"I just…I just ordered a drink," she said. "You want a drink?"

His lips tipped upward. "I don't need one."

She shifted. Excitement blooming between her legs.

"Right. Right." And she realized that she was just standing there repeating herself, and felt vaguely idiotic.

His lips curved into a smile. It echoed inside her. "If you want to have a drink, that's fine by me. We can stand here and exchange pleasantries for as long as you need to, but I feel like I need to make one thing perfectly clear—I aim to get you into bed tonight."

Her knees nearly buckled. And somehow, she managed to remain standing.

"We don't even know each other," she said.

"We've known each other for six months."

The truth of that burst in her chest. She had known him for six months. She might've seen him once, but she'd thought of him every night since.

And he felt confident enough in that to just *say* it. His confidence was intoxicating. An aphrodisiac and an inspiration. So she took a breath, and she decided she was going to practice that same amount of confidence. Because she wasn't Mallory Chance tonight. She was a mystery woman with the mystery man. And there would be no consequences, no nothing from this.

This wasn't anything.

And she… Didn't even know what that was like.

She'd first slept with Jared to keep him with her. Had been consumed with the idea of impressing him. Had worried about what she looked like, what she'd done, what she'd acted like, nearly every time since.

Everything about sex with him had been complicated.

From the desire to use it to bond him to her, to the trauma that had come as a result, to the way she'd felt like…like she was constantly paying penance for what she'd put them both through. And in fairness to him, he hadn't told her any of that. Had never said he needed it—as payment or anything else—it was just all this inadequacy in her.

Somehow, it had always been about him. About her desperate need to keep him with her.

But this was about her. Because she didn't need to create any kind of feelings in him. He just felt them.

And if she felt a burning, bright piece of guilt embed itself in her heart, she decided to go ahead and ignore it.

Because it had been fifteen years, and maybe she could have something else. Something for her.

And no one ever had to know.

So she reached forward and put her hand on his chest. And her heart was slamming against her breastbone, heat igniting in her body as she made that first contact. And suddenly, he wrapped one strong arm around her waist and pulled her flush against his body. He was hard. And hot.

Everywhere.

And she felt like she was going to… To… No.

Standing there in the bar being held up against this stranger's frame. She had never been this close to an orgasm this quickly in her entire life. Not ever.

"We can do a whole date if you need to," he said, his voice rough. "I'll buy you dinner. Whatever you need. Whatever it takes."

"I don't need that," she whispered. "I don't need a drink either."

"I'll pay the man," he said. "We can be on our way."

It was so casual, and at the same time, anything but. The tension vibrating beneath the words was radiant with heat. She wouldn't have been surprised if it left visible waves.

"I have a motel room," she said, her lips feeling numb, her tongue clumsy. "Just up the street. We can… We can go there. Now."

She had never done anything like this in her life. It was reckless. Crazy. But, she was reasonably certain that he wouldn't murder her, since he apparently came to this bar frequently enough that people would know him. And he came back to it. And… She should be fine. She was willing to excuse anything right now. Absolutely anything.

Whatever got her out of here. Whatever got her in his arms.

Because he was the reason. He was the reason she was here tonight. This was the reason.

Yes, the relationship with Jared had ended because of him. Because she had let it be exactly what it had always been. Had ignored the fact that she had changed and he hadn't. While she'd built shrines to the relationship that she *wished* it were. While she honored an investment of time that truly wasn't worth honoring. That only she cared about.

The truth was, his cheating had been the line in the sand. But there had been a moment right before that echoed in her head.

A birth for one of her clients.

The father on his phone, standing propped up against the wall while the woman was helped primarily by Mallory and her best friend.

*I don't know why she's with him.*

The friend had whispered that to Mallory when they'd taken a break and gone into the kitchen for a moment.

And Mallory had known.

She'd nearly defended it. Because without knowing the woman, she'd known.

And it had disturbed her down to her core.

It was why she'd had to be done. Just done when she'd discovered he'd been unfaithful while living with her. While sleeping in their bed.

And right now she not only felt resolute, but triumphant.

Because at the end of it all, she had a job that she loved, had a family that loved her and had what promised to be a night of incredible sex in front of her.

And Jared was just him. With no one to take care of him. A whiny manbaby who would have to find some other woman to foot the bill of his life. Because she wasn't doing it anymore. She didn't want to.

Her cowboy left a ten-dollar bill on the bar top and tipped his hat at the bartender, who waved slightly. And then, he wrapped his arm around Mallory's waist and started to propel her toward the door.

And a whole bunch of worries and doubts started to crowd her throat, trying to make their way toward her mouth.

What if this just wasn't actually *that* good?

Because that was the other thing. While a lot of her friends had engaged in one-night stands, they'd also said that the drawback to it was that the guy didn't have to care about your pleasure, since he never had to see you again.

And she thought privately that the man she saw all the time didn't care all that much about her pleasure.

That was the worry. The concern. She hadn't been able to get to completion more than half the time with the man who actually knew her body. So… What hope did she have with a guy who didn't know her at all?

What if he didn't enjoy himself? What if it was all a whole lot of… Excitement and buildup, and then it was nothing.

But then she found herself outside, and very suddenly, pinned against the wall of the bar, just around the corner from Main Street, in a shadow, concealed from the street-light. And he was right there, hard in front of her, his eyes glittering.

And then his mouth was on hers. And she didn't have the ability to think of any sort of objection. Didn't have the ability to think of anything. Because she'd never been kissed like this before. Like he was starving.

He consumed her.

Angling his head and sliding his tongue against hers. And she grasped on to him, clinging to his shirt, his shoulders, pushing her fingers through his hair. She rolled her hips back and forth against his arousal, already so close she couldn't believe it. She was slick and hot between her legs, and if he unzipped his jeans and pushed her dress up then, she wouldn't have said no.

In fact she would've said yes.

Emphatically, *enthusiastically* yes.

"Damn," he breathed. "Which motel?"

"Up the street," she said, breathless.

"Better make it quick."

She nodded and fumbled for his hand, taking hold of it and leading him down the sidewalk, her heart thundering so hard she was nearly sick with it.

She opened her mouth to say she didn't do things like this. Ever. But then stopped. Because he didn't need to know that.

They were strangers, and that was why it was exciting.

They were strangers, and that was why this was okay.

Because she needed to be free. She needed to have no ties.

She needed something different. And what better way to spend the inaugural night in Gold Valley than to banish the last regret from her relationship. Oh, not the last regret she would ever feel. She had a feeling regrets would pop up now and again for the next... Well, while.

But the last regret she could remember keenly experiencing because of Jared was that she hadn't been able to rush across the bar and do exactly this six months ago.

No more. No more at all.

Ever.

So she didn't tell him that. If he thought she did this every night? Fine. He could think that she was the very Whore of Babylon; it didn't matter to her.

As long as he wanted to get it on.

And he seemed to.

His hands were rough.

And she couldn't wait until they were all over her body. She didn't know who she was. All these desperate, sweaty images flashed through her mind. Raw desires like she'd never had before.

And why not make every demand that she'd ever had? Ask for everything she'd been afraid to ask for? Because it didn't matter. It didn't matter. The only thing that mattered was that she had fun. The only thing that mattered was that she had him. Her fantasy. This incredible, amazing fantasy.

She was grateful that the door to her room was exterior, so they didn't have to pass through the lobby or anything like that. It was dark, and no one was around. And no one saw as she fumbled with the key—the hotel had an actual key to the door—and got it unlocked, letting them both in.

She closed it firmly behind them and locked it again, chucking the keys on the table.

"So this is my…"

But the words were cut off. Because he dragged her back into his arms again, and he was kissing her, like he had done against the side of the bar, but it was more. Deeper. Because they didn't have to stop.

"Please God, say you have condoms," she said, between kisses.

"Oh, hell yeah," he responded.

"Good."

She didn't have them. She was an idiot.

But a newly separated idiot, so she didn't really… She hadn't thought of it. And she'd been in denial when she'd gone out tonight to see if he would be there, so she hadn't purchased any protection.

She'd been lying to herself. Telling herself she wasn't looking for him, and even if she were, it wasn't to do this.

But he had seemed like the kind of guy who would have some. And praise the Lord, he was.

"More than one," he said, biting her lower lip.

And she went liquid.

His hands moved down her waist, her hips to her thighs, and then he started to push them up, underneath her dress. Rough on her tender skin as they went around to cup her ass.

She moaned when he pushed his hands beneath the fabric of her panties, as he pushed his fingers between her legs and found her wet with desire for him.

Then she found herself completely stripped of her dress. He yanked it up over her head in one, fluid motion, leaving her breathless and standing there in nothing but underwear. She couldn't read his face. Because she didn't know him. But it was intense. Intense and wicked as he stared openly at her.

"You're so pretty," he ground out.

The way he said it. Like it hurt, like it cost him, made her melt. "Really?"

"Woman," he said, "I have made an endless fantasy out of you. But it doesn't match up to this." She had a lot of questions. A lot of questions, but she couldn't ask them, because he moved toward her again and stripped her bra from her body, made quick work of her panties. And she was naked. Except for her sandals. And suddenly, he was down on his knees unbuckling those. Fully clothed.

Then he kissed her ankle, the inside of her knee. Her inner thigh.

And... And...

She wasn't even going to have to ask him.

Because in fifteen years, Jared had never, not once, ever, gone down on her. And she'd always been afraid to ask. Because if the guy didn't want to do it... Well, what could you do? And asking felt... Well, a lot like asking for flowers. Which, you could do, but then the flowers didn't mean much.

She hadn't felt like she'd deserved to ask for it.

And suddenly, she didn't need flowers. Not ever. Because his mouth was *there*. On her. Slick and hot and doing wicked, terrible things that she had only ever been able to fantasize about before. Things that had never...

He was growling. Eating his way into her with a ferocity that defied even her darkest fantasies. And suddenly she was being propelled backward, those wide shoulders pushing her thighs wide. Her back was pressed against the wall, against some bland picture of a landscape, while he pushed her thighs up over his shoulders and pinned her there, his lips and tongue playing havoc with her senses.

And she thought she might die.

And then his fingers worked their way inside of her body.

She was so slick and greedy for him that it was easy. That all she could think of was more.

A desperate, deep need for more.

He worked his fingers in and out of her, pushing her up to heights that were dizzying in their splendor. Ratcheting her pleasure up to a degree that seemed impossible.

She was pulling his hair, pushing his cowboy hat off his head, and then, she shattered. Screamed. She was panting, unable to catch her breath, the waves of pleasure pounding through her not like a sweet, fluttering release, nothing quite like the tentative white rabbits of pleasure she'd experienced before.

This wasn't a shy, burrowing animal. It was a whole thunderstorm. A deluge that she couldn't escape. That wouldn't end.

And he didn't stop.

He kept on licking her, sucking her, thrusting into her. And on the heels of that first wave came another. Another. Sweat broke out over her skin, and she felt both more connected to her body than ever in her life, and somehow outside of it all at once.

And then he moved her legs down from her shoulders, no longer holding her up, and she slid down the wall, in front of him. Fully clothed, down on her knees.

"Delicious," he rasped, and she thought she would burst into flames again. But instead of that, she just kissed him, flinging herself at his fully clothed body, the denim of his jeans rough against her sensitized flesh, that slightly ribbed T-shirt abrading her sensitized nipples. He hadn't even groped her breasts. And in her experience that was right where a man would go first.

*That's right where one man goes first. Every single time. You don't know what men do.*

No, she didn't. And she was about to learn.

Except she had the sudden, depressing thought that maybe this man was an anomaly.

That she would never have anything like this experience again.

What had seemed comforting and freeing moments before seemed suddenly less so after the cascade of fantastic orgasms he had given her.

*It doesn't matter.*

*Even if it's only like this once and never again... At least you had it. At least you know.*

There was nothing wrong with her. It wasn't hard for her to come.

Not when the guy knew what he was doing. The flaw wasn't hers.

She wanted to scream it out the window at all the unsuspecting people in the motel parking lot.

It wasn't hard for her to come.

Her boyfriend had been too lazy to do it.

Because this stranger had gotten her off three times in ten minutes.

But, she couldn't think straight just then, because his hands were moving all over her curves, and she was restless and aching and ready for more. That quickly.

She stripped his shirt up over his head and separated from him so she could get a look at his torso. Which did not disappoint. He was all rippling muscles and golden chest hair, hard abs and an incredibly well-muscled chest.

He was gorgeous.

More than advertised.

He stood then, leaving her down on the floor, working his belt through the loops and pulling it off slowly. Then he undid the button on his jeans, slid the zipper down so maddeningly slowly. She moved forward, hooked her fingers down in the waistband of his pants, to his underwear, and pulled them off, taking his boots right along with them. He was glorious.

He made her mouth water. She'd never wanted to do this before.

But he made her desperate for it.

Granted, if you'd asked her how she felt about male anatomy before this moment, she would've said that it was fine, but she didn't exactly want it as art in her house or anything. But him… She would consider a sculpture of *him*.

He was big and thick and gorgeous. And she was absolutely overcome by her lust for him. She ached between her legs. Felt hollow with her need to feel him moving inside of her. But first. First she wanted to taste him.

She wrapped her hand around his thick length and leaned in, flicking her tongue over his hot, salty skin. She moaned. The smell of him… Musky and male, a deep aphrodisiac to her. Everything about him was like that. Gasoline to a lit match. Chemistry that went so far beyond anything in her experience, anything she thought existed.

She took him deep into her mouth, luxuriating in this. And how wanton she felt. How not like her. She didn't feel like frizzy, average Mallory. She felt every inch like the sex goddess she'd been certain she wasn't not long ago. Because this big, strong, gorgeous man was shaking as she touched him. Was pushing his fingers through her hair the same as she'd just done to him, grabbing onto her, tugging as she took him deeper and deeper into her mouth.

"No more," he said, jerking away from her. "I can't…I can't last."

"Well, I didn't last."

"You didn't have to. Besides. The great thing about women

is they can come as much as I can make them. If it's equal, I didn't do my job."

Well, if that wasn't the hottest damn thing she'd ever heard.

"Are you... Real? Or did my brain make you up?"

"If it's a hallucination, it's a pretty damn good one."

"Hell yes."

He picked her up from the floor, kissed her, walked them both over to the bed and laid her down on those unfamiliar sheets. The feel of his naked body pressed against hers, chest to chest, was amazing. She could lie there kissing him like that, flush against him, all day, except she wanted more.

He kissed her neck, her collarbone, moving down to her breasts, sucking her nipple deep into his mouth. He groaned.

"You're so beautiful."

"So are you," she said, letting her hands wander all down that gorgeous body. Watching as her fingertips dipped and moved with those rippling ab muscles.

"We need one of those condoms," she said.

He got off the bed, went back to his jeans, pulled his wallet out of them and grabbed three condoms out of it, throwing them down on the nightstand by the bed.

"Think that'll cover it?"

"Honestly? Maybe not."

"I will drive to the damn store," he said, taking hold of the condom and tearing it open, rolling it over his thick length quickly before positioning himself over the top of her.

"I like the way you think."

He kissed her, and as he did, he thrust home. She was so wet, so ready, that it was a relief when he filled her. He was thick, so big that she was utterly and completely filled. And she loved it. He started to move, that friction of his hard cock inside of her building her arousal to impossible heights yet again. She moved with him. Chasing that desire. He grabbed the back of her neck, lifting her head up off the mattress and kissing her as he continued to thrust, deep and hard into her.

And when they broke, it was together. The fierce growl of pleasure, the sensation of his body trembling, pulsing above her, set her on a long endless spiral of release that didn't end. They clung to each other after, breathing hard.

"It's a good thing we have two more," he said.

And impossibly, she laughed.

"It's an even better thing you're willing to go to the store."

WHEN MALLORY WOKE UP the next morning, the room was dark, and her bed was empty.

He was gone.

Of course he was. That was how these things went. She knew that. She did. And it was a good thing too. It really was. Because it was just a one-night stand. And she didn't know his name, and she was never supposed to see him again.

It had been the longest, most amazing night of her life. There were condom wrappers... In several places about the room. And there was a condom box that had been torn open with absolutely no finesse at all. She lost track of the amount of times they'd... Well, she could always count.

He had gone to the store.

The last time had been at the gray light of dawn. He held her close, entered her from behind, turned her head and kissed her mouth as he thrust into her with a slow determination that had driven her wild. That had made her have a whole different kind of orgasm. One that made her shake and shudder, one that hadn't seemed to end. One that had come from deep within her, racking her body over and over again.

And now he was gone. She lay there and looked up at the ceiling. This was her new life. She had started it with him.

And now she would go on without him. She would go on alone because it was what she had to do. Because it was why she was here. She smiled as she lay there. She had learned new things about herself last night.

There was nothing wrong with her. There was nothing wrong with her body. And another man could want her. Those were all things that she would save for later. There was no room in her life for a man right now. This was her new beginning. Her fresh start.

She'd been a wild thing last night, and if she ever had to face that man again...

She done things with him that she'd never even fantasized about before. She's been ravenous. She climbed all over him. She'd licked him like he was candy.

She'd take him over a lollipop any day.

And she didn't have to be embarrassed about any of it. She took a deep breath and lay back against the pillows. Against the sheets. Which were no longer unfamiliar. Which smelled of him. He was a stranger. She didn't even know his name. Except... In some ways she was now more familiar with him than any other person in the world.

She pushed that aside too. Because it was a pointless thought, and it wouldn't get her anywhere. And maybe she would just sleep half the day away, because she could. Because no one expected anything from her. Because no one even knew she was here.

She tried to recapture that feeling of freedom from last night, and she felt the spark of it flickering inside of her.

Today was hers. To do with as she pleased. And beyond that, her life was hers.

And she was good with that. She really was.

Last night had been a fantasy.

But tomorrow was the first day of the rest of her life.

# CHAPTER TWO

THE NEXT MORNING she got up with an actual bounce in her step and she put on red lipstick. She looked fantastic. She looked new. She didn't care that it was six thirty in the morning and that she looked ready for a night out rather than a trip to get a morning coffee.

She *looked* like a woman who'd had a successful one-night stand last night. Happy, relaxed and satisfied. Maybe even a little bit shameless and audacious—two things she'd never been in her life, since shame was a frequent companion, adjacent to guilt, and audaciousness had never really occurred to her.

She was proud of herself. She had gone after what she wanted, and she had paid no heed to any consequences. To the future. She had done the kind of thing she had long dreamed of doing. Okay, maybe she hadn't long dreamed of it. But she had dreamed of it the moment she had set eyes on him, and that was good enough.

An auspicious beginning.

She put on some nonsense high-heeled sandals that were practical for nothing but making her feel sexy and walked out the door of the hotel, deciding that she would walk to the nearest coffee shop, which she found easily, using her smartphone. The sun was already shining, and she knew that later it would be unbearably hot. That had been a little bit of a shock. Discovering just how warm it could be in Oregon, which she'd assumed was continually rainy. But no, it turned out. Not so. And it was often much warmer than the little pocket she lived in in the Bay Area.

In the summer, it was downright hot. You could take a drive about an hour out to the coast and find it a good twenty degrees cooler, but inland… Scorching was often the order of the day in summertime. But the mornings and evenings were beautiful. At least, this morning was. She sighed, drinking in deeply of the air and not caring that her internal phraseology was a bit dramatic.

She was renewed. Confident.

She had left her old skin behind and had made something new between the sheets with her mystery man. The thought of him made her feel somewhat melancholy, but that was good. It was to be expected. A woman needed something she could look back on with melancholy, and not just humiliation.

She walked into the coffee shop, pushing heavily against the black door, marveling at the cuteness of the place. Griffin had taken her here a couple of times when she'd been to visit. And the coffee was fantastic. The woman behind the register smiled as she took her order, a large ring sparkling on her finger as bright as her smile. She made her order and looked back behind the counter.

There was a guy on the shift that worked in the back who seemed really grumpy, but he was sexy in that sort of growly Viking way.

And she decided to go ahead and appreciate him.

Because while she might have had the perfect specimen of masculinity in her bed not twenty-four hours ago, that didn't mean she couldn't still appreciate men out and about.

She was single, after all.

That made her start whistling, and she only stopped when she became keenly aware that the man next to her was staring. She sidled over to the place where people picked their drinks up, moving around the corner of the counter and fading into the woodwork slightly. And that was when the door opened, and her heart hit the floor.

It was him.

*It was him.*

The man she was never supposed to see again unless she went to the bar. The man she really wasn't ever supposed to see. The one she'd tasted and clawed and kissed and licked. That one. That man. He was right there in the coffee shop, which was so mundane it was nearly laughable. A man like him shouldn't just be in a coffee shop in the broad light of day.

Hell, it wasn't *even* the broad light of day. It was the morning.

The early morning.

Sex gods of that proportion should not be up at six in the morning.

*He is a cowboy...*

She had somewhat convinced herself that he was a fake cowboy. Not the kind that rose early and worked the land and rode ranges. Because the real ones were never that pretty, were they?

It hadn't mattered. In the moment, he'd simply been a decorative cowboy. A sort of monument to the absurdity of all that she was doing. Staking her claim in a small town and doing so with an emblem of redneck debauchery.

Completely counter to anything she would normally do. Completely counter to anything she normally was.

But now he was there. Actually in front of her. Not just a fantasy. Not that human version of the late-night pint of ice cream that you ate under the cover of darkness, while pretending it never happened in the bright light of day. No.

Unlike the empty container of ice cream, he was now in front of her.

And she hid. She hid behind the post right next to the counter, praying that her coffee would come up soon and she could beat a hasty retreat, because she couldn't even fathom the idea of having to face him, speak to him, anything. He had seen her naked. More than that, he had pinned her against the wall and licked her... Down there.

And that had seemed perfectly reasonable at the time.

So many things seemed perfectly reasonable when you were turned on. At least, she had discovered that. Because she had done a whole lot of things with him that had seemed absolutely and completely fine. In the moment. Aroused beneath his touch spreading her legs and begging for more seemed as unremarkable as ordering a coffee.

But when fully clothed and not ready to beg for his touch, it seemed... A little extra.

And he'd seen that. He couldn't unsee it. She was sure that he couldn't, because she couldn't unsee him. She mentally undressed him. With every peek that she sneaked past the pillar, she saw his skin. Not the black T-shirt he was wearing. Not the black jeans. She cast a beseeching glance behind the counter, which did no good. She could hear him ordering. And she looked around again to see those masculine hands set on the countertop as he leaned in. There was a different girl at the register, with swinging butterfly earrings that looked young and silly, and no ring on her finger. She looked up at him and grinned.

Mallory felt churned up inside.

He chuckled, and she felt it down between her thighs.

Was he *flirting* with Madame Butterfly Earrings?

She darted back behind the pole again. It didn't matter. He could flirt with whoever he wanted. He wasn't her boyfriend—he was her fantasy. Her dirty secret. Yes. And dirty secrets could only be dirty if they were secret. And they can only be secret if they were secret. And she needed to get out of here right now.

She was dying. Of horror.

Finally, after what seemed an eternity, her drink passed across the counter just as he finished making his order. He started to come toward her, and she ducked around the other side of the post, holding her coffee. Then around to the other side. Her heart was thundering fast, and she could swear that she felt him. His presence. And she did a side step toward the front door, letting it swing shut behind her, her heart lodged firmly in her throat. She started down the sidewalk, trying to move as quickly as her legs could carry her, when she nearly ran into her sister-in-law.

"Mallory?"

"Oh," Mallory said.

"*Mallory*, what are you doing here?"

Mallory scrunched her nose and tried to smile, but she had a feeling she'd only just achieved a grimace. "Surprise?"

Iris shook her head. "It's crazy, but Rose told me that she thought she saw you the other night in the Gold Valley Saloon, and I told her that was impossible because you were in California."

"I *was*," Mallory said quickly. "In California. I'm here. Today." She was a liar. But hey, she was fiercely guarding her fantasy. Her fantasy that was currently right on her heels. And what small-town hell was this?

"I just… I was coming to talk to you and Griffin today. I… Have made some changes. And I… Need to talk to you about them." She finished extremely lamely.

"Oh," she said.

"Yeah. I… If you're around later… I'd like to come and talk to you and Griffin."

"Sure," Iris said. "I mean, you know you can always talk to me."

She didn't know her sister-in-law that well, but she loved her. Loved her effortlessly because she had brought Griffin back from the brink of the darkest pit any person could have ever been in. Griffin wasn't really living when he'd met Iris. Griffin was a man with one foot in the grave. His detachment from the family, his misery had been so intense that Iris had wondered if he would ever be able to come back from it. But he had. Through loving her. And because of that, Mallory loved her without question and without fail. But, this wasn't really a conversation she wanted to have twice.

"I better save it. I need to be caffeinated. Is there a… A time that would be good or…"

"Yeah, sometime this afternoon. Really, anytime. Griffin and I spend the later part of the day together. I'm just… Headed to the bakery. Did you want some cake?"

The door to the coffee shop swung open and she tried not to panic. Because it might be her man.

"Yes," she said. "Cake." And crossed the street quickly, arm in arm with Iris, toward the Cookie Jar, her sister-in-law's amazing bakery that she had just opened a few months earlier.

Griffin owned the building, and that was how the two of them had met. Mallory had a feeling that the version of the story they told was heavily censored, but it was okay. She didn't need all the gritty details. She sipped her coffee while Iris put together a box full of goodies.

"I'm staying by myself," she said, looking at the cookies, cupcakes and pastries that her sister-in-law had put into the box.

"Well. I don't know. Consider it a welcome gift? How long are you going to be here? Can you at least tell me that?"

"Awhile," she said. "I… Like I said, I'm making some changes."

"Well, I hope they're good changes," Iris said.

"I think they are. I hope they are. No, I know they are. I do. I'm… Oh, I really need them to be."

"Well we'll see you this afternoon."

"I'll be completely sugared up by then."

"Works for me."

But, she would need to tell Griffin that she was here. She couldn't just roll into his family dinner. And that was how she found herself driving up the long, winding dirt road that led to Echo Pass and the new house that her brother had finished building for himself and his wife.

Just the thought of it made her happier. Griffin being happy made her happy. When they'd been separated, when she'd been back in California and he'd been here, and she'd called him all the time, and sometimes he didn't answer… She had been sure she would lose him. She really had.

She hadn't believed that he could ever climb out of the hole he was in, and who could blame him? Who could even judge him? To lose his wife and child the way that he had… It was horrible. Beyond horrible. She wasn't sure if she would have been strong enough to make the decision to keep on going. But he had.

In the grand scheme of things, what she was going through was nothing. Particularly by comparison to the things that Griffin had endured.

The first thing that came into view was a small cabin, which she knew that Griffin was going to mention. And she knew that he was going to ask why she wasn't renting it. And then she was going to have to have an honest talk with him about... Everything. That was the problem. She had been interested in his life, in his recovery from his pain when he was out here hiding from the world, and he wasn't going to be any less interested in hers. That cabin, he had explained, was where he had lived while he was slowly building the house that he had never really intended to finish or live in.

Griffin had first purchased this lot of property when he was married to his previous wife. They'd had plans to leave California and move to Oregon, live in a house at the top of the mountain. When she died, Griffin had taken it upon himself to build the house as a memorial. Or rather, a punishment. Taking himself off-grid so that no one could get in touch with him, embroiling himself in a project he would never be able to finish. And then, Iris Daniels had come along, and somehow had pulled him out from the grave he was living in. He had finished the house for her. Had brought a whole team of men out to finish it, because the house was no longer a punishment, but a symbol of hope.

And it was a beautiful house. Modern and glinting in the sunlight, large floor-to-ceiling windows that were made to bring the view outside in. Nothing like the little place she was staying in. But then, she hadn't spent any of her adult life living in any kind of luxury.

Her parents had a very nice house.

And if she ignored the shame she could feel seeping out of the wallpaper, she could focus on the fact that she had grown up in a very privileged, plush surrounding.

But then she had gone out and gotten a job, and had spent the entirety of her adult life supporting a man-child.

She gritted her teeth. Thinking of all the start-up businesses she had invested in. All of the promises he'd made, and she would just have been so desperate to believe them.

She parked her car and shoved that to the side, and as she

got out and stood there in her brother's driveway, she realized that she probably should've called. There were two cars in the driveway, which meant that Iris and Griffin were probably home and hopefully expecting her since she'd talked to Iris earlier.

She didn't want to watch them in any sort of compromising position.

She heard voices coming round from the back of the house, and stopped. And then she heard laughter. Griffin's laughter. That was when he and his wife rounded the corner, holding on to each other, their hair wet. So they had definitely been out doing… Something. They both stopped when they saw her standing there.

"Mallory?" her brother asked, frowning, looking at her as though she might be an apparition.

"Yes," she said. "That would be… Me." She looked at Iris, who was looking apologetically at her husband.

"I wanted her to tell you she was here, especially since I didn't have details," Iris said.

Griffin looked at his wife, then back at Mallory. "What are you… Doing here? Are you with…"

Mallory sighed. "Let's go inside."

Griffin and Iris exchanged glances, like they were reading each other's minds with that simple look that passed between them. It made her feel… Strange. They hadn't been together all that long. Only a few months, and they could already communicate that way. She'd been with a man for years, and he could never anticipate her moods or her mind.

Or, he just didn't care.

She shoved that to the side. She was bogged down. In thoughts, and feelings. She hated it.

They walked up the front steps and into the house without saying anything, and then Griffin gestured to the couch. "Have a seat. Do you want a drink?"

"Beer if you have any," she said.

"Of course."

He walked across the large, open-plan space into the kitchen area, opening up the fridge and taking out a couple of bottles of beer. She noted that Iris didn't have any. She locked eyes with her sister-in-law, who smiled.

"Really?" Mallory asked.

"Yes," Iris said. "But it's early. So we're not telling anyone yet."

Her brother looked proud, but she imagined he was a little bit afraid. Griffin was more than familiar with just how hard life could kick you in the teeth.

"Congratulations," Mallory said, springing up from the couch and hugging them both. "That's wonderful. It's wonderful."

And she would be here. She would be here for her sister-in-law having a baby. She could deliver the baby. She loved pregnancy and birth. She loved the process of it. Medicine meeting miracle, every single time. And yes, it could be a little bit of a high-stress job, but it was part of the fabric of the world. It was the thing that made her feel truly connected to life. It was the process of humanity.

And this… This was an even more personal experience of it.

Her niece or nephew. Her throat went tight. Because she would never forget the first time she'd become an aunt. And even though her niece was gone, it didn't change the fact that she was the one who had made Mallory an aunt. It didn't change the fact that Mallory loved her.

"Yeah," Griffin said. "It's about that many feelings."

Griffin was eight years older than her, and their relationship had always been one of... Well, hero worship on her end. He'd been out living life while she'd still been growing up. But he was one of the people she wanted to emulate most in all the world. One of the people she wanted to make proud.

When he'd lost his wife and daughter five years ago, the grief she'd felt for him, for herself and their family had been unbearable. And then he'd taken himself away too. It had been like losing him as well.

Her parents hadn't known what to do, and Mallory had done her best to try to reach him. It had felt almost necessary to be the one to accomplish dragging him back from the brink.

To bring him back to them.

But he'd met Iris. And she'd transformed him. And now... Now they were having a baby. Starting a whole new life, which she knew he would never have thought possible when he'd been down in the depths of his despair.

"Well I'm really thrilled for you. And I'm glad that I sneaked up here so that I could find out before anyone else."

"My sisters are going to be mad," Iris said.

"Well, I'm his only sister. So. It just seems like I should get special dibs."

"Yeah, that seems fair," Iris said.

She really did like Iris. She was the perfect woman for Griffin. Perfect in ways she could never have imagined. Because not only could Mallory picture Iris with the man he'd been, she was also perfect for the man he was now. Just uniquely suited to everything he was, everything Mallory loved about him and everything that infuriated Mallory about him.

Actually, seeing Griffin and Iris together was one of the things that had started making her relationship with Jared feel... Wrong. And after that visit up here...

"So what exactly are you doing here?"

"Well. I broke up with Jared."

"Right."

He didn't look shocked at all.

"I *broke up with him*," she repeated.

"Yeah," Griffin said.

"No, I really broke up with him," she replied. "I mean, for good. I did it. He didn't leave—I kicked him out."

"Okay."

"He *cheated* on me," Mallory said.

That made her brother stop where he was, and his expression went fierce. "Really?"

"Really. And that's it. We're done."

There was a slight pause.

"You better mean it," Griffin said.

Iris suddenly looked uncomfortable. "I don't think that's the response people usually get when they say they've broken up with someone…"

"You've never broken up with anyone," he said. "How would you know?"

"You wanna test that?" Iris asked, smiling sweetly.

"I'd win you back and we both know it."

Mallory cleared her throat and kept staring at him until he shifted, his expression getting defensive.

"Yeah, well, you remember him," he said to Iris.

"I do," Iris said, patiently.

"And you know how I feel about him."

Iris rolled her eyes. "Everyone in a two-mile radius of the two of you was well aware of exactly how you felt about him. The only person who wasn't, was the person in question, since I don't think he much paid attention to what anyone thought. And even if he had, he wouldn't have cared. No offense," Iris said, directing that last part at Mallory.

"None taken. I've been fully marinating in what a self-ish asshole he is for weeks." And doing her best to eliminate memories of all the good and hard times they'd shared. She was working on making him as one-dimensional as her brother saw him, but that didn't mean she wanted to be hassled about it. "But yes, I would expect a little bit more... Of a reaction over us breaking up."

"You two have broken up a hundred times, Mallory. He's been with other women during those times."

"Yes, but it was different. He'd leave first. This time he was...he was still living with me."

"What the hell difference does it make?" Griffin asked.

"It makes a ton of difference to me," she said. "I thought everything was good. I thought he and I were good."

But as soon as she said it, all the sharp, bruised places inside of her lit up. Because it had always hurt. And she had always taken him back for some reason. Because she had spent fifteen years being wholly devoted to him mind and body, never kissing another man, never touching another man, and there had been... Oh, there had been other women. Because Jared was handsome, even if he was... That sort of easy that didn't grow, change or achieve. But he was fun to be with. And it was that... That thing that had always done something for her. She was so desperate to prove herself all the time, and he so deeply didn't care what anyone thought. He also knew how to make her laugh when she wanted to cry, and knew how to drag her out of a spiral when she was worried about what someone else might think of her.

But she wasn't going to focus on any of that.

Every time he'd decided to move out in the past, he'd always found another woman's bed to sleep in. God knew he could never seem to afford his own.

*Now you have, though. Now you've had Mystery Cowboy.*

*And he was better than Jared could ever be, and the sex was surely better than any he'd had with a random bar hookup.*

Because it was better than just about any sex ever. It had to be.

"Okay. I'm sorry. Judgment put on pause. You broke up with him, and…?"

"I sold my condo. And I'm moving here."

"Well hell," Griffin said. "Why didn't you say *that*?"

"That's what I've been trying to say. But, breakup news. Baby news. There was other news."

Griffin's whole bearing changed. "That's great, Mal. I'm thrilled to have you here. *We* are thrilled to have you here."

"Yes," Iris said. "Especially now."

"I have… I'm taking over a clinic here. I'm… I'm thrilled."

"Well, I wish I would've had it ready, but you know we have a guest room. And we can get the cabin prepared for habitation as soon as possible."

"I don't need it," she said.

"You don't need it?"

"No. I've got a place to rent already." She could only hope it was a decent place. She'd gone back and forth with the rental management company, but the info had been sparse. Rentals were thin on the ground in Gold Valley, it turned out.

"You didn't have to do that."

"I did. I mean, I sank most of the money from my condo into the birthing center. But, not all of it. And I wanted to have my own place. My own space." She looked up at Griffin. "I haven't lived on my own. Not for more than a month or so at a time. I… I've always been with someone. I've always been dependent in some way on someone."

"Jared was dependent on you," Griffin said.

Mallory closed her eyes. "You know, I would love to believe that. I mean, I would really love to just let myself feel that. To be angry with him, and with the fact that he sponged off of me financially for as long as he did. Because he did. But it's not that simple, Griffin. I needed something from him. And I have to figure out what that was."

As soon as she said it, she realized it was true.

She wasn't stupid.

She had a good family.

But somehow she'd let one mistake, one horrible, traumatic event determine how she lived her life. She'd committed herself to a relationship that didn't grow and change with her. So she'd tied herself into knots until she was a shape she hadn't recognized.

And she had to find the shape of *Mallory*.

Without all the weird baggage she'd tangled herself up in back home. Without Jared and her parents and everything else.

"I have to figure out what's next," she said. "And I'm hurt. That's the thing that gets me the most. That I'm really hurt by all of it. Even though I feel like... The visit up here, it was the beginning of me really seeing him. He wasn't polite to any of you. He was so obnoxious about the town. We were staying in this gorgeous little bed-and-breakfast, and he hated it. Because he didn't want to have to get up early to eat the breakfast. It was like being with a teenage boy."

She pushed her fingers through her hair—they stopped abruptly at a snarl because her curls would not be tamed—and started to pace the room.

"And I can see all that. I could see it then. I'm still hurt that he betrayed me. I still don't know what to make of my life now that he's not in it. Because he's not. He's really not. I'm done. For good. But the fact that it..." She swallowed. She didn't want to say it, because she felt like it was too easy to use these words, and she also felt like she didn't really lay claim to them, given all the pain that Griffin had been through. But it was really the only thing she had to describe it. "My heart is broken."

Her heart had been broken for fifteen years. And only Jared knew why. He hadn't done it. But he hadn't truly helped her heal.

"It's going to take time for me to figure out how to put it back together. How to put myself... Together. For the first time. As a grown woman."

A woman who was free.

She thought again of her handsome cowboy with the electric eyes, and then made herself stop that right away.

This had nothing to do with him.

"I just need to stand on my own feet. I need to be strong. For myself. Not for someone else."

Griffin made his way across the room and pulled her in for a hug. "You're perfect, Mallory. You just need someone who will see that."

She felt uncomfortable with that. It made her eyes feel like they'd been scrubbed with a cactus.

She didn't know how to respond to that so she didn't.

She spent the day with her brother and Iris. Iris made bread. Griffin grilled steak. They talked and laughed and she felt so free. She could stay as long as she liked. She didn't have to worry about Jared being bored.

She didn't make her move to leave until around ten at night.

"Hey," Iris said, as she was about to go. "Do you have plans Sunday? If not, you should come to my family dinner."

## CHAPTER THREE

MONDAY WOULD BE the last day in the motel, the last day before she went to her new house. And she didn't really know what she was doing going to this... Big get-together.

*You're doing something new. It's part of the new life.*

Yes. The new life. The new life which was... Well, she was looking forward to it. She was. It had been so nice to see Griffin and Iris so happy at their house. And she was just thrilled that she was going to be an aunt again. She was just thrilled that her brother had found so much happiness during this time.

And as for getting accepted into the whole extended Daniels family...

Well, she loved Iris. And Griffin had assured her that his in-laws were basically the best people in the entire world. They'd been through tough stuff, which was something that made Iris even more perfect for Griffin. She knew how to live. Even after everything she'd been through, she'd known how to live. And she'd been able to show Griffin the way back.

Maybe knowing them would... Maybe it would help her too.

She pulled her car up into the dirt driveway, beneath the sign that said: Hope Springs Ranch.

The road wound on a little ways until she got to the ranch house itself, which was eclectic—that much was clear even from the outside. There were muddy boots on the porch, along with a Bohemian rug and wind chimes. A bear that looked like it had been carved out of a log by a chain saw. A collision of country and hippie rolled into one.

Her brother's truck was already there. She had made sure to come a little bit late so that she wouldn't be coming up on a place full of strangers all by herself. She got out of the car and was greeted by an opening door and a passel of dogs. They were barking and wiggling, and Mallory backed up against the side of the car. "Oh," she said, looking down at the animals. "Hi. Hello."

"Mallory!"

She heard her sister-in-law's voice and looked up, to see Iris standing there with a beautiful blonde woman, who was clearly responsible for the Bohemian element at the place.

"This is my sister-in-law," she said. "Sammy."

"The lady of the manor," Sammy said, winking broadly.

Iris decided she liked her right away.

She opened her mouth to say something, when a dark figure came through the door behind Iris's sister-in-law and Iris. And Mallory's stomach dropped down to her feet. Yet again.

"Oh," Iris said, grabbing hold of the man's arm.

*Her* man's arm.

"This is my cousin. Colt."

HELL AND DAMNATION. The woman that had been haunting his dreams was standing right in front of them. Right in front of him. That was… Well hell. That was unexpected. Putting it mildly.

"Hi," Colt said, forcing a smile to cross his lips. He didn't smile much these days. He didn't do much of anything these days. In fact, the only significant thing he'd done in the last three months was standing in front of him.

"Colt," she said.

She looked like she'd been slapped with a fish. So, he knew that she was just as surprised as he was. And anyway, he couldn't think of any other explanation for it. Except pure, dumb, small-town luck.

If you could call it that.

He wasn't in any kind of space to be tangling with a complication. Not in hell. Not right now. Especially right now.

This was why he liked a transient hookup. He didn't deal with morning-afters.

And judging by the beet-red color of the woman's face, neither did she.

"Colt," she said. "This is Mallory."

"Nice to meet you," he said.

"Yeah," she returned. "Nice to meet you."

"Griffin's sister," Iris said, patting him on the forearm.

*Oh great.*

So, Griffin's sister had come through town, and he'd banged her. Well. There were worse things.

*Maybe.*

He hadn't been himself that night. Charm came easy to him, as did easy sex that pleased both him and his partner. At least, it had. He didn't think it was the stretch of celibacy that had changed him, though.

There had been something deep and raw between them, and it had all seemed fine because he wasn't supposed to see her again. He didn't want anyone to see how he was. Not right now. Didn't want any kind of the toxicity that existed inside of him to spill over onto the other people in his life.

God knew, his family had been through enough.

He was just sorting it all through on his own, as best he could. And his night with a stranger should've been just that. One night. With a stranger. But then this woman was here…

This woman.

He'd been something else with her.

The intensity unleashed in that motel room…

It had been an exorcism.

He didn't say anything, because his cousin was handily filling the silence, and when Iris wasn't talking, Sammy was. They went into the house, and Colt stood back in the living room, his eyes on Mallory.

*Mallory.*

It was the strangest thing. Because he'd seen her once six months ago.

Before everything had gone to hell. He'd wanted her then. He'd never experienced anything like that. Seeing a woman and knowing. Knowing that things between them would be explosive.

Yeah.

He'd wanted that.

He'd wanted her.

He'd told himself that it was one of those chance encounters that didn't mean anything. The little bit of attraction between himself and a woman he would never see again didn't really matter. That he didn't need to build it up and did nothing. But then, she'd been there.

Then, at one of the lowest points in his life, she'd come back. And she wasn't with that tool anymore. She was by herself. And now… Well hell.

He felt it still. Even after having her. And that was an entirely new sensation. He loved women. But one of the things that he'd always liked about them was the mystery. There was something kind of magical about sex with strangers. That you could go from not knowing each other to having each other naked in just a few seconds. That you could experience physical intimacy while keeping your emotions entirely separate. He'd always liked it. And he liked that rush.

Of uncovering a woman for the first time.

Seeing what color her nipples were.

How her breasts were out of her bra, if she wore one at all.

Did they sag just slightly or were they perky—either through nature or silicone. Frankly, he was into all of it. He liked wide hips he could grip and narrow, athletic builds. He liked women.

But, half of what he liked was that mystery.

That game. Unwrapping the gift.

He didn't like knowing what was already in the present. That wasn't really his jam. And the mystery of Mallory should be well solved.

He'd had that woman from every angle. Had tasted every inch of her. But still, looking at her now sent a rush of fire through his blood. He didn't get what it was about her. He really didn't. She was lovely. That sort of classic reddish curly hair, and pale freckled skin. She didn't particularly look like her brother.

Which really was a good thing.

"So," his cousin Ryder said, addressing Mallory. "What brings you to Gold Valley?"

"I needed a change of scenery. And Griffin is here. And... Well, I found out that the midwife is retiring. I had the chance to buy a clinic in town. A birthing center. That's what I do. I'm a midwife."

Sammy positively glowed. "That's great," she said. "Because we're actually expecting another baby."

It was clear that everybody in the room already knew, except for Colt. He felt a little bit irritated that Sammy or Ryder hadn't told him.

But maybe... Well, maybe he'd been a little bit more absent than he realized over the last few weeks. Maybe he hadn't been passing for okay quite to the degree that he thought.

"Congratulations," Mallory said.

"I had a home birth with Astrid. Do you only use the birthing center or..."

"It's going to depend on my insurance," Mallory said. "But ideally I'd like to give the mothers choice between home and the clinic. I want to be able to provide a flexible experience."

"Well I love that," Sammy said.

"Yeah, I love it less." Ryder looked uptight, which really didn't surprise Colt.

"I was fine last time," Sammy said, waving a hand.

"There are no guarantees in life," Ryder said. "But I'm glad that you feel so confident in the whims of fate."

"I ride the winds of fate like a mother of dragons," she said, tossing her head back. "Don't step to me."

"So," Ryder said. "You know Sammy now." He directed that at Mallory.

Mallory laughed. "It's not unusual for men to be concerned about the process. Particularly men who are more traditional..."

"Who said I was traditional?" Ryder asked.

It was Colt's cousin Pansy's turn to chime in. "The *everything* about you?"

"I'm being maligned," Ryder said. "Colt, help me out?"

"No, thanks," Colt responded, doing his best to keep his voice light.

"Wow. The thanks I get for raising you people."

It was a full house tonight, with Pansy and her husband, West, West's half brother Emmett, Logan and Rose, Jake and Callie, and Iris and Griffin in addition to Ryder and

Sammy, who lived in the farmhouse. There was also baby Astrid, who wasn't really much of a baby anymore, and was more of a holy terror on two chubby legs.

Rose was also pregnant, due in just a couple of months.

It was like everybody was moving into this phase of life that he just had no desire to get himself involved in. Hell, he didn't even… It wasn't about not being ready. It was more like it being his worst nightmare. The idea of being responsible for something so vulnerable as a baby. And a wife that was carrying one. A god-awful prospect all things considered.

Everything he touched turned to poison, and it was best if he never put his hands on anything quite that fragile.

He loved his family. He loved his niece, because the thing was, Astrid might as well be his niece, because Ryder might as well be his brother. He was Uncle Colt, whether that was his actual genetic title or not.

He liked kids well enough; he just didn't want any of his own. He liked to keep all his relationships light, not too deep. And he was good at it.

At least he had been. Usually with his family he smiled, he played football, he helped barbecue, he played the guitar—a light country tune with easy lyrics that meant less than nothing to him.

Far removed from who he'd been before his parents had died. When he'd been an overthinker who'd found music so personal he'd had trouble sharing his songs. Well once his parents had died, he'd quit playing his own songs. It had solved that problem. Made it all simple.

It was why he liked his sexual relationships easy and free. He liked everything that way.

The thing about one-night stands was you were never supposed to see them again.

And he should know, because he was an expert. He had been for quite some time. It was just how he lived his life. It was what he did. And he never had a particular sort of problem with it. Never felt guilt about it. But then, he had never thought obsessively about any of his one-night stands, over and over again.

Ever.

Until her.

That was the problem.

Mallory *haunted* him.

She had haunted him since that first time he had seen her in the Golden Valley Saloon all those months ago. And he didn't know why in hell that was. Unless she was some sort of omen. A ghost of a ship that was yet to come.

Shit, he hadn't known it was coming until it was too late. And now he was sitting there in his family gathering brooding about the whole damn thing, and *babies*.

There was just no point to it. Then, he imagined there was no real point to running away from the rodeo and licking his wounds on his brother's ranch.

*What's the alternative?*

All that easy and free had been messed up with Trent's death, and he was having trouble finding his way back to it.

"What's the matter with you?" His brother Jake made his way over to him.

"Nothing."

"Oh, other than the usual?"

"If you're going to tell me that I should be over my best friend's death…"

"I'm not," Jake said. "I think you know that. But if you want to be a jerk about something…"

"I'm not. I'm standing here drinking a beer."

"You're antisocial. Pick up your guitar. Play."

"Why don't I stand in the center of the room and do a line dance. Maybe 'Achy Breaky Heart'? Would that help you out, Jake? I wasn't a rodeo clown, you know. It's not my job to make people laugh."

Still, it was the mantle he'd picked up in the family all those years ago. But he was struggling with it now.

"It's not your job to save everyone's ass, either," Jake said.

His brother's eyes were too serious, and Colt didn't like it. He didn't like the fact that his brother was getting so close to his issues. Didn't like the fact that he seemed to have hit him right where he was the most sore.

"I know that you think you could've done something…"

"You know what I think, Jake," Colt said, feeling really irritated now. "I was done with the rodeo. That's it. You know, somebody dying in a riding accident is a really great reminder of the potential consequences to what we do."

"Since when do you care?"

A good enough question, since Colt Daniels had been known up and down the rodeo circuit as someone who just didn't give a damn.

He had thrown himself onto the backs of the meanest bulls, had challenged anyone who would let him to try and drink him under the table—nobody ever had. He was the kind of man who took risks that some saw as unnecessary. But he called it flipping a middle finger at fate, which she richly deserved.

It always felt that way. He had always felt like there was no point trying. Because if life wanted to take you out—it would.

It just damn well would.

There was nothing you were going to do to keep yourself here. If fate decided you'd live, you would. If fate decided you were going to die, it was about the same.

So he didn't see much point worrying one way or the other. Yeah, he figured that it was one of those predestined things. He figured that was one of those things that you couldn't fight, couldn't ignore, couldn't shake.

Then Trent had died and something had shifted inside of him. That kid... He'd had so much to live for. So many people depending on him. And it had uncovered old wounds. And it had exposed a whole lot of angry, festering, unhealed bullshit. He didn't like it. Not one bit.

"How about we skip psychoanalyzing me?" he growled.

"But it is my favorite pastime."

"I liked it better when we didn't talk."

"Cal says it's good for me to talk," Jake said, referring to his wife, who he'd married officially six months ago. That was what had brought Colt into town. His brother's wedding. And that was when he had seen her. But yeah, marrying Callie had changed Jake. Colt wasn't so sure he liked it.

"All right," came his sister-in-law's voice from inside the kitchen. "Who wants pie? Iris made it."

There was an enthusiastic chorus of yeses, but Mallory hung behind. She was new, and it was easy, he supposed, for everyone else here to forget that.

But he didn't.

Everybody filtered slowly toward the kitchen. Jake clapped him on his back and made his way that direction as well. And that was how Colt found himself standing there in the living room with her.

She looked around as if she was trying to find an emergency escape hatch. Sadly for her, there was none.

Then finally, resigned, she looked at him.

"Did you know?"

He hadn't expected that question. Her eyes were wide and filled with nerves, and his response to *that* shocked him more than his own response to her. It was about the only thing that could have. The fact that she looked like she might be genuinely terrified of him.

"Hell no," he said. "It doesn't suit me any more than it suits you to come back to haunt me."

"Haunting," she said. "Well, that is a new one for my repertoire."

"Don't act offended. It doesn't suit you."

"You don't know what suits me. You caught me at a weak moment."

"Excuse me," he said. "I *caught* you?"

She sniffed. "Yes."

"Talk to me about the part when I caught you. Was it the part where you put your hand on my chest? Or maybe it was the part where you led me down the sidewalk holding my hand?"

"Oh, I'm sorry, what about you? *We've known each other for six months.*"

"It's a good line."

"It was a good line." She practically hissed. "My panties came off in record time. But nonetheless… This is not something that I would normally do. Ever. Ever."

"Well, as it happens, it is something I would normally do. So, you can calm the hell down about it. There's no reason to get worked up. Or get your aforementioned panties in a twist."

The fact of the matter was, even standing there bantering with her, what he really felt was that he wanted to get her panties in a twist, on the floor of his bedroom.

Lust tore through him. Why the hell was that? Shouldn't be so easy for this woman to rile him up. But damn her, she did. From the moment he first set eyes on her. With that fiery red hair and that lithe body that seemed to call to him specifically, hell if he knew why. She wasn't the most curvy. The most *athletic*. The most anything.

Except, apparently, his particular vintage of whiskey.

"We're just…going to have to figure out how to… Work around each other."

"Like I said," he responded. "I don't have a problem with this. It was just another day in the life."

And it was a lie. It was a damn lie from the pit of his decaying soul. But he wasn't going to admit that. He wasn't going to admit that she had him all kinds of shook-up and that he had been in the middle of a dry spell the likes of which he had heretofore never known.

Before her, he had been pretty sure he would never be interested in anything that might make you feel good. Ever again. And the thing was, he was eager to get back to his penance. Work on the ranch. Go home. Drink. Sleep. Repeat. That was it.

He didn't drink to excess, though, not anymore. Just enough to dull the aches and pains of the workday. Just enough.

He had sworn off excess.

Because one thing he couldn't shake was that this kid that had meant so much to him had been on the fast path to hell this whole time, and Colt had been driving the train. He'd been the one Trent looked up to. The one he wanted to emulate.

And Colt had thought that was great.

He'd lost his own father, and… There was something about having someone look up to him. Something about having that kind of connection that had made him feel… Rooted to the earth, the way he had before. And then it had crashed and burned. Gone in a puff of smoke.

That kid had been moving fast, headed for a young death,

and it was clear. If you went back, looked at the evidence and paid attention. It was the only way that things were going to end. He drank too much and didn't take his safety precautions as seriously as he should. Didn't pay attention to whether or not he should be riding on a given day. But it was Colt who had taught him that.

Because it was Colt who had spent the better part of his life thumbing his nose at death. But death hadn't come to collect him. Yet again, it had come for the wrong person.

Let Mallory think otherwise. Let her think that he was still the Colt Daniels that he'd once been. He was certain when he was around her he would be able to put that on. That he would be able to cast himself back into that role. Because it was easy enough. Should be, anyway.

"Great. Great." She said the word twice, sounding less sincere upon the repeat than she had upon the first utterance. Then she smiled. It was a fake smile, but pretty all the same, because everything she did was pretty.

"Once upon a time," he said.

Her cheeks turn the delicate shade of pink, and he could've sworn that she stopped herself from licking her lips.

"Pie sounds nice."

"Sure does."

"Let's go have some pie."

Yeah, the fact that this woman was related to his cousin's husband was weird, but it was surmountable. It wasn't like he was going to see an obscure relation all that often anyway.

And it was fate. Because this kind of attraction had to be. It just did. It wasn't any kind of natural, or any kind of typical. And it had something to do with how crazy he'd been over the last few months—that he was sure of. It had to. It had something to do with the fact that he got a little bit unhinged when Trent had died, and it was now attaching itself to her.

"Before we go in," he said. "I'm Colt Daniels. I'm Iris's cousin. It's nice to meet you."

"Mallory Chance," she said. "Griffin's younger sister. Nice to meet you."

She got it. She understood. This would be a fresh start. It would be something new. Something different than it was before. They would put away the fact that they spent one night together burning off demons. At least, he assumed that's what she was doing. They could leave the demons there. They didn't have to bring them here. It wouldn't be that difficult.

And as he sat down, he tried to remind himself of a time when he'd imagined that one woman was pretty much like the next and it wouldn't matter if he'd slept with her by the time he saw her next.

Sex was only sex.

And this sex had been no different.

# CHAPTER FOUR

MALLORY WAS STILL wholly and completely rattled by the appearance of Colt Daniels—her mystery man—at dinner last night. She hadn't been expecting that. Of all the things.

She'd had that very near miss with him at the coffeehouse that next morning. She had been sure that was some kind of small-town anomaly. Something that happened once, but would never happen again. But now... Well, now he was sort of, by extension, part of her family.

"Oh gosh," she said, folding herself forward in her car and pressing her face against the steering wheel. She had to go out to the rental house today, but she was still feeling... Unsettled. The whole situation was just... An inauspicious start to her new beginning. She knew how she wanted to go. She knew how it was supposed to go. He was supposed to be a Declaration of Independence, who would then fade away into the annals of her personal history, not become some sort of Revolutionary War that she had to stand and fight in. She had no interest in that. Quite the opposite.

She'd had her fill of complicated. Of feeling wound up, tangled up in a relationship that was woven through every facet of her life to the point where she didn't feel like she could tug too far in any one direction because it was all connected.

Her life in California was inescapably bound up in her relationship with Jared, and her most real, crushing heartbreak.

The fact that he knew her in a way no one else did and that no matter how much she loved her parents, she was still—in so many ways—a teenage girl desperately trying to be the perfect daughter in front of them when it was just all a lie.

And in that moment when she'd seen that man, the father of a baby about to be born, more attentive to his phone than the moment... When the other woman had asked: Why does she stay with him?

Mallory had known herself. And it was like she'd seen clearly the long chain of events that had led her from being a teenager madly in love for the first time to a thirty-year-old woman, who couldn't even explain what she felt when she looked at the man she'd chosen to share her life with.

Her feelings for Jared had changed. She couldn't say the exact moment they had, only that they had.

She'd told herself obligation was love for a long time. And she was sure they'd both felt that to an extent. An obligation to each other.

But in the end... In the end the reasons they'd clung together at fifteen had long ago lost their sharp edges.

It was the time.

The energy. The fact that if she wasn't in the middle of that struggle, she wasn't entirely sure who she was. She had built her self-esteem, her self-worth all around that relationship. She oriented her position in the world by her positioning to him. It was insane. She knew it. But that didn't mean it wasn't where she was at. It was just... How it was.

It was crazy. But she hadn't known how to proceed without him.

She didn't know how to figure out if she was doing good or bad or indifferent if she wasn't with him.

And it just had to stop. It was why she couldn't afford to tangle herself up in knots over Colt Daniels. She wasn't in the business of tangling herself up in knots over men. She wasn't. And she wouldn't. Anyway. He was another problem. And if she had to—if she absolutely had to—then she would explain to Iris that she might need a little bit of warning if she was going to encounter Colt. But she wouldn't need to do that. She wouldn't. She was going to be on topic. Because Colt had nothing to do with why she was here.

She was done orienting her life around men. He didn't get to decide what she felt. Not about Gold Valley, not about the dinner that she'd had last night—which was quite good.

The fact that they had had some strange confrontation in the middle of that shouldn't mean anything. No. It should mean less than nothing. It shouldn't matter at all. That was it.

After her little pep talk, she started her car and began the route that would take her out toward the rental property. It was some ways out of town, a little bit more toward the coast.

Sunset Ridge.

That was the name of the place. At least, that was what she found via Google before she left. She knew better than to trust her cell phone to tell her where she was going out here. Sometimes she just inexplicably didn't have service. As if it liked to remind her that there were moments when Gold Valley wasn't entirely in this century.

*Oh, you think you're in a modern era? Nope, not.*

It had been like: Oh, are you thinking of starting a new unencumbered life? No, you're not. Here is the only man in town who's seen you naked. At a family function. That your brother is at.

She frowned deeply and kept driving.

He had *seen her naked.* There was a man in town who had seen her naked.

*Well, maybe there will be multiple men in town who will*

*have seen you naked by this time next year. You don't know.*
*You're in a new era of your life.*

Yeah. A new era that had so far been a little bit more inglorious than she had hoped it might be. But what could
you do?

She decided to think about other things. Consciously.

Because yet again, she wasn't going to spend overly much
time ruminating about a guy when she was driving toward
her new house. And once she got into the new house, she
was going to be buying things for it. Taking inventory. Setting up a life that was just for her.

She had never lived alone before.

She didn't even know what she wanted.

And just like that, the world was full of opportunities. Opportunities that had nothing to do with Colt Daniels.

So she breathed in deeply for the first time since last night
and rolled her window down. Then she turned some songs
up, singing at the top of her lungs about betrayals and folk-
lore. The paved road gave way to dirt, and there was a big,
green sign that read Sunset Ridge Viewing Area.

The house was past that. That much she knew. And
when she was about half a mile off that dirt road, the sig-
nal dropped out.

"I am smart," she said, looking down at her paper map.

She could just imagine the way this would've gone if Jared
had been with her.

*What are we gonna do now there's no cell service.*

*I printed out a map.*

*Who prints things out? You're such an old lady.*

Or, alternatively.

*I forgot to print out a map.*

*You're useless, Mallory.*

She growled. The sound vibrated inside the little vehicle.

She was still so angry.

She wondered how long it would take that to get better. Heartbreak was one thing—you kind of expected heartbreak when it came to a relationship coming to an end. But it wasn't strictly that. Not for her. Not anything quite so mundane as heartbreak.

How could you break what had been irrevocably destroyed so long ago?

This was a *fire*. A rage over all the years that she had wasted on somebody who just hadn't appreciated her. Someone who had stopped pouring into their relationship a long time ago, and had let her keep giving, and giving and giving.

Who had subtly, with his actions, by letting her do that, reinforced all of the things she had feared. That she only mattered if she was able to do something for him. That she owed him.

But still. It was just… Infuriating. "I don't need to be serious," she said, drumming on her steering wheel as she turned the music down and slowed her pace. She was looking now, because surely the place had to be close.

But the road just kept on going.

Griffin's house was way the hell out there, but this was even… Even more.

Honestly, it was crazy. For the first time, she seriously questioned herself. Because the town of Gold Valley was tiny, but she must be a good twenty-five minutes outside of it now, and it just seemed… Well, it seemed somewhat inhuman.

There was transitioning to small-town life, and then there was becoming a hermit on a mountaintop. She would need a falcon for this.

She didn't exactly know what she'd use the falcon for, but she'd seen shows where mountain people had a falcon.

Then she saw an old sign, rusted out and hard to read, that

said Sunset Ridge Ranch. She knew this was it. She knew it because it was on the paperwork she had gotten from the rental company. Of course, they hadn't mentioned just how far outside of town it was. And yeah, her instructions that she printed did seem to support this. It was just that she hadn't been fully able to take it all on board. Because it seemed so... So unlike any situation she had ever lived in before.

"Isn't that the point?"

"Yeah." She supposed it was.

But that didn't mean it didn't feel alien and strange. That was this whole experience. In fact, the only time she'd really felt confident in what she was doing was... Well, it was when she had decided to bring Colt back to her hotel room.

It was a good indicator that she didn't actually know what she was doing, and she should stop putting so much talking into gut feelings and just chill out.

The road narrowed and wound around several extreme S curves before spilling out in front of a rather rough-looking ranch house. That, she assumed, was the landlord's residence. The instructions from the rental company had said that the landlord would be there to meet her on Monday, and would take her up the... She frowned. "The less travelable road that will take you to your house."

*A less travelable road.*

She couldn't even imagine such a thing.

She sighed heavily and parked her car in front of the house.

So much for feeling completely proud of herself and her research.

If the main ranch house was this rustic, she had a feeling that the place she was headed to was going to be...

*New. Exciting. Something you haven't experienced before.*

She tried to latch on to the enthusiasm she'd felt the other morning. When she'd gotten up at six and put on red lipstick and had felt like she was free and full of possibilities.

She got out of the car. "Better to live in a ramshackle cabin alone than in a very nice town house with a soul vampire who eats your youth and joy."

She was going to make that her mantra.

She steeled herself, taking a breath and putting on her most pleasant professional face. She was not going to indicate to the landlord that she was having misgivings or concerns.

It wasn't worth it.

She didn't want to get off on the wrong foot. She was... Well, if she could learn one thing from this experience with Colt, it would be that small towns were *different*.

You were going to run into people, over and over. There was no such thing as seeing someone once and being guaranteed of not seeing them again.

It just didn't happen.

She had run into the man *three times* after all, and that should let her know exactly how she needed to go ahead and deal with the community around her.

She wanted to be a midwife here. That meant forging connections. It meant becoming part of the community.

In San Francisco, she'd had a community. It might've been a city, but the outlying areas that she served were her community. They were a part of her. She knew how it was. Women recommended you to their friends. They talked about you. And the experience of birth was such a personal and sensitive one, and everything you did was important.

Required thought and care. She would have to take every action in this town that way. No sniping at people who cut in front of her in line at the grocery store. No flipping people off when they cut her off on the road.

That would be a challenge.

In that sense, she was used to the anonymity of living in a city. There was really no anonymity happening here. She walked up the front steps of the porch and knocked firmly on the door. There was no doorbell. Which… Seemed obvious.

It took a while, but then she heard heavy footsteps coming toward her, and she knew a moment of concern. She had been liaising with the rental company this entire time, and had assumed that meant this was a safe process. But she didn't have any names. She hadn't verified anything. She had… Well, she had mace her purse.

So there was that.

She had this sense that she'd researched all this because she'd been to town once. Because she'd looked up a map of where the house was without actually having an idea of what that meant spatially. She hadn't…

Oh, she really didn't have any idea what she was doing, and it was far too late to be having that realization.

The door jerked open and she couldn't help herself. She laughed. Not just one burst of laughter either. A whole reel of laughter that made her entire body shake.

"You have got to be *kidding me*."

"I'm sorry," she said, doubling over, before she could look up again at Colt Daniels's irritated face. "I'm sorry," she wheezed. "I can't… I can't breathe."

"You think this is funny?"

"No," she said. "It's the opposite of funny. It's… It's absolutely ridiculous I have been in this town for four days. I saw you at the bar. I saw you at the coffee shop. I saw you at dinner."

"You saw me at the coffee shop?"

"I hid from you."

"Hid from me?"

"Behind the post."

He frowned. "Why did you do that?"

"Because of *this*," she said, wildly waving her hand back and forth between the two of them.

"What? That I'm your new landlord? At least, I assume that's why you're here."

"If you own this property. Then yes. You're my landlord. But no, that's not why I... This is ridiculous."

"You honestly didn't know?"

She moved her hand back and forth between them. "You clearly didn't know. If you didn't know, how would I know?"

The hysteria settled in her chest, leaving something surreal behind. The wind rustled in the pines that surrounded the property, and she heard birds chirping somewhere. It would be idyllic if she wasn't consumed by the heat from the man in front of her.

She tried to breathe.

She couldn't.

"Well, what are you going to do now?" he asked.

She sighed heavily. "Colt," she said, her heart thundering hard. Just saying his name did things to her.

He was the most beautiful man she'd ever seen, and she'd seen him naked. He'd seen her naked, and more than that... Deeply unguarded. It was not the most comfortable situation. On many levels.

But she was in it.

So what else could she do?

Maybe this was her lesson. That she was no longer allowed to sink into a state of avoidance. Of complacency. Because she had lived whole years with Jared that she hadn't even *felt*. They'd just sort of slipped by, like water downstream.

She'd been numb to them. To their interactions. And what she could say for certain about her new start in Gold Valley was that she hadn't been able to live a single moment of it complacent.

She'd felt each minute. Down in her bones, under her skin. Deep in her body where she had never felt things quite like that before.

Maybe this was the lesson.

That living, that feeling, wasn't easy.

But maybe it was better than what she'd had before.

"I... I need a place to stay. And I am... Desperately looking to start over."

"Why is that exactly?"

"Remember the guy I was with?"

"Yeah. He had a punchable face."

"He does," she said. "He just looks like someone you want to punch."

At least, he looked that way to her now.

"Yes."

"Well he...he and I had a really toxic, horrible breakup, and we were together for fifteen years."

"Guys that look like him are only ever toxic." The confidence in that statement irritated her. Like he'd seen in five seconds what it had taken her more than a decade to see.

"Yeah. Okay. You sound like my brother now." She let out a long, slow breath. "So yeah he...he cheated on me and..."

"Okay," he said. "I can figure out the rest."

There was something in his tone that indicated he didn't really want any more details. But too bad for him because she wasn't done talking.

"I just want *something*. We lived in a town house together for years. Everything was...the same. And now...now I need something different. *This* is different. I'd better take it. I need to. And don't worry. I am the opposite of looking for a relationship right now."

"Okay, good. Because I am looking for a relationship never."

"I need to be alone."

"I mean, I sure as hell like being alone too."

"Good. So… It's all fine. We were surprised. Both by each other at dinner and now… Maybe *we're cousins*. Maybe that's the joke."

He grimaced no. "I would… Rather that weren't case."

"I'm not saying I hope it's true. I'm just saying. The universe is being a little weird."

"The universe is an asshole. However, I don't see any reason why you can't stay there. It's not like we're going to be able to avoid each other if you don't."

"It seems that way."

"Come on then."

He walked out of the house past her, down the front steps. She followed on after him. "I have all the stuff in my car."

"It's a little bit of an intense trip up the road if you aren't used to it. If you want me to, I can drive."

"You want to drive my… My car?"

"I think *you* might want me to drive your car."

"I don't."

"All right, but I might catch a ride with you. I can walk back down, and I need to check out some stuff that way anyway."

"Go right ahead."

But when she got in the driver's seat, and he got in the passenger seat, suddenly everything around her seemed far too full of his particular brand of masculine energy. She just… She couldn't really breathe around it.

So much for telling herself that this was part of her lesson. Her body seemed to feel a slightly different wavelength than her brain.

She had never experienced anything quite like this. Her attraction to Jared was… Different. Yes, she had thought that he was beautiful, but there had been something else to it. Something that had made her feel validated.

She had constantly been seeking, searching for his approval. For him to give her the crux of his attention. Something about that had become addicting. It was gross, and she didn't like it. In fact, in hindsight it made her feel downright ashamed. But she hadn't been able to see it at the time. Not been able to untangle the many bonds that had held her to him, like a spiderweb with thin tendrils. On their own, not terribly strong, but they were a network, and there were so many of them—every time one broke there seemed to be more.

Until he'd broken them all.

The bonds that held her to Colt were simple. They were made of lust and desire. And they were… Well, they were strong.

And thinking about Colt and *bonds* in the same train of thought was…that didn't make things any more comfortable.

It made her sweaty.

"Which way do I go?" she asked.

"Just back out here," he said, and she did. "All right, now go this way." He pointed at the copse of trees that lined an extremely narrow-looking road that she might have called a deer trail if it hadn't been clear he expected her to drive on it.

"This seems cruel and unusual."

"You can make it."

So she did, nosing her car through the trees and gasping when she went right down into a pothole.

"You're fine," he said.

"Don't laugh at me." She was sweaty now, but not because she was thinking about Colt and the potential of bonds and being tied up. Because this was scary.

She kept on driving, and then when they came around the corner, the trees to her right faded away and there was a sheer cliff face on her side.

She hit the brakes. And the back tire skidded.

"Dammit," Colt said, raising his hand against the dashboard. "Are you trying to kill us both?"

"I don't want to drive," she said.

"You'll have to eventually," he said.

"I don't want to do it now." She scrunched her eyes shut.

"You said you did."

"But I don't. A woman has the right to change her mind, Colt. Drive the car."

She turned the engine off and sat there, waiting for him. He sighed heavily, then got out of the passenger side, which was thankfully the side that was on the rocky cliff face. She got out of the driver's side. She looked over at the other side and decided that she was not getting in. She climbed into the backseat still on the left-hand side.

"You're fine," he said. "And if you would've gone over there to get in the car you would've seen how much clearance you had."

"I have no clearance. A guardrail. You need to build me a guardrail."

"Do I look like the Oregon Department of Transportation to you?"

"You look like a man who's enjoying my suffering."

"Mallory," he said. "I only enjoy one particular way of making a woman suffer." He looked over his shoulders, those blue eyes connecting with hers and sending shivers straight through the center of her thighs. "This isn't it."

Heat prickled her scalp and she found herself breathless. "Fine."

She closed her eyes as they bumped and slid up the gravel road for what seemed like at least fifteen minutes.

"It was two minutes," he said.

"Oh," she said. "Well, I wasn't aware that I had given my estimation out loud."

"You don't like heights, do you?"

"I very don't."

You couldn't control a fall from any sort of height. Mallory liked control.

"I guess we should've gone through that on the rental listing."

"There *are many things* that I wish we had shared on this rental information."

"What do you think of the house?"

She got out of the car, and she was shocked to see that the house was… Not awful.

"I've been working on it. And as openly stated in the listing, there is a little bit more work to do. But I just bought this place."

It was small, but there were cute little flower planters out in front of the cabin, and the steps looks freshly replaced and stained. The little porch had chairs on it, which were lovely. Just the place you might want to sit and take in the view all around.

It was so much better than she could've anticipated, and for a moment she forgot about the awkwardness of the situation. Forgot about the fact that this wasn't going wholly according to plan. That she had just traversed a precipice to get here…

Well, it seemed like the journey to the top of a mountain now. Which it had been, literally.

But it felt like a spiritual journey.

"It's really beautiful."

"Get out."

She obeyed, but only because she was keen to see the rest of it. This felt like starting over. This felt like something new. You could hear yourself think here. She could take a full breath. She turned around and looked at the treetops down below... Well, that was why he made that drive. She could see all the way down the mountain, there were just... More mountains. A sea of green. Patchwork pine trees layered over the top of one another. It was beautiful. Truly beyond anything she had ever seen before.

"I didn't know they made green like this," she whispered.

"And it's your view."

Her view.

*Hers.*

"I love it."

"Are you going to need me to chauffeur back up here tonight?"

There was something about the request that sent a shiver over her body.

"No. I'll figure it out."

"Glad to hear it. Can I help you carry anything?"

He didn't wait for her answer, rather he was already getting into the back of the car pulling out boxes.

"You know, I didn't say that I need help."

"But you do."

"Well, you're very decisive, aren't you?"

He laughed. "Yeah, you could say that."

She sighed heavily, then ran back to the car, grabbed her suitcase and followed Colt up the steps of the porch. Their footsteps echoed hollow on the wood, and she looked around at the porch. There were some intricate carvings on the support beams. A moose. A wolf. An owl and a bear.

"These are beautiful."

"Passes the time."

"You…carved these?"

"I do a little bit of woodworking. I enjoy it. I've been adjusting to…" He cut his sentence off as if he regretted starting it.

She was curious. But she refused to press because she didn't want him to know that she was curious. She just followed him inside. The inside was… Well, it wasn't quite as well put together as the outside.

"I still have things to do."

The place was furnished, just as promised, but it was… A little bit shabby. It had definitely seen better days. It was overall habitable. The living room was tiny, with a little woodstove in the corner. There was a black couch shoved against the back wall, and a small coffee table in front of it. The cabinets were wooden and so were the countertops. The fridge and stove were a very distinct avocado green. There was no microwave. No dishwasher.

"It's pretty simple," he said.

"I mean… Simple is what I need. It is. Look, Colt…"

"Are you about to give me a lecture?" he asked.

"Not intentionally."

"I don't need a lecture. You're going to tell me that this is a very bad idea, right?"

"It *is* a bad idea," she said.

But he took a step toward her, and tension infused the moment. She could remember so clearly what it had been like.

To have his mouth on hers.

It was so strange to see her mystery lover in such mundane places. Except, his existence here, where they were alone, turned this into something other than mundane. And turned it into something spectacular, whether it should be or not. Filled the moment with possibility. And she didn't know she was going to be able to…

*What? Resist?*

He hasn't asked you for anything. In fact, he's telling you that nothing is going on. The same as you were about to tell him.

There's nothing to resist.

That annoyed her. Because he was getting to tell her first. It annoyed her because what she really wished was that she could've gotten it out first. Made her case. Be the mature adult.

Instead of the needy woman she was.

"Exactly," she said. She was all very *you can't fire me, I quit!* now. "It's not a good idea. Like I said. I was in a relationship for a very long time. I don't want entanglement. This next stage of my life is going to be about me."

"Yeah, I've seen the living you've been doing."

She huffed. "How old do you think I am?"

"Twenty-five."

*"Liar."*

"Twenty-eight."

"Thirty. Thank you for your more believable lie, though."

"So you've been in a relationship since you were fifteen," he said.

"Yes. I think the thing with us was something I needed. A one-night stand was something that I wanted to… Mark my spiritual growth with." That wasn't strictly true. She hadn't planned to want him. She just had. But it sounded good. Worldly and confident and a whole host of things she didn't actually feel like she was. "I just didn't figure that my chosen partner would be…so in my life. I want to spend some time…alone. Figuring out who I am and what I want."

"Totally alone?"

"Yes," she said. "I mean, no. I'm here because my brother's here. I'm here because I want to be part of a growing family, and I want to be close. Because he's the most important person in my life for… Griffin is very important. So, it isn't really about going it alone necessarily. It is about being independent, I guess. I don't know how to do entanglements without being dependent. I know other people do it just fine. But I don't."

"Don't get worked up about it," he said. "I'm not the kind of guy who does relationships, but I do hookups. I'm not necessarily used to being this close to my hookups after, but it doesn't bother me."

"So… You know, what we did was… Commonplace." She swallowed. "For you."

No call *getting worked up*, because she didn't have any real reason to try anything other than what he had. He should be the experienced one. It was good that he was having almost no reaction to her. At least, it should be. Because it should give her all the permission she needed.

To be guilt-free. Have no regrets.

This was who he was. And she should be appreciative because he was exactly the kind of man she'd needed. A man who could be that accomplished manwhore she had required. With skills to make her come like she had never come in her life.

And also had the necessary emotional fortitude to walk away, without her having to feel bad for using him or anything like that.

And still, it bothered her.

It bothered her that what was a singular experience for her had been one in a long line of such experiences for him. Nothing more than a blip on his sexual radar. He wouldn't even remember in a few months, after an untold number of women would take him into their motel rooms since she had.

"I didn't say that," he said, disrupting her line of thinking altogether.

"I… I don't understand."

"I didn't say that what we… I didn't say it was exactly like every other experience I've ever had. I said one-night stands were common for me."

She looked past his left shoulder. Right at the wall. "So this… Was different?"

"I don't want to answer that question. Because you want to be done."

"Yep. I do. I need to."

"Why?" he asked, his voice all low and gravelly. And the simple questions answered her more than a direct answer to her question.

Her heart fluttered. Her stomach went tight. She felt drawn to him. Even more intensely that she had at the bar. What was it about this? Because his eyes meant something to her. Because they spoke to her. Something about him seemed to reach inside her and draw her close. She couldn't understand.

"Don't do that," he said.

"I'm not… Doing anything."

"You are."

"I'm not."

"Don't look at me like you're begging me to come over there and kiss you."

"Oh, I assure you, sir, there is no begging."

Now she was imagining begging him, and it was far, far too easy.

He looked toward her, and she squeaked.

"Liar," he said.

"Fine. I'm having good memories of you. But my head will prevail. We are obviously connected in ways that we can't untangle. Griffin and Iris. They are both important people to us and even more so right now… Trying to find my place in this community and…"

"Right. Well."

He took a step back, and she could breathe again.

"This is fine. I'll be fine," she said. "I'll figure out how to drive up here. But you really won't install a guardrail for me?"

"How about I get you a guide llama?"

"Uh…"

"Guide raccoon? He won't be able to carry much."

"Going to pass on the guide. But thank you."

"You will find that I make a lot of these kinds of helpful suggestions. Meaning, not helpful at all."

"I guess it's good to know what I'm getting into."

"Just so you know, there's a few things in the barn that I haven't had the chance to move in. A coffee maker and a toaster, a few other small appliances."

"Oh…yeah I could use those. I mean, I have a coffee maker but it's old."

"This one is new. I bought some things, I just hadn't brought them all up."

"Where is the barn?"

"It's right next to the main house."

"Okay, I'll go through it and bring up what I need."

Then he turned and walked out of the house, leaving her there by herself.

She began to work at bringing in boxes, trying at the same time to mentally accept everything that had happened since she'd made her move. She'd already slept with someone, and she was trying to figure out how to cope with that.

Not bad for a woman who had clung to a relationship for a decade.

"Maybe that's the growth I'm waiting for."

She said it out loud because she was alone, and it was her house and no one would think she was crazy.

And that felt like growth too.

Though, this whole growth thing wasn't exactly clear or

easy, and after spending so many years in a vague state of unhappiness that she was only just now becoming fully aware of, she had been hoping, deeply, that growth would be easier. That somehow she would move here, and there would be magic. That she would be cosmically imbued with maturity and strength heretofore unknown.

Though what she seemed to have learned was that she made mistakes when it came to the men she chose to sleep with.

Images of that night filtered before her mind's eye, and she really couldn't call Colt Daniels a mistake.

It had been orgasmic triumph. Like climbing a mountain. Sexual Everest.

But she didn't need to climb it multiple times. She could just climb it once.

She had thoroughly scaled it. All was well. And now she could practice other things.

Like living in her own space. Being independent and not emotionally codependent.

"I am practicing," she said into the room. "I am practicing."

The first thing she did was set up her music so that she had something to sing to. And with that, she did her best to allay the lingering tension that she felt. Her mind continually straying back to the night she had spent in bed with him... Well, she was just reliving the climb.

It did not mean that she wanted to do it again. Didn't mean she would.

She was being a mature adult.

"Welcome, Mallory," she said to herself. "Maturity is yours."

# CHAPTER FIVE

"SHE IS MY DAMN TENANT."

"What?" Jake was looking at him like he was insane, and he realized that he had not introduced this story with any kind of explanation. But then, he hadn't decided yet he wanted to give his brother an explanation. Except... He'd said that, because it was the first thing that crossed his mind when he saw Jake on the back of his horse, getting ready to go out and ride.

"Mallory Chance."

"Griffin's sister?"

"The very same."

"Why exactly did you say it like that?"

"Well, it may surprise you to learn, Jake, that I have seen her before. Before dinner on Sunday."

"Really?"

He gave his brother a hard look.

"Oh," Jake said, realization clearly sweeping over him in that moment. "Well, Griffin is going to kill you."

"Griffin isn't going to find out, because we are never doing that again. But, imagine my surprise to discover that the sexy stranger I hooked up with last week is not only related to my cousin's husband, but she is living on my property."

"Well, maybe it's a sign you need to date her. You did sleep with her after all."

"I don't date. And anyway what year is it, Jake? You

slipped into some kind of 1950s fantasy that I should be aware of?"

His brother cackled out loud at that. "Right. Can you imagine Cal the 1950s housewife? If I told her to put on an apron, she'd slap my face." Though Jake didn't look upset at the idea.

"Another ringing endorsement for marriage."

"Hey, I'm glad to hear that you hooked up. I was getting a little bit worried about you."

"I don't deserve your happiness. It wasn't something I should have done. It's not something I'm interested in repeating. I promise you that."

"I mean, do you think she's hot?"

"You're not listening. It's Griffin's sister."

"No, I heard you. I guess I'm just wondering why it's such a bad thing, because what it sounds like to me is you've got a little proximity and a lot of opportunity, and I don't know why you're so intent on denying yourself."

"I don't want proximity."

He did not talk about this shit. But he was out here opening his damn mouth talking to his brother. That was the thing. They'd been talking lately.

Which was different for the two of them.

The entire family had always assumed they were close.

Because of course they had gone off to the rodeo together, so they must be the best of friends.

The fact of the matter was he and Jake might have gone off together, but once they'd left, they'd gone their separate ways more or less. They'd run in their own circles. Drank with their own friends. And he'd never talked about serious stuff to anyone.

But ever since Jake had gotten married it had changed.

When Jake had nearly lost Cal, Colt had been the one his brother had talked to about it, and it had been impossible for them to not end up talking about their lives. About their losses.

And the talk about the end of theirs parents' lives had strayed into territory Colt didn't want to wade into. Because it required mining those last moments of his father's life, and Colt just really didn't want to do that.

It was too painful.

Honestly, in general, he laughed about trauma stuff. Maybe that wasn't enlightened, but mostly he just felt like if you could go on, you should. Just dust yourself off and keep walking.

Those memories… Those memories lived somewhere deep. And sometimes they overtook him and he was forced to play them out from beginning to end.

More often than not, he was pretty successful at stopping them. That was the best thing to do. It was the best thing he could do—just get on with things.

But he wasn't sure why. That was the thing. Trent's death had made everything feel closer to the surface.

Because death felt like it was everywhere. All around him. Inescapable. The aftermath of it. The unfairness of it. The feeling of being left when you should be the one that was gone. It was one of those things you never explained to another person. He could barely explain it to himself.

"I needed to change some things. I was headed to an early death."

Except death seemed to skip him every time it came by.

"Yeah," Jake said. "I worry about you. I guess my question is, why do you suddenly care?"

"You know why. If I kept on living like I did, isn't that just spitting on Trent's grave? He was going to be a father, Jake. He had so much to live for. And here I am."

"You're not bound up in his death, Colt."

"I am," Colt said, his voice rough.

"Whatever gets you in a better space. If this does. I sure as hell have no desire to bury my brother, and I know the rest of them didn't see the kind of shit you pulled..."

He meant his family. They saw him happy, laughing. Playing his guitar at family gatherings. Even though they didn't see how the music in him had changed. How his own songs had gone away. They saw what he wanted them to see.

They'd never seen him dark and ready to defy death.

Jake had.

"Yeah it does. So there's some stuff I'm not doing anymore. No rodeo. No sex."

"You failed at that last one."

"Yeah, I don't have practice with abstinence unfortunately. Apparently I'm bad at it."

"We all have our strengths."

"But, I'm also not drinking to excess."

"Good for you."

Silence lapsed between them and Colt looked around at the valley below. He saw another horse coming up the hill, flying like the devil was on his heels. And on top was his brother's wife.

"There she is," Jake said.

Her dark hair was flying in the wind, her expression fierce. And Jake looked like he'd been hit with a ton of bricks.

It almost made Colt believe in love.

"Hey there," Cal said when she got to them, smiling, the brightest edge of that smile reserved for his brother. "I thought you'd like some lunch."

"You cooked?"

"No." She looked at her husband like he was an idiot. "I went and picked something up. But I'm taking a break from work too."

He liked that about Callie. His sister-in-law was the same as she'd ever been. Working with energy and optimism. The only daughter of the rodeo commissioner, Callie fought tooth and nail to be allowed to compete the same as the men. This season she was competing and doing well.

She fixed him with a direct gaze. "My dad asked me to pass on his condolences."

"I don't need that. But...same back to him. I know this has been hard for him too. I know it was the first fatality in competition on the circuit in his time as commissioner." It had been four months since Trent's death, but the pain hadn't let up.

"Yeah it was...really tough. But it's a dangerous sport. Everyone getting involved in it knows that."

It was dangerous, yes. But there was a difference between competition and competing when you were in the right head-space. When you were too cocky, drunk off your ass and thought you were bulletproof.

"Thank you."

"Mallory Chance is Colt's new tenant," Jake said, his tone making it clear why that mattered.

"Jake, I swear..." Colt growled.

"Oh, did they sleep together?" Callie asked.

"How the hell did you know?" Colt asked.

"The way you were looking at each other at Sammy's over pie. Like scalded cats. Well, I've seen plenty of rodeo cowboys dealing with barrel racers after a one-nighter where the guy didn't call. I know what that looked like to me."

"It's not that I didn't call," he said, defensive.

"So you did call?"

"We didn't exchange numbers," he said. "It was a mutual not intending to see each other again, I promise."

"And she found you anyway!" Callie laughed. "That is a funny story." He did not find it so funny.

"Yeah. Sure."

"Touchy."

"Don't tell anyone," he said.

"I won't," she said. "You men are as gossipy as a pack of hens. But I don't give a shit who you sleep with. If I spent any time worrying about women that grace your bed, Colt Daniels, I wouldn't have the time to worry about anything else. And I have better things to concern myself with."

"Is that so?"

"Yeah. Like your brother and what he's doing in bed." She leaned over on the back of her horse and kissed Jake on the cheek.

"I don't like this at all," Colt said.

"What?" Jake asked. "My joy?"

"It's the familiarity with your joy that I could do without. Take your joy over there."

"You know, Colt, if you need anything, we're always here," Callie said.

It was the sympathy from Callie that put him over the edge.

"My friend died. I've been through worse. Remember that time my parents died?"

Jake huffed a laugh. "As a matter of fact, I do."

"It doesn't mean this isn't also terrible," Callie pointed out.

Against his will, he had to soften a little. "Thanks, Cal. I appreciate it."

He didn't, though, not really. He just wanted to have things go back to how they had been.

Someday maybe he'd mean it. Someday, after he'd been living here for a while maybe… Maybe he could change himself into someone different. Just maybe. Maybe if he did that, he would feel… Alive again. Not so much like he'd died out there in an arena under the hooves of an angry bull.

Or in a plane somewhere over Alaska eighteen years ago.

## CHAPTER SIX

THE CLINIC DIDN'T have any patients today. But Mallory was meeting with Tirzah Marsden, the retiring midwife, to talk to her about everything she needed to know about the clinic. And to talk about the patients that Mallory would be having transferred into her care.

"We definitely don't have the most up-to-date equipment," Tirzah said.

"This is a lovely setup, though. Really."

It was beautiful, with a calm and serene waiting room. Each of the different birthing suites were set up to be like bedrooms.

It needed a face-lift, maybe, but it was still nice.

Overall, it was such an inviting place, and while Mallory had questioned herself a few times about buying something sight unseen, she didn't question it now.

She really was on the right track. Things might be a little bit weird with Colt, but this was where she was supposed to be.

She was confident in that.

"It's hard to give up," Tirzah said. "It's more of a calling than a job."

"I know what you mean," Mallory said. "I get so close to all my moms. I get to be part of such an amazing experience in their lives."

"Do you have children?" Tirzah asked.

"No," Mallory said. She was often asked that question. People wanted to know why she did this job. And sometimes potential clients saw it as a mark against her that she herself had never had a live birth. But she'd done the job for eight years. She didn't feel insecure about it. And the answer came easily these days. "I had a very traumatic stillbirth. A long time ago. It was that experience, the callousness of the doctors involved, that got me interested in midwifery. I wanted to become the advocate I didn't have."

It was a marvel, sometimes, that she could say all that without crumpling. That she could acknowledge her loss without lingering in it. But it was something she'd compartmentalized. It went here. In her work. She found purpose in her loss by being there to help other women when they experienced pregnancy loss and trauma.

That time in her life had been horrific. She'd been adrift. In denial for the whole pregnancy and so afraid of telling her parents. The only person she'd confided in was Jared. And he'd made her promises. With all the bravado of a fifteen-year-old boy. He'd promised to be there for her, and it had gotten her through.

He'd been there when their baby had been stillborn. And he'd been the one to hold her when she sneaked away from home to cry.

He'd cried with her.

He'd held her hand while they'd walked along the wharf in San Francisco and bought a toy sailboat from a small tourist trap store there. He helped her send it out to sea, a tribute to the daughter they'd never gotten to hear cry.

It had cemented their relationship, but it cemented it in a specific time and place. She'd been loyal to him because of what they'd lost together. Because he'd been the only person she'd had to help her through. Not her parents, her brother, her friends.

But she'd grown and changed since then. She'd found support and purpose in her job. She'd found strength standing on her own, and he just... Hadn't.

Hadn't grown, hadn't changed.

But in some ways she'd been afraid to leave him, because it would mean being separated from the only other person who'd known about her daughter, who'd grieved her.

It was amazing how much that realization allowed her to feel... Understanding for herself in a way she hadn't felt before.

She'd been berating herself for staying with Jared longer than she should have, but she hadn't really let herself remember.

That he'd been there for her. That he'd been good.

*Why does she stay with him...*

Of course, that couldn't go on forever, not when it wasn't good anymore.

"I'm sorry," Tirzah said, her smile kind. It was real sympathy without the kind of pity that turned Mallory's stomach. The kind that came from a woman who had seen every possible outcome of birth imaginable. "Like I said, it's a calling."

Mallory nodded. "Yes."

"It's why it means so much, but it's also why it's time for me to stop. This isn't a job that you can do halfway. It's time for me to see where my path leads me now."

"How many home births do you do a year?"

"Oh, it varies, though maybe thirty percent are done at home. It depends on insurance and the birthing cycle, of course. I feel this year will be busy. We're in the right phase for a birthing boom." Tirzah walked over to the front counter and took hold of a folder. "I have three expectant mothers who are extending out past my date, and I'm sure the schedule will fill up even more when word gets around about you. Lizzie Omak, Angela Litman and McKenna Dodge."

She handed the file to Mallory. "All three are in good health. Nothing concerning to report," she said.

"I'm looking forward to getting started," Mallory said. "I've been ready for this for a while."

She said goodbye to the other woman and spent some time looking around the office of the clinic.

There were surely some updates to make. But the way that it was positioned in an old house gave it a homey quality that she liked. Anyway, it wasn't in terrible shape—it just needed a little bit of TLC. And she could see how—when you were working by yourself, and also winding down—the aesthetics wouldn't be a priority.

There was a small office that was mostly cleaned out, and she assumed that it was Tirzah's and she figured that now it would be hers. She started mentally mapping out what she would need.

Everything to keep organized on her terms.

She would have a little bit more technology, that was for sure. But she liked to keep things both in hard copy and virtually. For security. She had a fair idea of everything she would need, and she had the money to do it.

The sale of her town house had put her in a great position to not only buy this place but to get some equipment for it. She wanted some updated ultrasound equipment.

She moved out of the office and into the bedrooms, and started to think about ways she could update those. They were pretty, but she wanted something a little more modern. Something that would bring in outdoor elements and smooth lines. Something very tranquil to enhance the birthing experience. If a home birth wasn't possible, and a mother still wanted this kind of environment, then serenity was absolutely the goal. And a sense that she was somewhere better than home.

A strange sensation tingled in the back of her neck.

Thinking about things like this made her happy. Taking care of people. Making herself... Important. It was something that she always cared about. And when it came to childbirth, the women in question badly needed to be cared for.

They were in a position where the experiences that happened to them during the course of a pregnancy and a birth could be extremely traumatic if not handled properly. Ensuring that things went as well as possible and she did the best she could... It was very important to Mallory.

She knew what it was like. To be in pain. To be confused about what was happening to her body. To be at the mercy of experts. And in her case it had been experts who simply didn't care. Who'd seen her as a young, unmarried girl who probably didn't care about her baby. Or who maybe didn't deserve one. Or didn't deserve compassion or empathy because pregnant fifteen-year-olds were sluts.

Or maybe they'd been busy.

She would never know for sure.

But no one she worked with would ever, ever be made to feel that way, and she made sure of that. She protected her mothers from feeling like victims.

As if it had come from a lightning bolt sent down from on high, she had a second epiphany, about how her behavior didn't stop with her patients.

She had forgotten over time that Jared wasn't a patient, but her boyfriend. As if she had forgotten that it wasn't her job to make his life easy.

To protect him from trauma.

To make up for trauma she'd felt like she'd caused him, even though she didn't think that consciously.

His trauma was his own responsibility. Hers had been up to her, after all. She'd moved on and made something with it. He wasn't a vulnerable woman at the mercy of the person with medical training, going through a physically demanding situation.

And as her behavior with him had shifted, he'd begun to act like he was entitled to the care she gave him. Wandering around acting as if life itself was a trauma for him and he needed to be handled with a soft touch, all the while dishing out nothing but passive-aggressive barbs.

He was a manbaby.

A babyman.

And she enabled him. He had gotten everything he needed from her while she got nothing in return. She had somehow rationalized that as normal and healthy because she was used to it when it came to her job. But that was a choice. And if it was her function and position in her job, when she came home to her regular life wasn't she…

Wasn't she allowed to be taken care of?

*An interesting thought, given that you're trying to be independent…*

Well. She was trying to be independent, it was true but… But. Except… No. This was good. She was learning. What she would need if she was ever to be in a relationship again. She would need to be both independent enough to walk away and not dependent emotionally. And able to ask to be taken care of when she needed it. There was nothing wrong with that. And somehow… *Somehow* he had made her feel like she couldn't do that.

Well, this place had already provided her with an epiphany, so she suppose that was a good thing. She looked at her watch and saw that Mckenna Dodge was due to arrive at any moment. She straightened and went into the bathroom, looking in the mirror. She had her hair tied back in a bun, trying to minimize some of the frizz caused by the warm weather, and was pleasantly surprised that it still looked okay. Her yellow prairie dress might be a little bit on the sweet side, but again, she was trying to give off that comforting aura.

Since the office was empty, she supposed she could conduct her first meeting with McKenna out in the waiting room. That was another thing to think about for the office. She would like something other than an exam room for those initial meetings, something that just felt like a place for a chat between two people. The door opened and a lovely brunette woman with a small baby bump walked in, with a large, handsome man in a cowboy hat behind her. He looked like an old-fashioned movie star. All square jaw and broad shoulders. But he had an extremely concerned look etched on his handsome face.

"Good morning," Mallory said, relishing the opportunity to slip into her role. Because she knew this. One thing about this move to Gold Valley was that she had been very much out of her element. And now... Now she was in it. "I'm Mallory Chance. I know that Tirzah spoke to you about the fact that I would be the attending midwife."

"Yeah," the man said. "She did."

"I'm McKenna Dodge," the woman said. "This is Grant. He's freaking out."

"That's very common," Mallory said, trying to be reassuring.

McKenna looked at her husband. "See? You're common. I told you."

"Maybe I'm common because it's normal to worry about your wife deciding not to have a baby in a hospital."

"He's fine," McKenna said, waving a hand.

Mallory was used to this. All of it.

She saw a mix of people, but this was definitely a scenario she saw a lot. It didn't bother her, and it didn't offend her. Giving birth was natural, but it was also a major medical event. And things could go wrong. She knew better than to ever promise anyone that everything would be okay. Because things did happen. She had been part of births that had resulted in medical emergencies and required transport to hospitals on more than one occasion. It was always scary, but she was always ready to make the call if it came up.

"Let's sit down and we'll just talk about a few things. You know, you're not marrying me," she said. "You can change your mind at any time. You can change your mind just before the birth if you're deciding this isn't working for you."

"Thank you," McKenna said. "I keep trying to tell him…"

"I'm not levelheaded," Grant said. "You're well aware of that."

She laughed. "Neither am I. But just not about the same things." She shook her head. "So what do you need to know?"

"Is this your first pregnancy?"

"Yes," she said, glowing.

The conversation went from there. When she was finished, she felt great. Everything had gone smoothly. She really liked the young couple and was genuinely excited for them. Grant had loosened up as the conversation had progressed, and it had come up over the course of conversation that McKenna was his second wife.

That he had been widowed some years back, and his reticence made perfect sense. He was afraid of losing someone. Everyone was, but someone like him, someone with an existing loss in his background, was bound to be a lot more concerned.

There. It was easy.

Easy for her to understand that, but so difficult for her to reach inside herself and make sense of her own emotions. She frowned. She sighed. If only she had read herself as easily as she could read Grant Dodge. For some reason, that put her in mind of Colt Daniels, and she banished all thoughts of him, and quickly. She stepped out of the clinic and onto the sunny street, careful to lock the doors behind her. She made her way over to the Cookie Jar, Iris's bakery, which was just a stone's throw away from the clinic.

She walked in and took a deep breath of the sugar-laden air. "Iris," she said. "This place really is a miracle."

Her sister-in-law poked her head up from behind one of the display cases. "Mallory," she said. "Good to see you. It's going to take me a while to get used to the fact that you're just here. I know Griffin is so happy about it."

"Well. I'm glad that he's happy. I know I'm really happy to be here." She chose not to think about Colt, and whether or not he was happy she was here.

He doesn't care, remember?

No. Of course he didn't care. She was just another one-night stand to him.

He said it was different…

Well, he implied it, anyway.

But there was no use dwelling on that.

"I need some cake."

"Well, you've come to the right place."

Mallory sat down at one of the small tables right next to the counter. "What kind of cake do you have?"

"All kinds."

"Well, what kind do you recommend?"

Iris regarded her closely. "You look like you're in a hummingbird cake space."

"That sounds like it could only be delicious, and I will not argue."

"Two slices of hummingbird cake coming right up."

A moment later, Iris joined her at the small table, a thick slice of cake on each plate that she set down in front of them. "I have to confess that it might be me in the mood for hummingbird cake," Iris said. "This pregnancy has me obsessed with sweets. Then, I'm always obsessed with sweets."

Mallory examined her sister-in-law. Iris was very pretty, but in an understated way. She kept her dark brown hair in a series of neat, elegant updos, and she favored sweet, feminine outfits. Usually, the only adornment on her face was a smudge of flour.

She was very different to Griffin's first wife, who had been sophisticated and polished, very outgoing. It was funny that her brother had fallen in love with two such different women, but Iris was the perfect woman for who Griffin had become. And Mallory was supremely grateful for her. She was also looking forward to getting to know her better.

*There. You thought about your future for a whole ten seconds without inserting Colt.*

Well, now she just lost the game, because she thought about it again. Just by thinking about how she had thought about it.

Iris took a delicate bite of the hummingbird cake, then gave Mallory an impish grin. "It's so good. If I do say so myself."

Mallory took a bite of the cake too and closed her eyes in absolute delight. It was all coconut and sweet, filled with tropical flavors, and she loved it. "You're right, this is great."

"I'm not one of those people who thinks something can be too sweet. Though, I obviously temper that a little bit with a lot of my baked goods here. You have to meet mainstream taste requirements. Though I like to make sugar bombs for Rose. My younger sister. You've met her."

"Yes. I remember Rose. She's..."

"She's a whole thing. Actually, I'll have to tell you about how Rose and her matchmaking are sort of responsible for Griffin and I getting together."

And so, Iris did. Recounting how Rose's attempt to set Iris up with a man who was objectively very, very boring had backfired and had sent Iris out on a quest to make herself more interesting—which had involved pursuing her dream of opening a bakery, which had led her to Griffin's door, back when he had been feral and barely human.

"I'm glad that you did," Mallory said. "Because none of us could have ever reached him. I know that I thanked you already, but really, thank you. Griffin is... I've always idolized him. He has always been everything I ever wanted to be. And seeing him as unhappy as he's been for all this time and not being able to do anything to help him...it was the worst thing. I did what I could, I called him, but I just wasn't..."

For some reason, she felt a slight twinge around her heart as the words that she had to say to her sister-in-law hit her. She hadn't thought them through before she started to speak them, and she hadn't realized that she felt any kind of way about them until it was too late. "I... I wasn't the person who could do it. I tried. I did. Maybe I should've driven up and brought him down from the mountain—I don't know. But I called him. All the time, even when he didn't pick up. Even when he didn't call back. But you're just the one, I guess."

How *petty*.

*How petty that you're hurt that the woman he has fallen in love with and married is the one who was able to reach him. That's the power of love.*

But not her love. Never apparently her love.

*Wow, Mallory. You could not sound more pathetic.*

But she'd...she'd wanted to rescue him because she knew what grief was like. Even though hers was private. Even though his own had made her more determined to keep hers a secret.

How could she ever tell her parents that they'd lost another grandchild? One they'd never known about? And what would the point be?

Still she'd wanted... She'd wanted to find another way to give meaning to what she'd gone through. Wanted to pull him back from the edge.

But that hadn't been for her to do. It had been Iris.

She was going to make an attempt to buck up, because she was sitting there being ridiculous while eating a delicious piece of cake with one of the sweetest women that she had ever met, feeling... Weirdly jealous of the fact that the woman had helped her brother out of the deep trenches of grief? She was grateful. That's all.

That was what she had told herself ever since Iris had come into his life.

And it was a surprise to discover that her feelings were slightly more complicated... Well, that it was a surprise... A shock, really, to discover that the center of her caregiver core was a deep, real selfishness.

She was almost... In awe of it. She had known she had it in her. Quite literally. She wanted to be the one who saved Griffin. Because somehow she'd imagined it would give her value. Give her loss purpose.

Redeem her.

She was uncomfortable with that. And she only grew increasingly more comfortable with that the longer she sat there across from Iris.

So she didn't say anything. She just sat there, eating her

cake. And she thought about telling Iris about… Things. About Colt. She was trying not to think about him, so she didn't really want to bring them up either.

"How did everything look at the clinic?" Iris asked. And that was when Mallory realized that her silence was probably uncomfortable.

"Great. Everything is great. I'm really excited to be here. I…" And then she realized it would be weird if she didn't tell Iris that she was renting from Colt. "I found out that my landlord is your cousin, weirdly."

"What? Oh, at the… The house. For a second I was still thinking about the clinic."

"Yeah. I… Colt. He owns the property with the cabin I'm staying in. I didn't realize it until I went there last night. I knew him because I… Met him. At Ryder's house." She realized everything she was saying sounded strange and lame and she was overexplaining things. And there was now no way the whole situation wouldn't sound a little bit weird, which had been exactly what she was trying to avoid.

"I haven't actually been up to Colt's new ranch. He just moved there."

"It's… Rustic," Mallory said. "But nice," she added quickly.

"Great. Well… If he's not nice to you, you'll have to let me know, because I'll beat him up."

"Is he… Not nice?"

And she realized that it sounded a little bit like she was fishing for information about him, but really, she was just making conversation. She was trying to kind of not think about her general selfishness regarding her brother, and also to find the exact appropriate amount of conversation to make about Colt that didn't make it seem like she had slept with him.

"Oh, I mean not any more or less than any of the guys in my family," Iris said, waving a hand. "It's just that they're all… You know, their whole thing. Colt and Jake specifically. Well, Jake was more one before he got married. But you know. Rodeo cowboys."

"I can honestly tell you that I have no experience of rodeo cowboys."

"Griffin is a cowboy," Iris said, somewhat archly.

"Kind of." Mallory relented. "More of a rancher."

"Well, okay, I'll give you that. That's how my brother is. Ryder. He's a rancher. And he's steady. You have to be when you work the land. You have to be up at a certain time every day. You have responsibilities. It's all about that. Rodeo cowboys on the other hand…"

"I can imagine you have to be kind of crazy to do that sort of thing." And she found herself extremely interested in spite of herself. "What… What event did he do?"

"He's a bull rider," Iris said.

For some reason, the thunderbolt of pleasure and need went straight through Mallory's thighs. A *bull rider*.

Was she having a full-on reaction to him? That was so… Primitive.

He made her primitive, she guessed.

She'd known that he was a cowboy, but she hadn't known he was like… A cowboy. It was so intense. He was a man who risked life and limb for… Well, a belt buckle, she supposed. She didn't actually know anything about the rodeo. Her entire reaction was based upon a sense of mystique that might not be at all real. But it made her tingle. In very interesting places.

*You're ridiculous.*

Yes, she was ridiculous. But she didn't really know what she could do about it. She seemed to be ridiculous when it came to Colt Daniels. But she had a whole different name for being here, and it had nothing to do with that errant attraction that she felt for him, so she was just kind of content to... Ignore it. But that didn't mean she couldn't... Sit here and enjoy this moment, with a healthy amount of distance between herself and Colt. She wasn't in danger of jumping him when he wasn't even here.

"Yeah. Well, not anymore. I guess one of his friends... Someone he was pretty close to died in an accident, and he quit. Though, he won't say that's why. That's what Jake says, though."

Suddenly, Mallory felt guilty. Like she shouldn't have that information. She had met Colt with no name. No knowledge of his occupation. No information about him, his family, his life. Nothing but a fantasy. And it had never occurred to her that he might be running from something that night they had hooked up.

He said that one-night stands were his modus operandi, and she believed him.

But there there had been something in their coming together, something singular and intense, and she knew that. Whatever he said, she knew that.

She might not have had a lot of sex with a lot of different people, but she'd had sex, and she knew what the mechanics were. She knew that there was something else happening between them other than just physicality. Other than just orgasms.

But they hadn't engaged in intentional intimacy. She didn't have the right to have secrets about him. About his grief. His dead friends. The reason he left the rodeo. It reshaped the fantasy that she had of him. She didn't want him to become a real person, she found.

And more to the point, she felt uncomfortable with it.

"I'm sorry to hear that," she said, looking away.

And Iris had no idea that what she was doing felt like a

breach of trust, because she didn't know that Mallory had a relationship with him that went beyond the one she'd confessed to.

*You don't have a relationship with him, you lunatic. You banged him. That's it.*

Yes, that was it. But still, it felt like a prior, existing connection that made it unfair for her to gain information about him through back channels.

"Yeah, but Colt doesn't like to talk about things," Iris said. "So... I don't really know any details."

That didn't help ease Mallory's mind. "Oh. Well. I should go. I need to go back to the clinic for a little while. But thank you. Thank you for the cake. Thank you for the cake and... Everything." She really tried to mean it. Really tried not to dwell on the tangle of complicated feelings that were rioting inside of her. "You know you're welcome to come to dinner tonight if you want," Iris said.

"Thank you. I'll probably stay home tonight." The word felt strange on her tongue. *Home.* Was this really home? She wasn't sure yet. She wasn't sure what it would feel like to be home, or when she would feel like she was even at home in her skin. Everything had changed so much in the last few weeks.

She was happy about it.

Mostly.

But... She also just felt strange. She wondered how many of these surprises she was finding deep down inside of herself had to do with the fact that she had been so distracted by her relationship with Jared it had prevented her from being wholly honest with herself about who she was and what she wanted. It had prevented her from really taking inventory of her relationships. It had been protective in ways she hadn't realized. And that was a very odd realization.

Tonight though, she would spend some time at home, her new home, putting it together. She would go into the barn, like Colt had suggested she do, and dig around for some of the things that she needed. And she would deal with that drive, even though it frightened her. She managed to make it down okay today; she would be able to make it back up just fine.

And maybe she would just spend some time thinking about herself.

That was another unpleasant realization. She had to wonder if the distraction of Colt was something she couldn't shake just because it was more interesting to ponder him than it was to think about her issues. Issues that she didn't really want to deal with. Because who did?

Nobody wanted to deal with their own issues.

Well, alone in a tiny, remote cabin where she didn't even have TV, she would have ample time to ponder them.

If only she could only keep herself from pondering her landlord.

# CHAPTER SEVEN

COLT'S ENTIRE BODY hurt like a son of a bitch. He could not believe how sore he was from doing ranch work. But putting in a new fence, moving hay around, dealing with heavy equipment and hefting building materials back and forth had made for a helluva day. He was dirty, sweaty, and he was in pain.

He still hadn't dealt with the interior of his house, which badly needed a face-lift, not because he was remotely fancy, but because he needed a bathtub big enough for him to sit in. He was too tall for a standard tub, and he needed to soak. Thankfully, he bought a hot tub off of a guy on the circuit, and he'd installed it out in the barn.

It wasn't the final stop for it, but he didn't have the deck built that he needed, and this worked fine for him. He went out to the barn and double-checked the temperature, then he walked in the house, opened up the fridge and got a beer. He took his hat off and set it on the counter, took his shirt off and wiped his chest down, then threw the shirt onto the floor.

He was beat.

He went back outside, the oppressive heat molding itself to his skin. He was over it. Whose bright idea was it to quit the rodeo and become a rancher?

He preferred eight seconds of glory to this bullshit.

No wonder he'd left Hope Springs when he'd been eighteen. It had been a solid decision.

"Whine about it, Daniels," he growled to himself as he wrenched the barn door open again, then pulled it closed.

He kicked off his boots, his socks and pants and underwear, and hauled himself, still holding the beer, down into the tub. He was still too damn hot for this, but it was what his muscles needed. Otherwise, he was not going to be human come morning, and Jake was still going to expect him to come out to the ranch.

Jake was establishing a pretty great equine operation, and Colt was impressed with it. He knew his brother was going to be successful with the endeavor, but it was requiring an intense overhaul of the property. Parts of it were completely finished, but with Jake looking to expand, it meant a hell of a lot of work for the two of them.

Of course, Colt could do something with his own ranchland. He owned land now. So there was that.

Hell, maybe he could even join forces with Jake in that way. Have some of the animals on his property.

But that all sounded very permanent. And he just didn't feel like making a commitment. Not entirely. Right now, he had a house, and it had decent bones. He could leave and rent it out if he felt like it. Lease his land. Go back on the road.

It had been some thirteen years since he'd been in one place for more than a couple months at a time. He just didn't know if he had it in him. Didn't know if he wanted to find it in him.

He let his head lie back against the rim of the tub. He tried to remember the rodeo. What it felt like. How much he enjoyed going out drinking after a hard-out ride. Picking up his guitar and playing a half-assed country song with more charm than skill. He… He hadn't touched his guitar for a few months. But then, he didn't much feel like he had the right to make music, any more than he felt like he had the right to party or win or fuck. Of course, then he'd met Mallory Chance.

And then, a vision of Mallory swam in his mind. Mallory, with her pale skin and firm, small breasts. Mallory, who had freckles in some interesting places, and he remembered each and every one. Remembered playing connect the dots with them, using lips and his tongue that night in the motel room.

He groaned, feeling himself getting hard beneath the water.

Nope. He wasn't going to do that. He wasn't going to go there with her. Talk about entanglement.

*Damn entanglement.*

She was his tenant. She was connected to his family by marriage. It was ridiculous. He didn't want this.

But then, he didn't want any of it. He couldn't remember the life that he'd had before, not really. It was like watching a reel of someone else's life. Watching a movie where maybe he played a part. But he didn't fit in this life either. Working with his brother, coming home, being angry...

Thinking about a woman who was not very far away, who he decided he couldn't have. It was all... None of it felt like him.

He wasn't sure he knew who he was.

The barn door opened, and he stood up reflexively, turning around to see what the hell was going on. And there she was. Standing in the doorway, backlit by the sun, her hair a glowing reddish halo, her eyes wide. She was wearing a demure little dress that was gently fluttering midthigh thanks to the breeze, and she was staring... Well at the part of him that had been getting a little excited thinking about her only a moment before.

"I... I'm sorry," she said, turning away from the door and practically running off.

"Hell," he growled, stepping out of the tub, yanking a towel off the nearby shelf and wrapping it around his waist. "Hey, don't worry about it," he said.

"I…" She turned back around. "I don't see how this is going to work."

In that moment, he didn't know why he would go after her. He didn't know why he cared at all. Any number of women had seen him naked. More than he could count. She'd seen him naked—he didn't care. But she was distressed, and his immediate instinct had been to go after her. It bothered her, and he couldn't leave it alone. Something was drawing him toward this woman. And it could be argued at this point that it was fate.

*Yeah. Fate. Your favorite.*

"It's fine," he said.

"I mean, you were naked in the barn. You realize that's ridiculous, right? Are you literally bathing in a trough? What is happening?"

"It is a hot tub, inglorious though it is. I bought it off a guy at the rodeo to help with my muscles at the end of the day. That's what I was doing. I don't have a bath in the house that's big enough for me."

"Well. I can… You are… Large." She waved her hand in a strange, circular motion.

"Large?" he asked, lifting a brow in spite of himself.

"Stop it," she said. "I need… I need to spend time with me. Dealing with my issues. Not… Dealing with all of this."

"What am I *all of*, honey? Because let me tell you, I didn't exactly ask for you to come crashing into my life. I didn't ask for any of this either."

"You said you didn't care."

"News flash. I lied. That's why I don't do relationships. I'd be bad at them, which I knew, but apparently, I would be a little bit of a liar. I don't like talking about feelings. I like dealing with them even less. But I am not ready to be dealing with you either. I don't want anything to do with women right now. I don't want anything to do with anything."

"That sounds… Well, sounds like you're pretty much out of luck, because there's nowhere you can go where there's nothing."

"Yeah," he said. "Imagine how irritating I find that."

"Well, you can't just… Do nothing."

"Sure I can. That's what I'm trying to do. Fade into obscurity. Work on a ranch."

"You're a bull rider," she said.

"Who have you been talking to?"

"Iris. We talked about you a little bit," Mallory admitted.

"Did you tell her that you slept with me?"

"No, I did not. Oddly, not a conversation I wanted to have. I don't really want to have it with you either."

"I feel like there's not really any avoiding it."

"What is there to say?" Mallory asked. "We discussed this already. We reintroduced ourselves. But then, you reintroduced me to your… Your penis. So, here we are. Talking about sex again."

The color had risen in her cheeks, and there was no way that he could remain in a neutral position when she was talking about his…his dick. It was just impossible. And she was right—the whole thing was a mess. He took a step toward her, and he was damn tempted to drop the towel.

But, he wasn't suicidal.

"I'm sorry, is it hard for you? Did somebody crash the new life you were trying to create for yourself? Breeze into town and screw up what little you'd managed to cobble together?"

"Yes, as a matter of fact. Except, there's a big inconvenience right where I moved. This is all supposed to be about me. Not another man."

He snorted. "I am not just another man."

"Well, I met you just a few days ago, and everything has become about you since then, so I would say you're not doing a very good job of distinguishing yourself from the rest of the species."

"You know, that would hurt my feelings if my ego wasn't so healthy."

They stared at each other for a long moment, and he felt attraction pouring through him. He knew why they were fighting. They were fighting because if they stopped for even a second, they were going to end up sleeping together again. And he knew it was a bad idea. Somewhere in the back of his mind. He knew that it was a bad idea.

He just couldn't think of why right at that moment.

Because there was no thinking. He was basically naked, and she was wearing a cute little dress that would be easily dealt with...

"No," she said, taking a step back from him.

"What?" He raised his hands, and the towel slipped. He put them back on the towel. "I'm not doing anything."

"No. You're not. I'm just saying that we can't. I realized today that I'm a terrible person. A selfish person. And I need to figure that out."

"Wait a second. Why do you think you're selfish?"

"I can't talk to you when you're naked. And you know, come to that, I probably just can't talk to you. So, we just need to not talk."

"Fine with me."

"I'm sorry I crashed your...bath."

"What was it you were after?"

"The appliances and things that you said were here. I need the coffee maker."

"Go on in and help yourself. Oddly, I'm not all that relaxed right now anyway."

He turned and left her there, heading into the house, ignoring the way that his blood was pouring through his veins. Everything underneath the skin felt hot.

*That woman.*

The thing was, she didn't even make him mad. Not really. She made him interested, and that made him mad. Because what he wanted to do was drag her inside and kiss her. And after he made love with her again, what he wanted to do was find out why she thought she was a selfish person. But he didn't need to know that. The girl had *project* written all over her, and that was what he was avoiding. He couldn't do it. Not again. Not ever. It just wasn't… No. It just wasn't. He wanted to do too many things with her that he just…

*How do you even stand yourself?*

He needed to get back to the rodeo. That was it. At least there he didn't… He didn't think about things. He just did them.

Except for all the free time. And there was too much of it.

And too many reminders.

And now he was as tense as he'd been before, if not more so. He went upstairs and slammed his way into the bedroom, pulling open his dresser drawer and rummaging around for some clothes. He got dressed, and then made his way back downstairs. He wasn't drinking to excess, but he definitely wanted a second beer tonight. Right as he opened up the fridge, there was a knock at the door.

If it was Mallory…

He swore, if it was Mallory, he was going to blow a gasket. Or haul her into his arms and kiss her, protestations from both of them be damned.

He walked over and jerked the door open, but it wasn't Mallory.

He knew the petite blonde who was standing there.

But she was holding a baby.

# CHAPTER EIGHT

MALLORY WALKED OUT of the barn, a blender, a toaster and a coffee maker in her arms. She was clutching them to her body like armor, because if Colt was anywhere near here...

*It's not him that you're worried about. It's you.*

He had looked amazing. Better than she remembered. He was a god. His body was honed. Lean and well muscled. She'd gotten an eyeful of him, all of him, when she first walked into the room, but then she just had to stare at his chest for... Well, for way too long. And it was... Incredible. Beautiful. And she was right back in the mind she'd been in that night they'd been together. She wanted to kiss him again. Lick all that golden skin.

He turned her into something she didn't recognize, and she just couldn't handle it. Not while dealing with all the other crap that was happening inside of her.

One thing was clear—neither of them were in a fantastic emotional space. There was no way they could deal with each other on top of it.

She came out of the barn around her car and stopped. There was another car in the driveway, and there was a woman on Colt's porch. Blond hair pulled up into a messy bun, dark roots showing through. She was in cutoff shorts and a top that barely covered her midriff.

Mallory shouldn't be nosy. It was his business, she supposed.

She shifted, just slightly, and Mallory could see that the

woman was crying. And then she moved even more, and Mallory could see a little bundle in her arms. If there was one thing Mallory knew, it was a little newborn bundle.

*A baby.*

Suddenly, the woman shoved the bundle into Colt's arms. His expression was grim and determined, his hold on the tiny delicate thing protective.

Mallory stood frozen to the spot, unsure of what to do. Unsure of how to react. The woman wiped tears away from her face and took a step back from Colt, who simply stood there grim-faced, clutching the tiny infant.

Mallory didn't know if she was watching a custody exchange or what. Did Colt have a *baby*?

That made her stomach twist, turn. She didn't like it.

Oh, she didn't like that at all. Didn't like the growling, groaning discomfort that roared through her at the thought.

Colt. A baby. Another woman.

*He said he was a whore. Why don't you believe him?*

She should take him at his word. What were the odds that he didn't have a random child if he really behaved how he said he did?

Colt hadn't moved. He was just standing there, the baby in his arms, a car seat at his feet. He looked up, and his eyes clashed with Mallory's. And she felt it. Just like she had the first time she'd ever seen him. Just like she'd felt it the second time they'd seen each other, that night at the bar when he'd taken her to bed.

But there was really no description for what happened to her body when she saw him standing there cradling that infant like he would destroy the whole world to keep it safe.

Even while she felt complicated emotions over the fact that he clearly... That that woman...

Whatever her emotions were about that, it didn't matter.

There was no denying that watching a large man holding a tiny baby was sexy on a biological level that she was just far too human to fight.

She shouldn't watch. She couldn't figure out why she was *watching*.

Her eyes went back to the woman.

This wasn't something routine. There was something wrong with that woman. The way that she was holding herself, the despair on her face.

Mallory knew that all too well. That hollow-eyed look.

Tired and grieving, even while she had a new life to care for.

And when it came to that, Mallory was an expert. As much as any one person could be without having experienced it themselves. And she clicked into gear. Her professional mode. Whatever Colt's relationship was to this woman it didn't matter. That woman needed something. She needed someone. And Mallory was going to be that someone.

She charged forward without further thought. "Do you need some help?"

The woman startled like a cat.

"I have to go," she said, breaking away from Colt.

"Cheyenne…"

"Cheyenne?" Mallory asked, jumping on the name immediately and moving to take control of the situation. The woman stopped. "Is there someone we can call who can meet you here? Someone who can talk to you? Anyone you want to talk to?"

Mallory knew, deeper than training, how much hormones could mess you up. Mallory knew how confusing this could be.

As she'd gone deeper into her own postpartum depression, she'd wondered if she'd have been just as bad if her baby had lived. If she'd have been able to care for her at all.

She'd never know the answer to that, but her sympathy—empathy—for women in these situations made her ache.

And she couldn't turn away from Cheyenne's pain.

"What?" The girl looked confused and tired, dark circles under her blue eyes.

"Does anyone know that you're here?"

She lifted a hand to her lip and started to chew a thumbnail that was half covered in blue nail polish. "I... I don't have anyone to call."

"Then can you talk to me? Can you tell me what's going on?" Mallory asked, keeping her voice as measured as possible.

The woman—that was a stretch, Mallory realized now that she was closer, she seemed more like a girl—looked angry then. "I don't know who you are."

"My name is Mallory Chance. I'm a midwife. I take care of mothers. That's what I do. And it looks to me like you're in some distress. I just wanted to make sure that everything was okay."

Cheyenne's eyes filled with tears. "No everything is not okay. Nothing's okay. And it will never be okay again. Ever."

"Those are just feelings. Those are just feelings it's not reality. I think what we should do is sit down and have a talk."

"I need to go."

"You don't want to leave your baby," Mallory said.

Those words came out harder, with more conviction than Mallory intended.

"I have to," she said.

And then the woman broke away from them and ran down the porch steps, running toward her car.

Mallory stood frozen for a second, her heart thundering, but when Cheyenne started to pull out, Mallory started to run after the car.

Because this woman was clearly in distress, and she had some concern that she would cause herself harm. If she had left the baby with Colt, then she must be worried about what she might do.

And she couldn't just leave her alone.

She couldn't just leave a woman who might be in mental distress.

She couldn't let her leave this baby.

This baby was alive.

This baby was here.

This baby needed her mother.

And as much as Mallory believed she needed to care more for Cheyenne right now, she couldn't stop those words from roaring through her like a flood.

She ran on the gravel until she slipped, fell onto her hands, her palms stinging. She was breathing hard. She looked down at her palms.

They were bleeding.

She closed her eyes and tried to process the last couple of minutes. Then she pushed herself into a standing position. She gazed down at her skin then, at the rocks embedded there and the blood starting to pool.

Dammit.

She was…

Broken.

She swallowed hard, her whole body shuddering.

*This isn't about you. This isn't about you.*

She pushed back against images of a small, still bundle that she'd barely been allowed to see.

And looked back at Colt.

He was still standing on the porch cradling the baby, the expression on his face one of fierce determination.

MAISEY YATES 121

She huffed and started walking back toward him, her steps unsteady.

"What were you doing?" he asked.

"I... She's obviously got postpartum depression, Colt. Somebody had to do something." Her hands still stung.

"Sorry. I didn't figure I could go sprinting after the car while I was holding the baby."

"She might hurt herself," Mallory said, insistent. "We need to call somebody. I assume you know how to get in touch with her?"

"No," he said. "I don't. I know her name, but that's all. We can call the police where she lives and see if they can do a welfare check on her in a few days, but other than that..."

"You don't know the mother of your child?" She couldn't help it. She was judging. Now she was full-on judging.

*You slept with him too. You don't have a lot of room to judge anyone.*

"This isn't my child," Colt said.

Well, that successfully shocked her. "It's not?"

"No."

Mallory felt thoroughly thrown off-balance now.

"Do you... Well, you know her, so you must know whose baby it is."

"Yeah, I do. I..."

"We need to call somebody," she said, charging forward, her brain running a million miles a minute. "We need to call the police."

She was starting to pull herself back from the past, from her moment of making this all too personal.

"No," Colt said.

"Give me the baby."

"Hell no," he growled, turning and walking into the house. Mallory followed.

"Give me the baby. I want to look at the baby."

"She gave the baby *to me*."

"And I need to make sure the baby is okay." She was sounding and feeling a little panicky, so maybe she wasn't as firmly back where she needed to be as she'd thought. "You don't understand. The mother is obviously in mental distress. Not just *upset*. Sometimes people in that state… They might hurt a child. Or themselves. That's my concern."

He looked at her like she might grab the baby and run away.

"I'm not going to *steal* the baby," she said.

He reluctantly handed the bundle to her. She rushed into the living room and laid the baby down on the leather couch. She unwrapped the blanket slowly and looked at her.

A little girl.

She was wearing a white onesie and pink-striped socks, but nothing else.

She had a shock of dark hair on her head—just the standard newborn fuzz that could become any color, really, because most likely it would all fall out.

She was new. *So new.*

And her mother had left her. Mallory's heart clenched tight. The idea that she had simply been… Shoved into Colt's arms and discarded…

*She's not well.*

It might have been the kindest thing Cheyenne could do for the baby right now.

That was true. If she was having some kind of an episode, than making sure the baby was under someone's else's care was probably a wise decision.

"She looks healthy. But of course I don't know her birth weight or anything like that. I have a scale, though, up at my house. We can weigh her, and then after we feed her… We can continue to track her progress, anyway. But I still think we need to call Child Protective Services."

"Why?" Colt asked.

"Colt, she abandoned her baby with you. And you still haven't explained sufficiently to me why she would've done that. What your connection is."

"I'm her godfather," he said gruffly. "I'm the person that's supposed to be left with the baby, aren't I?"

Her stomach dropped, and she looked back down at her hands, momentarily unsure of what to say or do, which she didn't like at all.

She liked to feel in control in these situations. The shock of it was what brought her own trauma back, when she'd spent a long time figuring out exactly how to do this work without overpersonalizing it.

Difficult situations had a healing effect for her. She could share her experiences without reliving them. She could help, which did something to soothe the helplessness that still resonated inside of her.

She hadn't been able to save her own child.

But she'd saved countless others.

It was the legacy of her pregnancy that had never been meant to be, and she accepted that. Jared had never been all that supportive of her getting into midwifery. He'd thought she was hanging on to her pain, punishing herself. She'd never seen it that way. It was giving herself a chance to experience birth in a different way than she had herself. To be there. To be the one to bring babies, crying and breathing, into this world when she hadn't been able to do that with her own.

"Oh," she said. His claim he was the child's godfather successfully shocked her. She hadn't expected… That.

"Can't a mother leave her baby with the baby's godfather?"

"Well… Yes. I suppose so. But that didn't look planned or… Or *happy* or anything."

"It wasn't," he bit out.

"Can you just explain it to me?"

"Her dad's dead," Colt said.

And suddenly, Mallory realized. His friend. *His friend who had died.* The reason he was here.

"Oh… I'm sorry."

He looked at her with a strange light in his eye.

"Iris told me," she said.

"Great," he said, his mouth a grim line. "Are you sure you didn't tell her we had sex?"

She laughed, but not because she thought it was funny. Because it shocked her. "I did not tell her we had sex, Colt. Because that's our business. Hell, I would say that's barely our business. Because we are persistently not dealing with it, which seems like it should be a great idea. It should be the best thing to do. Because it shouldn't keep continually being a problem. I rent a cabin from you up the top of the damn mountain. We should not have to deal with each other this often."

"Go then," he said.

"No," she responded. "Babies are what I do."

"You're a midwife. You're not a pediatrician."

She bit back a litany of tart responses. Because they would not be beneficial or helpful. And what was needed right now was help.

"No. But this baby is less than six weeks old. And I do home visits and check out on babies up until this age. I have the basic equipment to do a medical check. And no, I'm not a pediatrician, but as long as the baby is healthy—and I have no reason to believe she's not—then I am perfectly qualified to handle this." She breathed out a long, hard breath. "Anyway, it's not like I became a midwife because I don't like babies."

"Why are you a midwife?"

Well, this was getting closer to her issues than she wanted him to get. She had an answer that didn't include exposing the whole story of her past, but right now she couldn't think of it.

"I like to take care of people."

That was part of it.

And for some reason right now it didn't feel less loaded than the whole truth. Like the response that had risen up inside of her in the bakery with Iris over her thoughts about Griffin, Jared and the past decision she'd made, the answer suddenly felt like it was made of creeping, treacherous roots. Roots that might drag her down, and she didn't want that. Not now. She had to be competent. She had to be midwife Mallory, not slightly a mess just changed her entire life Mallory.

"I like to take care of people," she reiterated.

"Well, does she look healthy?" he asked.

"Yes. She looks fine."

"Look, if Cheyenne is having… If she's having a breakdown, I don't see how we can call Child Services on her. She did the right thing, right? She went and got help. She left the baby with someone she knew she could trust. And whatever I think about my own personal ability to take care of a child, or why anyone should look up to me at all… It doesn't matter. The fact is I took care of her and Trent when they needed it, and…" He shook his head. "I mean, I'm the reason…"

It was clear to her that there were some things tangled around Colt that he didn't want to contend with right now either.

"You're the godfather?"

"That's what Trent and I talked about before he died. Cheyenne knows that. Of course she does. It was… It was part of the plan. They're so young. She's… I don't know. Maybe she's twenty? Just a girl hanging around the rodeo. Probably barely eighteen when she met Trent. And I thought... I don't know. After the life that kid had, I was just glad that he found someone. I had concerns about the fact that they were so young. Hell, Mallory, I've never been in love. I don't want to be. And this kid just jumped right into it, in spite of the fact that he never had a family. He was a foster kid."

Colt's electric blue eyes met hers with a depth of sincerity that shocked her to her core. "He wanted to be a father to this little girl. More than anything. He wanted to break that cycle. I know he did. He was... He was a little shit. And their relationship was crazy. They were always breaking up and getting back together. It wasn't perfect. But neither of them had any example. In... That wasn't what he wanted for her. He wanted her to have everything. I can't risk her ending up in foster care. My responsibility is to stand guard over her if he can't. And he can't. I don't think that I should be in charge of anyone. Let alone an innocent... An innocent baby. But if it's me or Child Services, then it has to be me. So, no. We can't call."

Mallory's stomach twisted. This was tragic. There was nothing else to call it. An absolute tragedy. Cheyenne was a young mother who was without her partner. And that was what she had meant when she said it would never be okay.

The baby was maybe barely a week old.

"Cheyenne doesn't have any family?"

"As far as I know they never approved of her relationship with Trent. And weren't that thrilled when she got pregnant. I don't think there's really anyone she can depend on." His jaw went granite. "Hell. You know there isn't, or she wouldn't have come to me."

"Why not?"

"Because. She thinks I'm responsible for his death. She

made it plenty clear." His gaze went shaded. "She's not wrong."

"How…"

"Look. I don't want to talk about it. What I want to do is make sure this baby is taken care of."

"Colt, sometimes we feel responsible for things we never could have stopped." Her chest went tight. "That doesn't mean it's true."

"Does it mean it doesn't feel like shit?"

She shook her head. "Do you know the baby's name?"

"No," he said, and for the first time, he looked slightly at a loss. But that faded. Quickly. "Go get the car seat for me. It's still on the front porch."

He reached down and picked the baby up off the couch, careful to support her head. It was clear he didn't have a whole lot of experience with babies, but also that he was confident enough in his ability that he wasn't tentative. Didn't ask any questions. But then, his hands were so big, he could lay her across one forearm resting her head in his palm, supporting her perfectly.

"Car seat," he said.

"You could say please."

"Because you're so polite?"

She stared at him.

"Please," he said.

She rolled her eyes, then walked out of the living room, through the house. It was clear that the place was in a partial remodel. The kitchen looked uprooted, but the living room was lovely. The wood floors looking recently resurfaced, the couches plush and new. Colt had clearly done well enough for himself in the rodeo. Buying this huge piece of ranchland, working on this house. And owning the little cabin that she stayed in. She opened the door and picked the car seat up by the handle. It was still attached to the base. And fortunately, she also knew how to install car seats. She brought it into the house and set it down in front of the couch, detached from the base.

"We have to get supplies," she said.

"Yes," he agreed. "Obviously."

"Well, handily for you, I know how to install a car seat. I understand that you want to do this through sheer force of will and alpha determination, but there's an actual skill to making sure that a baby is safe. You can't just strap her to your chest and carry her around."

"That does sound like something we might need, though," he said. "A way to strap her to my chest."

"Yes," she said. "That does exist."

"I take your point, though. I need you to come with me."

"Oh, not for one second was I going to let you go to a store with a baby all by yourself."

"Let me?" He turned around and faced her, still holding the baby. "*Let me.* Look, lady, I don't even know you. We might have had a really good naked night together, but that doesn't mean we know each other."

Her face got all hot, in spite of her determination that she not let him fluster her. "Oh, I wasn't going to suggest that we know each other, but, I will take control of the situation if I have to."

"You don't know this situation," he said, angry now.

"Whatever. I'm going with you. And I'm installing the car seat." She picked the car seat up, both pieces, and took it back outside, realizing the entire thing had been counterproductive, since she had just brought it in. She growled, and then stomped over to his pickup truck, opening it and finding that there was no backseat.

"Then we'll take my car," she said, heading over to her

vehicle and opening up the back door. Then she heard him calling out from the front porch.

"What are you doing?"

"I'm getting ready to take her to the store."

"Why in your car?" he asked.

"Because we're not putting her in the front seat of your truck. If that was the only thing available, fine. But it is safer to put her in the backseat of the car in the appropriate position. So that's what we're going to do." She groused the entire time, wrangling with the clip-in system, which was always a pain, no matter how easy they said it was, before emerging victorious.

"All right," she said. "Give me the baby, and I'm going to get her put in the car seat and make sure that it's fitted to her."

He handed her the baby, but very reluctantly.

The little girl scrunched her face and scrunched her legs up like a little frog, and Mallory's heart melted. She held her to her chest for a moment, closing her eyes.

Then she breathed out slowly. "Okay," she said, talking to herself. She then set the baby down into the car seat, making sure that she was buckled in as tightly as she needed to be. And ensuring that her head and neck were in the proper position.

"Okay. I'm going to drive. You tell me where we're going."

And he got in the backseat. Folded that long, broad frame down into that tiny backseat, right next to the baby without even having to be asked.

In futility, she tried to imagine what would've happened if she had come home with a baby during her time with Jared. If someone had handed a baby to him.

*These are extraordinary circumstances. If it was a random baby, Colt certainly wouldn't be any better.*

Even now he wasn't… Paternal necessarily.

He was more like a giant, angry alpha wolf left in charge of a pup. Ready to take on the entire world to ensure the safety of the little one, but not necessarily tender.

But for some reason, her eyes filled with tears anyway.

"Okay," he said. "It's nearly an hour's drive, but we're going to head over to Tolowa. They have bigger stores, and they're open later. Also, less likely to run into someone we know."

"Yeah," she said. "That is a funny little feature of small towns."

"A shock to you?"

"I'm not from a small town."

"I figured."

"You know, I really didn't think I would see you again."

He chuckled. "I figured you were just passing through." He cleared his throat. "Turn left. I know better than to screw around in town unless I'm very certain of who I'm screwing around with."

*"Screwing around,"* she said. "What an interesting characterization of what occurred."

"Was it something else?"

"I don't know. But it wasn't… It felt heavier than that. That's all I have to say about it."

"Fair." The only sound in the car was the tires on the road. "Clearly we're both going through some shit."

"Clearly." She nearly laughed. She saw a sign that said Tolowa was forty-five miles away and figured she could continue to follow those signs for a piece.

But that meant that she and Colt were stuck in the car together for all that time. Maybe now was the time for her to unspool all of her complicated feelings. The real reason that she was a midwife. That deep need to matter to someone. To be important. To be able to be the champion. And how that spilled over into her relationships. Into her life. And had given her pieces of the things she wanted, but never the actual real thing that she wanted. How she was a woman who had been in a relationship for fifteen years, and of course she wanted a baby, but…

She'd been pregnant once, and she hadn't been the same after and why would she put them both through that again?

That was what he'd said.

Both times she'd brought it up.

She'd been unhappy, but she'd felt responsible. For so many things. For that horrendous loss and the unhappiness after, and he'd stayed with her, hadn't he?

So even though she'd been unhappy with the decision to not have children, it had never actually made her leave, when it should have.

*Why does she stay with him?*

At that point she'd just been so bound up in him. In their life.

"So, the rodeo. How did you get started with that?"

Infinitely better than unspooling anything.

"My brother Jake started doing it. Eventually I followed him."

Just like that. Nothing fancy or frilly, and definitely no more words than were necessary.

"So you… You're close to him?"

"Not especially."

"Right. Well. I mean, I know a little bit about your family because of…"

"Right. Because of Iris."

"Yes."

"Yeah, we're a whole tragedy. And Jake and I left. Which I guess makes us interesting in context with the rest of the family, who stayed. But… It never seemed like home to me.

Not after our parents died. You know, that was our house. The ranch house."

She took a moment to process that. "It wasn't Iris's and her siblings'?"

"Our dad ranched too. That was what he did. Their dad was the police chief. That's why Pansy, my cousin, is a police officer. She was following in her old man's footsteps. But yeah, no. It was going to be ours. But… In the end Jake and I didn't have any interest in it. Ryder was the one who raised all of us. He was the one who took care of us. And it just seemed easier to go our own way. Seemed better."

"Do you love the rodeo?"

He frowned. "No. I don't love it. But it gave me something to test myself against. You want to be needed. I don't want to be needed. Not by anybody. You want to help people… I never did. I just wanted to check and see if I was still alive. And believe me, you know the answer to that question when an animal that weighs several thousand pounds flings you around like a rag doll. So yeah. That was more what my rodeo dreams were about. And you know… I didn't want my parents' life. They weren't happy. So I threw myself into the circuit because it was like a party that didn't end. Booze, women. Danger. Glory. Defeat. All that stuff… Reminds you that death hasn't gotten you yet."

"Oh."

"Is that a little bit grim for you?"

"No," she said, squeezing the steering wheel. She wondered what that was like. Living every day testing how alive you were.

Her own trauma had pushed her into a place where she'd clung. To the familiar. To stability. His had pushed him into just the opposite.

"You must *feel* every day," she said.

"I guess so."

"Do you know how many days I just didn't feel?" she asked. "Days that I didn't even realize went by? When I have a birth... That's when I feel connected to the world. Connected to life. That rush... That rush isn't like anything else. It's amazing. And it reminds me of why I do what I do. It reminds me of why I'm here. But then I would go home to this... This guy. And I would go right back into this sort of numb space. Routine and... Not a good way. Because routine can be a good thing. But this wasn't. This wasn't good. This was something else... And I..." She shook her head. She guessed that she was going there. "If nothing else, meeting you...that reminded me I was alive."

"Me too," he said, his voice rough.

The baby began to cry, and she was sort of thankful for the interruption. Colt started trying to soothe her, bouncing the car seat gently.

"We need pacifiers. She's probably hungry. We need diapers. I can't fathom what she was thinking." Then she immediately felt guilty. "Obviously she wasn't thinking. I'm trying not to be judgmental."

"Yeah. I have no right to be judgmental. But I feel it all the same."

It wasn't long after that they came to an intersection that took them over a bridge and toward the town of Tolowa. It was a much more cookie-cutter town than Gold Valley. A practical town, filled with big-box stores and chain restaurants. But she would have to make a note of it, because if she wanted to do more major shopping, it might need to be here. Though, she had a feeling *major* would be overstating it, still. But there did appear to be an outlet mall. So there was that.

When she saw the Fred Meyer, she went ahead and decided to pull in. She knew that store would have everything they needed for a baby. He took charge of getting the baby out of the car, and the two of them walked through the automatic doors and into the store. She grabbed the cart and walked away from the produce, imagining the farther away they got from the food, the closer they would be to baby items. The first aisle they stopped at was one with formula, bottles, diapers and pacifiers. "I imagine that clothes and things like that will be somewhere else. But, we need a lot of things from here."

Every time she indicated they might need something, Colt put it in the cart. Sometimes two. By the time they had gotten through the aisle, she was pretty sure they'd bought almost everything, and most of it was completely unnecessary for the stage that the baby was at.

"How long do you think... How long do you think you're going to have her?" she asked as he grabbed the biggest box of newborn diapers in the aisle.

"Don't know." His simple statement was punctuated by deeply normal grocery sounds. The beep of a scanner, music from fifteen years ago and a couple of little kids begging for a candy bar. It was so aggressively normal it added to the strangeness of it all.

"I just... It can't be for very long."

"I don't know," he said. "And you know that I don't know. You know that I don't know because you were standing there when Cheyenne brought her. You basically heard the whole thing. There was maybe the tiniest bit that you missed, and I can tell you, it wasn't all that informative."

"Well... I just...you can't be thinking that you'll be caring for her long term."

"I'll care for her as long as she needs me."

She couldn't really argue with that. "You can't do it by yourself."

"People do it by themselves all the time."

"That's different."

"Is it?"

"What do you know about babies, Colt?"

"Jack shit," he said.

"Somehow I suspected as much."

"Do most people know anything about babies before they go about raising one? I never got the impression my parents were child development specialists."

Mallory blinked. The thing was, she was accustomed to people who had done a lot of preparation for their baby. People who had planned and waited.

And she'd told herself maybe it was a good thing she hadn't had to try and parent a baby she hadn't been ready for, because she'd seen all those people with their parenting books and nurseries done up to the hilt.

Maybe it was just easier for her to think that.

"I guess that's a good point," she said.

"It doesn't really matter if it's a good point or not. I didn't ask you. If you want to help... Great. Because you're right, there is a whole lot that I don't know, and you seem to know..."

"Everything."

"Everything," he said.

He turned the cart back toward the clothing section, and there they found some baby clothes. He stood there holding the baby while she chose a series of onesies, socks and a couple of little dresses, because she couldn't resist them. And then a few headbands.

"It's just all so cute," she said, her ovaries literally twisting into knots. "I really was trying not to be ridiculous about this, because it is a serious situation. But they're tiny. They're tiny and they're pink and they're adorable."

"Just get the kid something so she's not naked."

"Cute somethings," Mallory said, realizing that the cart was getting out of control.

And she wasn't going to examine what she was doing right now or how it linked back to her own issues, or her own unresolved...

Well, her loss could never be anything but unresolved.

Her daughter would be a teenager now if she'd lived, but she hadn't. And Mallory's life would be very different. She'd either still be with Jared, trying to hold it together for her, or she'd have left immediately when he'd proven to be a sucky dad.

Maybe he would have become a better man if she'd lived. If he'd been a father. If he hadn't been changed by that early loss.

Maybe Mallory wouldn't have finished school.

Maybe she wouldn't have been a midwife.

Maybe she'd have been a terrible mother. Or a great one. Maybe she'd have been the same person she was now, or maybe she'd be totally different.

And she couldn't know. Because there was no point in what-if.

Lucy had died before she'd ever drawn a breath.

"How long are you thinking the baby is going to be around?" he asked, pulling her thoughts to the present, and her focus back to shopping.

Onto the baby who needed her right now.

"Rude," she said. "These clothes and all the supplies can go back with her and her mother when she comes to get her." Concern lanced through her. "But promise me one thing."

"What's that?"

"I understand why you don't really want to involve Child Protective Services with all of this. I do. But, please promise me that when Cheyenne does come back, you'll make sure that she talks to a mental health professional. We need to make sure that she and the baby are set up for success. In my opinion it wouldn't hurt for her to have a caseworker…"

"No," Colt said. "A doctor, sure…"

"I would be happy with a doctor. We can make sure that they're taken care of."

"She doesn't have money, you know. Not insurance or anything. I wish that she had come to me if she needed something like that. But it's going to be difficult to get her to agree to the doctor thing."

"You can pay for it, right?"

She was making assumptions now, but the man did seem to have money.

"Yeah," he said. "And I will."

"Good."

Eventually, once they had added a pack and play, a swing and a little bouncy chair to their pile of things, they made their way to the checkout.

The woman beamed at them.

"Congratulations," she said.

"Thank you," Colt said, obviously forcing a smile.

She did her best to force one, but this was like some weird hell.

No one congratulated you when you were fifteen and pregnant. Well, no one had congratulated her because she'd *hidden* it.

And she'd never gotten to walk around holding a baby so she'd never had a random stranger congratulate her like this.

*Deal with yourself.*

"How old?" the woman asked.

"About a week."

She said it at the same time Colt said, "A month."

"It seems like longer," Colt said.

"Don't I know it," the woman said. "But the time goes by so quickly. Cherish it."

Mallory felt like she was standing in the middle of the Twilight Zone. Hearing platitudes that were meant for someone else, that were definitely not meant for her. Her throat felt scratchy.

It took way too long to ring everything up. And the awkwardness just sort of stretched. The baby started to fuss, and Mallory reached out for her. But Colt held her close, shifting his weight back and forth. He was a natural with the baby. In that way that he looked like he might take off the head of any passerby that posed a threat. He cradled her with so much strength and gentleness all at the same time...

And she looked away, focusing instead on the progress the woman was making with their purchases.

"All done. Enjoy your baby."

"We will," Mallory said, her smile dropping sharply as soon as they walked outside.

*"Enjoy your baby,"* Colt said.

"I don't know. People say strange things to people with babies." She assumed. She hadn't experienced it before.

Actually the whole thing was starting to make her stomach feel shaky.

They got everything loaded and got the little girl buckled up and put in the car.

"She needs to be called something. We can't just keep calling her the baby."

"Lily," he said, not hesitating.

And somehow she knew that if she asked him why, it would only make things... Well, it would push a further wedge between them, and she wasn't sure why she cared about that.

They didn't need to be close. They were dealing with this situation, and it was something that she wanted to help with.

"I like it," she said.

They didn't talk for a while, and when she checked her rearview mirror, she saw that his head was leaned back against the seat, and that his eyes were closed. His hand was set on the handle of the car seat, as if he was physically bracing it, keeping the baby safe even while he slept.

Lily.

Their little charge was Lily. And she still felt... Utterly shell-shocked by the whole thing.

She also felt... Maybe this wasn't her fight. Maybe she should just leave Colt and Lily at the house and not worry about it. He wanted to take care of the situation, so shouldn't she let him?

Right. This was a battle that she'd already lost inside of herself.

But her conversation with Tirzah played back in her mind. Being a midwife was a calling. Her connection to mothers and babies and all this kind of stuff... It wasn't just something that she thought was interesting. This baby needed her. And even though it wasn't strictly part of her job, it was part of who she was. And there was no way she was going to abandon her or Colt if they needed her.

She was grateful in some ways for the reprieve, not having to talk to him, because every time she did, it felt like the conversation was laden with secondary meaning and tension. It felt difficult.

But she didn't know the man, and part of her felt like she did, and that was something that she was having a near impossible time with.

They'd been naked together. Had engaged in intimacies that she only ever shared with one other man, a man she had known for more than half of her life—and it made her feel like perhaps she and Colt knew each other better than they did. Made her feel like she had a right to tell him what to do in this situation and also like she was connected to it perhaps on a deeper level than she was.

Well, who was she to argue with fate? Wasn't it fate that had brought him into her life?

Right. Fate. Or just hormones combined with the realities of small-town life.

Well, that made her feral. It was annoying.

And probably true.

Except… She couldn't escape that first thought she'd had about him when she'd seen him for the first time. That he was fate. That he was the lightning bolt. The thing she had never expected, the thing she had never asked for, but had found all the same.

Right. This angry, taciturn rodeo cowboy, who only turned on the charm when he wanted to get in your pants and was in general grumpy with you every other time?

It was true. All that charm he'd had on their first night had vanished completely when they'd learned each other's names.

Why did that make him more compelling?

*Because you like a project? Because then you don't have to figure out what you want? You just have to continue on proving you're valuable by throwing all of your energy into your relationship?*

That made her wince.

It wasn't fair, really, either. Because Colt was grumpy, sure, but he had never asked anything of her. He had never taken advantage of her in any way.

He wasn't an emotional or financial vampire sucking the resources and joy out of her simply because he could.

She couldn't make the comparisons between him and

Jared when they existed in entirely different contexts. He was her landlord. And that was it.

He was also a man she'd had a one-night stand with. Sure.

But he didn't owe her anything other than the repairs outlined in their lease agreement. Otherwise, nothing.

And she certainly didn't need to have facilitated this entire baby thing. And she didn't need to involve herself.

When she turned up the driveway that led them back to Sunset Ridge, she told herself that sternly and repeatedly.

But then they pulled up to the house, and the car slowing to a stop jolted Colt out of his sleep.

"Back again."

"Damn," he said, his voice rough and groggy. It reminded her a little bit too much of the morning after. "Guess I dozed off."

"I guess so," she said.

"I was pretty beat from working at my brother's."

"What do you do there?" she asked, opening the car door and then rounding to the back to open the trunk. There was so much stuff.

"Well, today it was fences. For more pastures. He's breeding rodeo horses."

"Oh. I thought maybe you did something with wood carving."

"Wood carving?"

"You made those beautiful pillars in front of the cabin."

"Yeah. But that's nothing serious. I told you, I just mess around with that."

"Oh. Well anyway… I don't really know all that much about ranch work. My brother had this really big equestrian facility down in the Bay Area. But I didn't spend that much time there. And when…" She suddenly felt sad.

"I know," he said.

She smiled. "Because you talked to Iris?"

"The keeper of all the secrets between us, I guess."

She huffed a laugh. "Except she doesn't know that we slept together."

"We didn't really sleep."

"True."

She cleared her throat, trying to do something to ease the tension in her body. She took the baby, and he carried all of the items into the house.

They got the things spread out in the living room, and they both looked around.

And then she burst out laughing. "This is crazy. This one tiny little creature necessitated all of this."

"Seems about right," Colt said. He shook his head. "I was just looking at my cousin's toddler thinking… Damn, I never want kids."

That made her lungs feel tight.

"Well, it's just temporary," Mallory said.

More for herself than him. She'd gone a little crazy with the baby clothes and she needed to not be… Forgetting what this was.

"Yeah. Temporary."

"Do you have an extra bedroom?" she asked.

"Yeah."

"Although, I can tell you, she might wake up a lot. And if she does, it might be better to have her in your room."

He nodded. "I'm going to have to explain this to my brother."

"I'll tell you what. Tomorrow I'll take the shift with her. You can work on what you want to say."

"Really?"

"Yes. I don't have anything scheduled for tomorrow. In

fact, I won't be all that busy for a while. I'll come to the house, and I'll take care of her."

"Nothing here is all that… It's not really set up for company. Or inhabitants that aren't me."

"It'll be fine. You're exhausted." Silently, she helped him get things set up. A bottle warmer in the kitchen. A baby monitor. Downstairs, upstairs, in the bathroom. Thankfully, he set the bed up, so she didn't have to go into his room. She didn't think she would've been able to handle that. You would think that a baby would do something to dull the attraction between them.

But no. That was functioning just fine.

Mallory took it upon herself to set up the little baby bath on the kitchen counter and give her a quick bath before dressing her in a fresh outfit. It gave her another opportunity to check her over. She made sure that she fed her, and the infant drank greedily from the bottle. Mallory stared down at her while she fed her, then kissed her little forehead. "It's okay, Lily. We're here. You're taken care of now."

And she realized that keeping that promise was the most singularly important thing in the world to her right now. She had the strangest sense of fate, yet again. That if she was here for anything, it was for this. That maybe she was meant to be here. Meant to hold this baby in her arms. Meant to stand in this spot, in this house right now for the sole purpose of caring for this child.

It was deep and certain.

And it terrified her all the way to her bones.

By the time everything was set up, and Lily was asleep, it was eight thirty.

"I'm pretty beat," Colt said. He laughed. "You have no idea how ridiculous that is. I used to stay out all night and drink and… Not anymore."

"Things change, I guess."

"I guess... I ought to sleep while she's sleeping."

"Yes," Mallory said. "You definitely should. And... Put her to bed on her back, and make sure that none of the blankets go up too high."

She wasn't sure that she could release her hold on this baby. She wasn't sure that she could... "Got it," he said.

He took Lily from her arms and held her, and Mallory just stared at them. She felt reluctant to leave.

"Thank you for your help," he said. "Honestly."

She hadn't expected that.

"I... I really want to. I want to help."

She took a step forward and put her hand on Lily's back. And that brought her in such close proximity with Colt that she could... She could smell him. The scent of the fields, and the woods, his skin. She was intimately familiar with him, but it was just that once. And so it lived inside of her like a whisper, so faint that she could hardly grasp it fully. But so real and deep that it seemed almost clearer than anything around her.

She looked up at him, their eyes meeting, and she felt a shiver run down her spine, going all the way to her toes.

"Thanks again," he said, his voice rough. "I think I'll head to bed."

"Okay."

She just stood there, watching him walk up the stairs. And then she turned around, heading to the door. She put her hand on the doorknob and she thought she might just... Wait. She would just wait.

He might need something. And yes he could call her, but if he needed her right away, she would just still be here. It made sense. It made a perfect kind of sense.

She paced around downstairs for a while, but he didn't come back.

And after a while, she moved herself into the living room and sat down on the couch. Then she pulled a blanket down from the back of it and lay down. And she realized she was crossing a line. Maybe. But what if he needed her? She would just lie down for a minute. Just a minute.

AN EARSPLITTING WAIL broke Colt out of his sleep.

"Shit," he said. The events of the day came flooding back to him. He was completely disoriented, he had no sense of time or space. But he remembered the baby. Lily.

*Lily.*

She was crying. Screaming.

All right. What did babies need when they cried? A diaper or a bottle.

He had never changed a diaper before. He picked her up, and he couldn't smell anything too intense. She felt slightly damp, and so he knew she would have to be changed. He had an actual changing table set up in the room, and he set her down on the table, unzipping the pajamas that Mallory had put her in before bed. There were wipes and diapers right there. And it couldn't be that hard.

It turned out, it was hard. And while the baby didn't stink in a conventional way, there was… A shitstorm. Quite literally. He had used almost an entire package of wipes and had a sweaty brow by the time he was done changing her. It was basically like dressing a fish. And the little thing could hardly move herself with any intention. But still. She managed to stiffen and flop at all the wrong times, and he was just afraid that she might break. He didn't want to hurt her. So he took it slowly, and she was getting madder and madder. *Because you're hungry.*

And finally he gave up on the clothes. He wrapped her up in a blanket as best he could and carried her downstairs. She ought to stay warm enough. But he needed to make a bottle.

And he could only hope that he remembered how to do that. Mallory had showed him, and he knew there were instructions. But he was still a little bit sleep groggy, and there was no telling how much of that he would actually be able to reenact in his current state.

He reached the bottom of the stairs, and nearly jumped back. Because there was someone standing in the living room.

"Colt. Sorry. I…"

"Thank God," he said. "I can't get her into the pajamas."

"I'm glad I stayed then."

"Do you know how to make a bottle better than I do?"

"I'm not that practiced with bottles. Not that I've never done it, but I'm not usually the one handling feedings. And even then, at the age I get them, it's mostly breastfeeding. Dressing and undressing though… That I can handle. Give her to me."

And he did. Gladly.

With his hands free, he felt a lot more able to sort out the bottle situation, and he found it wasn't all that complicated and didn't take that long. But by the time he was finished, Lily was dressed in a new pair of pajamas and had quieted slightly.

"She likes you," Colt said.

"I think she likes you just fine." She was just cranky because she was out of sorts. She held the baby up to him. "Feed her."

He cleared his throat and took her into the crook of his arm, pressing the bottle up against her lips, surprised when she latched on quickly and easily. She began to drink, making greedy little noises, along with an occasional sigh. His take on babies this size had always been that they basically didn't do much. But she was an expressive little thing. He had been able to tell when her anger was increasing with him, and he could see now that she took some delight in being fed. It made his lips curve up into a smile.

He held her and fed her, reflexively swaying slightly back and forth.

"I'm sorry," she said. "I should've left. I was going to. It's just that I…"

"Rightly got nervous that I wasn't going to have any idea what I was doing?"

"You look like you've got a handle on it."

"I'll tell you what. Come up to the guest room. If you don't mind. I mean… You shouldn't drive back up to the cabin, and sleeping on the couch isn't the most comfortable."

"Thank you," she said. "And if you need anything… Anything at all."

"Sure."

She smiled at him, and he followed her up the stairs, a tightening in his gut as he did. What he really wanted to do was ask her to come to bed with him. And weirdly, it wasn't even all that sexual of a thought. Right now, for some reason, he just wanted to pull her down onto the soft mattress and hold her close to his body.

He gritted his teeth. "This room right here. It's set and ready to go. I had all the bedrooms done already. New beds."

"Hey, be careful. You might end up with a roommate. This place is nicer than the cabin." She seemed to regret saying that. "No. I'm kidding. Because… Obviously that's a bad idea. Obviously."

"Why don't you just go get some sleep."

"Sure. See you in the morning."

"Yeah. See you in the morning."

He put Lily down to bed in the little cradle and shut the

lights off. Then he lay down in bed on his back, staring at the ceiling.

And he wished that he had invited her into his room. Because now, he didn't want to be in the quiet by himself. He didn't want to sleep. Because the only thing that was there for him was the unending pool of darkness and the icy fingers of death that seemed all too close when he tried to sleep some nights.

But it never took him. Not ever.

And instead, he felt mocked by the people who had gone before him. Images of his mother, his father. Images of those last moments he'd seen them.

When he'd stepped off the plane and traded places with her.

When the door had closed behind him. And he was waving.

And then to the last time he had seen Trent. Cocky and drunk and talking about how he was going to conquer that next bull. And he thought about saying something. Thought about telling the kid to slow his roll. But instead he laughed and patted him on the back. Because he had always cheated death.

Why wouldn't Trent?

But he hadn't.

And Colt was still here.

And he made a promise. A vow. That he'd be here for Lily. Because he was here when he shouldn't be. And so he would be here for her. Because it was about the only worthwhile thing he could think of.

It was about the only reason he could think of that he might still be left behind.

# *CHAPTER NINE*

MALLORY JERKED AWAKE SUDDENLY, and she wasn't quite sure why. The baby wasn't crying.

The baby wasn't crying. The baby should have cried.

Her heart was pounding. She wasn't sure why she was so absolutely awake, or so absolutely certain of what was going on, only that she was. It was as if she hadn't fallen asleep at all. She was in the guest bedroom at Colt Daniels's house, and they were taking care of the baby. She had fallen asleep on his couch in the middle of the night and he had woken up. And then he had sent her to the guest room. Where she had slept all the way through the night.

She got out of bed and realized she was still fully clothed, and that her dress was wrinkled. She tugged it down as best she could and pushed her hair back off her face, walking out of the bedroom and looking down the hall. The door to his bedroom was cracked open, and she pushed at it. Then she heard sounds coming from down the stairs.

Dishes clattering. She walked downstairs, and when she hit midway down the staircase, she could smell… Bacon.

She turned left and went into the kitchen, and there he was. Lily was sitting in the little chair that they had bought for her, dozing, and Colt was scrambling eggs, frying bacon… And then he took a tray of biscuits out of the oven.

"What is this?"

"I have to get to work soon," he said. "And I get hungry

in the morning. Pretty much don't usually stop for lunch. Plus, since you're staying all day... I figured I owe you a thank-you."

"You... You made biscuits."

"I opened a can of biscuits. That's not really the same thing."

"But still."

"Mallory, this is about the easiest cooking a person can do."

"Oh, I know that. I cook this kind of breakfast all the time. It's just..."

She couldn't remember the last time someone had cooked for her.

Her parents were wonderful. They really were. But the thing about Mallory was she had been a late in life baby. Something of a surprise. Griffin had basically been an only child for a very long time. And then when they were kids... He had done most of the entertaining for her. He had cooked for her and taken care of her. And then he went off to college. Her parents had reconnected with each other, found their spark after their oldest child had left home. And that had been wonderful. But they had gotten a babysitter a lot. They had gone out to dinner, gone on vacations. She had stayed with her grandparents, who she also loved dearly. It wasn't that there weren't people in her life who were there for her. There were.

But there was still something... There was something quite notable about a man cooking breakfast for her.

"I'm just... Thank you."

"No problem."

"Did she... Did she wake up a lot last night?"

"Two more times. But it wasn't a big deal. I got it taken care of."

"I was here so that I can help..."

"You're helping all day. There's no reason for you to have gotten up last night.

"Coffee's over there."

That jolted her out of her strange fugue state. It was just incredibly weird to be in this moment. A lot like playing house. And it left her disquieted. She moved around the kitchen until she found the coffee mugs and then poured herself a generous helping. She made her way to the fridge and opened it up. But there was no half-and-half to be seen.

"No cream?"

"No. I have milk. But... I drink it black."

"Oh," she said, feeling a little bit more crushed than was necessary.

"Sorry about that."

"It's fine," she said, grabbing the carton of milk and pouring a dollop into her coffee, grimacing when the liquid turned a sort of thin brown, rather than the lovely, creamy color that she preferred.

But the disappointment about the coffee was forgotten quickly enough, because it was nice and strong, and it wasn't bitter. And then there were eggs, bacon and biscuits. With lots of butter. She filled her plate up, and so did he, but he didn't sit down. He basically ate standing up, halfway out the door. "I'll be back midafternoon. Thanks again."

"Sure. What exactly are you going to... What are you going to tell your family?"

"I'll figure it out. I haven't exactly made the decision yet."

"No. Understandable."

"So just... Don't tell Iris. Don't tell Griffin. This has to stay between you and me."

"I probably won't talk to them today. I might... I might

drive her up to the cabin. But only if you feel okay with that. My driving skills on the road are just fine now."

"If you're feeling comfortable with it, I'm fine with it."

"Okay. I just have a few more things I want to do up there, and it might be easier if I just bring her with me."

"All right. Well, I'll bring something back for dinner."

"Sounds good."

And then he was gone, leaving her with Lily.

"Okay, little one," she said. "We've got some stuff to do today."

If she kept moving, then she wouldn't linger on the domesticity of the morning. Of the situation. But as she looked at the tiny, sleeping baby, she was overcome by the realization that it was going to be easier said than done to remember exactly what was happening here. To remember that Lily was temporary, and this wasn't going to be anything more than...

"Your glorified nanny," she said. "Not even glorified."

Though he had cooked her bacon and eggs. So there was that.

But seriously, if her emotions could be bought with eggs, she needed therapy a lot more than she needed anything else.

COLT URGED HIS horse forward, bringing him to a gallop. He was absolutely avoiding having the conversation with his brother that he should have. The one about Lily.

Eventually, he was going to have to talk to his family about the situation, but honestly... He thought that maybe it was going to end up being exactly like it had been with Mallory, and he didn't want to have the argument again. She had come around to his way of seeing things in...

Just then, he looked back over his shoulder to see Jake and Cal bringing up the rear. Both on horseback, both grinning from ear to ear.

And he realized that Cal would be his ally. He didn't know how he knew it, only that he did.

"You guys are slowpokes," he said.

"We were just too busy flirting," Callie said, grinning.

"Great. Glad you're happy."

But he found he meant it. He kept coming back to that night that he and Jake had talked. When they had finally spoken about their parents. And about the things that Jake knew about their father. That their father hadn't been a man planning to stay with his family. And that made the conviction and Colt's gut burn all the harder.

"I've got something to tell you," Colt said.

"What?"

"Callie," Colt said. "I feel like you're going to understand what I have to say."

"What's going on?" Jake asked. "It sounds serious."

"It kind of is. You know Trent."

"Yeah," Jake said. "I know Trent."

"Did you know his girlfriend was pregnant?"

"Yeah. Hell. It really is awful."

"Well... Cheyenne showed up at my place yesterday."

"She did?" Callie asked.

"Yeah. And she... She left the baby. With me."

"What?" That question was followed by a slew of profanity from both of them.

"I know," Colt said. "Look, Trent had asked me to be the godfather to the baby before he died. He was...he was scared, after he found out Cheyenne was pregnant. He didn't have good parents, he didn't know how to be a father and he... he looked up to me. Poor idiot." He let out a painful breath. "And Cheyenne just said that she needed me to take care of her for a while. She's in a really awful space. Mallory... Mallory is a midwife, right? And Mallory said that it was postpartum depression. She tried to catch Cheyenne and talk to her, but she was unable to. But I got everything I needed to take care of the baby… And… I'm taking care of the baby."

"I don't know, Colt, it sounds to me like you should call somebody," Jake said.

"No. Cheyenne called someone. She called me, more or less. I'm the person that has to fix this. I'm the person that has to… I need to be here for this kid."

And it was Callie who nodded. "You have to do what you have to do."

"If this is more of your survivor's guilt…"

"Don't," Colt said. "Don't you dare throw our lives back in my face. The shit I have to live with. It's not for us to talk about, Jake. There's a reason we spent that many years not talking. So don't ruin it. Not now."

"Fine," Jake said. "I won't."

"Anyway. I might need you to explain it to… Everybody. But I need Pansy to keep out of it."

"If Pansy needs to be involved…"

"Why would she need to be involved? It's perfectly within her right to leave the baby under Colt's care if she wants to," Callie said.

"Fine," Jake relented. "But the thing is if you're doing this because of guilt…"

"Of course I'm doing it because of guilt. Why else does a person do anything?"

"Sometimes I forget how Catholic you both are," Callie said, laughing.

"What?" Jake and Colt asked simultaneously.

"I'm just saying, you find guilt and martyrdom to be powerful motivators."

Both of them huffed and snorted uncomfortably.

"So is… Who's with the baby?"

"Mallory." They both stared at him. "What? She wants to help."

"It seems to me like you're getting pretty involved with her," Jake said.

"I'm not involved."

"Why is she helping you?"

"Because she loves babies. And she happened to be right there when it all went down."

"And you're not… Attached to her?"

Colt ground his teeth together, stared off into the distance at the stunning view of the massive mountains, shocking and green against the backdrop of a deep blue sky. "I don't do *attached*."

"No, of course you don't," Jake said. "You barely do *attached* to me. Why would you be attached to some woman."

"I'm *attached* to you," Colt said, frowning.

"Are you?"

Something shifted inside of Colt, uncomfortable and heavy. "Sometimes I question why I'm back here."

"I know I do," Jake said. "You're going to work here on my horse ranch forever?"

"I don't… Are you rescinding the job offer or?"

"No. But you have your own damn money, and you don't seem to like the work very much, so I'm not sure what you're doing."

"Penance," Callie commented.

Colt shot her a glare.

She shrugged. "I call it like I see it."

"Are you just punishing yourself?"

"No. Apparently I'm here to be second best for everybody. How about that? To be the one who came back from almost going on that trip to Alaska. When we all know you would've been better off if you'd have had Mom. To be the one left behind on the circuit, when if anybody should have died because of dumbass, drunken behavior, it should've been me and not a kid who was about to be a father. Because he had a woman who loved him. A little girl who would've loved him. And now about all I can say for it, about all I can say about anything is that... I'm here. And I can take care of her. So I will. And I don't know why the hell else I'm here."

The words felt like they left a trail of fire up his throat. They never talked about this before.

Of course, Jake knew full well what had happened the day of his parents' accident. It had been Colt who was supposed to go with his father. Because the state of his parents' marriage had meant that his mother hadn't wanted to go on the trip to Alaska. But then things had changed. They gradually began to mend things, or so it had seemed. But, Colt was still going to go on the trip because he had been invited, and his mother hadn't thought it was fair for Colt to lose the chance to go on the trip just because their marriage had improved. But at the last minute Colt had wanted...

He'd wanted to be a part of fixing things. Of making them better.

And for what? It was possible his father had been planning on leaving them all anyway.

It had cracked him open inside. Because really, really what was the point of the farce that they had engaged in? The one that had saved his life and condemned his mother to death. The one that had put her on a plane bound to break apart over the ocean and had taken him back to safety.

He didn't know.

He only knew one thing. That the one good thing he could do right now is take care of Lily. Maybe the only good thing he could ever do.

"You know that's not how anyone sees it."

"You're the only one who knows the truth, Jake."

"It doesn't matter. It's never mattered. I don't even think about it."

"Because if you did, you'd drive yourself crazy. God knows I do."

"Colt…"

"No. I'm done talking. I've explained the situation with Lily. Now you know. She'll be coming with me to Sunday dinner. Mallory probably will be too."

He stared at them both. "I mean, she might as well. She's practically family."

And with that, he went to go finish riding the fences.

## CHAPTER TEN

MALLORY STAYED UP at her cabin until the late afternoon. By the time she had finished doing all of her chores—most of which were accomplished with Lily strapped to her chest—she was a lot more exhausted than she could have ever anticipated.

She never would've thought that a one-week-old baby could be that taxing. Well, obviously she *knew* that babies were tiring, but that was when you were taking care of one instead of sleeping. Last night, she had gotten a very good night's sleep, so she hadn't really anticipated being this exhausted just carrying one baby that she knew for a fact weighed under ten pounds on her chest.

She had put Lily in her little weighing apparatus earlier. What she did was place the baby in a shawl, which hung from a scale and provided an easy, cozy way to get a read on her weight. Lily seemed healthy. She was having a good number of wet and messy diapers, and she had a hearty appetite.

She seemed alert, but not too much. Really, she was an unremarkable newborn. Except, Mallory found her quite remarkable. She was already attached to the little thing, and claiming that she wouldn't get attached... It was silly.

She could get attached to a particularly good cookie while she was eating it.

How much more was she going to get attached to this sweet little life?

"It's okay. I'll take good care of you until your mama can come back."

She ran her fingertips over the baby's fuzzy head. She was definitely ready for Colt to take a shift. But… He was probably tired.

He would probably want to get into the hot tub again.

And then she started thinking about him in the hot tub.

What wildly inconvenient streams of thought. Babies and naked men. It was a whole lot for her hormones.

And then she heard the sound of his truck, and her whole body did a weird little shivering thing.

One boot-clad foot exited the truck, kicking up dust around where he made contact with the ground. And the rest of the man followed. He looked dirty from the day's work. His dark hat had flecks of some kind of clay on it, and his forearms were streaked with the day's labor. He was carrying a grocery bag and another bag that looked like it contained foam cartons. Her stomach growled. She hadn't realized how hungry she was. This morning's breakfast seemed a long way away. She stepped back from the door, so that she wouldn't look overeager, and went into the living room, then paced back out into the entry. Just as the door opened.

"Oh," she said, patting Lily's back. "Hi."

"Hi."

"How was… Work?"

He chuckled. "Great. How was… This."

"She's great," Mallory said. "I mean, not that she can really do much right now. But I was able to get a lot of things accomplished in the house. It's starting to feel very homey."

"Well. Good." And it was unspoken between them, whether she would spend the night down here or up at the cabin. She should go back to her house. She knew that. This odd situation of her setting up down here wasn't really… Well, it was strange. Bottom line, it was a little bit strange.

He opened up the plastic bags, and inside were a few different things, but also, a carton of half-and-half.

"Oh my gosh," she said. "You got me cream for my coffee."

"Yeah," he said. "You mentioned that it's how you liked it."

She was completely and totally stunned. "But you remembered. And you did something about it without me asking."

"Yeah," he said. "Is that weird?"

"Yes," she said. "That's… I mean… It was very thoughtful of you."

"Mallory, you must have had a whole lot of people in your life that were bottom of the barrel."

"Not a whole lot of people. Just one. For a long time."

"Right. That tool you were with at the saloon the first night I saw you."

"The very same."

"I'm going to go get washed up. Feel free to start dinner… Without me."

"Oh… I… I can wait I… I mean unless you want me to start eating without you. Because it's not like we need to eat dinner together."

"Come on," Colt said. "This isn't high school. Eat with me if you want—don't if you don't want."

He turned and walked up the stairs, leaving her standing there. She did her best to remove Lily from the sling without waking her. She got her situated into the little sleeping cot that they had downstairs—*they*, dangerous way to think of things—and started to rummage around for plates. She didn't touch the bag of food. She opened up the fridge and stared at the carton of half-and-half for a second. She felt… She didn't know what. It had been a very nice gesture. But maybe she shouldn't think it was so nice. Maybe it was not all that extraordinary, and the fact that it seemed like it might be was…

She heard footsteps behind her and turned around, her heart slamming against her breastbone.

It was cold. His hair was damp, and he was wearing a white T-shirt and a pair of faded blue jeans. His feet were bare, and she didn't know why, but that felt impossibly intimate.

It felt… Well, it was sexier than it had the right to be.

"Dig in," he said.

"Okay," she said.

She closed the fridge, then went over to the food bags. "Is this the kind of thing you do… Okay, don't take this the wrong way," she said, taking the first container out of the bag. She opened it up and groaned. It was entirely full of grilled meat, onions and peppers. The next container had rice, and the following one refried beans. There were corn and flour tortillas wrapped in tinfoil in the next one.

"Hope you like fajitas."

"I really do. Thank you so much."

"You look exhausted."

And she somehow didn't even take it personally that he'd said that. Because it didn't seem mean. It didn't seem anything but an expression of… Concern.

"I am."

"You were about to say something?"

"Yes," she said, loading her plate up with chicken, steak, peppers and onions.

"Well, say it."

"Don't take this the wrong way."

"You know, anytime someone prefaces something with 'don't take this the wrong way,' it makes someone awfully curious. Because that means there's a wrong way that I could take it."

"Yes," she said. "When you date a woman, is this the kind of thing you do? And I don't want you to take it the wrong way because I understand you aren't dating me by getting dinner..."

"I don't *date*."

"Oh."

"I'm serious. I mean, I guess I had a couple of girlfriends in high school. But... I was fifteen when my parents died, and it... Pretty much blew everything to hell."

"And so you don't have relationships?"

"No."

"Well—so this is just how you treat people then?"

"People need to be fed. And they ought to have the things they like. It's not that difficult to listen when someone tells you exactly what they want. The odds were kind of stacked in my favor, here. You actually have to be pretty damn obtuse to fail at something like this. You told me exactly what you wanted for your coffee, and I got it for you."

"You know, I used to think that I had to have it all together because I was in a long-term relationship. Like it mattered just because it existed."

She sat down at the bar right next to the kitchen island. And she started to assemble her first fajita. She put on extra sour cream, because this conversation required it. "I just... I thought it made me special. Or proved that I had arrived at some kind of emotional milestone. And even six months ago, if we would have met and you would've told me that you never dated anybody, I would've thought there was something wrong with you. But, I'm not really sure that's true. Or at least... There might be the same kind of wrong with us. I don't know."

He chuckled. "Oh, there's definitely something wrong with me. Do you want a beer?"

"Yes," she said.

"Coming right up." And he went toward the fridge, opened it and produced a cold one for her, handing it to her after popping the top.

"I feel like I've woken up in an alternate reality. I am so used to being taken for granted. That just you handing me a drink feels like a big deal." It was funny that she just… Said things to him. But there was something about this relationship, the supposed temporary nature of it, and the deep intimacy that had come with it that just made her feel like… Why hold back what she thought?

Why hold anything back at all?

She'd been holding too much in for too long.

"I knew that guy was a dick," Colt said. "I really did. Because I remember when I walked into that bar and I saw you."

His eyes went intense, and she couldn't look away. "I wanted you. Then. We were sitting there with him. And I thought… I could probably seduce you away from him."

"You probably could have."

She felt her cheeks getting hot.

"Now I wish I would've tried."

"Oh, he would have been incensed."

"Well, all the better reason to do it."

"He's… The only man that I…"

"Yeah, I get that. You know, from the whole timeline of the relationship and everything."

She nodded slowly. "I figured it was probably pretty obvious."

"There's nothing obvious about you, Mallory. That's the thing that gets me. What I don't understand. What I really don't understand is why you— And don't take this the wrong way, it's just that you're not my usual type at all. But damn, woman, I saw you... I couldn't forget you."

She took a bite of her fajita and started to chew. She took an extra long time with it, because she was going to say the next words that were on her mind, it was just that she was a little embarrassed about it in advance. But they were having a real conversation, and maybe this conversation was the first step to dealing with things. Because obviously, they were in whatever situation they were in. So maybe they needed to be a little bit more honest with each other. Maybe they needed to have a conversation.

"I was having sex dreams about you," she said in a rush. "When I was still with him. After I saw you the first time. We made eye contact for thirty seconds in a bar. And I started having... The dirtiest dreams about you. I couldn't forget it. I had an orgasm during one of them."

"Damn," he said, his expression going completely stoic. She shifted in her seat, regretting it now, because she was getting turned on. Because it would be so easy... It would be so easy to cross the space and kiss him again. Except Lily was right there asleep. Except she was renting from him. Except so many things.

But the biggest thing was that the cream seemed like a big deal.

And she had to figure that out on her own. She had to get her head on straight. Because right now she was ready to leap into bed with a man just because he had brought her takeout and handed her a beer. Because he had remembered what she wanted in her coffee. And maybe she needed those things to feel a little bit more commonplace before she went and... Yeah. Maybe.

"I don't know why," she said. "Except... That should've been the sign. Right there."

"Yeah, we can change the subject anytime, because there's a baby sleeping right over there."

"Right. I just…" She took a big breath. "When my whole life blew up, I came back here, and I would be lying if I said part of me didn't hope that I would see you again."

"You just didn't want me to see you again, and again. And again."

"Yeah, pretty much."

"Understandable."

"What about you? I mean… I know why I jumped into bed with you."

"I already told you, that's just what I do."

"I don't believe it, though. Because you remember me. Because like you said, the first moment that you saw me… And you brought me half-and-half. So, please just tell me this. Because I've already… Shown you how sad I am. And I'm sitting here eating fajitas and baring my soul, so maybe give me a little bit of something in return."

"It's not going to be baring my soul. You don't want that, anyway."

"All right, it doesn't need to be that. Nothing quite that dramatic."

"I can't explain what happened the first time. Maybe it was just lust. I'm used to generic lust. I'll admit that. I spent a lot of years on the road. And the excitement of meeting eyes with a pretty girl from across the room hadn't been a big deal for a long time. When I was a kid, sure. I'd see her, I'd wonder what would happen. And look, I love women. I really do. But I was working a steady diet of buckle bunnies, and anybody in my position tends to end up there. Easy quarry. Or maybe that's the wrong word. We're their quarry, they're ours. It's a mutual hunting situation. And after a long ass day of traveling, after competing in events, drinking…

That's about the speed you want to go. So I don't know, I guess I was jaded. And then…"

She looked down at her plate. Away from him, because she sensed that he needed her to do that.

"Trent died. And it was like part of me went with him. I can't explain it. But look, I've experienced loss in my life already. You know that. You already know our tragic story. How our parents died when we were teenagers. It's a terrible thing. And I thought that I'd accepted that the world was random. That life sometimes handed you shit on a plate and you had no choice but to eat it. Yeah. I thought that I knew that. But seeing a kid like him die…"

"You said that you felt responsible for it."

"I am. I met him when he was… Man, that kid was a hellion. Sixteen years old and nothing but trouble. He was a runaway. Out of the foster care system. I kind of… Hell, I… I had never taken responsibility for another person in my life. Out of all the boys, I was the youngest one to be left behind. There was Ryder, Jake, Logan. And then there was me. I was the kid brother. And I resented them trying to… Take care of me. I resented it big-time. I didn't want to be taken care of because I didn't think I…"

"Right." Of course he hadn't thought he needed it. Teenage boys always thought they were grown men, didn't they?

"I met Trent when he was trying to steal stuff out of the back of my horse trailer. And rather than call the cops on the kid, I gave him some jobs to do. I tried to help get him on his feet. What I did was get him involved in the rodeo. And it turns out I'm a pretty bad person to emulate. I drink too much. I sleep around too much. And I could see him doing all these things that I did, and I didn't like the look of it on him, but I didn't know how to tell him what to do when I didn't know how to do it myself."

"It sounds to me like he was a kid who had a lot of life experience before he met you."

"True enough. But I just… The drinking was really out of control. And I knew it. I knew that it was going past the way that we partied after rides. That he was starting to take risks he shouldn't. But again… That's me. I was the life of the party, Mallory."

She looked at the grave, tired features on his handsome face, and she had a pretty hard time believing that. "Were you, Colt?"

"I was. And then… Everything went to hell. He did his last ride drunk. He was floppy like a rag doll, and not in a good way. When he went off the back of that bull… He couldn't save himself. And I… I can't get it out of my head. I watched him die. We all did. We watched that accident like a train wreck, and no one could get to him in time."

Her stomach twisted. "Did you try?"

"Of course I did. I…" He closed his eyes. "I couldn't stay after that. I couldn't stay in the rodeo. Everything had to change."

"Yeah. And Cheyenne was angry at you, wasn't she?"

"With good reason. She told me that he wanted to be like me. She told me that he saw me take risks, saw that I didn't wear a helmet, that I stuck with a cowboy hat instead of all the safety gear. That he didn't drink any more than I did… And that he was there because of me. And she's not wrong. He was. I was the wrong person for him to look up to." He looked over at Lily. "And now I'm taking care of his daughter? I shouldn't be. But I can't get rid of the responsibility of it either."

She swallowed hard. "Colt, I'm going to admit to you pretty readily that I haven't been through half of the things that you have. You had a much harder life than I have, and there's no denying that. I have great parents who model the loving marriage for me. A brother who fell in love and married a wonderful woman. And even though she died, I saw him in a healthy relationship. And still, somehow..." She swallowed hard, knowing she was omitting things, even while she feigned honesty, but she just didn't want to talk about her stuff. "Still, I was in mine. Still, somehow I didn't take those lessons on board. People were all around me modeling a healthy life, and somehow I didn't." She took a deep breath. "And I guess what I'm trying to say is that people are going to do... They're going to do what they're going to do. And you can't control that. They're going to make their own decisions. Griffin was my hero, and I still didn't turn out anywhere near as healthy as he did."

"That's nice. I mean, that's nice of you to say."

"But you don't believe me."

"I just know that he wouldn't have been in the rodeo in the first place if it weren't for me."

She reached out and put her hand on his. "It sounds to me like he might have been in prison or dead long before he ever got to twenty-two if it weren't for you."

He closed his eyes. "You know, I used to think... You couldn't outrun your fate. And maybe that's true. Maybe it is just fate."

"But you feel responsible somehow anyway."

He shrugged. "None of it's logical, is it? Why do we do anything we do, or think anything we think?"

"Yeah, why do we stay with someone who makes a random guy buying half-and-half seem like a miraculous gesture? I guess that's the question."

"Honestly, the question of why we hooked up... In the entire array of questions, that's a very easy one."

"It is."

She stuffed the last of her second fajita into her mouth and set about building another one. She was suddenly very sad, and she felt like her feelings would pair nicely with overindulgence.

"Are you going back up to the cabin tonight?"

"How about I stay here? I mean, until everything is settled. Until you feel a little bit more comfortable with her and with preparing bottles in the middle of the night..."

"Sounds good. Is there anything you need in the bedroom?"

"No. But... I might go back up and grab an overnight bag."

"Okay."

She let out a long, slow breath. "I'm really not propositioning you."

"I believe it."

"This is a lot."

"Look, Mallory," he said, his voice rough. "Before you... Since Trent died, I haven't even been tempted to be with someone. There's something about you..."

"But you don't want it to be there."

"I can't offer you anything."

She considered that for a beat. "I don't want anything."

*Except...*

She wanted him. She wanted him in spite of everything. In spite of everything she knew to be right.

"Okay. I'll be back."

She headed out toward her car, and she took a breath. It had been hot the last few days, and now it seemed like there might be a storm coming in. She took a breath and tried to get a handle on herself. Wanting him did not mean having him. There was Lily to think about. And honestly... Just both of them. It was a minefield. The two of them were. And wanting each other didn't have to make it difficult. And it didn't have to matter quite so much.

She had to laugh though, because her entire intent in moving here had been to get out there and experience life. Had been to get out there and experience something other than the kind of fake domesticity she'd been living in for so long. And what had she stumbled into? Taking care of a baby. Playing house with a handsome man.

*And so the one thing you absolutely must not do is sleep with him again.*

Renewed, she drove back up to the cabin and collected her things.

She was going to make sure that Lily was taken care of. And that was the bottom line of all of this. It wasn't about her; it wasn't about Colt. It was about Lily. And she was committed to ensuring that Lily got the best care possible.

It was easy to shove her feelings to the side when she kept that in the foreground.

And she would just have to keep on doing that. As many times as it took.

She was just about to walk out the door when her cell phone buzzed in her pocket. She sighed and picked it up without looking at it first.

"Hello?"

"Mallory."

She felt like she was having a short circuit. So she just stood there. "Jared?"

"Yes. Why have you been being so ridiculous? You should pick up when I call."

"Oh. Should I?"

"Yes," he said. "For all I know you're dead somewhere."

"I mean, obviously I'm not."

And she waited. Waited for the things she was afraid of.

Waited for the reason that she had fled to Oregon to appear, blooming in her chest like a great growling monster. Longing. Nostalgia. All the things that she was afraid would send her back into his arms.

Except… It made her want to laugh. She couldn't even fathom it. It wasn't because of half-and-half.

But she was here now. And she was already more enmeshed, more involved in this life than she had been in that previous life of fifteen years. She was so… Active right now. She was caring for a baby. She had just talked about deep, dark wounds over Mexican food with a man who made her feel flushed and ridiculous. A man she couldn't touch again, but the fact remained, he made her feel those things. And that night they'd been together, he made her feel all kinds of things that she hadn't known that she would ever be able to feel. Thing she had thought were beyond her.

Because of the man she was on the phone with. He made her feel broken. He'd made her feel like there was something wrong with her. And… And then there was Colt.

Colt made her feel beautiful.

Even though that part of their relationship had concluded, sitting next to him made her feel a kind of feminine that she never had in her life before. That man…

That man.

And this one… He didn't even register. One night with Colt, and she was genuinely, one hundred percent, absolutely ruined for Jared.

Possibly for anyone.

No. She wasn't going to think that. That wasn't productive. Wasn't helpful at all.

"Well?" he pressed.

"Well what?"

"Are you going to explain yourself?"

"I'm sorry. Did the packing up the entire house, moving, not answering your calls, all after I screamed at you about cheating on me… Not explain things for you?"

"Just… What the hell?"

"What do you mean what the hell? You cheated on me."

"Not technically. I mean, we were kind of broken up. Because we had that fight…"

She'd spent a lot of the last couple days processing her relationship. Remembering why she'd stayed. Remembering that he'd been there for her when she'd needed him.

Now wasn't the time for that.

Now wasn't the time to be fair or measured or any of that.

"You know what? I'm glad that you cheated on me. I'm not going to let you wiggle out of it, but I'm not upset about the cheating. What I'm upset about is that it took cheating to get me to leave you. Because you are useless. You're a deadbeat. And you'll find some other woman to sponge off of, because that's who you are. And unfortunately there are too many women in the world out there that are like… Like me. Who are afraid if they let go of a person who says that they love them, they'll never find that again.

"But love isn't just words," she continued. "Love is doing things. And I did that for you. I did. I gave you my heart. I gave you my body. I gave you a house. And together we…we made a child and we lost her. And we never did figure out where to go from there, except we were just…stuck, weren't we? I guess that's why I was still with you."

"Hey," he said, his voice changing, taking on that placating apologetic tone that he always affected when she was mad at him. When he was losing an argument. "Baby. We've been together for so long. And I guess I started to take you for granted. And I'm sorry. That's not who I am. That's not what I want."

"It's what you did, though. And you know what, it's not even nostalgic for me anymore. So whatever you could've done, however you could have used this… It's not going to work that way for me anymore. It's not going to grab me anymore. Because I don't love you. I love myself too much for that now."

Because she had woken up. She just had. She had suddenly breathed deep, and she had realized how shallow it had all been before. She was awake now.

"I came to town, and I found the hottest man you have ever seen, and I banged him. And it was amazing." She was breathing hard now, her words pointed like a dagger, and maybe she wanted to hurt him—she sort of did. But even more than that, she wanted to claim something for herself. This victory.

"It was the best sex I've ever had. I didn't know sex could be that good. Do you know why? Because I only ever had sex with you. You're bad in bed. You're whiny. You're selfish. You're less accomplished than I am. You don't want a girlfriend. You want someone to be your mom, and if you could've had me wipe your ass, you probably would've asked for that too.

"But I'm done. I'm done. Because even though all I have here are fragments of a future, they are better than what I had with you. I'm still piecing it together. I'm still figuring out what I want. But the one thing I'm absolutely certain of is that it will never, ever be you. Not ever again. So yes, I'm glad I answered this call. I hope that things seem clearer to you now."

"You're such a bitch sometimes, Mallory."

"Yeah," she said. "I'm a big old bitch. Go fuck yourself." Then she hung up the phone, her heart beating fast. And she laughed. Because that wasn't the high road, not even close. And she wasn't even sorry.

She felt elated. Electric. And suddenly, she started to cry. Not because she was sad, but because she felt like she had well and truly shed a heavy, painful burden. Because she felt like she had actually, finally separated herself from that millstone. He would've pulled her down beneath the surface of the water. He would've drowned her. But it was over. Now it was over.

And she was free.

And here, in Gold Valley, she had a one-night stand she hadn't been able to escape, a helpless baby that needed care, a clinic that needed to be revamped and new patients to get to know. She had her brother, her sister-in-law and a new niece or nephew coming. And she wasn't sure yet how all those pieces fit together. But they were pretty amazing pieces.

And they made her feel alive.

# CHAPTER ELEVEN

OVER THE NEXT few days Colt, Mallory and Lily settled into a routine. It worked so well to have Mallory staying in the house that it had stopped becoming a question. He felt bad, because she had gotten her cabin all set up, and she wasn't really inhabiting it, but it just didn't make much sense for her to go up there when she was taking every other night with Lily. They had decided that trading off would help with work. And on days when she didn't have clients, she took Lily down to the clinic, while a couple of other days Colt had stayed home.

He was going to start bringing her to the ranch, but he needed to make sure that he had the right kind of sling that would support her fully while he rode on the back of a horse.

And in the back of his mind the whole time, he kept thinking that any day Cheyenne might come back.

True to his word, he had the police do a welfare check on her. He knew that she'd gone back to her house. But he hadn't been able to get in touch with her. He had called once, and she hadn't answered. Then after that, her phone had been off. But he kept thinking that soon, soon she would come back. But he continued to amass baby items and continued to get more deeply entrenched in the situation, regardless of the fact that he knew that it was only temporary. And finally, it was time for the family dinner. Mallory decided to go with him, and he decided to bring Lily, which he knew was a little bit of a gamble. But... Part of him wanted to share her.

Wanted them to meet her. Because she was Trent's little girl. And that had mattered. He mattered. Sharing her seemed... Like a decent thing to do, really. When he walked into the living room, Mallory was already there cradling Lily, who was dressed in the frilliest pink dress he had ever seen.

"When did you get that?"

"I saw it in a boutique on Main Street the other day, and I couldn't pass it up."

"That's really something."

"She's so cute," Mallory said, smiling.

And there was something about the glow on her face as she looked at Lily that made... Well, it made his chest do something strange. And it was bad enough... The sexual tension, because that was a hell of a thing. But then there were all these moments that felt like something else. Something deeper, and he didn't like them. Of course, talking to her about his actual damn feelings over fajitas probably hadn't been the best idea, but it had happened. So what could you do.

"I have a headband too." She popped a little pink band around her head, a large rose on the front.

He groaned. He took Lily from her arms, surprised at how natural it had become in just a few days. She was so tiny. That he really wasn't used to yet. "All right, Silly Lily," he said. "Frilly Lily." And he laughed.

"Was that a dad joke?"

He suddenly went stiff, his whole heart turning to cement.

"No," he said. "I'm not her dad."

Mallory blinked, her face falling. "I know that. I'm sorry. I was making a joke. Apparently a bad joke."

"Just so we're clear."

"Clear," Mallory said.

He felt like a dick. "It's just that Trent…"

"I get it," she said. "He was her dad, and that's really important to you."

That, and the idea of him being someone's dad… It made him want to peel his skin off.

"Let's go."

They got in her car—which was what they did when they took Lily anywhere—but this time he was driving. It was one of those strange things that couples did. Drove each other's cars. And they were not a couple. Just how hard up he felt right now was testament to that.

He sighed heavily and didn't even bother to hold it back. There was no point even thinking about it. Not any of it.

They were in a screwed-up situation. It wasn't like anything else. They certainly weren't a couple. They certainly weren't a family.

But it was amazing what a few days of sleep deprivation and caring for an infant could make you think about.

It was the way people were wired, he supposed. If he believed in fate in any capacity, he supposed he had to acknowledge that.

They were designed to do this. Produce offspring. Pair off and take care of it.

When they drove underneath the big sign that read Hope Springs Ranch, Mallory made an amusing sound. "Has it always been called that?"

"What? Hope Springs?"

"Yes."

He nodded. "Yeah. I guess the man who discovered the actual springs called it that because finding water like that brought him hope for success. The name stuck for the ranch. I always thought it was kind of a sick joke."

"Because of your parents?"

In more ways than one.

"Yeah."

"I'm sorry. I mean, I'm really sorry. I know it's not the same. But I loved my first sister-in-law very much. And my niece…"

"Yeah," he said.

He hadn't even really thought about that. He was aware of course of Griffin's losses from all those years ago. But he hadn't really connected them to Mallory. Or how they would've hurt her. But losing a child in a family…

That made his stomach clench tight. Turn over. He had known Lily for only a few days, and he wasn't blood related to her, but the idea of something happening to her nearly sent him into a full rage. She was so tiny, so vulnerable, and it felt like it was his responsibility to protect her from… Everything out there in the world. At the same time he felt wholly and totally unequipped to do that. He had failed to protect so many people in his life.

"That must've really hurt," he said, his voice rough even to his own ears.

"It did. I can't help it, but I think about her sometimes when I look at Lily. I have dealt with countless babies, but my niece was really the only child I took care of more long-term. It's been a long time, but that's not something that you forget. It's not really a grief that eases. You just kind of have to make room and learn to breathe around it."

"Is it difficult to take care of Lily?"

She shook her head. "No. Actually, it's kind of… Healing. To care for her. Actually, it's healing in a lot of ways." She reached up and wiped a tear off of her cheek. "Jared called me." He stopped the car in front of the ranch house.

"Really?"

"Yeah. I quite literally told him to do something ana-tomically impossible with himself. And I feel really good about it."

"Well I'm glad to hear that."

"I was afraid I would miss him." She looked out the car window. "But I don't. I really, really don't."

"Good for you."

"I'm ready for dinner. I'm starving. The biggest problem with taking care of Lily is that I forget to eat during the day."

"I never eat during the day."

She looked at him, and her eyes dropped down to his mid-section. Her admiration was open and frank, and it affected his body in a sharp, intense way. "Well, that explains a few things about you."

"Are you hitting on me?"

"Well." The air got thick.

Tension.

It was always swirling around them. And damned if part of him didn't enjoy it. Because what he'd said to her the other night about buckle bunnies was true.

It had become a sure thing. And in some ways, a little bit boring. This… Well, this really did remind him of a dif-ferent time of his life. One that was less complicated. Ironi-cally. Because it was also about the most complicated time in his life he could remember. But it also reminded him a little bit of that innocent need you could feel for a woman. That sense of what if. Mallory Chance was a mystery that should be solved, and yet she also felt like an infinite one. It was the strangest damn thing, and he found that he kind of liked it.

It was amazing that in the middle of all this, he could like much of anything. But there were moments. Quiet moments in the middle of the swamp.

"Let's go," he said.

He got out of the car quickly, eager to put that moment behind them. He grabbed the diaper bag and hefted Lily out of her car seat, not that it was much of a heft. She was such a little peanut. He couldn't see her mother or her father in her face. Mostly because she had that squishy little newborn look that was pretty much standard issue on them as far as he could tell. Though, she was an exceptionally cute standard issue in his opinion.

He shoved aside the heavy feeling that settled on his chest and fixed a smile on his face.

His family wasn't used to seeing him in an intense mood. And hell, he wasn't really used to being in one. It was just the last few months. It had been impossible to shift. And the whole situation had brought up a bunch of things that…

Yeah, everything was just kind of out there.

He hated that he couldn't put on that smile anymore. That he couldn't do what they expected of him.

Maybe they just expected this now.

The door burst open, and practically the entire family was shoved into the doorway, looking out.

"Hi," he said.

Iris and Griffin in particular were staring.

He knew that Jake had more or less explained the situation to Ryder at least. But he had forgot to ask Mallory if she had talked to Griffin.

"This is Lily," he said, indicating the baby. "She's staying with me for a while. Mallory is helping."

Mallory half waved. "Hi."

Iris and Griffin exchanged glances that held clear and weighty words.

*Great.* So this was going to turn into an interrogation at some point. He was confident in that. Because when Griffin met his gaze, it was sharp and a little bit too intense.

And if he held the baby a little like a shield at that point, it wasn't his fault. Everybody backed up when he walked into the room.

"Should we do rapid-fire Daniels questions?" he asked.

"So she's Trent's baby?" Ryder asked.

"Yes," Colt said.

"And my sister is involved?" Griffin asked.

"Yes," Mallory said. "Your sister is involved because she is an expert on babies. And she happened to be standing there when the baby was pushed into his arms." She sighed. "Also, how can you not get involved with babies?"

"She's beautiful," Sammy said.

Pansy, still in her police uniform, took a step forward. "And everything is okay with her mother?"

"Pansy, I know this is a strange situation, but there's really nothing... Look, before she goes back with Cheyenne we'll make sure that everything's okay," Colt said. "I'm not going to let her go into an unsafe situation."

"I know," Pansy said. "It's just that I like to make sure everything is aboveboard, and this is a little bit... Middle of the board."

"It's not."

"He's her godfather," Mallory said. "We are going to have to get the baby set up with a pediatrician, though, and as we are not legal guardians, that is a little bit tricky."

"That's what I mean," Pansy said. "It's going to get complicated."

"I'm not afraid of *complicated*," Colt said. "Since when has our life ever been simple?"

"Fair point," Rose said. "We don't do simple. We only do convoluted and slightly dodgy. I'm referring to my marriage." Her husband rolled his eyes and sighed audibly. She looked back at him and smiled broadly.

"Okay, are we done gawking? Can we eat?"

"Sure," Sammy said. "Eating."

And just as he'd suspected, while everyone else filtered into the kitchen, Griffin grabbed hold of Colt's shoulder.

"So what exactly is happening with you and my sister? Because it just seems odd to me that she's suddenly helping out with the baby."

"Believe me when I tell you, I couldn't get her to not help with the baby. I tried."

"That does sound like Mallory. She's... Persistent. And I mean that in a good way. She was the person that called me. Pretty much every day when I was out here trying to disappear into the mountains. She... She wants to help."

"She has helped. I don't know what the hell I'm doing. But it's my responsibility. I would think that you'd be the kind of man that understood that."

Griffin regarded him. "Yeah. I do."

"But, that doesn't mean I know what I'm doing." He sighed heavily. "Honestly. She's been amazing. And essential."

"She's fragile," Griffin said. "And I know she doesn't act that way. I can absolutely picture her charging right in and getting up in your business, but I really worry about her. She was with that... I *hate that guy*."

"Jared?" And just like that, he felt a little bit revealed. Because that was making it clear he knew more about her personal life than he might if she was just helping out with the baby. If they hadn't had... A prior situation.

"Yeah," Griffin said.

"Look, I like your sister," he said, because that was true. "And she's helping me out with the... Quite frankly an insane situation. And I appreciate it. But I respect you. And more than that, I respect her. And I'm well aware that I'm too messed up to get into any kind of situation. Particularly with someone that… Is apparently involved in multiple aspects of my life."

"That's weird, though," Griffin said. "How you pretty much knew what I was going to ask. Almost as if…"

"No as if. What, do you want me to lie and say that I find your sister unattractive? Because she's beautiful. And I'm not blind."

"Okay," Griffin said. "Settle down."

"You're the one who pushed the subject."

"Yeah, but I didn't mean to push it *that* way."

"Okay. Well. Don't do it again."

"You're an asshole," Griffin said.

Colt turned around and smiled, still holding Lily, cradling her fuzzy head with his hand. "Yes, yes I am." He walked in, and there was only one seat available, one right next to Mallory. So he took it.

"Do you want me to take her?"

"No," he said. "I'm fine."

Dinner was a fantastic feat, but it always was with the women in his family involved. There was homemade bread, steak and salad. And it took a while for him to figure out how he was going to eat it with one hand, but he managed.

He was about halfway through his steak when he realized that mostly everyone was looking at him, and not eating.

"What?"

"It's just weird," Logan said.

"What? I'm doing what any of you would do. Hell, Ryder. It's basically what you did. When shit goes down, and you have a responsibility, you do what needs doing."

"Fair," Sammy said. "But please watch your mouth in front of my baby. And… Yours quite frankly."

"Sorry," he said.

Astrid looked up, her eyes shining bright. "Don't repeat him, mite," Ryder said.

"She's more likely to get in trouble repeating you," Sammy said, dryly.

"I watch my language."

"Unless you happen to hit your hand with a hammer."

"That happened one time."

"Yeah, but you dropped so many F-bombs they're practically embedded in the walls."

"I can take her now," Mallory said, taking Lily from his arms. "You finish dinner."

And somehow, that seemed weirder. And he felt a little bit like he'd lost his shield.

But there was pie on the table, and he determined that he would focus on that, rather than anything else.

MALLORY TOOK LILY into the living room with a bottle and sat on the couch. Colt should visit with his family. She was basically... The babysitter in tow. She didn't need to sit at the table. Granted, her brother was here, but they could visit another time.

She heard footsteps and looked up and saw her sister-in-law standing there.

"Hi."

"Hi," Mallory said.

"So how are things. I feel like I haven't seen you in a little bit. I mean, I get why."

"Yeah. It's... Kind of crazy? But it's happening. For what it's worth, I told him that he should call the police. But he... He feels really strongly about taking care of her..."

"Something happened between you two, didn't it? Or is happening?"

Mallory went stiff. "Is it that obvious?"

"I don't know if it's obvious." Iris grimaced. "Yes. It's obvious. Even Griffin was twitchy. Which means he probably picked up on it too. And he's a man, and therefore not all that in tune with human nuance."

"Nothing is happening now. Okay, you know how Rose said that she thought she saw me in the saloon before you found out I was in town?"

"Yes," she said slowly.

"It was me. I came into town, I hadn't talked to anyone yet. I was really messed up from the breakup." She cleared her throat. "Well I… I met Colt."

"Oh my gosh."

"Yes. And then… Everything."

"Oh my gosh," Iris repeated.

"Yes. But… Now we're taking care of Lily."

"A little tip about wounded men," Iris said. "They get under your skin quicker than you could believe."

Iris was talking about Mallory's brother. Obviously.

Mallory looked down determinedly at Lily. "It's not like that. I like him. I really do. But I need…" She looked back up at Iris. "I don't know. I don't know what I need. I'm here to figure it out." Those ugly feelings rolled around inside of her. Those ones that she felt earlier. The last time she'd talked to Iris. "I think I'm jealous of you, Iris."

"What?"

Mallory hadn't expected the words to come out of her mouth, and she could tell that Iris really hadn't expected to hear them.

"It's just… You… You got to Griffin in a way that I never could."

"Well, trying to be delicate about it, Mallory, there are aspects of my relationship with Griffin that are…"

"Look, I know. It's romantic. And you love each other

that way. I get it. It's just… I love Griffin. Very much. He was my idol growing up. And you have no idea how much I missed him when he was gone. But he didn't want me to come see him. He barely called me back. And I am grateful to you. Forever. For pulling him out of that pit. I really am. But I just wish that I…"

She had wanted to redeem herself by fixing him. Because…above all else she felt like she'd failed. In the most important relationship she could have had.

That she'd failed to bring her baby safely into the world.

And she had wanted, so very badly, to bring her brother back. As if that might be some form of atonement.

It didn't matter that she knew, intellectually, that Lucy's death hadn't been her fault.

She felt like it was.

Iris put her hand on Mallory's. "I understand. Believe me. As someone who spent a lot of her life being afraid she wasn't enough… There are moments and places and people that can unlock things inside of you. But just because Griffin started healing after he and I met, it doesn't mean what came before wasn't enough. Sometimes you have to prepare the soil before you try to plant anything in it. And I really do believe in my heart that if you hadn't worked on Griffin the way that you did, if you hadn't loved him the way that you did, he never would have been ready for me."

"Oh," Mallory said, her eyes filling with tears. "I just… Iris I feel so guilty even thinking that. I should just be happy he's okay…"

"Don't feel guilty. Do you have any idea how… Ridiculously sad I was that I was the last person in my family not to be paired up? I couldn't even be as happy for them as I wanted to be."

"Well, you weren't the last."

"No." She looked back toward the kitchen. "Colt is kind of a special case, you know. I don't know that any of us really knows him. He used to be so happy. But I don't know that that was ever real. And now that I realize that… It makes me sad. It really does. It's obvious now that there's something wrong, but we all knew. And for years… We're both each other's biggest champions, and sometimes each other's own worst enablers. We know what each other went through, and we make a lot of assumptions about what each other feels. And sometimes that's good. But sometimes… Sometimes I don't think it helps."

"You must help each other well enough. If you didn't none of you would be quite this functional."

"Well. I guess we function okay. Though, we kind of arrived to a functional place dramatically."

"I'm starting to think that maybe none of us make it without a little drama."

Iris wrapped her arm around Mallory. "Well, one thing I know for sure, is that all the drama I've been through in life has been worth it to get where I am. It's made me who I am. And as difficult as everything that I… It's why I was able to be there for him. And like I said, I really do think the reason he was able to accept that was because of his family. Because of you. Because of the way you loved him. Even when he couldn't quite accept it."

"Thank you," Mallory said.

"And I love my cousin. If you could quite possibly help him heal…" She shook her head. "That's not fair. I know you're here to deal with your own self, not heal Colt."

"But I seem to be in the middle of all this, regardless."

Iris laughed. "True." She reached out and stroked Lily's cheek. "She's beautiful. You look so natural with her. I hope that I'm as good with babies. I don't have a lot of experience with babies. Even though I am the oldest girl. When they were tiny babies… I know a lot about little kids. That, I'm good with."

"Do you want to hold her?"

"Yes," Iris said.

She transferred Lily to Iris's arms, and right then Colt walked into the room.

"I wanted to hold her," Iris said, looking over at him.

"You're a natural," he responded.

They lingered for a little while longer, and when it was time to leave, there was something inescapably right about all of it. The warmth in the air, standing next to him. And as she got into the passenger seat and buckled up, she did the best she could to banish it.

Because this was good. It was good. She'd talked to Iris, and she… Suddenly, she found herself blinking back tears.

"What?" Colt asked.

She looked over at him, not able to see his face in the dim light of the car. And she knew he couldn't see hers either.

"How did you know that I was crying?"

"The way you were breathing. I know what it sounds like when you get all emotional. You do it when you look at Lily a lot."

Her heart crumpled. "Oh. Just a conversation that I had with Iris. About Griffin. I've been feeling sorry for myself about a few things. And she… She really made me feel better. She made me feel like… Like maybe I'm wrong about some things."

"You? Wrong about something?"

"I know," she said, laughing. "Shocking, right?"

"I don't think I'll ever recover."

An oncoming car sent a slice of light across his face, and her heart tripped over onto itself. If she wasn't careful, it would be easy to think that this was something it wasn't. If she wasn't careful, it would be easy to get comfortable again. And she wasn't here to be comfortable. She was here for moments like she'd had tonight. Ones that stretched her and grew her. Changed her and shifted things inside of her. That's what she was here for. And that's what she was going to put her focus on.

Not Colt Daniels and his wicked smile. Or the way he made her heart hurt when she looked at him.

# *CHAPTER TWELVE*

THE THUNDERSTORM THAT had begun to make itself evident a few days ago made itself manifest that day. Colt had decided to stay home that day, figuring that he didn't need to be out riding in the fields when the weather was this miserable, particularly not with Lily. Mallory had patients to see to today, and it just worked out best if he stayed with the baby.

She had been with him for nearly two weeks. And that meant that Mallory had been with him for that amount of time as well.

And the house was beginning to feel too small. That woman...

Sometimes there were moments where the air seemed to stop around her. Where time itself seemed to stop. And all he could do was stare at her. At her shining eyes, her full, beautiful mouth.

She was becoming a craving. And he didn't think he could attribute it to the lack of sex, because in that case, wouldn't every woman he passed incite such an internal riot inside of him? But they didn't. It was only her. Only ever her.

He was feeling particularly pissed off about it today too. He had a sleepless night with Lily, and the house now seemed extra quiet. Because of course she was sleeping. He lay down on the couch for a while, but he didn't like to be idle during the day. No matter how exhausted he was. He stared at his guitar in the corner for a while, but he left it. It had dust on it.

His dad had taught him to play the guitar. That was one of his happy memories. His dad in the living room playing a country song and laughing.

Ever since his conversation with Jake a few months back, it felt tinged with an extra layer of loss.

Had his dad really intended to leave them? In some ways, Colt didn't think so. Not given the conversations they'd had right before the trip. He didn't want to play guitar.

He picked up a block of wood and his knife, and he started to fiddle around with it. "You might like this," he said, addressing Lily, who didn't care at all, and was asleep in her bassinet. He began to make a small fox. The corner of his lips kicked up into a smile when it began to take shape. This particular fox had a ridiculously out of proportion tail. But he thought it was something that a little girl would probably find cute. Maybe he would send it off with her when she left. He sighed heavily and curled his hand around the piece. All right. There wasn't going to be any sitting around today—it wasn't doing him any favors.

His phone rang, and he picked it up. "Hello?"

"Colt Daniels?"

"Speaking."

"This is Doctor Elizabeth Fielding."

"What?"

"I'm calling to schedule an appointment with baby Lily. I just spoke to Mallory about the circumstances surrounding the situation, and while normally I wouldn't go ahead and make the appointment, I appreciate that the circumstances really are extraordinary."

"I didn't ask Mallory to schedule an appointment," he said.

"Yes, she mentioned as much, but we got to talking in line at the coffeehouse this morning and…"

"She's using small towns against me."

"No one is using anything against you, Mr. Daniels."

"I…"

He looked out the door at the pouring rain. And suddenly, it looked better than sitting in here. "I'll have to call you back."

Fury licked through his veins. She had gone behind his back and contacted a doctor. Okay, it sounded like she got to chatting to one in line at Sugar Cup. But it didn't really matter the circumstances. The fact of the matter was, she'd put Lily at risk. At risk of being taken by Child Services. And that put… It put Cheyenne at risk. And everything that Trent wanted. And what the hell was the point of any of it if Colt ended up compromising the custody of Lily?

And somewhere inside of him, he knew that he was being unreasonable. Because Mallory was looking out for the physical well-being of Lily. Because well-child visits were important, and they knew next to nothing about Lily. Including her actual age. They didn't have a birth certificate. He clenched his teeth. Yeah, he knew the situation wasn't going to work long-term. But it wasn't supposed to be long-term. Things would work out. They just would.

Something had to. God couldn't be that mean.

Colt picked up an ax and walked over to the wood pile, where a piece of wood was already set up on end. And he brought the ax down on it. Hard. Splitting the wood in two pieces.

That's what he would do. He would chop wood. In the pouring rain. "How's that for martyrdom, Callie," he muttered, directed at his sister-in-law, even though she couldn't hear him.

His shirt has started to stick to his body, and he stripped it off over his head, flinging it into the mud. And he kept chopping wood. Mud and debris flying back against his face, rainwater dripping down into his eyes. But he didn't care. His heart was pounding so hard he thought it might go through the front of his chest. He didn't care.

And that was when he saw her car coming up the driveway.

Lucky for her, he was still furious.

WHEN MALLORY PULLED UP, her heart nearly stopped. Because there he was, in a kind of glory she had never even seen before. He was angry, that much was clear. And he was standing there... Half-naked. His chest was splattered with mud and rainwater, his hair wet and plastered down to his face. His jeans rode low on his hips, revealing those deep cut lines that were just so damn sexy. His body was like a finely carved piece of art. Like something he had chiseled himself using nothing but a knife and wood.

His eyes made contact with hers where she sat in her car. Then he looked away, grabbed a piece of wood and set it up before bringing the ax down on it, splitting it violently.

She got out of the car. "What are you doing?"

"What does it look like I'm doing? I'm chopping wood."

"Chopping wood in the rain. Shirtless."

"Yep."

"Okay."

"What the hell were you thinking?" He charged toward her, holding the ax down at his side. He looked menacing and glorious.

He looked like the alpha wolf.

And suddenly, she knew exactly what the problem was.

"Colt... Don't be angry."

"Oh," he said. "Okay. I won't be angry. I'll just continue being fucking furious."

"I'm sorry. I didn't know that she would call you right

away. Usually it takes a doctor a really long time to actually..."

"She's very prompt. How dare you do that without talking to me? Lily isn't your baby. This isn't your mess. It's mine. You chose to stick your nose in it, and I can't control that. But this isn't about you. She's not part of your path to healing."

"Oh," she said. "She's yours? Or is she a human being who needs to be taken care of."

"*I'm* taking care of her," he said. "And you're overstepping. You know that. Don't you pretend that you don't understand that. Don't you pretend that this couldn't... I couldn't forgive myself. If she ended up getting taken by Child Protective Services, if she ended up in foster care, on top of everything else."

"That isn't the goal. That isn't what the doctor wants. It isn't what I want. But we do need to make sure that she's healthy..."

"I have an idea," he said, closing the distance between them, breathing hard. The rain was coming down in big fat drops, and her dress was starting to stick to her skin. His eyes were electric again, but this time, it was with rage. Rage... But there was desire there too. His well-muscled chest heaved with the force of his breath, water droplets rolling over his muscles. "Why don't we find better ways to keep your mouth occupied."

He dropped the ax on its head, onto the muddy ground with a thunk, and it landed next to him, splashing water up between them. Then, he wrapped his arm around the back of her head, cupping her and drawing her toward him, bringing his mouth down on hers in a fierce claiming. This was nothing like the first time they had come together. That time had been intense, filled with a mutual need that had absolutely nothing to do with each other beyond the instant electric chemistry that had combusted between them. But it wasn't about who they were. It wasn't about Colt. It wasn't about Mallory. But this time… This time it was. He might be angry, but this… This was intimate. The kind of intimacy that had been absent from their first time. Because now she knew.

She knew that his friend was dead. That he was trying his best to make his way in this world. That he had left behind his dreams. That he was the sort of man who would take a baby that was handed to him without explanation on the front porch of his home and do his best to take care of her. Would defend her with everything he had in him.

She knew that about him now.

And what did he know about her? That she was frustrating, she supposed, because he was definitely frustrated with her now.

But that he wanted her all the same, and somehow that was even better. Even better than the way that he had wanted her when she was a stranger. He wanted her infuriating. He wanted her when she opposed him. He wanted her when he was absolutely and completely displeased with her in every way.

He wanted her so much.

The fierce growl that rose in the back of his throat as he opened his mouth wider to taste her deep proved that. And then his other arm came around her body, his palm pressed to her lower back as he let her feel the hard steel of his desire at the cradle of her femininity. He wanted her. And he couldn't deny it. And she wanted him. And it wasn't like a gentle, gauzy desire. It was something sharp that cut her all the way through. It was something that made her feel bright and brilliant. Angry and filled with joy all at once. And he was like a freight train. All muscle and testosterone and unstoppable desire.

She fed off of it.

Off of the way he made her feel both empowered and fragile all at once. Off of the way his masculinity consumed all that was soft and female about her.

The rain poured down on them, cold and insistent, but it did nothing to dampen the ardor between them. Nothing could. It could have been a whole bucket of ice and it wouldn't have stopped this heat. Never.

It was an unquenchable flame, and she didn't fear it. Not now. She wanted to be consumed by it. By him. By all of this and everything. And it didn't matter if it was a terrible idea. Because nothing about what was happening was a good idea. Because all of these fragmented pieces of her new life were impossible. Disparate and insane, but one thing was certain. One thing was absolutely certain. She wanted him. And she wouldn't be denied.

Because this was rare. This need. Like flecks of real gold shining at the bottom of the stream. Like the gold this valley was undoubtedly named for. Small little bright spots of fragile perfection that existed in a world full of bedrock. And why shouldn't she live in it? Why shouldn't she revel in it? Why not her?

Why should it be consigned to one night? A moment of pleasure.

It was that mindset that made her feel like small gestures of kindness were exceptional. Because she did. She limited herself out of fear. Out of fear that she might be alone. Out of fear that she might not be enough.

But hadn't Iris just told her something entirely different? Hadn't Iris just set her world on its head by suggesting that while she might not have been there for the ultimate outcome of Griffin's healing, that she had been instrumental in it.

And that made her mindful. That perfection may not come immediately, but that every moment on the road mattered.

And so maybe this moment mattered. Mattered in ways she might not yet be able to know, so she had to seize it. Capture it and claim it.

She wrapped her arms around his neck, reckless now. Impassioned. They were slick from rainwater, and between her legs she was slick with need, and it was everything.

In this moment, it was everything.

He lifted her up off the ground and walked them both back up toward the porch. They made it up the steps, and he pressed her up against the side of the house, the sound of their breathing amplified in the covered space. He held her chin steady as he kissed her, his grip like iron, and it made her feel safe. Something about being held tight by all that strength, something about his certainty... It made her feel protected.

This was not a man she could control. This wasn't a man who was dependent on her. But he was a man who needed her all the same. For this. In this moment.

And that made her wild.

He wrenched his mouth away from hers, kissing down her neck, his hands moving over her curves. Her dress was soaked through now, and it offered no protection from the searing heat of his hands. And she loved it. He moved his hands down her hips, down past the hem of her dress, and then he shoved it back up, the fabric peeling away from her skin as he yanked it up over her head, leaving her standing there in nothing but her bra and panties right there on his front porch.

"Colt," she said.

But his gaze was that of a wild man's, and she could see that he wasn't in a space to be rational. And she wanted to join him there. And so she did. She just jumped right in. She didn't care what happened. If someone saw. She didn't care about anything but wrapping herself in this all-consuming need. He tore her bra away, leaving her breasts exposed, her nipples beaded tight from the cold and from desire. He lowered his head, sucking one deep into his mouth, the deep sound of satisfaction he made as he tasted her nearly pushing her over the edge right then and there. He cupped her with his other hand, teased her and toyed with her, and she squirmed, the wood rough against her back, Colt hot and amazing at the front.

He pulled her away from the wall and spun her around, and she couldn't figure out quite what he was doing as he stood back and looked at her. "Damn," he said.

"What?" she asked, her voice shaky.

"Just looking at you standing there, naked outside. The trees behind you, and your hair all wet. It's like you're magic. Made from the forest. I want to take you out to the middle of the woods and have you there. Just you and me." The words were hot and desperate, and they sounded as if they had been pulled from somewhere deep inside of him. And she didn't know why, but it made her want to cry. That open, frank appreciation that was like nothing she had ever experienced before.

Because he made her feel like she was created from those words. From that desire. He knelt down in front of her, slowly peeling her underwear off, leaving her entirely naked. And he looked up at her, his gaze filled with banked fire. He leaned in, angling his head, and he bit her inner thigh. Her breath hit his through her teeth, the pain on her tender skin a glorious shock. And then he was standing, picking her up like she was precious and fragile, moving his hand through her damp hair as he carried her into the house. And up the stairs.

"Lily…"

"Asleep," he said, his voice rough.

"And the…"

"Baby monitor is on."

It was her last moment of sanity before she dissolved completely, so she'd decided to use it to try and be responsible. But that was over now. Because she was naked, held against his firm body as he kissed her deep. As he walked her toward the bathroom that connected to his bedroom. He turned the shower on, and then stripped off his jeans, boots and underwear. He divested her of her shoes, and as soon as the water was warm, he dragged her in beneath the spray. Their bodies were slick, and she wiggled against him, reveling in being skin to skin with him again. Finally.

She stepped back, admiring the view of his naked body.

"I didn't imagine it," she said.

"What?"

"How… Sexy you are," she said. "Sorry. That sounded a little bit… Cheesy?"

"Nothing that you could do or say right now would be cheesy to me," he said, looking down at his rock-hard arousal. She wrapped her arms around his neck and kissed him, and then there was no more talking. It was all hands over water-slick skin, and deep groans of desire. He pressed her firmly against the wall, and slid his hand down her ass, squeezing her tightly before moving down to her thigh and lifting her to get up off the ground. Then she felt him push against the entrance to her body. And she gasped as he thrust deep inside. He cupped her face, his forehead pressed against hers, his eyes never wavering as he thrust deep and hard into her. She'd always thought shower sex sounded like it was overrated. Like something perilous and more trouble than it was worth. But…

She had been wrong. Because with Colt it was wonderful. With Colt…

It wasn't a question of making the decision to be here. Making the decision to do this. It was about being swept up in the moment. Utterly. Completely.

And then, everything reduced. To the slide of him inside her, to the feel of his hands bracing her. To the sight of those electric blue eyes boring into hers. The water on his skin and the smell of him. Soap and the sound of the water, the sound of their bodies moving against each other. She was made entirely of feeling. Of passion. And for someone who had been all about the feelings of others for so very long, not because she was so good, but because she needed to find ways to make herself important, just accepting that she was enough in this moment was a bright and brilliant triumph.

Pleasure rioted through her, and suddenly she couldn't think anymore. She could barely breathe. She dug her fingernails into his shoulders and clung to him as he thrust inside her. And when she cried out her release, it reverberated over the shower walls. He growled out his own, and when it was done, they were breathing hard. He shut the water off, wrapped her in a towel and carried her back to the bed. She lay on her back, staring at the ceiling.

"I'm sorry," he said.

"Why?" she mumbled, sleepy now.

"I didn't use a condom. I swear to you, I have never done that before."

She had a moment of panic. Where her stomach hollowed out and she felt fifteen. Even though she knew she didn't need to. Even though she knew she was protected.

But she doubled up. It was just what she did. It only took one unplanned pregnancy to make her hugely paranoid.

But she was on the pill. It was okay. It would be okay.

"Don't worry about it. I'm on the pill, and I..." She didn't really want to have this conversation. This was probably part of why she'd stayed in the relationship she had. There were things you didn't have to talk about. "I always made him use one. Because I didn't trust him. And it turns out I was right to do that. And I really wanted to make sure that I didn't get pregnant. So, there was always doubling up."

"Good," he said.

Weirdly, she did not feel paranoid about Colt at all. Either health or safety or getting pregnant with his baby.

The very idea made her dizzy. Because she felt like she could... Handle this. Like if she were to get pregnant, even if he didn't stay with her, it would be fine.

She wanted a child. She did. Someday, even if not now. But it wouldn't be bad if she had a child now. Colt would be a good father. And they'd figure something out. He was a good man.

Not light or easy, but... What could she do but laugh?

"What?"

"No matter what... No matter what happens in my life... I'm going to be okay now. And that makes everything feel a lot less scary."

He rolled over onto his stomach and made a low, masculine sound. "What's that like?"

It was clear that he was tired, and she reached over and pushed his hair off his face. The familiarity didn't dampen her desire for him, and she had expected it to. That once he wasn't the fantasy object, it would be different. And it was. It was something deeper. Something more intense. And she couldn't really articulate what it was.

*Or you don't want to.*

"It feels pretty good, Colt," she said. "Because if you can get happy with yourself, apparently everything else... Feels manageable."

"What if you think you might be a mistake in the world?"

The words stopped her breath. But before she could say anything, his eyes closed, and his breathing deepened too. She looked at his muscled body, sprawled out over the bed. And she knew that they weren't actually at peace here. Because he was still angry with her. Of course he was. He was still mad that she had talked to the doctor, and she couldn't really blame him. And they needed to discuss it, eventually. They just would have to. It was nonnegotiable. But right now, everything was paused. Because they'd given in to this desire between them, and that was a good thing. It was. It made her feel rested. At peace. Happy. And in the moment, it was something she could take, even knowing that eventually they were going to have to deal with reality again.

*This is reality*, she told herself. And that realization made her heart lurch in her chest. This was reality. This moment. With him. The intensity with which he wanted her. When it had been a one-night stand, it had been something outside of reality. Something outside of the moment. But now it wasn't. Now she was acknowledging that this was real. That it was not separate from life, but part of it. And that made her feel empowered. It made her feel strong. But it also made her feel afraid. Because it made this feel like something she could have… Maybe something she could have for keeps.

She blinked furiously, trying to banish the tears that were building in her eyes.

There was no point getting attached to the man.

Just like there was no point getting attached to Lily.

*You're attached to yourself. And that's a good thing. That's what matters.*

Yeah. She would tell herself that. Over and over again. And it would have to be enough.

She would have to keep believing she was enough.

## CHAPTER THIRTEEN

WHEN HE WOKE UP, Lily was crying. And he was still wrapped around Mallory.

*Wow.*

He had gone and spectacularly blown up his intentions with her. He hadn't stuck to any kind of plan as far as she was concerned. And he... Wasn't all that regretful about it. He really wasn't. Because that had blown his mind. Because that had made him feel alive. And if he couldn't feel happy about being alive, at least he could feel something other than dead.

He was naked, and he rolled out of bed quickly and found a pair of athletic shorts, pulling them on and walking downstairs where Lily was, still asleep in the cradle. He saw to her diaper and her bottle, but she was still fractious, and he tried rocking her gently, but didn't make any progress. And then his eyes fell to the guitar in the corner of the room.

And something stirred inside him that he hadn't felt... Well, he'd felt it the first time he'd seen Mallory. He recognized it now for what it was.

The beginning of a melody. A vibration that seemed to exist in the deepest parts of himself begging to be let loose. For a melody to be formed, so that a feeling could become something real. Something you could hum and sing.

He hadn't realized it, but it was there. From the moment he'd met her, and growing stronger now, stronger as he looked at Lily.

"Well," he said. "Hasn't done much for me recently, but might as well try."

He crossed the room, and for the first time in months, he picked up the guitar.

MALLORY STRUGGLED TO wake up. She heard Lily crying, but it had felt like half a dream, and when she finally did pull herself fully into wakefulness, Lily wasn't crying. But she could hear music coming through the baby monitor. A pleasant-sounding singing voice and a guitar, familiar in some ways, but also something she hadn't heard before. She wiped her eyes and went downstairs. And she stopped, her foot held on the last step. And everything became clear. It was cold. She looked around the corner, and she saw him, sitting on the edge of the couch, facing the cradle where Lily was. He was quietly strumming the guitar, and he was singing.

And suddenly, she realized she still didn't know this man. This man who was so taciturn, but who played beautiful music. Who carved creatures into wood and didn't think that he was supposed to be alive.

There were so many layers to him, and she had no idea how to dig down and get through them. Maybe there was no way. But there were these moments. Unguarded and beautiful, when she could see bits of the depth of him. And she had a feeling that not even he really wanted to see it. That he was in denial of all the things he was. And she could understand it in a way, because she didn't particularly like to examine pieces of herself either.

It made her feel vulnerable. And she suddenly felt unaccountably sad that people spent so much of their lives running away from the truth of what they were because they were afraid it could hurt. Because they only had the life they got here on this earth, and whatever came after was a mystery. But living for the sole purpose of protecting yourself, of denying everything that you were, your center…

Of only having these few quiet moments in the dark, where you could sing…

Her heart clenched.

And in that moment, she forgot to guard herself. She let herself dream. She let herself imagine.

What a future with Colt might look like. And she didn't care if she was supposed to want it. She didn't care if she was supposed to be waiting for something. To change, to be made new. She wanted to just be here.

*Now.*

Standing there watching this man sing to Lily. And it might not go beyond this moment. There might be nothing after it. Lily's mother could come back at any time, and that was something that Mallory should be rooting for. She and Colt would probably not have futures that intertwined with each other's. But still.

*But still.*

In this moment, she just admired him. And he would make a wonderful father. He truly would. Her womb clenched tight just thinking of it. Oh, she could imagine having a baby with him. She could imagine being with him. Even knowing all that she didn't know, she knew this. She knew that he thought to bring her half-and-half after just one mention of what she wanted in her coffee. She knew that he was a phenomenal lover. She knew that he would put everything on hold to see to his responsibilities. And then there was this… This tender care. It was extra to everything. It wasn't simply about keeping the baby alive, or keeping her safe, or honoring a memory. He had uncovered a piece of himself and used it to bring Lily comfort.

So on some level he must know…

He must know he had something to offer the world. Because here he was. Offering himself.

*And what about you?*

*Are you still waiting to figure it out?*

*Why does she stay with him?*

A tear slipped down her cheek, and she moved away, because she didn't want to interrupt this. She didn't want to intrude.

Her own feelings were building, growing, the memory of that birth echoing in her.

Why does she stay with him?

Mallory had known. She'd always known.

She stayed because he was the father of her child.

Thinking that, really thinking it, took the wind from her lungs.

She had stayed with Jared because he was the father of her child. Because in her heart, Mallory was the mother to a baby she'd never hold in her arms.

She wept silent tears as Colt's voice carried through the hall. She leaned back against the wall, her hands clasped behind her back, pinned there, and she swayed silently to the music. To the grief in her soul. To the joy in her heart that built, impossibly, even through the sadness.

She held her baby girl in her heart. Just on the other side of the wall from the baby she'd spent the past while holding in her arms.

The man she held at night.

The man she…

It was like the past, the present and the future were all too clear just now, and she felt like she couldn't hold it all.

But maybe she could put some of it in its proper place.

Jared was over. She'd finally found the courage to let go. To admit she was holding on out of grief. She'd finally realized she could still be Lucy's mother without being Jared's girlfriend.

The future… She didn't know what would come.

But right now, she had Colt. And Lily.

And if he looked complete with Lily, complete without her, she chose not to focus on that.

And she tried not to let her own words from earlier rebound on her.

That she was sure everything would be okay.

Because she wasn't sure what her life would look like without Lily and Colt in it.

She'd come here for a fresh start. For independence. She'd found something else that she didn't want to put a name to.

And when it ended…

She would have to start all over again.

# CHAPTER FOURTEEN

MALLORY SHOULD BE happy to be invited over to her brother's house for dinner, but she found that she was only resentful. In large part due to the fact that she wanted to see what was going to happen with Colt tonight. They hadn't discussed it. They had slept together all night last night, though he'd slept on top of the covers, she had noticed. But he had come back to bed after putting Lily to sleep, and she hadn't mentioned that she'd seen him singing to her. And then he had taken Lily and gone off to work at the ranch, and she hadn't had the chance to… Kiss him. Rub up against him. Say that she really wanted to keep sleeping with him as long as she was staying at the house, because really, why not?

Yeah. That.

But, Griffin had asked her to dinner, and she did want to go. She cared very deeply about Griffin, after all. And he was the reason she was here.

"*I'm* the reason I'm here," she said out loud as she got into her car and started to drive toward Griffin's cabin.

She was the reason she was here, and that was becoming more and more apparent every day. Her work at the clinic was rewarding. Carving out a place for herself that was hers alone, making a space for herself in the community… It was gratifying. Just for her. And that was the conclusion she was coming to. That ultimately, whatever happened here, this was the right place to be. She was looking for a magic fix.

It was just that slowly, over the course of time, she was becoming more at peace with what was. And that was... Her.

She'd felt isolated by the experience of her pregnancy and the loss of it. By the fear and shame she'd felt, the fear she'd disappoint her family and then the devastation of dealing with Lucy's death alone.

She'd processed a lot of her grief, but there were things that remained.

Being in Gold Valley was for her, and she had to remember that. For her independence and her sense of self. Her acceptance of herself.

She thought a lot about what she'd realized last night. About vulnerability. And she just sort of let it sit there the whole drive through the winding, two-lane road, letting the pine trees blur all together.

She got out of the car and walked up to the front door, knocking, where she was quickly greeted by her sister-in-law and her brother.

"No baby?"

"No," she said. "She's with Colt."

"Okay," Griffin said.

"I'll just be in the kitchen—you guys get caught up," Iris said, fluttering out of the room in a very unsubtle manner. And suddenly, Mallory felt a little bit caught.

"How have you been?"

"Good," she said.

"The clinic is going well?"

"Yes. I have some new equipment coming in next week, and I'm going to focus on getting some new decorations going. The outside needs a face-lift. It's just a little bit run-down. But I have some ideas, and things are going well. I really like all of my new patients."

"Good," Griffin said. "Good."

"What's happening, because I feel like you just sat me down to tell me that I'm in trouble? The way that Iris made herself scarce was just a little bit too neat."

"I just… I'm a little bit worried about you."

"Why?"

"You're off… Playing house with her cousin. And it concerns me, because you just got out of a relationship. And this baby… The baby is going to have to go back to her mother."

"I know that," she said. "I do. And I'm not playing house with him. I… I'm actually very aware that sometimes it feels like that. But that isn't what's happening. And I'm thirty years old, Griffin. I'm not a kid. I get that you feel protective of me because of the whole thing with Jared."

"I don't necessarily trust your decision-making skills."

That stung. And she felt rage turn in her gut. At the beginning of all of this, she might have given him that. She really might have. Because she had felt pretty damn bad about her own decisions. She hadn't felt that awesome about her own stake in the things that she'd done with her life that had made it suck. And she knew… She knew that she had made bad choices. But… How dare he? How dare he, particularly after she had such a great realization last night.

"I'm sorry," she said. "What gives you the right to comment on my decision-making, Griffin? Because it's a lot of commenting. You completely cut yourself out of my life for five years."

"I was going through something," he said, his tone dark.

"I know that. I know, and I'm not angry at you. Except… I don't know how you can possibly tell me that I did something wrong when you haven't been in my life for a…a long time. You don't know what I've been through, or how I've grown. You were dealing with your own pain, and I get that, but I wasn't frozen while you were gone. I was growing and changing and figuring out what I wanted. I'm the one that made the decision to fix things. And I didn't do it because of the snide comments that you made about him. And whatever I do now is not going to be because of the comments you make either."

"Mallory… That's not what I meant. I'm just concerned about you."

"Why? Are you… You have worries about what?"

"I just don't want you getting involved with him…"

"You don't want me to sleep with him."

"I didn't say that."

"I *have* slept with him. Already. So you can just chill out."

He closed his eyes. "Iris told me that you… That you met him a particular way."

"Look at you," she said. "Such a prude. It's not really any of your business. Yes, I met him a certain kind of way. And… Things are continuing in that vein. But I'm not a child. And I'm not stupid. And I deserve… I deserve to be happy. So what—you met Iris and the two of you shook hands?"

"You know that's not true."

"Oh, okay. So, you're allowed to meet somebody and start a physical relationship with them, but I'm in danger of hurting myself. You, who were in a pretty terrible place in life, were totally able to make your own choices."

"No," he said. "And Iris probably should've stayed away from me, frankly."

"But she didn't."

"Yes," he said. "But I'm not… I shouldn't be the poster child for who you think can be redeemed. That's what worries me. You're always trying to save people. You're always trying to rescue them. Me. Jared. Everybody that you work with. That's what you do, Mallory. And you came here to rescue yourself. And I'm just worried that you're caught up in the rescue mission. I'm not saying that I'm better than you. I'm not. What I'm saying is that I see how tender you are. And I see how you can get hurt here. And I don't want that."

She swallowed hard. "I get that. And I get that you're coming from a good place, Griffin. I do. But what is the point of living if all we're doing is protecting ourselves? If that was the point of living, then you should have just stayed at the top of the mountain by yourself, shouldn't you?"

He didn't say anything for a long time. "Yeah, I guess it's easier for me to imagine risking myself than it is to worry about you being hurt."

"I might be," she said. "I know I'm going to be sad when Lily leaves. And it's complicated. Because I'm rooting for her mother. I want for this to be something that's fixable. I want for it to be something that can be redeemed. But I'm also... Desperately attached to that little girl. And I'm going to be really sad when she has to go. But I'm not going to regret loving her. Because it was a choice that I made. And this was something that I actually decided on. That was the thing with Jared. I quit making choices. And I just kind of let myself sit there and forget everything. I just kind of let myself forget that I was in control of my life. I made one choice and I just kind of sat with it. I know what I'm getting into with Colt. I'm not fifteen. The first time I was with Jared I was too young to understand that I didn't have to try to make it forever. And I could never quite... I could never quite come to the conclusion that it was okay if it didn't last. By the time I didn't care anymore, I had quit thinking about it. But everything here I've gone to willingly. And I'm happy with that. Whatever happens. I hope you can understand that. And I hope that you can respect it even if it does concern you."

"I'm sorry, Mallory. When you said all that I realized... You're right. I haven't been as close to you as maybe I like to think. Maybe I don't have as much of a right to intrude in your life as I feel like I do."

"I appreciate your involvement, actually. I moved closer to you so that we could have a closer relationship again. But you don't need to lecture me."

"Sorry," he said. "I know that you were hurt. Really, really hurt by losing Mel. And I think part of me feels responsible for that. Because I loved her, you loved her. And sometimes I feel like I hurt all of you with that loss."

"You know that's not true."

He nodded. "I do. I do know it's not true. And thank God for Iris. Because not only has she shown me the truth of a whole lot of things, she's helped me live. Really live."

"That's what I want."

"You know, I want to tell you that you're too good to be some guy's Band-Aid. But you know... My wife is..."

"The best woman you know? It's okay, you can say it."

He chuckled. "She is. And she's been more than a Band-Aid. She's been a tourniquet. A lifeline. And I'm damn thankful for her. And I'm not really sure if I'm in any position to deny Colt that, if it's what he wants. But the thing is... You do have to want it at some point."

"I don't know if he will, Griffin. I promise you I'm not banking on it. I'm not thinking about it." But that was a little bit of a lie. She could acknowledge her vulnerability, but she didn't need to share it. Vulnerability could be private. She was okay with that.

"Well, if he breaks your heart, I promise I'll be here for you. And I'll spare you the lecture."

"Because you gave me the lecture in advance."

Iris came back in then. "Did I miss it?"

"Were you trying to?" Mallory asked.

"Yes," she said. "I was desperately trying to miss the awkward conversation. Thank you."

"Why exactly? You're the one who ratted me out."

Iris looked genuinely aggrieved. "I had to tell him. He's my husband. I can't keep things from him."

"I feel strongly that he didn't want to know that," Mallory said.

Griffin grunted.

"I'm sorry," Iris said. "But if it's any consolation, I am against the lecture. I think that you have to be able to make your own decisions. And I stand very firmly on that as someone who experienced a lot of familial concern over my connection with Griffin."

"That's different," Griffin muttered.

"Was it?"

"What was their objection?" Mallory asked.

"Something about virgins and big bad wolves," Iris said.

Mallory's head snapped around and she looked at her brother. *"Griffin,"* she said, her tone shocked.

*"What?"*

"You really have no right lecturing me," Mallory said.

"Defender of the innocent," Iris said, rolling her eyes. "Except me."

"What's for dinner?" Mallory asked, desperate for a subject change.

"Meat pie," Iris said. "I have a recipe from New Zealand."

And then thankfully the conversation went away from Mallory's love life and Lily and went to the bakery, and Mallory genuinely enjoyed herself. But she was never fully in the present, and she wasn't actually sad about that. She was glad that she was excited to go home. And glad that she was excited to see Lily and Colt.

Colt.

Her heart fluttered a little bit.

She was having a great dinner with her brother, and soon she would go home to see two more people she cared very deeply about.

And she had to marvel about the fact that her life had shifted so deeply that now she had many wonderful things to care about. And it was different. It was different to care like this than it was to simply be in service of another person. Than it was to simply be in some kind of strange codependent relationship. This was a choice to care. And she could understand that Griffin was worried about her, but he didn't need to be.

Even without any certainty, she was happier than she'd ever been.

COLT WONDERED IF she would come back to his house tonight. He was pacing the halls, wondering if she was going to come back tonight. He had thought about her all day. How much he wanted her. It was impossible not to. Last night had been… An explosion. Of anger. But of need too. He had suppressed everything that he felt for Mallory for so long that he had damn near exploded with it.

And he should regret it. But he didn't.

And then she was back. The front door opened, and before he could even think about what he was going to do next, he grabbed her, pulled her against him. And he consumed her. This woman. This woman who had gotten underneath his skin, who had peeled back layers of his grief, and who made him… Who made him regret some things less. And he kissed her. Kissed her like he might die if he didn't, because he didn't know what else was rooting him to the earth. Maybe it was just her. Maybe she was what he had been waiting for all this time, and until her, everything felt difficult and wrong. And so did he. But in her arms, he felt like something else. And while it might not make any sense, he was more than willing to take that kind of crazy. He carried her right upstairs and took her into the bedroom that she was staying in, because Lily was asleep in the cradle by his bed. He laid her down on the mattress, and he let a tornado of desire consume them both. When it was over, he couldn't breathe, and he didn't want to. Because if he had no breath in his body, it was because she had taken it. And he would gladly surrender that to her. He would gladly surrender to her entirely.

And he never felt like that, not in his entire life.

No, he'd surrendered his entire life to fate. Except, it hadn't been in a glorious or grateful sort of way, no. It had been a middle finger at death. It had been a dare.

Come at me.

Come take me.

And then it had taken the person closest to him instead.

He buried his face in her hair, inhaled her deep. And she wiggled more closely to him, her soft curves molding to his.

"What are you doing tomorrow?" she asked.

"Really? That's what you want to talk about? My to-do list for tomorrow?"

She huffed a laugh. "Actually, I was planning on sitting down with you when I came in the door and having a rational discussion with you about what exactly is happening between us. But then I walked in and you started kissing me. So that kind of answers that question."

His chest went tight. "Does it?"

"Yeah. We're doing this. For now."

And suddenly, all that tightness dissolved, collecting at the base of his sternum, turning into lead. "Yeah. For now."

"So," she said. "What are you doing tomorrow?"

"Nothing that can't be moved? Did you need anything?"

"As a matter of fact, I do. What I was wondering was..." She moved, her chin resting on her hands, which were resting on his chest, as she stared at him intently. "Will you come look at my clinic tomorrow? I have some things that I need to fix. I want to consult with someone who obviously knows a thing or two about wood."

A laugh escaped him, without his permission. "Is that a double entendre?"

"Well, no," she said, moving one hand and sliding it down his body, curving her fingers around his already reinvigorated arousal. "But it could be."

"Mallory," he said, her name strained. "You're killing me."

"Good."

"Yes. I will come down to your clinic."

"Thank you," she said, nuzzling against his neck. "I'm glad that I came here, Colt. I feel like maybe you were fate after all."

"Fate?" That word sat unsteady in his mind, tasted like metal on his tongue.

"That's what I thought. The first time I saw you. But I think it was bigger than I thought. I mean, I was just thinking I was attracted to you. But... Now I can't imagine this without you. Without having met you. Without Lily."

"Mallory," he said. "I can't..."

"Oh," she said, her head popping up slightly. "That's not what I mean. I don't mean like happily-ever-after fate. But we are friends. And I will always be happier because I know you. I'll always be a better person because of this. Because of you."

"That's giving an awful lot of credit to my... Wood."

It was her turn to laugh, and he'd said that to try to make her laugh, but he still felt uneasy with it. Because he'd intentionally worked to lighten a moment that he wasn't sure could be lightened. That he wasn't sure could be anything but the same kind of heavy.

But he was tired of heavy. Right then. He'd taken it as his punishment. As his due. Had worked to get strong enough to hold it, but right then he just didn't want to. Because she was looking at him like he might be something great, and that wasn't something he was supposed to want. Not anymore.

Because the other person who thought he was great was Trent.

His heart squeezed. He thought of Lily, and the way he played her to sleep last night. He hadn't seen the point in music. Not until right in that moment. And he had to admit to himself that he missed it. That it was a part of him that he was ignoring, denying. Another form of punishment, rather than simply a lack of desire.

"It deserves a lot of credit," she said.

"I'm glad you think so."

He tipped her chin up and started to kiss her again. He was ready. Ready to have her again. Under him, over him, in front of him. However.

Just then, a thin cry split the air. He laughed, rolling onto his back. It wasn't a laugh because he thought it was funny. It was mostly just because… He wasn't sure what the hell his life was right then.

But then, he'd been constantly stunned to be alive since the age of fifteen. And right then, with Mallory's naked body on one side, and the sound of a crying baby coming from the next room, he felt outside of his body. Like he was living someone else's fate. Someone else's life.

"I'll get her," he said.

Mallory kissed his lips. "No. I'll get her. You sleep."

She patted his chest, and he was about to say no. About

to say he didn't need sleep. But somehow, right then… He wanted to rest. Because Mallory had said that he could. And there was something about the way she looked at him, like he deserved to rest and so, Colt rested. And when he closed his eyes, it was her face that he saw.

# CHAPTER FIFTEEN

COLT STOOD OUTSIDE the clinic, a little arts and crafts–style house that was the worse for wear on the outside. It was neat, but it definitely needed a bit of a tune-up.

There was a broad, sweeping tree out front that offered shade in the little yard. And it was definitely... Tranquil.

"This is it," Mallory said, turning around and spreading her arms. She had Lily in the front pack, at her insistence—since he was going to be put to work she'd said—and she looked... Damn, she was beautiful. Her curly hair was especially buoyant today, and she complained about it whenever it was like that, but he really liked it. He more than liked it. He didn't really think there was a word for what he felt about it. The way that it moved with her. The way that it was wild and refused to be tamed. She was wearing another of her simple little dresses. This one a ribbed fabric in a mustard yellow that clung to her curves. And she would probably be horrified to know this, but when she walked, sometimes the fabric clung to her ass in such a way that he could see the whole shape of it, and he considered it a true gift.

"It's great," he said.

"But?"

"I didn't say *but*."

"It was implied. But..."

"You're right. It needs a little TLC."

"Come inside," she said.

"All right." He followed her into the building. The waiting room was open and nice. He didn't really have any opinion on decor.

"I was thinking," she said, "that it might be nice to have some kind of a big carving. Like a tree of life. And I could put it in here. And maybe something like that echoed on the front. Nature and animals. Women and children. Something that shows the connectedness of birth to all of nature."

"Mallory Chance," he said. "You're a hippie."

"I'm not." She mused for a second. "Okay, I guess I'm a little bit of a hippie."

"I don't know—that might be a deal breaker."

"I'm a little bit of a tree hugger too. But just a little."

"How much of one?"

"The bark chafes, so I try to save it for weekends only."

He chuckled. "So basically you want to commission me to do a bunch of... Art?"

"That's exactly what I want to do. A bunch of big, granola crunchy artwork."

"That's not really what I thought you wanted."

"Colt," she said, "I can hire anyone to do carpentry work. But what you do... What you did in the little cabin... It's really extraordinary. I feel something every time I look at it." The way she was looking at him... "Maybe it's because you made it. But either way, I would love to have something that you made in here. Actually, I would love to have several things you made."

"Sure. I can do it."

And that was how he found himself deep in a bigger wood carving project than he'd ever been involved in before. He already knew that he wanted to take Lily's little fox and hide it somewhere within the larger piece. Make it a removable component at the bottom of the tree. And after he thought of that, he decided to do it with a lot of the woodland animals.

Make them light enough that they wouldn't fall and hurt anyone, and big enough that they wouldn't be a choking hazard. But something that children who were waiting for their mothers could play with. And there was something he enjoyed about carving something like this.

Something that used natural material, that was beautiful and functional. Before long, he had a big piece of wood carved into the shape of a tree with branches that arced upward. And in the base were all the little animals.

When he got it hauled down to the clinic, Mallory nearly erupted.

"This is amazing," she said. She knelt down on her hands and knees. "The little animals," she said.

"I made one for Lily a couple weeks ago. It just… Seemed like something that might work here."

"It works amazing."

Lily was strapped to his chest, and he put his hand on her back. It was amazing how much she'd changed in the last month. She'd grown so much, and she was working on holding her little head up. She made more noises. Looked around and turned her head to the sound of their voices. She heard Mallory exclaiming over the tree and was craning as much as she could in the carrier, but it didn't take long for her to tire and let her head relax again.

"She's excited that you're excited," he said.

Mallory moved over to him and dropped a kiss on Lily's head. When she looked up at him, their eyes met.

"I'd kiss you," he said. "But we are in a semipublic space. And there is a baby present."

"And?"

"I can't keep it PG."

"I don't really mind…"

"Sure. But… Don't you have patients today?"

"Yes," she said.

The door opened, as if on cue, and a young woman came in that he vaguely recognized, followed by a man he definitely recognized.

"Hey, Grant," Colt said. "Good to see you."

Grant had been a lot older than him, but everybody knew the Dodge family. They were somewhat infamous, like his family, though for different reasons. And he clicked that his wife would be one of the Daltons. One of the secret Daltons. They were a more infamous family than either the Daniels or the Dodges.

"Colt," Grant said.

But clearly, Grant was more focused on the discomfort of dealing with his pregnant wife and being in this situation at all.

"Wow," McKenna said, looking at the tree. "Is this new?"

"Yes," Mallory said, touching him on the arm as she spoke, as if it were the most natural thing. And with that touch, she linked them together, whether she knew it or not. He could see it in the way the woman's eyes followed that touch. In the way Grant regarded them.

"Well it's amazing," McKenna said. "Do you do… I need something for the nursery. We need something for the nursery," she said to Grant.

"Well I…"

"He can pay for it," she said.

"Thanks," Grant said.

"What? I want a tree like this in the nursery."

"Give me your information," Colt said. "I can get in touch with you. I'll need measurements and things like that."

"Yes. Thank you. This is amazing."

Surprisingly, that happened to them a couple more times, and by the time he moved to the pillars on the outside, he had other business owners stopping to ask about his work. He had made a large Mother Earth sort of figure in one of the posts, a tree on the other, with animals twined around both. He kept to a similar look and shape of a craftsman pillar, while bringing art into it. And it was something that apparently resonated with the local community.

"I have about six commissions just from working in the front of your clinic," he said to Mallory that night at home.

"Well, everything looks amazing."

"Yeah."

"Have you thought about making this your business?"

"No it's…art, I guess. I never thought about doing that for money. I mean I love it…"

"Then shouldn't you do it? I think you could charge whatever you wanted. And please, charge me," she said.

"No," he said. "You're helping me with Lily."

"And you're not charging me rent while I help with Lily. You can't do all this work for me for free too."

"I can do whatever I want." He set her down on his lap and dug his hands into her hair. He'd been waiting to do that all day. Then he kissed her.

They spent most of Sunday lying low. Doing tummy time with Lily, which he learned was something important to her development. They had gone to the pediatrician that week. And everything had been fine.

And he knew that he was intentionally ignoring reality, but he didn't care.

"The flowers on those headbands are getting bigger," he said, looking at Lily as they prepared to walk into the ranch house at Hope Springs.

"Impossible," she said. "Because Lily is getting bigger."

"I think you have a stash of ever-expanding flowers."

The door opened, and they were greeted by everyone. And Lily was immediately taken out of his arms. She was a favorite. At this point, Iris's pregnancy was public knowledge, Rose was nearly due, and Sammy was beginning to show.

It was a baby parade.

Little Astrid was particularly fond of Lily, and watching her try to be a little mother to the baby was pretty damn adorable, even he had to admit it.

"I think you're getting soft," Jake said, nudging his knee when they sat outside later that night with beers. Ryder was leaned back against the side of the house, his feet kicked out in front of him, the porch light shining down over his cowboy hat. Logan was seated on the railing, West, Pansy's husband, propped up against one of the pillars. Griffin was sitting in a rocking chair nearby. Emmett, West's half brother, was standing in front of the porch, throwing rocks in the general direction of the digger squirrels that were darting around. He wasn't going to hit one.

"What the hell is that supposed to mean?"

"I saw you making faces at the baby earlier."

"Babies like it when you make faces. I'm not an animal."

"I don't know. I've heard some rumors," West said.

"All greatly exaggerated. At least these days."

"Soft," Jake said.

"If I'm soft, big brother, you're marshmallow."

"Admittedly," Jake said.

"So, what exactly is the plan, Colt," Ryder said, lifting up his beer bottle and using the lip of it to push his cowboy hat up. "You been back for going on six months now. You haven't committed to any kind of work. And you've got this baby for... An open amount of time."

"As a matter of fact," Colt said. "I'm thinking of starting a custom woodworking business."

"Really?"

"Yeah," he said.

"News to me," Jake said.

"Sorry," Colt said. "I was planning on talking to you about it. But he asked what was going on in my life instead of just making fun of me."

"Well, I'm your brother. I'm supposed to make fun of you."

"I can work on your ranch still," Colt said. "It's gonna take some time to get it up and running. And I need to buy some equipment. I got cash to spare, but I need to be... You know, smart about all that. It's not like I have the kind of money coming in that I did when I was winning pots in the rodeo and getting endorsement deals and things."

"Sure," Jake said.

"So you know, I'll be... Careful. But I've been doing some things down at Mallory's clinic."

That earned him a grunt from Griffin. Everybody looked at him. Griffin shrugged. "What? It looks nice."

Griffin's discomfort with him was still pretty apparent. While Iris was completely okay with it, her husband was definitely a little bit skeptical.

"So you're going to stay," West said, looking at him directly.

"Yeah, I figure I'll stay."

The door opened, and light spilled out onto the porch. Sammy came out holding a wiggly, fussy Lily, and Rose was behind them, holding a guitar. "She's grumpy," Rose said.

"Mallory said that she likes music."

And that was how he found the guitar thrust into his arms. "Play a song."

He hadn't played at a family thing since Trent had died.

He had played just a little bit at home, mostly at night when Mallory wasn't around. But last time Lily had been overly fussy, he done it.

And he didn't feel like he could very well say he wouldn't do it now.

He took the guitar, and Sammy held Lily so that she was facing him. Everybody was looking at him. Then he smiled. Then he started to play something upbeat. Something his father would've played. Old John Denver that always made his heart lift, even though he couldn't ignore the unfortunate similarities between his father and John Denver. Not the gift for country music. Their tragic end. But even as that settled on him, he kept on singing. About country roads, because he hoped that eventually something might lead him home.

But for a moment there wasn't anything but the music. But the people dancing around him. His family. And for a minute, he could pretend that he was in a different time. A different time that still somehow had Mallory and Lily.

Lily laughed, and Iris grabbed her arm, and the two of them twirled on the porch as he played.

And it wasn't until the song was over that everything real crept back in.

"It's been too long since we've heard you play," Ryder said, nudging his elbow.

But Lily had stopped crying, so he supposed that was a good thing.

He cleared his throat and stood up. He put the guitar away, and they stayed for just a little bit longer.

And for some reason, after that clean, clear moment when everything had seemed fine, the past felt more present than ever. And when they got into the car and started driving back toward the house, he turned to Mallory, and he didn't know why he said it, but he couldn't hold it anymore.

"Lilies were my mother's favorite flower. That's why I called her Lily." He swallowed hard. "My mother is dead because of me."

MALLORY HAD SENSED the heaviness that had settled over Colt when he had finished playing. It had been like he'd been infused with light when he'd been singing the song. His voice was beautiful in her opinion. Made goose bumps stand up on her arms. Made her want to jump right into his lap and do unspeakable things to him, even with his family standing right there. But she had refrained.

In that moment, he'd seemed light. It was the same when he carved those pillars for her. When he was creating, when he was making something beautiful for the world, he seemed… More at peace. And otherwise, there was this. And she was so very aware of it now. But she hadn't expected him to say that. Who could have?

And she didn't say anything. Because she sensed that he didn't want her to. That this was a story he was going to have to tell at his own pace. But this was something he was going to have to sort out on his own. There were so many moments where Colt talked about his own fault in things that she knew were impossible. But it didn't matter if they were possible or not. He felt it. In his soul, and that much was clear.

"My parents' marriage was falling apart. They were unhappy. And it was… It was hell. We lived in a house, the ranch house, on the same property as the cousins. And every time they came over, my parents would smile so wide it was like their faces were going to break. Every single time. And then when they were gone, it was like it was worse. We felt like we were holding on to this terrible secret. That the Daniels family wasn't perfect. That we weren't one big happy clan.

"Well, my parents wanted to go on this trip to Alaska. A couple's trip. And it was getting… It was getting tense as hell. My mom didn't want to go. She didn't want to go fishing in a frozen tundra. And she was mad at my dad because she felt like he knew that, full well. That she would rather go somewhere warm. That she would rather go to the beach. But he always had to do what his brother wanted. And finally, my dad just said he talked to his brother. And he did admit what was going on.

"I guess he did, but they clearly didn't tell Ryder and the others. Doesn't matter. Jake and I knew. Well, I loved fishing. I loved Alaska. I'd been kind of obsessed with it since I was a kid. Because I just… I wanted to see what was out there. I wanted… To test myself against something wild, and Alaska seemed like the place to do it. And I was fifteen, and…"

"Why you? Why not Jake?"

"Jake was seventeen. And I think he was getting laid." He laughed, but it sounded hard. "Yeah. I think it was something like that. I hadn't discovered that mystery yet, so the tundra seemed like a pretty good prospect. But it could've been Jake. Except it was me. I was the one that was supposed to go. Something happened, I don't know. There was a big fight. And then… And then it was like things had changed between them again. Like they'd made up.

"You know, now that I'm older, I can fill in some of the blanks. Because they disappeared to their room for a long time, and I have a feeling I know how they were working things out. Either way. It changed. Still, my mom didn't want to take my spot on the trip. But I felt… Well, I felt like it was something I could do. Something I could give to them.

"I waited, until the last minute, because I was struggling with being selfish about what I wanted. But finally I called my mom, while I was still sitting on the plane, and I told her to come back. She was seeing us off. And I said… I said she should get on the plane instead. She did."

He was silent for a long moment. The road noise, the tires on the gravel, the wind whipping by the windows—it all became deafening. "I remember it. Clearly. Hugging her, standing there on the plane, then brushing past her and walking out the door. I watched the door close, and I waved at them. Watched it take off. Watched until I couldn't see it anymore.

"I only had my learner's permit then, but I knew how to drive. We drove all over the ranch. It was a long drive from the takeoff point to home. So I went home. And by that night… Everything had changed. It would've been me, Mallory. It's not a could have been, might've been. It would have been. If not for that last-minute exchange… I'd be dead."

"Colt, I don't know what to say. I don't know what to say except that's just one of those things. One of those things that most of us never get a chance to know about. I'm sure we've all had near misses and never had to confront them. I… I assist with birth. I see the thin line between life and death so often in those moments. The baby's cord can be in the wrong place. Something can take too long. Distress can occur. A moment that seems normal can turn into something altering in a terrible way. It's just that line… It's so thin."

She knew it deep. Far too well. She lived, Lucy didn't. The world still turned.

"How are you supposed to live knowing that?"

She didn't speak for a long time, because there was no pat answer for it. They were clearly both living. But he wasn't living whole, and that was clear enough. She could see it. She knew it. And she didn't know how to fix it. Didn't know how to fix him. Obviously, if it were that simple it would be done. He would've fixed himself.

"The way we've been doing it, I guess," she said. "One breath at a time. A moment at a time."

"I'm tired," he said.

And her heart broke into a thousand pieces. "I know. I can feel it." She reached across the space in the car and put her hand on his. "Maybe you don't need to have all the answers."

"I've never had them. And I kept thinking that someday I would. Someday I would see it. A purpose, a point, to all of this. But all I have is more unanswered questions. All I got was another loss that I can't explain."

"You're not at fault for what happened. Not to either of them. You aren't responsible for bad weather that takes down a plane. Or for the decisions the pilot made. Or just... Mechanical errors. You're not responsible for the drinking that a young man did. You're not responsible for the fact that he chose to ride. And you know... You did enough stupid things to know that sometimes you walk away from those things."

"Yeah," he said. "But he didn't. And that's hard for me to accept. I've had infinite chances to be a dumbass. To pretend like I didn't give a shit about my own mortality because if it came for me, it came. Do you know what that's like? To feel like fate must've spared you. It doesn't feel like glory. I think some people might take it that way. But I never did. I just thought... What a terrible weight. What a horrendous burden. Because I never felt like I was very special. And I couldn't help my family any. It would've been better if they'd been left with my mother. Not with me. What was I going to do to help anyone? Ryder had to take it all on his shoulders because there were no adults left. One fifteen-year-old kid that couldn't help anybody..."

"Maybe you don't need to fix anything."

He didn't say anything to that. And she just wished that she could... She wished that she had the right words. But if the right, easy words existed… That all of this would be simple. And she knew that it wasn't. She carried around a whole host of blame for a relationship that she'd been in with a crappy guy. And yeah, a lot of it was down to her decisions. But it was taking time to sort through that, and it wasn't anywhere near the kind of trauma that he'd experienced in his life. It wasn't even comparable.

"I feel like I should. My mom was a good woman, Mallory. Maybe the best. She… She used to call me brave when I would sing my songs."

Those words were like a knife twisted directly in her sternum. She could feel his pain, and also his reluctance to continue. No, not reluctance, his inability to continue. Because it was too much, this. Too painful. She could feel it in the weight of every word, in the raw scrape of them against his throat. It was clear. Abundantly, painfully clear.

"I love your songs," she said.

"You've never heard my songs."

Her eyes stung with unshed tears, and they didn't speak again as they drove up the driveway to the house.

And when they got there, there was a car parked in front.

# CHAPTER SIXTEEN

COLT WAS STILL feeling raw from the conversation in the car, and it was one he had never intended to have. Not at all. Not even a little bit. He had never spoken those words out loud to anyone. He never had to. Because Jake knew, and nobody else ever needed to know. But he'd told her. And it had come from somewhere deep inside of him that he preferred never to acknowledge or think about. That he preferred never to access. And he'd given her the keys to it.

What the hell?

But then they pulled into the driveway, and the car was there.

And he knew exactly whose car was.

"Colt…"

"It's okay," he said.

But he didn't know it was okay. He didn't know what to think or what to feel, and fundamentally, he could see right now, looking at Cheyenne's car in that driveway, that he had been heavily in denial this whole time. That he hadn't really known what he was hoping for.

And it wasn't right or fair. Because Cheyenne was Lily's mother. And Lily wasn't even Lily.

She was whatever Cheyenne called her. A name that Colt didn't even know.

But he had poured more of his heart and soul into that little life than he had given to anything in a long time. Had found pieces of healing with her that he hadn't known were possible.

"It's good," he said. "It's the right thing."

"It doesn't feel right," Mallory said, her voice a broken whisper, and it made him angry. Because he didn't have any damn control over it. And there was something about her being sad that made it even worse. Because he hadn't chosen this.

But he didn't say that. Instead, he put the car in Park, went to the back and got Lily out of her car seat. Cheyenne saw them and opened up the driver's side door, getting out. She looked across the expanse of gravel at them, leaning against the car, picking at her nails. She looked better than when they'd seen her six weeks ago. Her hair was freshly colored, and it looked like she'd been sleeping more. She didn't have the same agitated look to her demeanor, but she didn't look happy either.

"She looks good," Cheyenne said. "She's big."

Colt clenched his jaw together and held Lily even closer. "She is," he said. "Cheyenne, I'm glad you're back, but I can't send you home with her tonight. Because we're going to have to go talk to somebody." And he was resolved in that. Because he would need to be absolutely certain that Lily was going to be taken care of before he sent her anywhere.

"No," she said. "That's actually not why I'm here. I can't take her back."

He was shell-shocked by that, his stomach hollowed out.

"I've been thinking a lot. And I feel bad, but I don't know how to take care of her. And when I left her here... I was devastated for a while. But then, it felt like everything was okay again. Like I could figure my life out. I haven't been able to breathe since Trent died. And then I had a baby, and I had to take care of her, and I did a terrible job. I didn't want to do it, and I was angry at her. And every time she cried I was furious. Every time she cried I... I resented her for it and she's the baby. It's not fair. I know what it's like to have family who doesn't want you around. I don't ever want that for her. I never wanted to be that mother. But I should never have been a mother this early, and I can't do it by myself. I could've maybe done it if he was still here. But I don't know how to be without him and be a mother. I just don't know how to do it. And... I don't have anyone to go to. I didn't want to just abandon her, and I know that Trent would..." She laughed, a small, bitter sound. "Well, he would've died before he saw his child in foster care. That's what's going to happen, isn't it? If I give her up, she's going to end up in foster care."

"No," Colt said. "She won't. She won't end up in foster care because I'll adopt her."

He hadn't known that he was going to make that decision until the words came out of his mouth, but once they did, it seemed so obvious. Once they did, it was so certain to him. It seemed... Obvious. That it was going to end up here. It was always going to end up here. Because she wasn't just a responsibility, she was something else altogether. She was the kind of salvation that he had known he'd been looking for.

A kind of purpose.

And he felt broken open by it.

There were so many things... That conversation that he had in the car with Mallory swirling around inside of him... So many things that he was trying to make sense of. That he was trying to find. Truth about his life and about why he lived the way that he did.

But the fact was he had been looking for his purpose ever since he found out that he was still here while his mother had died. Because she'd known her purpose. It was taking care of them. Being his mother. Encouraging him. He lost his way somewhere. Been unable to get back to what he might've been if she'd still been around. Because he'd been brave.

He'd been brave to her when he'd written songs and played music, and he'd decided that he didn't want to be that kind of brave, because it hurt too much.

So he'd been the kind of brave that didn't make you feel or make you think.

He'd flung himself around the back of angry, snorting animals, and he'd put his life at risk, because he'd decided that that was the sort of brave he should be.

When in reality that sort of brave was easy. Because he'd been angry. Because he had been certain that he shouldn't even still be here. Because he'd found it a whole hell of a lot simpler than having to feel. And then he met Trent and he thought maybe that was his purpose, to mentor this kid, but he'd lost that too. And then he'd just felt… Like he didn't have a purpose at all. But here was a chance. Here was something.

Here was the gateway back to that other kind of brave. That required softness and a different sort of strength than he had touched in far too long. But he tested out that other brave, and it was destructive. It didn't help anyone.

It wouldn't have made her proud.

He felt that ache in the back of his teeth.

"You will?"

Mallory was standing beside him, completely quiet. And it was Mallory, her presence, her words from before, just her, that made him resolute.

Mallory and the melody she'd brought back to his soul.

"Yes," he said. "I'll adopt her."

Cheyenne's face crumpled, for just a moment. Then she took a breath. "That would've made him really happy." She nodded. "He would have trusted you. To take care of her."

"Sure. Glad I can help in some way."

"That's more than just… Helping," she said.

"It's helping me too," he said.

"There's like… Legal stuff we'll have to do, right? I have to… Sign things."

"I'll contact a lawyer," Colt said. "I think that's the way to go. Can you make sure that I have all your contact information?"

She pulled a scrap piece of paper out of the car and started to write on it. Then she shoved it into his hand, careful not to make any physical contact with Lily.

"I don't know what else to do," Cheyenne said, looking lost for a moment.

"Cheyenne," he said. "You're sure this is what you want?"

"I don't want any of this. I didn't ask for it. I didn't ask for him to die. I didn't ask to be left by myself. I didn't ask my brain to get so messed up. None of it is what I want. If I had what I wanted then I would have the family that I dreamed of. But I can't ever get there… I can never get there if I can't get out of this. I'm just going to end up being a bitter, angry person the same way that my mother was, and I don't want to do that. I can't do it. I don't ever want her to grow up feeling like she's responsible for the bad things I feel. And I just wish that my mom had been brave enough to let someone else take care of me if she didn't want to do it. I wish my dad had been brave enough to make the decision, instead of coming in and out all the time. Trent doesn't get to make a choice—nobody asked him. He's just dead. But I can. If you'll love her…"

"I already do," he said, the words scraping his throat raw.

And Cheyenne burst into tears. He didn't know what the hell to do. But fortunately, Mallory moved. She wrapped her arms around the woman's fragile frame, and she held her while she cried. They both leaned against the car, and Mallory stroked her hair.

And he was undone by it. Witnessing this. This broken, battered love that came from a place of just doing its best.

And it made him feel like an ass. For spending all these years not doing it. Not connecting with the people around him because why? Because he didn't feel worthy? What Cheyenne was doing was hard. Giving up this baby, taking on all the guilt that came with that, all the judgment that would result. Going through the work to make that choice. Love didn't look one way. And love didn't need to be worthy, really. And this unworthy love was something that cut deep. And that mattered.

It mattered a hell of a lot.

So he was going to take all the imperfect love inside of him and give it to Lily. He was going to honor this. Even if it was hard. Even if he didn't feel up to it in some ways. He could take care of her. He wouldn't resent her.

She was giving him something that he needed.

Something he hadn't even known he'd been desperate for. And it was the damnedest thing. Because all of this— from meeting Mallory for the first time—to this moment, felt like something that was written in the stars. Stars that he'd never been able to see. Inscribed on pieces of himself he didn't know how to reach. But he wanted to.

He wanted to.

"Are you going to be okay?" Mallory asked. "Do you want to… Do you need a place to stay?"

She shook her head. "No. I've got a place. And I can make it back before too long. I'll just get a coffee."

"We want you to be safe," Colt said.

"I promise I will be. I mean… I feel better. It hurts. But I know this is the right thing to do. I've had all this time to think about it. And I can finally... See the way forward. And I just don't think that either of us would make it if it wasn't like this. And that's what I want. More than anything. I just want us both to make it."

"You'll do more than make it," Mallory said. "Someday. Someday you'll realize that. That you're going to do more than just survive this. You're going to live."

After that, Cheyenne got in her car, and she drove away. And he was left standing there with... His daughter. Because he was going to be a father. He was going to be her father. He already was. That was the crazy thing.

He knew it.

Deep in his bones.

That this was something meant to be. That this was fate on some level. Even though there had been a whole lot of terrible to get here. He was certain in this moment. In this one thing and it had been over eighteen years since he'd been certain about a damn thing, and it was like... It was like a revelation. Like the sky had opened up and poured stars down on him. And he didn't have another way to explain it.

"Colt..."

"I need a minute," he said.

He swallowed hard and carried Lily back inside. Walked upstairs and went into his room. He closed the door behind him and settled in the rocking chair that he'd moved into the place. And he sat there, and he looked down at this child. This child that he was going to raise.

This child he was going to call his own.

That was all he could do. Just stare at her. And from the depths of his soul came the most profound pain that he'd ever known. There was a fear biting at the back of it, one that he could scarcely quantify.

He had never felt anything like this. Like the ceiling was

pressing down on top of them, like the floor was rising up to greet him, like the whole universe was going to swallow him whole.

And there he was, made of stardust and impending doom and responsible.

Responsible.

For this life. Because this moment had come toward him and he'd had to meet it. He had no choice. He wouldn't have made a different choice even if he could have.

He looked down at her, and her wiggling there, all helpless and tiny and small. And she wasn't part of making any of these decisions—people were just making them for her. "I know how you feel."

That's how he felt… For most of his life. Ever since that moment he lost his parents. Like that great big cosmic hand was just doing things, and he hadn't been consulted.

And he looked down at Lily. And no, she didn't have any control, but he had her. He had her. His chest seized up, because right then he wondered.

If someone had him too.

If he'd been held this whole time and he didn't even know it.

He swallowed hard, and he felt it then. This sense of being safe. Of being held. Of being right.

This moment. This was the moment he'd been running from for eighteen years. Because here he sat, in a house he bought, holding his child.

His mother's grandchild. Her first grandchild.

"You would be proud, Mom. You would be proud."

Because this was brave. The kind of brave she'd always believed in, not the kind of brave that threw himself on the back of a bull and chased glory in the rodeo. This kind of love, and the softness it took to hold the baby, the strength it took to decide to step up.

That was the kind of brave that she'd seen in him, and it was the kind of brave he'd been running from.

Because this kind of brave took his whole heart. This kind of brave took your soul. And it had been devastated the day that she died. And he told himself all kinds of stories about it. But this was what remained, and it didn't matter what he thought was right. It didn't matter what he thought was wrong. It simply was. So it was what was supposed to be, because there was no other choice.

There was no other reality.

And if he believed in fate, then he had to believe that he belonged here. If he believed in faith, then he had to believe that this moment was made for him. And he was made for it. And he was strong enough for it. He was brave enough for it. And it was just love. That was all it came down to. And it was the most singular, most terrifying thing that he had ever known.

Because he was made to be her father. Because all the steps had been leading here. Because it mattered. Because he mattered.

And it was the hardest thing. The hardest thing. To believe in that. Because it made him want. It made him feel. He didn't want to feel.

He'd spent all these years trying not to feel. But Trent had gotten under his defenses and made him want to be a better man. Made him want to be someone a person could look up to. He'd taken blame on himself because it was easier. Because it made grief feel just a little bit softer. Because guilt was easier than just trying to live.

That was the truth.

With guilt you could be stuck in bargaining forever. But once you let it go, you just had to move on. And then what? You had to be brave.

He hadn't wanted to be brave.

Oh, he told himself he was brave.

He was masculine; he was reckless. Fearless. But not brave.

True bravery was harnessing all your strength and making it tender so that you could care for the vulnerable.

It was looking inside of himself and asking if he could find a way to remember his parents. So that he could be a good father. So that he could give to this child the things that they'd given to him. It was asking himself to be that boy he had been. Sensitive and raw. That boy who'd lain down and wept the night his mother had died. The night he lost his father. Who wanted to do good, before he told himself that when he tried to help he only broke things.

Because that was an easy thing to tell yourself. It was damned easy. If you could convince yourself that you only broke things, that you never tried to hold the beautiful or the delicate, and you never tried to care. And damn, he'd spent a long time doing that.

But now there was Lily.

And downstairs there was Mallory.

And all of these things were bigger than him. Bigger than this one moment. They were the culmination of things. And it made him feel...

"I'll protect you, forever," he said. He wanted to speak vows to this child. So that she would know. "And if it was all for this. If it was all for you... It's enough. And I'll be the best I can be. Because that's what you deserve. You don't deserve any less. There's a lot of imperfect love inside me."

But he was beginning to realize that perfect or not, love was what mattered. Perfect or not, it was what carried you through.

And he told himself a lot of tall tales because it meant he didn't have to care.

And caring like this broke you open.

He was broken open.

A flood of grief, a river of pain. But within that there was beauty.

Within that, there was joy.

Because for the first time he felt... For the first time he felt right. And like he was exactly where he needed to be.

## CHAPTER SEVENTEEN

COLT DIDN'T NEED HER.

As Mallory sat down on the bottom step, that thought thundered through her like a herd of wild horses. He didn't need her anymore. Not at all. He had in the beginning. Because he hadn't known what he was doing. But he did now. Full well. And he'd stepped up, he said that he was going to adopt Lily. Adopt her. And she was... She was overjoyed.

Sad, too, because poor Cheyenne.

That entire moment had been fraught. But she'd been able to help. She stood there and she'd comforted the mother of the child, which was something that mattered to her. It was a calling in life. One that meant the world to her. But it made her feel displaced. Because Cheyenne was gone, and Lily was taken care of, and she... Had to go back to being her.

*You were okay with that, remember? You knew you had to do this.*

She was. She was, of course. And she wasn't going away. It was just that... The situation with Colt was intense anyway, and it was one that she probably shouldn't encourage. Things had reached a head tonight, and they'd broken down, and it was... It was a lot.

She took a breath and stood up, feeling the dull thud of her heartbeat echoing in her head. Because this felt like breaking, but it shouldn't. Because actually everything was fitting together exactly like it needed to, so it was a good thing.

She slipped out quietly, taking Lily's seat out of her car and making sure to set it in the house. He was going to need to get a family vehicle. But that was a conclusion he could come to on his own.

Because Colt Daniels wasn't a manbaby.

He didn't need a mother.

He was a father.

That made her heart clench. She had helped. She had done exactly what she'd set out to do. Lily was safe. Cheyenne was hurting, but she would be okay. She had to believe that.

And now it was time for her to get back to her life. Because that's what she was doing. She was building a new life for herself here, and she needed to go ahead and get back to that. She'd sought shelter with Colt and Lily. And there had been something singular and wonderful about it, but it was time for it to end.

He didn't need her anymore. And if he didn't need her anymore then… That was that.

It meant she needed to get back to the business of the life she was building here, or the rug really would get pulled out from under her. She really would end up rebuilding all over again. And she just… Couldn't.

She sighed heavily, her chest feeling like there were fragments of glass resting inside of it. It was silly that she was feeling like this. But normal. She was attached to them both. She cared for them both. She blinked, her eyes feeling like there had been sand scrubbed into them, and got into the car, taking the drive up to the cabin. And once she was inside, she shot Colt a text letting him know that she'd gone home. Giving him and Lily this time. She opened the door to the cabin, and it was strange. She meant to make a home here, but she hadn't done that. She'd gone and set about making a home inside Colt's, and that was the wrong thing to do. It had been silly.

If she was hurt, it was her own fault. She should know better than that.

She wasn't supposed to build her healing around someone else. That just caused pain, and she knew it, because she'd done it already.

She pushed that to the side. She wasn't dwelling on that. Not on any of that.

She wasn't dwelling at all.

She realized that she'd left all the appliances down at Colt's house. Because she fished them out of the barn six weeks ago, and had never meaningfully stayed here since. She puttered around up here once, but that was it.

"You're a fool, Mallory Chance," she said.

So she crawled underneath the blanket and lay on the couch and watched a streamed movie on her computer, and then she took herself off to bed. But she felt restless, because she missed his arms.

And that was as good a reason as any to put things on pause. It didn't mean that they would never…

It didn't mean that.

She had spent her life so married to the intensity of being in a relationship. But she and Colt weren't that, and they'd never been. They helped each other. They were friends. And sometimes they had sex.

All right, pretty much every night they had sex multiple times, but that was how it was when they were living together because it was convenient. It wouldn't be like that now. But it would be better. They would have some kind of reasonable separation. She would be… Important to Lily, she hoped.

*Until Colt gets married, because now he's taking on this kind of traditional life…*

She shoved that to the side. And she decided she was going to sleep instead of think. Because right now thinking hurt too bad.

She woke up to the sound of thundering footsteps in her house, and she startled, windmilling her arms.

Wrapping her blanket around her, she scampered to the door, conscious of the fact that the early morning light was filtering underneath her bedroom window curtains. She hadn't realized she'd actually fallen asleep. Apparently she had. She cracked open the bedroom door, the blanket over her head like a hood, held tight right under her chin by her fisted fingers. And she heard... The sound of sizzling bacon. And smelled that not long after.

"Colt?"

"The one and only. Were you expecting another man to be in your house cooking breakfast?"

"I wasn't expecting... You in my house cooking breakfast."

"We always eat breakfast together. And I had a feeling you didn't actually have any breakfast supplies up here. I brought your coffee maker."

"Oh... Thank you."

"The house was awfully quiet."

"Even with a screaming baby?"

"She doesn't scream," he said.

Lily was strapped into her car seat, happily grabbing at her feet.

"But she could," Mallory said. "At any moment, really."

"A risk I'm willing to take."

Still sort of shell-shocked by his appearance, all she could do was stare.

"You know, if you're not going to fill the silence, you leave me no choice but to ask why the hell you took off last night without saying anything?"

"You didn't need me. I mean… I don't mean to say it like that. It's just… I didn't want to intrude. This is… It's a big thing that's happening. And I didn't feel like I wanted to go and make it about me."

"Since when have you ever second-guessed making it about you?"

She frowned. "Ouch."

He shrugged a shoulder. "I didn't mean it in a bad way. You've thrown yourself in the middle of my business since you first came into town."

She cleared her throat and sat down at the small bistro table in the corner of the room. "I fail to see how you picking me up in a bar was me flinging myself into your business."

"I'm going to ignore the obvious pun available here. All right, maybe we kind of crashed into each other. And ever since then we kept on crashing. So why the hell stop now?"

"Things are changing," she said. "And when it was all sort of uncertain and… You needed my help. But now you… You don't. It's okay, Colt, because I have this whole new life thing that I'm trying to do. And you know, I should probably focus on that instead of just being involved in yours."

"Okay, there's a few things wrong with that. The biggest one being that you're acting like you being involved with Lily and I wasn't somehow just part of your life. Because I think it was. Not mine alone, is it?"

She took a deep breath, and suddenly a mug of coffee appeared in front of her, and her heart contracted. "Colt," she said. "I just… I feel a lot like I replaced one crutch with another, you know? I'm supposed to be independent."

"Okay."

"And you needed me. Because you didn't know what to do with her, and I was really happy to help."

"Okay," he said, sounding maddeningly placating.

"And," she said, "now that you don't need me…"

"You keep saying that. You keep saying that, and I don't know what the hell it means. Maybe I want you. Is that something? Does it not matter?"

"You… You want me?"

"Yes, Mallory. I want you. I enjoy having you around, Lily enjoys having you around. I don't know why that seems impossible to take on board."

"I just don't know what it has to do with anything."

"Why were you with him?"

She blinked, feeling a little bit like she was staring down at the darkened bottom of an abyss that she didn't want to traverse. She let Jared go. She told him where to shove it. She was proud of that. Happy with it. But now he was dredging it up like it was still a factor. Like it was still part of what she was reacting to, what she was doing.

*You spent fifteen years in that relationship. Did you really think that you were going to banish it in a month?*

She didn't want to think about that. She didn't want to give weight to it.

But he was looking at her with those eyes, and she'd never been very good at staying neutral when he looked at her.

He made her feel things. All kinds of things. Big and bright and far too much for her frame.

"I was with him because… Because there was a time in my life when I was very lonely. I had trouble making friends and… My parents weren't very interested in me. Griffin was gone and… And Jared was interested. He was interested in me and it felt really good. He was funny, and I wasn't. I was too insecure, and he never was. And I could do things for him that other people wouldn't. It made me popular. Because I was the first girl in my group of friends to have sex, and then everybody wanted to know what it was like. I'd tell them. And then later... I guess it didn't change. I guess I kept on liking what happened when I did things for him. It made me feel safe. It made me feel worthy. To be needed."

The words felt frozen on her lips.

"Well, you know you can be with someone for different reasons than that."

"Right. Well, you're adopting a baby and you want..."

"Don't tell me what I want. I'm still figuring out what I want. Mallory you're the only person I've ever... I've never talked to anyone about my mother. About how I feel about living while she died. I know all about trying to figure out how to feel worthy."

"Colt..."

"And I have let those fears dictate what I'll be, what I want and don't want. Whether or not I sing." He looked like a revelation had just crashed down on him. "Mallory, I've built my whole life on that loss. On the pain of being sure that if my dad hadn't died, he'd leave. And I can't ask him, can I?"

"No, you can't..."

"You thought I didn't need you or want you, but I do. I... I don't know what he wanted. I..."

He crossed the room, knelt down in front of her, and then he kissed her. Hard and deep and long. It was decisive. And it cut through all the fog inside of her in a way that... Well, damn near terrified her.

"Mallory, look how much damage it does when you think you know."

"I should be here, though. I mean, this is my house, and I should be... Here."

*I'm not playing house with him.*

He was setting up a real life, a permanent life, and he needed to be able to be in that. And she needed to not trick herself into thinking she was part of it. Because it just wasn't... It wasn't a good thing, that much was certain.

"Do whatever works for you," he said. "But it doesn't work for me for you to disappear with your tail between your legs, suddenly acting like we haven't been living together for weeks. You didn't ask me what I wanted, Mallory."

"I just figured..."

"What? You just figured because now I knew how to change a diaper I wasn't going to want you?"

"I... It's not practical."

"Who the hell cares about practical? Have you met me? I'm a former bull rider with issues out the ass, and I just said that I was going to adopt a child. None of this makes sense. None of this is practical. But I know what I want. I know what I'm going to do. You figure into that somewhere, Mallory, you don't get left out."

And then she couldn't look at him. She just couldn't. She had turned her gaze away to focus on the ground.

"Well, I..."

"Well nothing. Eat breakfast."

"Okay."

She didn't have a choice. So she did. Because she might have been able to slip away last night in a little bit of self-preservation, but when he was looking at her like that, even if she was looking at him, she couldn't deny it. Couldn't deny him. Even if she wanted to.

She should have told him the truth. The whole story. But it... She had never told anyone outside of work. She told people in a very specific context and not...

Not when her heart was involved. Not when she already felt so tender.

Not when she felt like she would be confessing a failure. So, instead she just ate her bacon.

# CHAPTER EIGHTEEN

FOR THE FIRST time in a good while, Colt let himself remember. It had started with that conversation—that confession—he'd made to Mallory in the car.

He'd finally said out loud what haunted him, and the world hadn't come down around him. Mallory had listened. And she hadn't run from him.

It had made it feel...

It had made it feel okay to remember.

He had been working alone on Jake's ranch all morning, and he got into thinking. He had Lily in a carrier strapped to his front, and he had a feeling this was just what his life was going to look like for a while.

It didn't bother him.

No, he felt more settled, more grounded than he ever had. It was a weird thing to accept his life rather than fight against it. Different from where he'd been ever since he was a teenager. It was a strange thing that happened when he set aside the anger. The rage against fate.

Yeah, there were a whole lot of things that weren't fair. Still a whole lot of things that didn't make sense, but what was in front of them right now did make sense. This moment. This kid. This life.

And it was the strangest damn thing, because he felt the melody and lyrics stir inside of him that he hadn't heard on the radio, and he hadn't had access to that in a long time.

Even when it had happened in the last few years, he'd done his best to shove it down because he hadn't wanted to think about it. Because it was too painful. Too painful to remember what it had been like. When he'd written music and poured out his heart and his mother had praised him for it. When she'd been excited and happy about his gifts and what he might do with them. Because it made him hopeful and excited too, and he learned to put that away. Because in order to write songs he had to touch part of himself that he decided now he didn't want to.

Right now it was like he didn't have a choice. Because these changes in his life had started to pry his chest open wide, and he could no longer keep thoughts and feelings out of them. He didn't even want to.

And when he heard music, he saw Mallory's face.

That sense of freedom was what set him out to finding Jake. Because he wanted to talk to his brother. Really talk to him. Because he was beginning to understand what had changed inside of him. Why he wanted to talk about things now when before he hadn't.

He was beginning to understand, and even if it still... It terrified him a little bit, he was beginning to get it. And he was wanting to... He was wanting to explore it. Wanting to see.

"Come on, sweet pea," he said to Lily. "Let's go find your uncle."

Jake was somewhere at the back end of the property, and Colt was surprised that he was by himself. He half expected to stumble upon him and Callie making out, but he supposed that they had to work sometime.

"Been looking for you," Colt said.

"Hello," Jake responded. "That's the most surprising thing I've heard in a while. Usually you avoid me."

"Yeah. Been thinking, though."

"You?"

"Yeah. I'm adopting Lily."

"You're adopting Lily."

"That's what I just said. There's no need to repeat me. Waste of time."

"I'm just shocked," he said.

"Yeah, well, I keep feeling like I should be. Like I ought to be completely stunned by the fact that I decided to take on being a father. But with everything … I don't see another way that it could be. I don't see another reason for me to be here. I don't… Because the more that I pull away, the more that I try to make my whole life about achievements and all of that… The less it makes sense to me. Being here with you and Callie makes sense to me." Mallory made sense to him, but he wasn't going to say that.

"I'm glad to hear you say that, but… I feel like there's a but."

"No but."

"I guess I'm just surprised because… You know, everything that. I mean, I'm going to be a dad someday. Callie and I are going to have children once it fits in with what she wants, but there's just a whole lot of… Shit, you know? Because of how Dad was going to leave us."

"I've been thinking a lot about that," Colt said. "Thinking a lot about Mom. It hurts to do that. It hurts too much. But I have to think about it. I have to go over it. I have to. Because it's the one thing I haven't done. I play out all that trauma. Being on the plane, getting off the plane. But I never think about who they really were. It's easy to focus on how we lost them. It's easy to think of Dad's…those plane tickets after. But I was with him on the plane. We talked before

Mom got there. I think he might've changed his mind, Jake. I really do. I think he was going to stay."

"We don't know that."

"No," Colt said. "We don't. We can't. Just like I can't know... If you all would've been better off if I would've stayed on the plane and Mom would've gotten off. I can't know and I can't change it. I keep wanting a guarantee. I keep looking around trying to find some final, extra firm sense of purpose. I can't lie—Lily is giving me that. I can't lie. But it's more than that. It's more than just finally being able to say, hell, I guess I'm supposed to be here because I can take care of this kid and make sure she turns out all right. I don't even know if that's the grand plan. There's probably a thousand people that would be better at taking care of a kid. But I... I've got to choose this. I got to choose this moment, because of fear. I've got to step up to it. Not just because she needs it, but because, hell... I think I need it. More than I can possibly articulate or understand. I need to be in this moment. I need to be the man for her. I can't have guarantees. But somewhere in there, I just hope that Dad... That the moment I had with him on the plane before I got off, when he said that he wanted Mom to go, I have to hope that he was deciding to be the best man that he could then. And I have to trust it."

"How?" Jake asked.

"I don't know. But it's like you deciding to love Callie, I guess. At a certain point you just have to choose to believe. In something bigger than yourself. It's something better."

"Yeah, but you've always believed. I'm the one whose faith suffers sometimes."

"I haven't always found the comfort. Because yeah, I've always believed. That someone—probably God—was guiding something, but I couldn't see my place in it. A lot of times

I felt like it was a joke, or a mistake. And it was random, maybe I wouldn't feel like I needed to find a purpose. But it never felt random. So I searched for the meaning of everything. I was always looking for actions. I was staying the hell away from feelings. Because feelings are… Feelings are the problem. But now I think feelings are the point. I thought brave was throwing myself into the rodeo. I thought brave was taking risks. But it's not those kinds of risks that make a man brave. It's this," he said, touching Lily's back. "This is what makes you brave. Deciding to try something when you don't know if you can handle it. Deciding to be strong when you don't really know if you're strong enough. You're the right man for the job. You become the right man for the job because the job is there. As you do it. And that…" He shook his head. "That's what I hope our dad did. That's what I hope he was."

"I've always admired your faith, Colt. And I admire it even more now."

"We have to choose a story. Because we don't know what it was."

"I guess you're right about that," Jake mused.

"But it's not me that's really impressive. I'm choosing a better story. But you know… You chose to make a life with Callie—that's pretty damn brave."

"Yeah, not easily. You remember. I wasn't exactly a poster child for going quietly into loving feelings."

"Because it's hard," Colt said. "It's hard." He shook his head. "Mom used to…used to say that I was brave. I'd write songs about everything I felt, wrote it all down. And she said… That's brave, Colt. It's a damn hard thing to talk about what you feel. I quit doing it. Because it hurt too much. Because I quit being brave. When they died, I just lost it. I told myself it was brave enough to go and ride bulls. I thought…

I'll go make you proud, Mom. I can still show you what I can do. But I want to be the kind of brave that she would've wanted me to be. Somehow, it all connects. It just, it does. Believing the best. Opening myself up to things. Talking to you. It really annoyed the hell out of me when you started talking."

"I know," Jake said.

"I'm glad you did now. I'm really damn glad."

"You know I worried about you," Jake said. "Because it has been so hard to reach you. And I sure as hell didn't know how. I was as messed up as you were. I met Callie and things changed. I wanted to change. Even back then. When she was just a kid and I was mentoring her. And then... And then later. When things changed again. She makes me want to be better. If you found the thing that makes you want to be better..."

It wasn't just one thing, though. Colt didn't quite have the words for it yet. And while he was damn glad he was able to talk to his brother now, there were just certain things that needed to be considered in dark rooms by himself. Certain truths that needed to be come to by himself.

"You know, I thought a lot about my legacy," Colt said. "About what the point of it was. But I haven't thought a whole lot about my life."

"Well, the greatest legacy is living. Life is pretty damn sweet."

"I'm starting to think so," he said.

And that was the thing, he tempted fate, tested death all those years when it had felt like the biggest, grandest unknown out there. When he felt unworthy of the breath in his lungs and uncertain what to do with the time he'd been given that he felt like was borrowed and maybe not his own.

But he suddenly felt the sun extra warm on his skin and

the air clear in his lungs. The scent of pine, dirt and grass. The sensation of being on the back of his horse, the feeling of Lily's weight in his arms and her steady breathing. Life. It felt like a gift just then. A gift that he'd handled roughly. A gift that he hadn't fully embraced. Because he had been waiting for the other shoe to drop, because he had been afraid to care too much, because he had been too afraid. Too afraid.

Because he hadn't been brave. Because the scariest thing of all was acceptance. Was truly accepting that his parents were gone. That Trent was gone. That it was the hand that life had dealt, and there was no amount of anger holding on or fighting it that could bring them back.

All he could do was honor them. By honoring himself.

By living all that life afforded to him.

There was no amount of guilt, no grand demonstration of martyrdom that was ever going to balance the scales.

What if there were no scales? No balance. If it wasn't about achieving any great purpose. Because the greatest purpose that he'd found so far was loving this child.

And investing in the hope that she would love him too.

The love of his family. His brother.

Maybe it was just that simple. Not some cosmic equation to figure out. But the love that you gave and took every day, that you spent and held tight and cherished. For the land and the sky and the people around you.

And maybe that was just living.

"I guess I better get back to work," Colt said.

"Yeah. See you after."

"See you after." He turned his horse around, but then he paused. "You know I was always thankful for you. I love you."

Jake looked like he'd been hit in the face with the cowboy boots. "Oh. Well… I love you too, Colt."

"Just wanted to say it."

"Appreciated," his brother said, his voice husky. And Colt's chest felt tight then too. Deep, real living.

Because maybe the purpose was life. A more abundant life. With rich unfathomable layers that took bravery to feel. To want. To care for.

It was loving the fragile things in a dangerous world that required real bravery.

And that was what he wanted. From here on out.

# CHAPTER NINETEEN

MALLORY STOPPED ON the porch of her clinic, touching the intricately carved posts there.

Colt's work was amazing.

Colt. Just thinking about him made her heart clench and her body get hot. That man...

The last thing she had expected this morning was for him to show up cooking breakfast for her. And say he wanted her. Kissing her.

It made her... Well, it made her want to run a mile, and she didn't even know why.

She was here, at the clinic, getting back to the business at hand. It had been a good day so far, complete with a couple of home visits. She had gotten to visit Grant and Mc-Kenna and see the place where they wanted to give birth to the baby. It was looking like everything was going to work out with her insurance and that it was going to be able to be a home birth just like they wanted, which was all for the best, because while she was getting everything in shape at the clinic, it was going to take a little while for everything to come, and for her to get it all set up.

"Mallory?"

Mallory turned and saw one of her clients standing there, an expression of concern on her face. Lizzie Omak was clutching her baby bump, her brows pleated.

"Lizzie," she said. "We don't have an appointment, do we?"

"No. I was having lunch down the road. I… I'm bleeding."

"You did the right thing coming in. Come on," Mallory said. She put her hand low on Lizzie's back and began to lead her up the stairs, pushing her inside. "How much blood?" she asked briskly, leading the way down the hall into one of the exam rooms.

"I don't know. Um… A tablespoon, maybe?"

"Okay. Brown, bright red?"

"Kind of… Bright, but dark."

"Okay." She took a breath. "Can you get undressed please, I'll be right back."

She walked out of the room, heading to the bathroom to quickly sterilize her hands. She heard the door open, and Colt called her name. "I'm in the back, I'm with a patient," she said.

"Okay," he said.

"Don't leave."

She knew how to handle emergencies. This wasn't her first time ever dealing with a client hemorrhaging. And she had a feeling they were going to have to go to the hospital. But she would look at her first. Mallory was not one to take any chances. If a mother or baby could be served better in a medical facility that had more resources than she did, then that's where they would go.

She rushed back into the exam room, keeping her expression neutral. "How are you feeling? Do you have any cramping?"

"I… No. I… I need to call my husband."

"Yes. We will call your husband. Let me examine you first."

Lizzie winced. "I'm having cramping now."

Lizzie was twenty-eight weeks. If she had to deliver, it was… It was not ideal. Survival was possible, that was definitely true. It would just be better if they could keep her pregnant.

But Mallory was beginning to have doubts. Lizzie was lying back on the bed, and Mallory felt her abdomen, checking for signs of rigidity. Lizzie winced.

"My concern is that you may have had a placental abruption," Mallory said after a moment. "We need to go to the hospital."

Lizzie started to cry, immediately. "I don't… I don't have a car, and my husband works an hour away…"

"I'll go with you. I'll sit with you. Colt will drive us."

"I need to call my husband," she said, her breathing getting sporadic.

"It's okay." She got out the Doppler and put it on Lizzie's abdomen. The baby's heartbeat was still strong. Lizzie wasn't bleeding uncontrollably, but based on what she was feeling in her uterus, Mallory was definitely concerned. "But I do want to take you to a hospital. We need you to have more intense monitoring than what I can offer you."

Lizzie dressed, and then Mallory helped her from the exam room. "Colt," she said. "Will you drive us?"

She noticed that Lily wasn't with him. "Where's Lily?"

"I'll explain later," he said. "My family has her. Don't worry about it."

He picked up on the situation immediately, and she felt a little bit bad about co-opting him, but he didn't seem to mind. Instead, he did everything she asked him to do absolutely seamlessly.

She sat in the back of her car with Lizzie, and Colt drove them toward Tolowa. All the while, she monitored Lizzie for distress. She had thought that sending her in an ambulance would only create more trauma, and since the baby's heartbeat was strong, and so was Lizzie's, it made more sense for them to drive.

Her husband was also on his way, and Colt had done the hard work of calling him too. When they arrived at the hospital, Colt dropped them at the front entrance, and they went inside. "You won't leave me, will you?"

"No," Mallory said. "I'm not going to leave you. As long as you want me here, I'm here. You can trust the doctors, but if you need me…"

"I need you," she said.

Mallory explained the situation to the nurse at the emergency room. Rather than staying in the ER, they were immediately taken to the birthing center. At that moment, Lizzie was with it enough to text her husband and let him know where they'd gone. When they were settled, Mallory texted Colt. It took an hour, but Lizzie's husband finally arrived. At that point, she had already been examined by the doctor. She had begun to bleed more, though the baby's heart rate still looked good.

Mallory was thankful that the doctor was respectful of her desire to stay. It was important to her that whatever Lizzie needed, Lizzie got.

"What am I going to do?" Lizzie whispered. "What if I lose my baby?"

Mallory blinked. Tears were pushing against her own eyes, but she tried not to show them.

"I don't know if it'll all be okay," Mallory said. "The miracle of birth is not always a simple one. And sometimes… Sometimes in life bad things happen. But you are strong. We don't know what will happen. But what I know is that you can keep breathing in this moment. Just focus on breathing now. On staying calm. Focus on what you can do."

Hours passed, and the situation remained in flux. And so Mallory stayed.

It was everyone's goal to keep Lizzie pregnant. But it became clear as the bleeding worsened and the baby began to enter into fetal distress that they were not going to be able to accomplish that. And when they took Lizzie in for the C-section, it was just her and her husband. It was also nearly midnight. Mallory stumbled out of the room and was shocked to see Colt sitting in the waiting room.

"You're still here."

Sitting in those mauve chairs under fluorescent lights. Her cowboy in very shining armor.

"Yeah," he said. He stood. "I saw them take her out."

"She has to deliver. I want to... I want to wait. Is that okay?"

"Whatever you need."

"You were just there, the whole time?"

"Yes," he said. "I was there the whole time."

"Thank you," she said.

She sat next to him, her legs giving out. And she leaned her head against his shoulder. "Tell me about it."

She looked up at him. "She had a placental abruption. She's only twenty-eight weeks. The baby can survive. But... I hate this. I've seen happy and sad outcomes. You don't work in the business of childbirth without seeing things you wish you didn't."

"You didn't have to stay," he said.

"No. I had to stay. It was important that I stay."

"This isn't an easy business, is it?"

She shook her head. "No."

"Why do you do it?"

A sob shook her shoulders, and she knew she couldn't keep it back. Not anymore. She had to tell him. Because it just felt right. Sitting here in this hospital birthing center that reminded her so much of the one that she'd been in all those years ago. "Because I know what it's like," she said. "Because... Because I had a baby. And she was stillborn." She looked at his face, waiting for something. Waiting for horror or judgment or anger. But it wasn't there.

It was very carefully neutral, in a way that scared her a little bit, but at least that neutrality gave her space to speak.

"I was fifteen. Nobody knows. Nobody but... Nobody but Jared. And I guess... I guess that was why I stayed with him. Because we went through that together, and he was actually good. He was a fifteen-year-old boy who had gone through something adults struggle to cope with, and he helped me. And I was... I hated it. I hated that loss as much as I hated being relieved by it, and in some ways I was. But it was always tangled up with the fact that he was the father of that baby. The father of that baby that was gone. A connection to something that I... That I still grieve, Colt. I really do. And it's a terrible thing, because I can't really miss her. Because she was never... She was never here. But I miss what might've been so much. I think about it. I think about it sometimes... How old she would be. To be fifteen. And I would be struggling to figure out my life and hers at the same time. Except... She isn't. She isn't here."

"Mallory," he said, his voice rough. He pulled her into his arms, putting his chin over her head and kissing her hair. "You are the bravest woman I've ever known."

"How am I brave? I've kept that a secret, you know. I kept it a secret from everyone. How is that brave?"

"You're carrying all that so that no one else has to. Is that the truth? I know all about that." His eyes looked at her, intense and shining bright.

Electric blue that touched her in ways nothing else ever had. And had, from the moment she'd first seen him.

"Maybe," she said, blinking hard. "When I told you I understand how thin the line is… I really do. Between here and gone. Because I was going to have a baby, and I hid it from everybody. And then she was gone. Then she was gone, and I never had the chance to tell the world. I regretted it. In the end I regretted it, but what can you do? Especially… I got to a place I thought I might be able to share with everybody and then…"

"Your brother."

"Why would I ever heap that much pain onto my family? It just feels cruel at this point. Like such a hideous and terrible thing to do to them after everything they've already been through."

"But it's part of you," he said.

She thought about that for a moment. About how angry it made her when Griffin underestimated her, not having any idea the kinds of things she had gone through. The kinds of burdens she carried. "Maybe," she said, her voice muted. "Maybe that's true."

"I'm sorry," he said. "I'm sorry that you went through that alone."

"You come out stronger…"

"And you chose to share that strength with other people. I'm not sure I ever managed that trick."

She put her hand on his. "That's not true. Whether you know it or not… You shared it with Lily's dad. Trent got strength from you. He wanted to learn how to be a man like you. He wanted to be a father like he knew you could be. I think that you were like a father to him."

The corner of his mouth turned up a little bit. "I hope so. All I can ever think of is… I think of the ways that I failed him. But then, I spend a lot of time thinking about the ways I felt like my own dad failed me. But after talking to you… I went to speak to my brother, Jake, about it. I don't know what my dad was thinking. I don't know if he was going to leave. I don't know if he was going to stay. But I can't know. I can only accept what is. I guess you know something about that too. You can't help but wonder sometimes. Think about the way your life could have gone if you hadn't… If you hadn't lost…"

"Yes," she said. "I know. I… I'm trying to accept it. In a way I don't think I ever did before. That she isn't here, so I don't need to hold on to things that don't fix anything. I think I held on to Jared for so long because it was like keeping her." She blinked, her heart twisting. "It's hard. To accept the bad that happens."

"I think if you don't, you don't ever get around to accepting the good."

His words tumbled down somewhere low inside of her chest and hit something tender. But just in that moment, the doctor came in. "Mom and baby are stable," he said. "She's going to need some assistance in the NICU. But I'm optimistic." And if there was one thing Mallory knew it was that doctors were never needlessly optimistic.

"Thank you," she said. "Thank you."

"The husband said you could go home now. His wife is still in recovery."

Colt helped her up out of the chair. "Thank you. We'll call tomorrow."

And she found herself being propelled out of the building and back toward the car. She sat in the front seat with him on the way back to the cabin. And he stayed there with her all night, holding her in his arms.

For a minute, she thought about resisting. But in the end,

his own words kept echoing in her head. Because he was right. There were a fair number of terrible things in the world that you couldn't do anything with. There was nothing to do but accept them. So why couldn't she accept this good thing, even if just for tonight?

COLT'S DATE PLANS had been blown all to hell by what had happened the night before. But he had no issues delaying it for a day, and Iris and Griffin were happy to take Lily again. He wanted to do something special for Mallory.

Mallory.

The revelations of last night had only cemented everything that he already felt about her.

Finding out about her loss... Well, it damn near killed him. But... It left him in awe of her. Even more than he already was, which was an incredible damn thing.

Because it was Mallory who had brought him to the place where he could even begin to be what Lily needed. And he saw that now, for sure and certain.

That Lily was why everything fit together now.

That Mallory was the start, the spark of all the change in him, of the ability to become the man that he needed to be. It was her. And more than that, the feelings that she aroused in him. That she had brought out in him since the first moment he'd seen her. The real reason that he hadn't been able to forget her, even though after that first time he'd gone back to the rodeo, gone back to pretending that he was the same man he'd been before he'd seen her.

But he hadn't been.

She had created a storm inside of him that had washed away the remnants of what he'd been. A storm that had brought with it destruction then new life in all manner of brilliance, that had brought a new dawn into the darkest night he'd been living in for so many years. The hope he hadn't imagined possible for a man like him.

She was a revolution all in herself. She was his fate, with beautiful curly hair and a floral dress. And she had been from the first moment they'd seen each other, and if they'd both been brave enough to step outside of that life they'd been living then, they could've had each other that much sooner. If she'd known then that she should leave that boyfriend of hers. If he'd understood then, without Trent dying—without a baby coming into his life—that happiness was never going to be found for him on the circuit, no glory wrapped up in winning prize money.

But they both needed something else, something big. And he'd failed at the first big shift in his life—he'd let it make him afraid. He'd let it close him off. But not again. Not again. He wouldn't do it again. He was going to rise up now, and he was going to take hold of everything beautiful left in this world.

He was going to embrace fate rather than curse her; he was going to claim it all, rather than running away.

He heard the sound of a car engine, and he stood up from his position in Mallory's living room. He was going to have to hope that she forgave him for co-opting the space and making a few improvements.

She would see his truck parked out front, which was just as well, because he didn't want to scare her or anything like that, and he had a feeling that if she just walked in to see a dark, shadowy figure standing in her living room, it might make her feel uncomfortable. And that was the last thing he wanted.

He heard footsteps on the porch, heard the door open, and she stopped as soon as she got inside. "Colt?"

"I hope you don't mind, but I thought we might have dinner in. After last night I figured you'd be tired."

"I am."

"How is Lizzie today?"

Mallory smiled. "She's doing well, and so is baby girl. I'm so... I'm so happy for them. It could have gone very badly and it didn't."

"She had an amazing midwife on her side."

Mallory ducked her head, compliments still obviously not sitting easily with her. "Oh," she said. "It smells amazing. Did you cook?"

"Yes. I made everything but the bread. You mentioned you liked fettuccine, and I figured that I would... Make some for you."

"You actually made Italian food."

"Yeah."

"Because you remembered that I said I liked it?"

"Yes," he said.

And as much as it made him want to punch her ex in the face, he would never get tired of the wonder on her face when he fed her. When he touched her just with affection.

Because it healed something inside of him, and made him feel... Made him feel he was worth more than he'd ever imagined he might be. And for a minute that made him feel guilty, because it came from a wounded place in her, but maybe that was all part of it.

Maybe the broken pieces in her just fit the broken pieces in him right enough. Maybe that was the point.

Because nobody made it through life without a few cracks, without scars and bruises. And maybe it wasn't about making them go away. Because that might not be possible. Maybe it was about finding the beauty in those things. And the ways that they could heal each other.

"I don't know what to say. That's…" She frowned. "You burned your hand. Did you do that cooking?"

He looked down at his knuckles. "Yeah. Not a big deal. You know I've been hurt way worse riding bulls—pasta is not going to take me down."

"Colt." Then she just sighed and closed the distance between them. She didn't kiss him. Instead, she wrapped her arms around him and laid her head on his chest. The feeling that sparked in him was entirely unexpected. His heart felt like it was two sizes too big and he felt…

Transformed. New. He was beginning to recognize this feeling. This feeling that reached deep places in his soul, places where he usually housed creativity, creation. Yeah, that's what it was like, but it didn't take work or effort. It just sort of bloomed. Inside of all that he was. And it was some kind of brilliant miracle, this gift, in the middle of a broken, difficult life.

What a wondrous, amazing gift it was.

"I FEEL LIKE I should get dressed up."

"You don't need to do that," he said.

"No," she said slowly. "I want to. Hang on just a minute."

The minute turned into twenty. She vanished into her bedroom and appeared a while after. And it was worth it.

She was wearing a tight, mustard-colored sweater dress that conformed to her curves, that made him want to peel it off slowly and deliberately. She was so beautiful. But it was more. And he wasn't sure he would ever be able to capture what that more was so that he could hold it for a moment. So that he could look at it, put words to it.

Like trying to put light in a jar and hold on to it for a moment. So that you can examine the fractals and the glitter. So that you could try to make the ephemeral into something material. What moved through you and sustained you and showed you the lay of everything.

"I love your hair," he said, taking a step toward her and moving his fingers through the curly mass.

"Seriously?" she asked. "It's frizzy."

"It's beautiful. Just like you."

A shadow fell over her eyes for a moment. "That's nice of you."

"Look, I know you said he was good to you at one time, but what did he say to you during all that other time that made you feel like you weren't beautiful?"

"I'm over him."

"It doesn't matter if you're over him or not. I can see how he made you feel about yourself. About what it did to your self-esteem and how much you value yourself."

"You don't need to try to fix me."

"I'm not. I'm not, but somebody has to say that you're beautiful. More times than he ever said you weren't. Why would anybody not need that? Living with a person who doesn't treat you the way you deserve, no matter how small or subtle the comments, that's the kind of thing designed to break a person."

"I'm not broken."

"I know. You're brave and strong is what you are. Brilliant. Beautiful. Last night you were incredible, and now that I know…everything you've been through, Mallory, and what you use your strength for… You deserve to be told how great you are. Always." *And I need you.*

When those words echoed inside of him… He wanted her to understand it wasn't in the same way that her exboyfriend had claimed to need her. That it wasn't because he wanted to use her. He wanted to give to her. He wanted her to give to him. He wanted to share a life. A whole life.

One held together by the brilliant threads of light that he couldn't quite name.

*Can't you?*

She looked uncomfortable, and he could sense her shrinking away. "Why won't you let me tell you that? You're beautiful. Take that from me. Let me help you. Let me drive you home from a late night like last night and cook for you. Let me hold you. Let me take some of your pain."

"I'm trying to be independent. I'm trying to make a new life, and I don't want to go getting dependent on you. Besides, Colt, you have enough pain of your own. I didn't need to dump all my stuff on you."

"It's not dependent to have relationships. Real relationships. That bullshit that you had with him, that's not real. And you did not dump your…stuff on me, you shared yourself. Whoever made you feel like that was too heavy—him again, I assume—that wasn't love."

"I know that it's not love," she said. "But it's definitely the only relationship I know how to be in. And I need some distance from that. I guess I'm just… I'm wary."

That was like a punch to the chest, because he wanted to ask her for more. He wanted to ask her for everything. He wanted her. All of her. Wanted her to be his woman.

What he'd said… Hell, yeah, that was real. His woman. *His.*

Her body, her pleasure, her mind, her heart. He wanted it all. But he wanted equally to be hers. Wanted to be her fate in the same way she felt like his.

"What if I told you I wouldn't mind if you were dependent on me?"

"I don't… I don't know what to say to that. Because you know, that's not really healthy and…"

"How would you know?"

"Because I've been dependent on people. On their approval, on their… It's exhausting."

He remembered what she'd said. About how she hadn't told anyone about the baby. She'd been afraid of losing approval for a long time.

"It doesn't have to be. That wasn't you being dependent on other people, that was making them dependent on you. That's different. I want to do things for you. I want to be there for you. I want to make you dinner. And I want to make you come. I want this."

She looked away from him, her cheeks going red, and he put his finger underneath her chin and tilted her face toward him. And he kissed her. With everything he was, with everything he felt deep down inside of him. He kissed her. He kissed her because there was just nothing else to do. He kissed her because he needed her.

And he couldn't list all the ways, couldn't list all the reasons. But that was just it. It wasn't a list of attributes or gifts or wants or even needs. It was something bigger, deeper.

Something more than he'd ever experienced in his life, and he'd experienced a whole damn lot. It was music; it was art.

It was brave.

It was her.

From the moment he'd seen her, something had shifted inside of him, the world had begun to change. From that very same moment.

"Mallory," he said, the words rough, the words scraping his throat. "I'm in love with you."

And as soon as he said it, he knew it was true. As soon as he said it, he knew there was no point fighting any of it. He was all in. All in to this, all in to her. It was funny how… Up until this moment he'd been pushing off thinking that. Up until this moment he pretended like he didn't know what he wanted. He did. He wanted all of it. Every last bit. He wanted to make a family with her.

He wanted to be Lily's father, but he wanted Mallory to be Lily's mother. He wanted to go to bed with her every night and wake up with her every morning. There was a reason that when she left the house it had felt wrong. And she kept talking about need. She kept saying that he didn't need her. But she didn't understand need the way that he did.

He'd made a life of being self-sufficient. And within that, he made a habit of not connecting with people. But now he'd done it. And this was exactly why he hadn't wanted to. Because he knew how deep it went. And how much it cut when you lost someone. But he couldn't deny it anymore. It wasn't living. It wasn't honoring the reasons that fate had left him in this world.

"Colt... I don't know what... I can't... Colt, I came here to start a new life."

"Start a new life with me. I love you. I love you."

And he saw fear fill her eyes, and it reminded him of that night they'd come together. Of when they'd seen each other after. It was connection. It terrified her. Made her want to run the other direction.

"Don't say anything."

He couldn't hear it now. And he couldn't say any more. He could only show her.

That first night they'd been together, it had been all about the physical. All about lust, all about passion. And in the time since then, feelings had begun to braid their way into the interaction. Desire mingling with something intimate and more specific.

But he could see it all clearly now. The tapestry of their relationship. Because feeling had always been there. From the first.

And he would've said that love at first sight was impossible because you couldn't know ahead of time. You couldn't possibly love someone you didn't know. You couldn't see ahead to all the things that they would become to you.

But, hell, he believed in fate and the hand of God.

He believed in all that, maybe because he had to.

And he knew that it had been love. From the first. It was why the sex had been different. It was why they hadn't been able to escape each other.

She was meant for him. And he was meant for this moment. For this woman.

And if he couldn't tell her, he would show her.

He kissed her, his tongue sliding against hers, his heart beating faster. The blood in his veins was fire, and his body was hard, ready. This was like nothing. Like nothing that had ever existed before. Desire mixing with feeling. He felt undone. Like all of the protective layers inside of him had been ripped away, leaving him exposed, bloody and open. To anything. Any pain that she might wish to throw at him. She could destroy him now with a few carefully chosen words. And he... He didn't move to protect himself. He wouldn't change anything.

Because this was what had to happen. Because he'd lived his life protected. He'd lived it separate. And it hadn't solved a damn thing. But this... This.

He moved his hands behind her back, ran them down to cup her rear. Then he moved them down farther, sliding his fingers beneath the hemline of her dress, pushing it slowly up her thighs, past her hips, her narrow waist and her breasts, until he took it completely off her body. And when he saw her, his stomach went completely tight. She was dressed in yellow lace that barely covered her curves. He could see the dusky hue of her nipples beneath the whisper-thin bra, and the shadow of curls between her thighs.

He looked at that body with renewed respect. That body that exhausted itself for others. That body that had carried a child, no matter that it had resulted in loss. It had been changed by carrying that life.

She had been changed by it.

Into the woman before him. The woman who had saved him.

"Thank you," he said.

"What?" she asked, her breath coming in short, sharp bursts, her eyes darting back and forth. She looked afraid.

She looked afraid, and he had felt guilt for that before. He had felt the desire to put her at ease. But he knew now that he had to push her through it. Because he knew her now. And he understood. It was their connection that terrified her. It was the feelings that were rising up inside of her. She wasn't ready.

Well, she could join the club. Because he hadn't been ready for this either. Hadn't been looking for it, hadn't wanted it. Not in the least. But he loved her.

And he hadn't gotten to choose.

But of all the things in this damn world that he hadn't gotten to choose, at least this was beautiful. At least it was bright. At least it healed rather than destroyed. It was a gift.

And he'd been dished out enough bullshit that he didn't take that for granted. And he wouldn't let her run away from it, not without a fight.

Not without a bloody-knuckled fight.

"For getting dressed up for me," he said, his voice rough. "You're so beautiful. The most beautiful woman I've ever seen."

"You keep saying that," she said, her voice trembling.

"I already told you. I'll say it now. I'll say it again. I'll say it forever, Mallory." He cupped the back of her head, smoothing his thumbs along the line of her jaw. "I'll say it until everything the world made you believe about yourself is gone. Until I can build something new inside of you. Until you start to see everything I see. Until you believe it." He moved his thumbs down her delicate throat, paused at the base of it, feeling her pulse thundering wildly beneath his touch. Then he moved down between her breasts, fanning them outward and teasing her nipples through the lace. He felt them get hard. Even in her fear, even in her uncertainty, she wasn't immune to him. Not even close.

She was held just as captive by this as he was, and she had been from the beginning. That was the thing. It had always been bigger than the two of them. And it had always gotten them both. It had always been them together. And he needed to get her where he was now.

He traced down her rib cage, her waist, and she breathed sharply, her breasts pitching upward. And he couldn't help himself, because he was only a man. He lowered his head and kissed her, right on the plump curve of one breast. Licking the edge of that place where lace met skin. Then he closed his lips over the top of one distended nipple, sucking her through the bra. She arched, wiggling, and he held her steady, smoothing his hands down to her hips, his mouth following that same path. Then he tipped her back on the couch, moving her thighs up over his shoulder.

"I…"

He had done this for her a few times, and every time, she got uncomfortable. She screamed at the end, but was hesitant in the beginning. He had to get her mindless before she could be okay with it.

"He never did this, did he?"

Her body went red, her cheeks a deep shade of pink. "I…"

"Of course he didn't," Colt said. "Because he's an idiot. Because he didn't want you like I do. Because I love you. And I love everything about you. Damn, woman, I crave your taste. You have no idea. I'd rather do this—" He turned his head and kissed her inner thigh. "I'd rather taste you than have you go down on me any day. If I had to choose. If I didn't have to choose, obviously I'd take both." He moved down lower, hovering right above that lace. "But this, this I couldn't live without." He kissed her there, featherlight over the fabric, and she squirmed. She closed her eyes and threw her arm over her face. "No," he said. He reached up, grabbed her wrist and pinned her arm down to the back of the couch. "Watch me," he said.

Her eyes flew open wide in shock. And he leaned in again, kissing her there. She wiggled, and he could tell that she was aroused, tell that she was trying to fight it. "You watch me taste you," he commanded. "And you believe it when I tell you that I want you. That I'm crazy for you." He nuzzled her tender flesh, and relished the whimper of desire that escaped her mouth.

With his free hand, he traced the crease where her femininity met her thigh, then slipped his finger beneath the elastic there, finding her wet with desire for him. He teased her, before slipping one finger inside of her. And she gasped. Then he gripped the edge of her panties tighter, popping them free of her body.

"You've got to quit doing that," she said. "I liked those."

He felt a brief step of regret. "I liked them too. But I like this more." And then he was tasting her. Unencumbered by any clothing. Just her. Her desire. Her need for him. That essential part of herself that he felt was… For him. Because she was for him.

This was for him.

There had been other women in his bed, but never in his life. And there had been another man in hers, but it had never been this. He knew it. Down in his bones. Because this moment, this pleasure, it was all theirs. And it didn't matter who had come before.

Because it was never this.

Nothing else ever could be.

He tasted her, sliding his tongue through her folds, zeroing in on that sensitized bundle of nerves there. And he pushed two fingers inside of her, teasing her as he continued to taste her. And she gasped, her hips bucking up against his mouth. He looked up at her, and their eyes met, and she burst into flame. He could feel her climax rippling through her entire body, in the way that her thighs tensed, in the way that she cried out his name, her fingernails digging into his shoulders.

He was so hard it was painful.

"You're always getting me naked before you take off any clothes," she said.

"Because I'm impatient."

And he looked at her then, sprawled back against the couch, her bra still on, her panties decimated. He stood back, slowly removing his own clothes, taking some pride in the fact that she couldn't take her eyes away from him as he did so. In the way that she clearly enjoyed the look of his body. It was beyond intense, this thing between them. That he just about lost it over her looking at him. Over the way she moved her eyes over him like she wanted to devour him. Like she wanted to consume him whole.

He wanted her to. Wanted to be consumed in this, consumed in the two of them.

She took her bra off, sliding the bright yellow fabric down her arms and tossing it onto the floor. Then he bent down, picked her up from the couch and carried her back toward the bedroom. He nuzzled her neck, kissing her gently as he laid her down on the mattress. "I want you. So much. You can't even know."

"I do," she said, curving her hand around his neck and kissing his mouth. And for a moment, it felt like enough. For a moment, in that bedroom, with just the two of them, it felt like everything it could ever need to be. And he knew that when it was finished, they were going to have to talk. And he knew that when it was finished, it wasn't going to be that simple. But right now it was.

The next breath he took blended into hers, and now it just seemed to go on. As she moved her hands over his body, as he lost himself in her. And he remembered thinking—it seems so long ago—that she wasn't a conventionally beautiful woman. That she wasn't the kind of woman he usually chose. He couldn't even see that now, because she was the kind of beauty carved out specifically for him. As if each part of her had been made to appeal to a part of him.

As if they were Adam and Eve.

He pulled her down over the top of him, her silken body over his. She pressed her hands down to his stomach, and he looked up at her, reveling in the view. Her wild hair falling over the plump curves of her breasts, her skin pale and lovely, unknowing, with a smile on her lips.

And then she rocked her hips just so, and brought the slick entrance to her body over the head of his arousal, and he nearly lost it then and there. She was the only woman he'd ever been with without using that barrier of protection, and once she'd said it was fine, well, they'd dispensed with condoms entirely. He had never been in the kind of relationship where he would do that. And with her... With her there were no barriers. With her there was nothing but this. He rocked his hips upward, plunging deep inside of her, grabbing hold of her hips and bring her down as he moved out. She gasped, letting her head fall back. And then she began to move her hips in a knowing, sensuous rhythm. Because she knew him. And her. The secrets of their pleasure together.

She began to whimper, fractious little kitten sounds coming up from her throat, and then he gripped her hard, reversing their positions, bringing her down onto the soft mattress. Because he couldn't wait anymore. Couldn't take her teasing anymore. Because he needed her to know.

That this was real. And she was his.

She was his.

He released his hold on his control, pounding hard inside of her, letting his body say what words felt insufficient to express.

The depth of how much you need her. Of how much he wanted them to be one. Because they were in this. In their desire for one another. She looked up at him, and there were tears in her eyes, and he felt an answering expansion in his chest. Emotion flooding him, filling him.

Mallory.

Fate.

Every step, every broken piece of that rocky road that he walked...

It was worth it to be here.

In this moment.

With this woman.

Everything was worth it.

He pressed his forehead to hers, his release threatening to overtake him. But he couldn't take it, not until she had hers.

"Oh, Mallory," he whispered. "Please."

And as if she knew exactly what he was asking for, she shattered. Bright and brilliant beneath him. Her cries of desire were the most wonderful thing he'd ever heard. The most essential thing.

He swallowed them as he tasted her lips, as he shuddered and spent himself inside of her.

"I love you," he said against her mouth.

So she could hear it. So she could feel it.

So she could know.

That everything she'd said she didn't want, they became.

That everything he knew they needed, they were.

## CHAPTER TWENTY

MALLORY'S SKIN WAS sweat slicked, her body buzzing from the release she just had. From him. He was still thick and hard inside of her even though he'd come, and he was looking at her so...

She had to look away. She couldn't keep looking at those eyes.

"Colt," she whispered.

"I love you," he said.

And those words that she'd been trying to deny, trying to ignore, rolled over her like a wave. She had tried to shut her ears, trudged up the mountain, tried to pretend that it wasn't happening. The dread that had bloomed low in the pit of her stomach that first time grew. A creeping vine of terror that made her want to escape the room. Escape her skin. That made her want to be anywhere else.

"I'm not supposed to be doing this right now," she whispered. He held her down, held her fast, his hand the strong grip on her jaw.

And that was when she realized something that frightened her, sickened her. Not at him, at herself.

She couldn't control this man. She couldn't put a limit on his feelings, she couldn't make them something comfortable. She couldn't put him in any position in her life and tell him to stay there. Ply him with housing, with sex twice a week, with fake moans of desire when she wasn't in the mood, but didn't want to hear complaints.

She couldn't hold herself distant from him. It would be this. All the time. Every day. This demanding, greedy thing.

She couldn't turn him into a patient and have office hours. She couldn't treat him like a child and give him an allowance and send him off on his way.

He would feel what he felt. He would make demands that he expected to have met.

He would require the deepest parts of her. Every day. Relentlessly. And she would have no defense against him.

She couldn't control him, she couldn't contain him, she couldn't fashion him into the image of a boyfriend in the way that she wanted, because Colt would never be anything quite so domestic as a boyfriend. He never could be. Men like Colt were never boyfriends. Lovers, sure.

Husbands. Yeah, they could be that.

Tears filled her eyes and she tried to get away from him. But she couldn't. Until he let her go.

Her heart was pounding, in terror, because this was the culmination of everything she had sensed from the first moment she had seen him again that morning in the coffee shop. There was something bigger than this, something bigger than them, and she couldn't do anything to find it. To escape it.

And not only was *he* something she couldn't control or get away from, *this* was.

Of course it was. Because hadn't it turned out that Griffin was related to him by marriage? That she was renting his cabin?

And she was everything terrified and small. Like a nervous rodent that wanted to go back to her den.

"I can't do this right now," she said. "And neither can you. You have… You have Lily, and you need to think about her. I have to think about starting my business, and I have to think about… Colt, I can't go from living with one man to living with another. I have to… I have to be by myself. I have to get my head on straight."

"Why?"

"Because I have to," she said. "This is… This is surrogacy for the independent life that I'm supposed to be building, and it's just another crutch. I can't go doing that. I can't hobble myself forever because I went from one relationship to another."

"Don't you dare compare what the two of us have to anything that you had with him."

"You know… It's healthy for somebody to be by themselves after they've been in a long-term relationship."

"You know this as well as I do," he said, his voice hard and firm. "People die. They die every day. They die sooner than they were planning on it. They die when their children are grown, they die before their daughters are born. I've seen it happen. Too many times. I've loved too many people that I've lost. I'll be damned if I wait. Because there may not be a later, Mallory. There may not be a future to go and get healthy for. You've got love now. Isn't that healthy? Isn't that what everybody wants to find? Isn't that the thing that we're all healing *for*? What we're all breathing for? To love somebody. To be loved back. It's the one thing that I could never accept because it was the one thing that terrified me. It was one thing that I knew could hurt the worst, but it's the only thing that was ever going to fix the shit show that is my emotional baggage. I was protected for a time. By my own inability to connect. By the guilt and the grief that I kept wrapped around me like a shield. But I wasn't living. I was looking for purpose because that was easier than looking for love. But you… You opened me up to something completely different."

"That was Lily," she whispered. "That was Lily that did that."

"No. Because without you I never would've taken Lily in. Without you, I wouldn't have thought that I could love her. Wouldn't have thought that I could be a father to her. Without you, it never would've happened."

"No, you just think that. You just think that because…" And that nervous, scurrying thing inside of her moved around until it found something he could get purchase on. Something that made sense. Because this didn't make sense. And this terrified her. But this one excuse, well, that made it all feel better. And it made it easier to say no. "And now you think you need me."

"Oh," he said, gripping her chin. "I know I need you. I know full well that I need you. To be my partner. To be my wife."

She shrugged away from him, standing up from the dead. "To be your wife so that I can be Lily's mother?" The words made her stomach ache, made it feel as if her chest was caving in on itself.

Here was a man standing there offering her the world. Dreams that she had carried around inside of herself and she couldn't… She couldn't bring herself to believe it. Not really. She was waiting for the catch, she was waiting for the other shoe, and she would make one, collaged together out of desperation if she had to, so that she wouldn't be blindsided by it later. Because that was the one thing she couldn't stand.

She couldn't stand to be blindsided.

She couldn't stand to live this… Raw unprotected life. It was too dangerous. And she would only end up being hurt. She had learned that a long time ago… But it didn't help to be soft. You didn't win anything by being soft. You just had to keep doing things so that… They stayed busy enough, so they stayed important enough.

But she wouldn't be able to keep her distance with him.

Because he was demanding everything from her, and what would happen if he decided later that he wanted nothing? What would she do?

She would die of it.

She had watched the way that Griffin's grief had nearly consumed him.

And she already knew what it was like. To lose her own love. To lose her dreams. To be exposed, vulnerable and grieving and to have no one who was able to comfort you because you were too ashamed to confess your sins.

She couldn't be that needy again, that vulnerable again.

Oh, there was a reason she'd stayed with a man who hadn't had access to her innermost heart, and there were a thousand things she'd told herself. A thousand reasons she'd given. Guilt and necessity and history.

But he'd kept her safe. Because he'd wanted nothing. Given nothing she couldn't live without.

And Colt would want everything. He'd see everything and know everything and she just… She couldn't.

"I can't do it. Can't be this thing you need me to be. You want a nanny, and I get that."

"I want a wife."

"Put out an ad, then, Colt," she said, her voice breaking. "I bet like three hundred women would answer it in the first day."

"No. Dammit, listen to me, Mallory. I want you to be my wife. Stop taking what I said and making it mean something else. I want you to be my wife. I want you to be the one that I come home to every night. I want you to be the one that

I… That I unload this unimaginable grief on. I'm sorry. I know I'm asking a lot of you. But I want you to be the one who understands me. The one I let in. I want you to be the one I write songs about. Because I'm going to write songs. I want you to be the one that's with me when I freak out because Lily started driving. And you know what, I want to have more kids."

His voice fractured, and the shards of it dug into her soul. "With *you*. I'm going to be afraid the whole damn time. Afraid that something's going to happen to them because I know the world to be relentlessly cruel. I want you to be the one to hold my hand through that. You're right, I guess. I do need you. I don't need you to pay my bills. And I don't need you to be my mother. I need you to be my partner. I need you to shoulder a hell of a lot. And I think you can. Because I think you're my fate, Mallory. But we have to take it. It doesn't ask, believe me. It just takes what it feels like. But when it gets here, you have to put your hand out. You have to grab on. Because it doesn't force your hand and it never will. And that's why it can feel like it's relentlessly cruel. Because you're passive when it's taking. But you've got to show up for the giving. You just damn well do. So I'm here, and I'm showing up. I'm opening my hands. I'm saying all, take it all. Hold it all. What do you need me to carry, Mallory? Because I will carry it."

But she couldn't. She couldn't put that on him, couldn't expect that of him. She just couldn't do it. How could she give him all of her… Her mess.

She'd wanted to be happy with herself.

But that was easy.

This… This was impossible.

"I don't want this," she said. "Colt, the things you want…

I don't even know if I can give you. I already lost a baby. What if I can't carry one?"

"I don't care," he said. "It doesn't matter. I'm sorry I said that. I just… I would love to have a baby, but if we can't, that's fine."

"You say that but you don't know, and it's…it's too much. I need time. I need to start my clinic. I need to spend more time with my brother. And this wasn't part of the plan. I just can't… I can't be that for you. I'm sorry. But I can't. I won't."

"I'm going to need you to find a new place to live, then."

Her heart slammed against her breastbone. "What? Are you… You're punishing me for rejecting you?"

"No," he said. "But I can't look at you if I can't have you."

"I thought we were at least friends. Lily is attached to me and I…"

"You can't be halfway with her either. I'm not doing this. I'm not playing a game with you. I opened my damn self up. I feel it all. Everything that I've been protecting myself from for all these years, I feel it now. For you. But you can't have one foot in this. You can't have one hand holding on to me. I realize you had an entire relationship like that for fifteen years. But I am not him. I am not some whiny ass mama's boy who needs your money. I need your heart. I need your damned soul, Mallory Chance. If you can't give that to me then you can't give me anything."

"It's not fair," she said.

"What's not fair?" he asked, zeroing right in on her tentative handhold. Zeroing right in on everything she feared most. "That I won't let you turn me into something easy? That I won't let you make me into a shield? I don't really damn well care. I don't care if it's not what you want. I don't care if it's not what makes you comfortable. I want you to be uncomfortable. Because I'm bleeding. My mom said that I was brave, and I took that to mean that I needed to do something dangerous. I told myself that's what it meant. Because I knew that the kind of brave she really saw in me, the kind of brave she really wanted me to be would destroy me. But here I am, daring your destruction. Because I'll have it all, or I'll have none of it. Because we are not playing at intimacy. It won't be sex without love. Or a relationship without intimacy, or a transaction. Is that it?"

He took a step toward her, his eyes far too keen. "You want a transaction. You were fine when you were helping me out. You left as soon as you decided that I didn't need you. That had nothing to do with me. That has to do with you. You're afraid. I wish I knew why. Who made you feel like you couldn't be loved, Mallory?"

She felt like she was running. Her heart was pounding so hard, her eyes filling with tears. "Stop it. Stop acting like you have some deep insight into me just because you've seen me naked."

"I do. Because I know you. Because I've told you all of my shit. You told me about your boyfriend, but you didn't tell me how you came to be in a relationship with that bastard. And I want to know."

"I don't want to talk about it. I don't want to talk about any of this."

"Then, like I said. You must decide where you're going to stay."

"That's just… It's not fair."

"No," he said. "What isn't fair is that you're alive. You're alive—Trent is dead. You're alive—my parents are dead. You're alive and you don't want to live. And believe me, that would've been the pot calling the kettle black just a couple of weeks ago. And I realize that now. There is no point in going on about everything if you're just doing it to stay safe.

I love you. And yeah, I want it all. The deepest, messiest parts of you. I want you to need me, the way that I need you. I want you to be mine. The way that I want to be yours. And when you can take that. When you can handle it… Well, then you can find me."

He dressed, and she watched him. Was powerless to do anything to stop him. And she waited. For fate to intervene, because hadn't it done so already with them? More than once? And it made them find each other repeatedly.

And the words exploded out of her mouth. "You don't want me," she said. "How can you? I am…broken, Colt."

His face went flat. "What?"

"I felt wrong always. And Griffin was so…he was so great, with trophies in every case and…and so many friends. I was never that. I was just me, and it never felt special. And I thought I was special when Jared liked me, and so I slept with him. And then I got pregnant. I was afraid. I was so afraid of what my parents would say because Griffin would never…he would never." She choked on those words, her throat burning. "I hid it, but I thought… I thought I'll show them though, that I can handle this, but I kept being afraid to tell them, and then… I had a stillbirth. My…the doctor just didn't care about me. I was just another dumb girl who got herself in trouble to him, and he didn't even let me see the baby. He just…they just took her. The nurse said I didn't want to see her anyway because it was early, but I wish I had. I wish I had. I…" Her throat felt raw, emotions thick there and expanding, bigger, wider. "I failed her. I got myself into trouble, and I couldn't even… I couldn't make it right by being a good mother. I couldn't… I never even held her."

She wasn't supposed to be reliving it. Hurting all over again.

"I named her Lucy because she should have a name. Even though she didn't get a birth certificate."

He took a step toward her. "Don't," she said. "Don't. I don't want to do this. I don't want to relive this. I don't want...*this*. I can't try again and not be good enough, and not be what you need. You know... Jared was easy because he wasn't good enough for me. He wasn't. You're right. And I never had to worry about being less when I was with him either."

She didn't know how else to say it and she didn't want to. She didn't want to go deep. Didn't want to show him her heart, her soul.

It hurt too much.

She couldn't bear the rejection. Inevitable. Painful.

"Mallory, is it Lily? Is it too painful to..."

*Yes.* Yes it was too painful. Because she wanted to be Lily's mother, and she couldn't let herself do that either. "No," she said. "It's not Lily. It's you. This. Us. I'm not the woman you want me to be. Not the woman you need me to be. And I don't want to try. I'm tired. I'm tired and I'm... hurt. And I just want to..."

"Hide?" he asked.

That hurt. Because it was true. "What's wrong with that?"

"Remember when you told me you had years you didn't feel? That's what hiding gets you."

"How would you know?" she asked. "You were hiding too, just with adrenaline. How do you know you aren't doing it now? Trying to make yourself feel better by putting all the right pieces in order. Child, wife. I'm not saying there's anything wrong with that, but don't act like your coping mechanisms are better than mine."

"This is not how I'd choose to cope, Mallory," he bit out. "I'm sorry. About your baby. I'm sorry that you were hurt.

Someday though, you're going to have to let someone in. Prove that they won't hurt you."

"No, I don't." She could have gone on, but she decided not to. She just stood there and stared him down until he turned.

Until he walked away.

Until he walked out.

But once he was gone, she realized, that he was right.

Healing wasn't going to be magical. And if she could have done it alone, she would have.

But it was going to require her peeling back layer after layer. It was going to require her to sit with herself. It was going to require her to confront all the deep dark things that existed underneath the surface, and her own fear along with it.

And sitting there, she just didn't know if she was that kind of brave.

She understood now. Why a man would join the rodeo.

Because if this was learning to heal, learning to love, then even she would rather take being trampled by a bull any day of the week.

Because she thought that she was running away to Gold Valley to start a new life, but in reality, she had just been coming to find more of the same.

Something that was all hers. Something she could conduct, control.

Removing herself from any kind of accountability.

But even though she could see that, she didn't know what else she could do. Even though she could see it, she didn't know how to find the bravery in herself to go after them. Because the bottom line was, he'd said that he loved her.

And she knew that to accept it would be to surrender. To something that would take it all from her. All her emotions. All her everything.

And she didn't want to give that to someone else.

She didn't want to expose herself to loss and rejection.

Not ever again.

But this was the alternative. And it was hell.

And unlike that day in the hospital, that day of loss and pain, this was a hell of her own making.

But she didn't know how to climb out of it. She never had.

If she had… She would have done it fifteen years ago.

*He offered you his hand. You didn't take it.*

And she worried that now she'd be stuck down here forever.

# CHAPTER TWENTY-ONE

COLT WAS SITTING in his living room, holding Lily and drowning in misery. He'd said that he loved her. He tried to get her to see what he felt.

And all that pain had poured out of her, and he hadn't been able to stop it, or help it.

And he wasn't a man given to misery, not after all the things he'd been through. He preferred guilt. He preferred a good healthy dose of martyrdom and shame. Because all those things went well with liquor. And this was just heartbreak, and that was something he wasn't equipped to handle.

He looked at Lily, sleeping in her bassinet, and his heart did something strange.

"Someday," he said. "Some asshole is going to come into your life. I'm going to hate it. I'm going to have to figure out how to deal with your heartbreaks. I'll tell you what. I'm never going to let you date a man like Mallory did. Because he did a number on her."

But it was more than that. He knew that. The loss of the baby was a grief that hurt her still. But there was something more too.

He also didn't know what to do about it. Didn't know what to do to make her see that when he said he loved her, it wasn't a manipulation tactic. That when he said he wanted forever, he damn well meant it. Well, there's always been one way he'd known how to express himself. But he hadn't written a song in a long time, and he sure as hell hadn't written about grief. About loss. About love.

He picked up his guitar and began strumming. Lily shifted, and maybe it was a coincidence, but he saw a little smile on her face. He was broken. But he was determined not to close himself off again. Because he had to be better for Lily. He had to do better for himself.

For his family.

And he started to strum, and as he did, a melody came straight from his heart. That Mallory melody.

And with it, lyrics, the first that he'd heard inside his soul for years. He strummed until he found the progression. The one that matched the echo in his heart. And then he started to write. It wasn't for anyone. Just for him. But it was something he'd stopped himself from doing after his parents had died. He only played other people's music. Because it was easier. Because the words in his own soul were something he didn't dare give voice to. He would now. Even broken. Even bleeding.

In the end, there was one truth that was before him, glaring and bright and brilliant as the sun.

And that was that he could love her whether she ever loved him back.

But he could love exhaustively, even if she did say no. Because eventually love would win. Eventually, it had to.

It was the only thing that could heal.

It was the only thing that gave him the strength to get through it—the very same thing that made her breathe was the same thing that was going to make sure she survived.

All that imperfect love.

It didn't need to be perfect.

It just needed to be brave.

# CHAPTER TWENTY-TWO

MALLORY WAS AFRAID that it was too late. Because she felt hollowed out and stunned, the way that she had when her sister-in-law and niece had died.

But fear gripped her, fear kept her from going after him. And she just sat there in that cabin that he told her to leave, feeling small and wounded.

*He loved her.*

He'd said that he loved her.

But how would she ever...

She had never been enough. That fear had driven her for her entire life. Every time she'd felt compared to Griffin, and been found lacking. Every time teachers had said *oh you're Griffin's sister!* Only to be met with her average performance by comparison with her exceptional older brother.

*You can do it, Mallory. You just have to apply yourself.*

Except she had applied herself, and it had all been... Average.

And then she'd thought she'd found a place in school. And then, even though she'd felt shame over her pregnancy, she'd also felt a fire inside her. Maybe she could show her parents...that she could do that. Overcome that.

But she hadn't. And then her performance at school had slipped even more. She'd wound herself more tightly around the boyfriend they didn't approve of, and they'd never understood why. They'd just...

*Not everyone can be like Griffin, Mallory, it's okay.*

Supportive, but painful. She'd wanted so much to be special like he was. And she just hadn't been.

She was afraid she still wasn't, and as the years had gone on, she didn't even have a clear idea of what it was supposed to mean. It was just a feeling.

This desperate, clawing inadequacy that had become part of her identity. A lifestyle of atonement.

And wasn't that why it hurt so much when she hadn't rescued Griffin and returned him to her parents?

Even Lily…well, Colt had rescued her.

And he felt like maybe Mallory had rescued him. He'd said that, her beautiful Colt, who had given to her like she mattered before he ever even knew who she was.

She wept. Fresh tears.

Like her whole body might break apart. Because how was she supposed to ever… It was exhausting, feeling all of this. And the only way that life had been bearable up to this point was the barrier that she had placed between herself and the people around her. Because she had learned.

After years and years of trying to make her parents proud, that it was better to just… Just do things that made them happy, not make waves, go on her way being accepted because of what she could do.

She'd stuffed all her pain deep down; she'd stopped trying to be like Griffin. She'd decided to get on with things and…

Her parents had learned that they could rely on her, and that was better than proud. Or at least, it was the only kind of satisfied she'd ever figured out how to be.

The only way to protect herself. And she had, good Lord, she had. She'd never told them about what felt like her biggest failure, her biggest pain.

She'd stayed with Jared. One part unresolved grief, one part punishment, one part self-protection.

And all of this, all of this with Colt, there was no defense. There was nothing. Nothing but feeling, and she didn't know how to make it okay. Because it was everything that she had done her best to guard against from the time she was fifteen years old.

And she'd realized there was just nothing she could do. And she found other small ways to be acceptable. Ways that had carried her through graduation, through not getting accepted into college. Through ups and downs in her relationship with Jared. Through the loss of her sister-in-law and her niece. She had found things she could *do*. And people appreciated that, and even if she couldn't be exceptional, she could be someone people needed.

And keeping busy meant there was less to feel. Less to…

She blinked hard, trying to keep herself from weeping.

And then she found herself in her car, driving toward Griffin's house, because she didn't know what else to do. Iris was the one who opened the door.

"Mallory," she said. "Come in. You look… Terrible."

"Thanks," Mallory said, sitting down on the couch, her legs numb. "I feel terrible. Nice to know that I'm… An accurate portrayal."

"What happened?"

"Colt…"

"That bastard," Iris said. "I will gut him."

She looked up at Iris, feeling miserable. Her sister-in-law was the sweetest person on the planet, and if she was offering to disembowel someone, it was because she felt really passionately about something. "I think I'm the one that you should gut."

"Why?"

Griffin chose that moment to walk into the room. "What's going on, kiddo?"

"I… I broke up with Colt."

Both Iris and Griffin stared at her. "Well, if you chose to do that, shouldn't you be… I mean it was the right thing to do then," Iris said, looking visibly disappointed.

"I don't know if it was," she said. "But I don't know how to say yes to him. I don't know how to… Griffin, how did you do it? You lost someone, and now here you are. But I don't know how to do the right things to make this work, to make myself feel okay. I don't know how to not be scared."

"I don't know how to not be scared either," he said. "Honest to God truth. I'm scared all the time. I'm scared for Iris's health. I'm scared about the baby. I'm scared because I know that I can't trust in a happy ending, not when there are so many forces in the world outside of my control."

"How do you stop being scared?" Mallory asked.

She felt so small. So small and so… Inadequate. And hadn't she always next to Griffin? Her favorite person, her idol. The person she could never measure up to.

Her fears felt petty next to his.

Her fears of loss and rejection, because as much as her grief stung, it didn't create a lasting fear of loss, but of failure. Heaped on failure.

"Tell me what's going on."

"I just… Griffin, you understand. After Mel died, and you left, Mom and Dad fell apart. They were worried for you, yes, but also you know… You're their favorite. I don't mean that they don't love me, they do. They were just always so impressed with you. You were their firstborn son, the one that they planned. The only child they ever intended to have. And… Then came me. I'm just not you. You were brilliant, and you went out in the world and you made your own fortune and you did all this stuff that just blew them away. Griffin, they love you so much. Everything about you. Everything you are. And it just isn't the same for me. And…"

"Mallory," he said. "You are exceptional. All on your own. We're not the same person, but we don't have to be."

"But…"

"Does he love you?"

"He says that he does. I'm afraid. I'm afraid that I'm not going to be enough for him. I just…everything I've tried at I've fallen short." The words stuck in her throat. The whole truth.

"Remember," Iris said. "Remember what I said to you? About how sometimes it's that right kind of love. Maybe you have to trust that you're that for him. Because my cousin… He has kept himself separate. From everyone and everything for years. If he said that he loves you, then it's real. And you have to trust in your love for him."

"What if I can't? Because if he hurts me then I'm going to… I'm never going to recover. I… I chose Jared for a lot of reasons, but one of the big ones was… I didn't worry about being special enough for him. I didn't fear losing him, and I always knew he'd be back. I always knew that I had the upper hand, that I was the better one in that relationship. And I can't… I can't control this. He wants everything from me. And he even has a baby. I love her so much. I love him so much. And it's like my heart is being pulled out straight to my throat, and I'm just afraid that I'm going to get hurt." It sounded so lame. It sounded like an excuse, because it was.

"Life doesn't come with guarantees," Griffin said. "It's the love that makes it worth it."

She broke down. And she told him. Everything. About the baby. About how she'd been alone in her pain, her failure, her misery.

And he held her while she cried, and Griffin wasn't disappointed in her.

"I just wanted to do something right. And I knew it would have upset them at first that I got pregnant so young, but I thought once I had the baby and gave them their first grandchild, and showed I was responsible, they'd accept it. And I just... I couldn't even do that right, Grif. I couldn't keep my baby alive."

"Mal," he said, his voice rough, breaking. "I know how that feels."

She shook her head. "You went through so much worse."

"No," he said, his voice rough. "Grief is grief. Loss is loss. You don't need to hide yours. Honey, don't make it second best to me. You're not. Your feelings aren't."

His words rocked her to her core.

Because it was true.

She'd been so sure she was second—and she'd decided her loss was second too—that it didn't matter, or that worse it was her fault.

She was the one who'd decided, before anyone else could, that she didn't deserve the support. That she wasn't worthy of it.

And that was how Mallory found herself driving back down the freeway. She didn't sing. She went with the radio off. Because she didn't really feel rebellious so much as desperate. She felt sad, unable to sort through her emotions.

Underneath them though, underneath was fear. And it drove her fast and far.

By the time she arrived at her parents' house just outside of San Francisco, she was gritty eyed, starving and emotional. And when her mother opened the door, she burst into tears.

"Come in," she said, ushering Mallory inside.

"Please tell me it's not that ass again," her dad said.

"No," she said. "It's not. It… It's me," she said. "I…"

"Come sit down," her dad said.

She ended up sitting at the kitchen table, cups of tea in front of all of them, though she felt like she wasn't strong enough. Not for the conversation they had to have.

"I know that I was a surprise," Mallory said.

"Today?" her dad asked.

"No. I mean… Me. As a baby. And that Griffin is so much older than me and…"

"You're a blessing," her mom said.

"I… You said that. You have. But I just always felt like Griffin was… Like he was the gold standard. Like maybe you would've been better off with just him. Because I struggled to do so many things that he did easily."

"Mallory," her mom said. "You made our family complete."

"No, I…" She put her hands up against her eyes. "I need to finish what I'm going to say. Because I'm not trying to make you feel bad. But… You say all these things, and you said all these things. But it doesn't change the way that I feel. Every time I would bring home a report card and it was Bs and Cs you would tell me I just needed to keep working and it would get better. Because Griffin had straight As and… I just could never be that. And I felt like I wasn't being good enough. But I was good at other things. I gave my friends lots of advice I… I got important in my group of friends for being mature. And that made me feel special. I was important because I had a boyfriend."

"Oh, Mallory," her mother said. "Is that why? Is that why he was so important to you?"

"That is a longer story."

And over hours and tea, long into the night she told her

story. About Jared. About loss. About how she had hoped that it would make her special. And about how she couldn't figure out how to tell them when it was over. About the great conflicting fears she'd had inside of herself. Because it was impossible to explain and rationalize even in her own head, the shame that she had felt combined with being certain that once she'd had the baby everything would be okay. And then when that baby was gone, the crushing failure that she wasn't good enough. And that all it had been was a mistake. A punishment maybe.

"I wanted to be special," she said, her voice thin and scratchy from so many hours of talking. Of crying. "And it was just... In the end, I was nothing but damaged. In every way. And then I started doing worse in school and I... I don't know. I figured it out. I figured how to pick myself up. But I didn't go to med school. And I didn't become a huge success the way that Griffin did. And I... I didn't want to hurt you."

"Mallory," her mom said, her eyes red from her own tears. "You are special. And I hate that you went through this alone. But the worst thing is I'm not sure how we could have handled it. How we would have. Because regardless of the kind of parents I think we were, we obviously left you with scars. I can't tell you how much I regret that you didn't know how to talk to us. That you dealt with something that deep, that painful on your own."

"It's my own fault," Mallory said. "I just... I decided that I thought I knew what you felt about me, and I let it dictate everything that I did. And I don't know the answer to it. I don't know how to make myself feel like I'm good enough. I keep waiting. And there's a man in Gold Valley, and he thinks I'm great, but I'm so afraid that someday he's just going to see all the failures that I see. That I'm going to spend years trying to live up to this love that he's offering me, and I don't know if I can."

"Mallory," her father said, speaking after a long silence. "I wish I would've said this to you years ago. I wish I would've had the words to say it years ago. But *special* does not come from what you do. It is not grades on a report card, or a degree on the wall. It isn't money in the bank. Special comes from being loved. When people love you, you occupy an essential place in their world. You are special, Mallory. Because we couldn't live without you. Simply because you're you. And I'm sorry that we did a bad job of making sure you knew that that love wasn't dependent on anything. I'm sorry that our encouragement became impossible hoops for you to jump through. Because it was never meant to be."

Mallory nearly dissolved, right there. At three in the morning with the weight of the world resting on her. And she knew then that it was true. She hadn't missed Griffin's trophies or grades or achievements when he had gotten married and gone away. She had missed him. She hadn't missed his beautiful house or his job when he had lost Mel and the baby and moved to Oregon. She had missed him.

He was special because she loved him. And maybe that's what she'd been missing all along. Maybe he wasn't the most amazing human being in the entire world. Maybe she just loved him a whole lot.

"I don't understand why... Why I don't just know this."

"You have to love yourself too, Mallory," her dad said. "Because if you do... Maybe you'll start to see what the rest of us see. Maybe you'll start to see what this new man of yours sees."

So she did that. For a full minute. Just sat there, trying to look at herself through the eyes of her parents. Colt. She wasn't perfect. But what she saw was a strong, determined

THE TRUE COWBOY OF SUNSET RIDGE

woman, who had made mistakes and gotten up from them. Who did an awful lot to care for the people around her. And yes, some of it came down to martyrdom. Martyring herself to the cause of becoming indispensable. Of earning favor.

But there was a whole lot of care in it too. A whole lot of good.

"I know better," she said finally. "Than to believe that my baby being stillborn was my own failure. I literally made it a career to learn everything I could about it and try to find a way to forgive myself."

"Did you?" her dad asked, softly. "Or were you looking for ways to condemn yourself?"

The question dropped the bottom out of her world yet again. Because wasn't that true? Hadn't she always been looking for ways to continue condemning herself so that she could stay in that safe and protected place that didn't ask herself to try again.

She'd been so certain that she wasn't afraid in the way that Griffin was. That she wasn't protecting herself in the way that Griffin was.

But maybe she was. Maybe in the end, she was.

"It's all just fear," she said. "Isn't it?"

"That's most of life. Being afraid and figuring out how to do things anyway."

"I love him," she said. "But what I'm struggling to figure out is why he would love me. But maybe I'm really just afraid. That it won't work out anyway. That there's nothing I can do to improve myself, to be better, because actually maybe I am good enough and it still won't work out. What if I've been good enough the whole time? But it still won't... It still won't make everything work out in the end. If it's not my fault... It's not my fault then I guess losing Lucy was random. If it's not my fault then..."

"Then it's life," her mom said. "And that is scary. I didn't do a very good job of sharing this with you, Mallory. That much is clear to me. I was certain I couldn't have more children, and then I got pregnant with you. And I was afraid that my initial misgivings over the pregnancy would cause me to lose you. And then you were born, and you were beautiful and perfect. A gift. Not something I earned. Just something I was given. And that's the way the world is. We are given all sorts of good and bad things we don't deserve."

And she knew then, that there was never going to be a guarantee. And she also knew that it was about making a choice. A choice to live, no matter what. Because she had seen in obvious terms what it looks like when someone didn't—Griffin—and his retreat into the mountains. Those years of separation.

But she was no different. She had been around her parents, yes, but she had held herself separate, using the barrier of a boyfriend she knew they didn't like to go ahead and keep their disapproval where she could see it. Manage it. At acceptable levels. She had also used him to keep herself from being in a relationship she cared too much about. To keep herself frozen in a particular space that didn't require any more healing than she was ready to do.

Now she needed to decide if she was going to live. Really live. Push back her fear of not being enough. Push past her grief.

"I want to do that. I want to live. I really do. How do I do that?"

"I think you start by saying yes. To the scary things. The new things. The next thing," her dad said.

Mallory bit her lip and blinked hard, trying to keep tears from falling. "I think I'm in love," she said. "Really in love. Not like I pretended to be with Jared. I was pretending for myself, so that I could… Keep on hiding. But he doesn't want that version of me. That one that just takes care of everyone and doesn't actually share anything, the one who feels a lot of sad, messy things. And it scared me. It really did. I knew I needed to… I knew I needed to do this before I could ever say yes to him. I knew I needed to be honest with you."

"He'll be lucky to have you," her dad said. "Truly."

"I hope so. Because I know I'm lucky to have him."

She'd been on a quest to find herself. And she said all that stuff to Colt about being happy by herself, but of course she thought she could be happy by herself. It wouldn't challenge her. It wasn't about that. It was about feeling worthy of being with another person. Of being loved by another person. Of being needed—not as a piggy bank—but as an emotional partner. And the only way she could feel that was if she *decided* that she was worth it.

And if she decided that her heart, her soul, was worth it, no matter what anyone else thought.

She had to decide. No one else could do it for her. Least of all her parents.

"What's this guy like?" her mom asked, slowly.

"Oh well…" A smile touched her lips. "He's a cowboy."

## CHAPTER TWENTY-THREE

COLT HAD AVOIDED Sunday dinner. It wasn't that he didn't want to see his family, but he was too raw from everything that had happened with Mallory.

He would've said that he didn't have the capacity to be hurt. But he did. This was heartbreak. For sure and for certain. It had been three days since he'd sent her away. Since he'd seen her. He felt guilty, like he shouldn't have kicked her out. But then anger would kick through him, and he would go back to feeling like it was completely reasonable to not want the woman who'd rejected him to live on his property. It was an interesting thing. Because he had never been in love before. So, he'd kind of imagined that he would be one of those people who would be just fine with an ex, making her a friend.

But no. He wasn't. He wouldn't. Couldn't. He was too damned hurt.

But his feelings for her weren't gone. He loved her still, as sure as anything. There was a knock on his door, and his heart did something strange. Kicked up into his throat and pushed itself out. He went downstairs, his heart thundering like a son of a bitch, and opened the door. It was Jake and Callie.

"What are you doing here?"

"Came to see you. Iris and Griffin told me what happened."

"Damn. Of course they did. You know, from the beginning, she was way too up in my business."

"Yeah, well," Callie said, breezing in after Jake. "I'm babysitting. He's taking you out drinking."

"I don't feel like it."

"I'm not letting you revert to type," Jake said. "You don't get to go back to being inside yourself just because she didn't work out for you. Come on."

"I vote no," Colt said. "I'm brooding."

"You're going to do it with me. Over a drink."

And that was how he found himself in his brother's old ass pickup truck, headed out to the Gold Valley Saloon, a place he had not been to since the night he picked up Mallory. He didn't like it.

"You're mad," he said.

"Yeah, I'm mad. I told her that I loved her. After giving her the best sex of her life. She rejected me."

"Oh, you're *mad* mad."

"Yes," Colt bit out.

"And hurt."

"Fucking heartbroken," Colt said. "You know, I think you're an even bigger dick now than I did that night out on the porch at Ryder's, when you told me about how you rejected Callie. That hurts. You don't even know."

"I have a fair idea. Because I wasn't feeling so hot myself. I imagine your lady isn't either."

"Right. I'm sure she's feeling fine. It was her choice."

"According to Iris and Griffin, she was pretty broken up about it, actually."

"Then she shouldn't act like an idiot." He felt a mild bit of guilt over saying that, since he knew she'd been through hell.

But she hadn't given him a chance.

To be better.

To be better than her parents or her ex. To prove himself.

"We all act like idiots, though. You thought that she was supposed to be fine just because you up and healed from your stuff? I'm sure she's best on her own."

He thought about Jared. He thought about the fear that he saw in her eyes whenever things got too real.

He thought about all the soft, placating thing she said, the way that he was the one who ended up sharing while she just talked, probably about feelings, but never about details.

"I know she is."

"Yeah well. Would you give her a chance. To make it right?"

"I don't have a choice. I'm miserable without her. I... I wrote a song about her," he mumbled.

"Oh, well, now that is a miracle."

Just then, the door to the saloon opened, and he knew already that it was going to be her before he even saw her clearly. She was wearing another of her pretty, girly dresses.

"Did you know that she was going to be here?"

Jake clapped him on the shoulder and winked. "I'll see you later. Don't worry about Lily. Callie and I have it."

She walked over to him, looking pale, her eyes large. "Come here often?"

"I think you know I don't," he said.

"Yeah, but I wanted to be clever. An echo of the first time we saw each other. Because... That was real then, wasn't it? It was real, and I was... I was hoping to make it into something less. I was hoping to make it into just sex. Because that seemed easier. But... Colt, I think I've loved you from the first time I set my eyes on you. I just... I learned to make myself look so functional that nobody ever knew I was struggling. I did everything. Took care of everyone. And it allowed me to control how happy everyone was with me all the time. It let me feel like I controlled my…my feelings of inadequacy. And allowed me to stay in control of my feelings for the people in my life, so that I'd never be blindsided by loss again. When you said that you loved me… When you looked at me like that, I realized I didn't have any control. Because you do make me want to curl up and take a rest. To let you take care of everything. You make me just want to *be*. You make me wild, and you make me feel things that I didn't know I could feel. And it's… It's terrifying. Because you reached down inside of me and you exposed a place that I want to forget exists, because I know… I know how it will hurt if I can't make myself enough for you. If I fail at this. I wanted someone who needed me more than I needed him, even though I didn't realize it. But I need you so much, Colt. And you can't be placated or shoved aside—you see me. You really see me. And you call me out when I need it. And… You make it impossible for me to hide behind anything. And I want you. I want Lily. I want to love you both. But I don't know how to handle my fear."

He took a step toward her, and he couldn't be angry. Not now.

"Give it to me," he said. "Trust me. I will trust you. Neither of us have ever had a lot of trust in the world. Except… We found each other. I knew something from the moment I set eyes on you. The same as you knew me. It's not an accident."

"Do you really think we were meant to be?"

"I do. I feel it in my bones. Mallory," he said, "I've been cut off and broken for most of my life. Guilty and questioning, but when I'm with you, it all makes sense. When I'm with you, I know that I'm supposed to be here on this earth. When I'm with you, everything makes sense. You have to trust that."

"Colt, when I'm with you, I want to open up. I want to feel everything. I want to depend on you. And that's the scariest thing, because I've always thought I needed to be strongest so that I couldn't be let down by anyone."

"You can rest with me, sweetheart. I guarantee it."

"I want to."

"I love you, Mallory Chance. I have this whole time, even while you infuriated me."

Her throat worked, but he saw that it was a struggle for her to get the words out. She did, as tears filled her eyes and began to fall down her cheeks. "I love you."

"You'll come with me?"

She took his hand and led him out of the bar. Took him down the sidewalk and toward that motel. Where she already had a room.

"You planned this," he said.

"Yeah," she said. "Because… I realized that I had a lot of work to do. You. And me. And this is where I came that first night I was here. To hole up and make some decisions about myself. But you're right. You know, I've actually been alone this whole time. I used that relationship as pretense that I was fine and healthy. But I was just using it to make myself feel good. I avoided intimacy in that relationship, and it was easy. I kept my hopes, my dreams and my heart all to myself. I didn't even realize that I was doing it. While I played the blame game with all the things he did wrong, I didn't realize how much I set those expectations. How much I trained him to be a boyfriend. Because it suited me. Because it can be safe. Because it kept me from loving somebody that I couldn't live without. It's scary to love someone like that."

"I know," he said. "Believe me I know." She started to strip his clothes off of him, leaving herself fully clothed.

"Since I'm always naked first," she said.

"Yeah, but my heart was naked first," he said, pulling her up against him, letting her feel how much he wanted her.

"I know." She stepped back, stripped her clothes off, and when she joined her body with his, she said she loved him. Said it over and over again. And this time, when they were finished, he didn't leave that motel room. He just kept on holding her.

"I want you to marry me," he said. "Be my wife. Be everything."

"Lily's mother too?"

"Yes."

"I want that," she said, her words hushed, her voice thick with tears. "I want to be your wife. And her mother. I want it so much that it scares me. I fell into that... I thought it was a fantasy, Colt. I didn't think you could ever love me."

"Mallory, I could never love anybody else. Believe me. If I was going to, I would have at some point in the last thirty years, but it didn't happen."

"I'm still afraid," she said. "It's why I hid in that relationship for so long. It's why I never talked to my parents. Nothing has felt secure or safe or okay. I never felt like I had proven myself worthy enough to drop that sort of disappointment on them."

"I know. But we're here. And we get to choose." He pressed his forehead to hers. "We get to make the choice, and we can't ever know for sure what will happen down the road, but we can keep on choosing each other. Every day. I love you."

She sobbed. "Please love me. I am needy, and I love you so much that it makes me hurt. Please don't ever leave me. Please..."

He cut her words off with a kiss. "I do," he said. "I will. Forever."

MAISEY YATES

"Me too."

Colt had spent his life wondering what his purpose was. And lying here with Mallory Chance in his arms, he knew it. As deep as he knew anything. Right the way down to his bones.

To love. To be loved.

By her.

Forever.

# *EPILOGUE*

IT WAS HIM. The man. The fantasy man. Colt Daniels, standing there at the head of the altar in a black suit, black cowboy hat on his head, his blue eyes looking electric. Her parents were here, her mother holding Lily in her lap, the level of frill on Lily's dress completely out of control.

Today they were getting married. Today they were also signing Lily's adoption papers before the judge. It had been a little bit of a long road to get here, but after all the temporary guardianship and paperwork and relinquishing of parental rights, they were here. Here for the final day. Where they would become part of each other's lives on paper. The sealing of what was already meant to be, woven into the fabric of time.

She felt like family already.

Colt was the most beautiful man she'd ever seen in her entire life. From the first moment she felt like he was a cowboy god. But it was more than that. Deeper than that. She took his hands, and looked into his eyes. He was that missing part of her. And he made it not so scary to open herself up to love. Because she could trust him. He made her feel like she could trust herself.

And when they were done with their vows, and they kissed, he bent down and took Lily from her mother's arms and held her up between them.

"Well, I didn't think when you showed up in Gold Valley nine months ago that this is where we would be now."

"No I didn't. But you know, there's just some things you can't even know to hope for. And you're one of them. You were too good for me to imagine."

"Have I told you today that you're beautiful?"

"You have," she said. "But I'm happy to hear it again."

"And I love you."

"I love you too," she said. "Big and brave and forever."

And that was the kind of love they were both determined to teach Lily. Because even though she suffered some loss, there was plenty of love. And it might be imperfect, but it was real. And it was more powerful than any other force on earth. More than shame. More than fear. More than grief.

And they grabbed it with both hands.

\* \* \* \* \*

# THE COWBOY
# SHE LOVES TO HATE

This one is dedicated to my childhood favorites: Jimmy Spoon; Caddie Woodlawn; and Sarah, Plain and Tall. They're part of what shaped my love for Westerns. Books make all the difference.

# *CHAPTER ONE*

SHE WAS AT his front door. And damn if her hair wasn't in pigtails.

Nelly Foster was standing there, arms crossed over her chest, her expression bright and determined. "It's my birthday," she said.

But he was fixated on the pigtails.

When Taggart McCloud was thirteen years old, the one thing he'd wanted most in the world was to pull Nelly Foster's pigtails. Okay, maybe not *most* in the *world*, but the thing he'd wanted most while sitting slack-jawed and bored out of his mind in the one-room schoolhouse that he and all the other ranch kids attended on the sprawling property that contained Garrett's Watch, McCloud's Landing, Sullivan's Point and King's Crest and collectively made up the Four Corners Ranch.

And now that he was thirty-two, he found he still wanted to do it.

She was prissy, stuck-up, thought she was better than him… But she had been the teacher's daughter. And now she was the librarian of the largest town adjacent to Four Corners, which was not large at all.

At least, he'd heard tell she was the librarian. He'd never been in the library to see it with his own eyes. Tag wasn't a sit-still-be-quiet kind of guy. Tag was a get-shit-done kind of guy.

He had said that to Nelly, the adult equivalent of pigtail pulling, quite honestly, on another birthday of hers, nine years ago.

Her twenty-first birthday, to be exact, when the Sullivan sisters had dragged her down to the saloon to get drunk.

After twenty minutes of being there, all she'd succeeded in doing was sticking the tip of her tongue into the shot glass and screwing up her face into a horrified, disgusted expression. Which had made him laugh so hard he had damn near fallen out of his chair.

"Is something amusing to you, Taggart?" She had said his name like he might be in trouble. He had never understood how or why she could do that so effortlessly. She was younger than him. She had no call getting on his case about anything.

"You," he said, from his place in the corner. His brothers hadn't laughed, as he'd assumed they would, and his buddy Landry King had simply given him a sideways glance and said: *You have a death wish?*

A death wish.

He wasn't afraid of Nelly Foster.

"That's not how you do it," he said, standing up from the table and making his way over to the bar. Then he picked up the shot glass and downed it in one, setting it in front of her, making sure to maintain eye contact. A strange current of electricity shot between them. Like it always did. But it made no earthly sense.

Tag liked to have a good time. Nelly was so buttoned-up it would take a half hour to get to the potential good time, and even then, she would probably call it an early night because she had to get up in the morning to feed her cats. Or something.

"I'll take another shot." The color mounted in her cheeks, and that surprised him more than anything. But one thing he did know about Nelly was that when she was challenged, she dug in. She was as mulish as she was repressed.

Which was *a lot*.

The other whiskey shot appeared, and she looked at her friends, then back at him, before taking it to her lips and knocking it back. She swayed in her stool, then slammed it down on the scarred, wooden countertop. "More?"

He sat across from her, taking his jacket off and pushing up his shirtsleeves. "Sure."

It wasn't fair. He was going to drink the little mite under the table.

Two shots later and she was bright-eyed, but determined.

"I'm cutting you off," he said.

"No," she said. "You don't get to win. You always think you win." She was slurring slightly. "You don't know every-thing. You don't know everything about me."

"Oh, I don't know everything about you. I've known you since you were five years old."

"That means I've known you since you were seven," she said. "And that does not make you better than me or more mature than me." She stuck her tongue out at him. She was drunk. Nelly Foster was drunk. And his initial re-action to that was to be afraid, because her mother had been his teacher, and he could imagine Mrs. Foster coming for him with a switch. And the fact of the matter was, his dad wouldn't have lifted a finger to stop her. No. Seamus Mc-Cloud would've said that Tag was reaping what he sowed.

"I've never claimed to be more mature than you. But then, you were born a sixty-year-old spinster. I wouldn't be sur-prised if you came out holding a box of kittens."

In his drunken haze, that seemed like a real zinger. The problem was, he had started drinking a while ago, so these were not his first three shots of whiskey. He was ahead of her, which was fair, because she was probably an alcohol virgin.

That word stuck in his head. Stuck there hard.

*A virgin.*

"Is that the best you've got," she said, tipping her glass back and letting the last drop fall into her mouth. "You must've come out holding a bottle of Jack Daniel's and a note that says *I give up.* Because you've been nothing but a screwup since day one. And we all know it."

"There's a few things I'm good at," he said, something burning in his chest.

"Name one."

A smile tugged at his lips, and he knew that his mama would slap him upside the face for saying what he was about to say to Nelly Foster. But he was going to say it anyway.

"*Fucking*, Nelly. I'm damn good at fucking."

Her face turned bright red, and she slumped slightly in her chair. "Some people don't care about that," she said.

"Only because some people don't know what they're missing. Am I right?"

He forgot that his brothers were there. That they were watching. He forgot that her friends were sitting next to her, until they moved slightly, clearly ready to slap him or something if need be. But Nelly waved them off. "I don't need to know what I'm missing to know that I don't want it."

"Suit yourself. But I'll tell you what. My birthday gift to you. If you're curious. Cash in your chips."

"What?"

"Any birthday. From this to… To your thirtieth birthday. If you don't find some nice boy to teach you what it's all about, come see me. My door's always open." And then he got another ill-advised shot, took it down straight, and got up from the counter and left.

And if he had thought about that occasionally on her birthday—and remembered her birthday at all—he didn't tell anyone. In fact, no one ever talked about that night.

Not his brothers. Not Wolf.

Certainly not him and Nelly.

But here it was. Her birthday.

If he wasn't mistaken, her thirtieth birthday.

And she was here. At his door.

And then she did something very unexpected. She grabbed the large bag that was slung over her shoulder and lowered it, reaching inside and grabbing a bottle of whiskey. "Did you need this?"

"I'm sorry, what?"

He was still standing in the doorway; she was still standing on his porch, the light illuminating her brown hair, giving it a coppery, halo effect. He would be lying if he'd said he never noticed that Nelly had copper in her hair. He had. His brother Gus had once said that Nelly looked like a small brown mouse, and he argued. Because she didn't look like a brown mouse. Her hair was not dull or dusty, but quite something in the sun. Her eyes had that same sort of hidden vein of metal in them. You just had to look.

And he looked.

"Did you need whiskey? To remember. To get through it." She huffed a breath and then shoved past him right into his cabin. At least the place was clean. Not so much because of him, but because he had the cleaner for the main house come by once a week and give it a once-over. He worked too hard on the ranch to do much of any kind of housework. But he lived alone and he was out before dawn and home after dark. So there wasn't really another person or another time to get it done.

Not that it mattered what Nelly thought of his house. He didn't think she'd ever been in his house before.

"Honey, most people don't drink whiskey to remember. They usually drink it to forget."

Her cheeks went pink. "But we were drinking whiskey when…"

"When?" He knew. Because the memory was sitting sharp on his mind, and then it had been there, right there, the minute he had opened the door to see her standing there. Along with memories of her pigtails and how he found it irresistible to poke at her whenever she was around. How he found… How he found himself drawn to her, regardless of the fact that it didn't make sense. That they had nothing in common. That she was…

That she was her. And he was him.

"When you made your offer. For my birthday present. And I want it."

She walked over to his couch and sat. She set the bottle of whiskey down on the floor, folded her hands in her lap and locked her knees together.

And that was when he looked at her. Really looked at her, for the first time. She was wearing a floral dress with a little white collar that went all the way up to the base of her throat. The skirt of the dress fell past her knees even when she was sitting. She had on white socks. Black shoes. He didn't know why the white socks stuck out like they did. He didn't know why he found the white socks sexy, but he did. He should find nothing about her or this moment sexy. Because she was clearly having a breakdown of some kind or she wouldn't be here. And she was dressed like the librarian fantasy he would say he did not have.

*Right. Like you haven't had fantasies about her for years.*

Sure, he'd tried to keep them half-formed and vague. But sometimes… Sometimes.

And he always felt ashamed about it. Because there were plenty of women—bright, easy women—who really enjoyed a one-night stand. Who enjoyed having a good time with him and then saying goodbye in the morning. Or more accurately, later that same night. Nelly wasn't one of those women. Never had been. Still, there were times when it was tough for him to remind his body of that.

Right now being one of them.

Especially because she was… Well, hell.

"You want it."

"Yes," she said, clipped. She unfolded her hands for a moment, grabbed the top of the whiskey bottle, and scooted it to the side slightly, as if she was reminding him it was there.

"Why the whiskey?"

"Like I said. If you needed to jog your memory, or to blur the moment. Whatever you need to get in the mood."

"To get in the mood to… To be very clear, Nelly, are you asking me to fuck you?"

She bit her lower lip, her feet flexing, as she brought the toes of her black shoes up off the floor. "I do wish you wouldn't use such coarse language."

"The terms of the offer involved coarse language, so I'm not really sure why I would revise it now."

"I am uncomfortable," she said.

"There's no place for being uncomfortable in situations like this, Nelly, and if you are that uncomfortable, I suggest you walk your pretty self right back out the door."

"I walked all the way up here. I'm not leaving now."

She had always been stubborn. Stubborn and impenetrable. And the one time she had ever let her guard down was that night they'd done whiskey shots at each other at the bar. And since then it had been nine years of barely saying much of anything to each other. Anytime they had one of the big reunion potlucks at Four Corners over the summer, her mother would come, and Nelly would stand dutifully by. She always made polite conversation, particularly with the Sullivan sisters, who were a shade more civilized than the rest of them, it had to be said. And he would always get that impulse. That impulse to go and badger her. He was never sure why, that was the thing. But then when he got older, he started to understand. Whether it made sense or not, he was attracted to her. You didn't get the impulse to go over to a woman if it wasn't rooted in that. At least not in his world.

It was the stubbornness, he realized then. And the fact that she didn't melt or get silly around him. A lot of the girls at school had. They were a collection of different ages, all thrown together in one classroom, because the number of kids fluctuated so much from year to year, depending on who was working at the ranch, and the actual public school was so far away that it made more sense to just keep the kids close. Often there were new girls, and they were usually impressed by him. Hell, they were impressed by any number of the guys, but he'd always had an easy way with women. But not with Nelly. And it was that… The fact that she was work that appealed to him, and he couldn't quite say why.

"Are you going to tell me why?"

"All right. I was humiliated when you said that to me on my birthday. I was humiliated that you knew. And I'm humiliated that I'm here right now. But you weren't wrong." She swallowed. "I don't really know why, Tag, but you have been like a piece of gravel in my shoe since I was ten years old. Just… Always there, and always annoying. But I also know that you… Look, you're a decent guy."

He laughed. "Did it choke you to say that?"

"You are. Don't go being a dick about it now."

*"Dick?"*

"Well," she said.

"Salty language from the lady."

"You started it," she said. "The salty language. Anyway. This is the last year. The last year that you gave me to redeem the…the… The offer."

"And you want to redeem the offer."

"Yes. Because I'm tired of this. I'm tired of being me. I am a small-town librarian who has actually never seen a naked man. I'm a cliché, and I hate it. I want to be done with it. And you know what, it might as well be you. Because you already think I'm ridiculous. You already… You looked at me and you knew. You knew then. That I'd never been with anybody. So it's not a surprise to you to find out that it still hasn't changed."

It actually was. Hell, he'd been not entirely confident in his declarations that she was an obvious virgin back then. It appealed to him, and that was another thing that he couldn't quite sort out. Because virgins weren't really his thing. He preferred a girl who liked an easy good time. And already, this was several miles short of easy. This was something else entirely. And he couldn't quite put his finger on what. But the thing about Nelly was, he thought… He always thought that there was more to her. Like copper hair that was more than just brown. Like fire that seemed to rest just beneath the surface of all of that uptight… Everything. And so, it had been easy enough for him to imagine that she was kind of a freak. That maybe she took trips down to a bigger town and found herself men to indulge her appetites. It was just as easy for him to believe that as it was to believe that she actually was at home with her cat and a book on Friday nights. Because he had always sensed depth in her that wasn't all that simple. To contain, to define.

"All right. So, you're here because you're embarrassed, but you figure it's all right if it's me because you don't think I have a high opinion of you."

"That's right."

"Well, that's a hell of a thing," he said, pacing back and forth in front of her, his long legs eating up the length of the floor. "Nelly, don't you know you shouldn't go having sex with a man you don't think has a high opinion of you."

"I'm past caring," she said. "I just need to change. I'll take any man."

"Wrong answer," he said.

"I didn't realize there were strings attached to the gift." Suddenly, tears filled her eyes, and that shocked the hell out of him. "If you don't want me, I'm not going to beg. I can't take the humiliation. But you shouldn't have… That is the meanest thing that you've ever done. Say that you would, and then… And then, when I get up all my courage to come up here, you…"

And he couldn't take it anymore. So he reached out, hauled her up off the couch and into his arms, and he kissed her.

# CHAPTER TWO

FOR AS LONG as Nelly Foster had known Taggart McCloud, she'd thought he was irritating. And it wasn't until she had gotten older that she'd realized the feelings that she had for him weren't about irritation at all. But rather about the fact that what she wanted was to kiss him, right on the mouth. Just like he was doing right now.

She wanted to cry. Except that she already was. Humiliatingly. Crying in his arms while he gave her her very first kiss.

She didn't have the words to explain why she was here. Or why she felt all these... Things. It was just that her mother had always warned her to stay away from men. Especially charming, handsome men. Men like Taggart McCloud. And there was good reason for it. She herself had alternated between being afraid of all the feelings that he aroused in her and being angry about them.

Afraid because she had been conditioned to be. Her mother's own fears had imprinted on her from a young age, but still... Tag had reached past them.

She could remember the very first time she'd realized that she wanted to kiss him.

She had been fifteen, and he'd been seventeen. Tall and rangy and beautiful in a way that made her skin feel too tight. The thing was, there were any number of handsome men in his family and on the ranch. If you liked cowboys, they were a dime a dozen at Four Corners. But they had never mattered to her. They had never irritated her, never appealed to her and never frightened her. It was only Tag. It had only ever been Tag.

She had gone down to the lake with the Sullivan sisters and Breanna Lawson, and they were playing on the rope swing. And then Tag had shown up, along with Wolf Garrett and Landry King. She'd asked her friend Fia if the boys had to be there, but she had explained prosaically that the McClouds' beach was right next to the Sullivans', and she couldn't ask him to leave.

Anyway, they all shared the rope swing. And that was how they had ended up swimming with the older boys. And there was a point where she had ended up shivering on the bank, and Tag had given her that cocky grin of his and sat down next to her. And it had made the hair on her arms stand on end to have them so close. A droplet of water had slid from his hair down the bridge of his nose to his lips, and she'd watched it. And suddenly, everything in her had gone fluttery. Which had never happened before. Not quite like that. And that was when she'd realized that Taggart Mc-Cloud was beautiful.

And even worse, that her brain was composing some sort of bad poetry about wanting to be that drop of water on his lips. She'd scrambled up and run away. And she had not let herself read books with romance in them for at least six months, because every time she did, she ended up inserting herself into the scene with Tag. And she knew better.

Still, it had all felt fun and giddy even with all of the dire warnings of her mother in the back of her mind. Her father might have tricked her, might have hidden who he was and gotten it past her that he was a dangerous, evil man.

And then, on her twenty-first birthday she had gotten

tipsy for the first time. And she'd been so… So angry and so intoxicated to have him in her sphere. That was the thing about Tag. He always seemed to be there. And it didn't make any sense, because she was plain-Jane Nelly Foster, and he was… The sex god of Four Corners.

Well, one of them. There was a weirdly high number of hot cowboys there.

But either way, it never made sense that he was there. But he was. Always. And she hadn't been able to resist the push and pull between them, not with her defenses lowered. But then he'd gone and… Pointed out her virginity, to everyone that was there. And then, on top of that, he had… Basically offered her pity sex. And that had lived in her head rent-free all the years since. And every year on her birthday, when she was faced with a quiet evening at home, dinner at her mother's house and then a sedate movie before bed or… Asking Tag if the offer was still on the table, she had… She had thought about it. And she had been angry that the thought was even in her head.

And this birthday, this birthday had been looming. Thirty. Never been kissed. Never anything. And Tag was her fantasy.

If she was ever going to change, if she was ever going to… Be something other than she was, the Nelly Foster who had never managed to escape her past pain, no matter how much she wanted to… Well, he felt like a mountain that she needed to climb. And it was mostly because he had essentially given her a box of climbing gear and told her that she could.

And he was kissing her now.

And it was… It was incredible.

Better than fifteen-year-old her could ever have imagined.

She didn't want to be a waterdrop on his lips. She just wanted to be the woman that was being consumed by him. Because that's what it was. And it didn't feel like pity.

He moved away from her, gripping her chin between his thumb and forefinger, and it occurred to her then, ludicrously so, that she had never been so close to another human being before.

"If you hadn't realized by now, Nelly, I actually do have a high opinion of you. I have always thought that you were a strong, interesting sort of girl that I wished I knew a little bit better, but didn't know how to."

She blinked. "What?"

She always thought that he was… A mythical figure. Fascinating. His confidence and swagger were so intimidating she had barely been able to look directly at him. And he found her interesting?

"I'm bookish," she said.

He chuckled. "And strong enough to stand up to me, to anything I ever dished out to you. And I always wondered why. How. Because yeah, you seem maybe a little bookish, but you also seem a whole lot like a warrior. And I've always wondered what all that was about."

"The world is dangerous," she said, "and filled with dragons."

"Dragons, is it?"

"Yes," she said, not wanting to have a discussion about dragons right now per se. Metaphorical or otherwise. Because she was here for one thing. And it wasn't to talk things out with Tag. He wasn't a talker. He would be the first person to say it. He had said it to her before. He was a man of action.

And that was what she wanted from him.

All of the other things that she still had left to process she would do on the other side of this. This wasn't a night about grief. Not a night about the way she felt shaped by her mother's anger and haunted by her best friend's death. This was a night to go back to that moment when she had first wanted to kiss Tag. And be a woman who could. Everything had gotten ruined after that. She had a couple of years of a heady, sweet crush on him, and then it had all gotten destroyed. She had gotten destroyed. And she knew that wasn't fair.

And that was what she kept coming back to. Breanna was gone. And while she felt a mountain of guilt for the way things had been left with her friend in the end, the fact that there were certain things she just couldn't bring herself to do, the fact that she felt frozen at a very particular point in time... That was a poor tribute. It just was.

She didn't think every day about how badly affected she was by that loss. But there were just some times when she would realize. What she didn't do. Where she didn't go. And most of all...

Well, if she didn't have issues around men in relationships already, courtesy of her mother, her last words to Breanna would've done it nicely enough.

But she happened to have a combination of both. And that made it even more difficult.

"I would like to skip the pleasantries," she said. "I think we've known each other long enough that we don't need to engage in any kind of witty banter," she said.

He lifted a brow. "Well, that is the nicest damn thing you have ever said to me, Nelly Foster."

"What exactly?"

"Well, the implication that I might be capable of witty banter."

"Your great tragedy," she said, "Taggart McCloud, is that you are not the idiot you would like the world to think you are. You never have been."

"Well now, I don't know about that. I'm not particularly

well versed in literature, but there are other things. Other things I'm quite knowledgeable about."

"I have no doubt," she said. "It's why I'm here."

Except that was such a simplistic thing. It implied that it wasn't tied directly to him. This sex quest. It implied that any man would do. And really, she hoped that after this, any man would.

But she needed to get over her Taggart McCloud fixation.

"All right then," he said. "No talking."

And he kissed her again. And she felt like she could fly.

She didn't know if it was good or bad that she couldn't seem to divorce emotion from this moment. Sure, in her mind, she had imagined racing up here and getting caught up in the heat of desire.

She might be a thirty-year-old virgin librarian, but she was well familiar with what it was like to be aroused. She knew her way around her own body. And if her own body was often guided by fantasies of Tag, so be it.

She also really liked the show *Outlander*, and it did a lot for her.

*Right. Going to pretend it's not a general fixation with Scottish men...*

Not that Tag—or anyone in his family for generations— was directly from Scotland, or had the kind of accents that often made their way into her fantasies. But as the name suggested, they were proud of their heritage.

The idea of Tag in a kilt made her heart do a little flip.

"You seem some speechless," he said.

"I might be."

"I'm halfway there."

"Well," she whispered, "that is a miracle."

Her lips felt swollen, her body shuddering with need. She really, really wanted more of this. More of him. And that was the real miracle. That she had been brave enough to get here, and that she felt brave enough to go on.

Because thirty years was a long time to not do something. To suddenly decide to do it... Well, it was a little bit scary.

"I don't really want to talk anymore anyway."

His kiss became hungrier, going deeper. She parted her lips for him and wrapped her arms around his neck, and he took her up into his hold. He was so muscular and broad, and she felt small, fragile and sheltered all at once.

Her mother had woven cautionary tales about men and their physical strength. But she hadn't said that it could be wonderful. That it could make you feel treasured and beautiful. All she'd ever known was that it could make you feel small and afraid.

But Tag didn't make her afraid. Tag made her feel like she could fly.

Like maybe she was flying already.

He lifted her feet up off the ground and began to carry her down the hall of his small cabin, back to the bedroom. The bed was surprisingly nice. Well put together, and she had to wonder if it was because...

"Do you have a lot of women up here?"

"Don't come into the den of iniquity asking questions if you don't want to know the answers."

"Right."

"Nelly, I am nothing if not everything I have ever appeared to be."

"I guess the same goes for me," she said, suddenly feeling nervous. Because what did he think about those other women that he had laid down on this bed? Would he only picture them?

"How many virgins have you slept with?"

"I'm sorry, what?"

340   THE COWBOY SHE LOVES TO HATE

"How many virgins have you slept with? I'm genuinely curious. Is this sort of a lesson space... Or do you tend to prefer women with more experience?"

"Well, now you've gone and made me feel predatory. I do not have sex with virgins."

"Except right now. You still didn't answer my question."

"Pretty sure none," he said.

"None? Not even in high school?"

"Look, not to be... Not to be disrespectful, but I believe the despoiler of virgins is Landry King, and most of us were getting his castoffs by then."

"Really," she said, "Landry?"

"Hey, I'm just saying."

"So this isn't something that you do."

"Why does it matter?"

"Well, I'm not going to be better in bed than any of the other women you brought up here before. Not even close. I don't know what I'm doing. That's kind of the entire point. So I guess the idea of being at least a novelty experience suits me."

"Oh, you find it soothing, do you?"

"Yes," she said.

"The idea that you're a novelty."

"Exactly."

He took a couple steps forward, and suddenly his face was... Predatory. So unlike Tag in any way she had ever seen him before. "Nelly Foster, you are not a novelty. And you are not just one of an endless parade of women that have come to my bed. The parade is not endless—hate to disappoint you. Long though it may be. But even though there is a parade, you're not a part of it. You are singular to me. I have wanted you for a long damn time. And it has driven me crazy. Because why the hell a guy like me, who knows that all he wants is easy sex and a good time, should be fixated on a girl who was bound to grow up to be the town librarian— that much was apparent from day one—I don't know. I've never known. And you know what, I don't like not knowing things. Because I may not know everything on a test, and I may not be the smartest kid in class, but I know about life. And I damn sure know about attraction. But I wanted you from the moment I started wanting. And I amused myself with easy, because I figured easy was about all I could handle. But you're here now. I'm not about to turn you down."

"You wanted me?" she asked. "You really wanted me?"

She was so turned on she didn't really want to stop to have a conversation, but it was... It was tempting. To linger in this. Because Taggart McCloud could certainly have any woman he wanted—and she'd assumed that he had.

But apparently, all this time he had wanted her. He had wanted her.

"You know, there's this thing. Chemistry. You have it or you don't. And it has nothing to do with whether or not someone is the most attractive person on the planet. You can put two perfectly shiny, beautiful people together, and they may not have the greatest sex. Because sex is about chemistry. And, Nelly, we've had it from the beginning. We struck sparks off each other. Day one. And it was building to this. Why do you think I offered myself on your birthday. I got it in my head that you might be a virgin, and the idea obsessed me. Now, I was pretty sure you would've taken care of it between then and now. But... Yeah, that night, the minute it entered my head, I had to know. And I really wanted to be the one to do something about it. But that would've been a mess. Because I was twenty-three and a dumbass."

"No offense, but aren't you still kind of a dumbass?"

"Yes," he said. "But less of one. Anyway, I know better how to handle this moment than I would have then."

"How exactly?"

His mouth was on hers again. His large hands roaming over her curves. And she felt... She felt completely overwhelmed. The sensory... Everything was almost too much. The heat, the press of his body against hers, the sound of their breathing. His breath, his heartbeat. Her own. She felt dizzy. She felt transformed.

And she thought of dragons again.

She had sort of thought of this—of him—as a dragon to be slain.

But maybe it wasn't about that. Maybe it was about being strong enough for the dragon. Maybe it was about becoming the kind of woman who could stand up to it.

And so she stopped worrying. About what she might do. About what he might feel. And she just let herself embrace her own desire. Let herself get caught up in it. When he stepped away from her, he stripped his shirt up over his head, and any thoughts that she had about being blasé quickly evaporated.

It had been a good while since she had seen Tag without a shirt on. He had lived up to every promise his body had made to her at seventeen, when she'd last seen him shirtless down at the swimming hole. And then some. His chest was broad and muscular, covered with dark hair now, a big difference between back then and fifteen years later. And she was confident that she wouldn't have been able to appreciate this back then. But oh, she was ready for it now.

She pressed her hands against that chest, moved her fingers down in wonder, watching as they moved over his muscles. Every indentation. Every line.

"Oh my," she said.

He grabbed her wrist and pulled her against him, kissing

her again. And somehow, he managed to get her shirt and bra off while still holding her in his arms.

She didn't have time to be embarrassed, because she was too busy being breathless. And it was a gift. A beautiful, wonderful gift. That she could be with a man who affected her so deeply that her desire for him superseded her virginal nerves, of which there were legion.

The frank male appreciation in his gaze was stunning. Because she didn't think anyone had ever looked at her like that. Like she was fascinating. More than that. Like he wanted to eat her.

And then he proceeded to do just that. He fastened a kiss to her collarbone, worked his way down. And then he took one nipple into his mouth and sucked hard.

She knew about sex. She liked sexy books. She had a rich fantasy life, because that was what you did when you were afraid to have an actual life. It was what you did when you felt too guilty to give yourself nice things. So she had gotten very accustomed to that realm. And she knew exactly the kinds of things that men and women did with each other. She was in favor of them. But somehow it was also much more than she had imagined. The scrape of his whiskers against her skin, the fractured quality of his breathing. And the stark, sharp sensations that had nothing to do with her own hand. That, that was what shocked her the most. How different it was when she wasn't in control. Because it was him. The pressure that he put on her body. Where he touched her. The unknown. It was so intense. So heady. So glorious.

And when he moved away from her, his green eyes hard on hers, it was also inescapable that this was Taggart Mc-Cloud. And it was the fulfillment of a fantasy that she had been withholding from herself all this time.

Because she had felt she didn't deserve it. She still didn't think she deserved it. But she was here. She was thirty years old. She had made it this far. This was her life.

And she felt awash both with hope and despair at that thought. He took a step back, undoing the button on his jeans and lowering the zipper slowly. Then pushing them down his lean hips. His thighs were muscular. His calves were nice. She was basically looking everywhere but...

And then she finally did.

Oh, this was going to hurt. It had to hurt. Because he was... He was so thick. So... So long and...

*Did you really want Taggart McCloud to be disappointing?*

No. She hadn't. But, he was not a beginner model. Too bad she had chosen him to be the person to initiate her. The decision had been made. The die was cast. So she was going to have to risk the pain that would come with the impalement.

"What?"

"I'm just..." She cleared her throat. "Engaging in risk assessment."

"Risk assessment," he repeated.

"That is *huge*," she said.

"It'll fit," he said.

"You don't *know* that."

"Pretty sure I do." He closed the distance between them. "As much as I like the shoes and socks..." He knelt down in front of her and slipped off her shoes, then her socks. And the brush of his calloused fingers against her skin somehow felt erotic.

Then he kissed her ankle, her calf. Right beside her knee. Up and up until he was at the edge of her panties, and she shifted.

"I'm going to make you feel good," he said.

"I... I know what you're about to do," she said.

"Of course you do," he said. "You're a know-it-all, aren't you, Nelly Foster?"

"I believe you already know the answer to that."

"I think I can surprise you. Because you might know. But, honey, you don't know." And then he slipped her panties down her thighs, leaving them down at her ankles, and leaned in, pressing a kiss right to the cleft just there. Then he slipped his tongue through her folds, and she gasped. It was like white-hot fire, blazing over all of her. Every bit.

She began to tremble, her whole body alight. He licked her, slow and leisurely, like he had nothing else to do in the entire world except pleasure her.

Then she found herself being lifted off the ground. Lifted, while he crouched in front of her. Like she weighed nothing. And he managed to get her thighs over his shoulders, all while he held on to her back, never once abandoning his attentions to her body.

He maneuvered her to the wall, pressed her up against there, and ate more deeply into her. She was grasping for something, anything, lacing her fingers through his hair and clinging to him. She bucked her hips against his mouth, begging for release. This was too much. There was no way a human woman could possibly endure this. He would take her right to the edge, and then he pulled back, his mouth so wicked, so expert, he seemed to know exactly what she needed, and he seemed to excel at denying it.

So unerringly it was clearly intentional.

Then on a growl he pulled her away from the wall and took her down to the bed, his face still between her legs as he kept on pleasuring her like that, sliding one finger deep inside of her slick channel, adding another. He pumped them in and out of her body, and she arched her hips up off the bed.

"By the time we get to that part," he said, his voice a rasp, "you're going to be begging me for this. You're going to be begging for me. And I'm not going to feel too big. It's going to feel just right. In fact, it may feel so good you don't want another man's ever."

And she had no trouble believing that. None at all. He pushed a third finger inside of her, and she felt uncomfortably stretched. But he did it slowly, managing his movements so that she had time to acclimate. The most amazing thing was that she realized she trusted him. Then he brought his mouth back on her again, until she fell over the edge. Until she was sobbing his name. Her internal muscles clenching tight around his fingers.

Then he brought himself back to her lips, kissing her slowly. Holding her close.

And to her horror, she felt tears prickle at her eyes. Because it wasn't just that he had made her feel searing pleasure. He made her feel cared for.

Truly, what he'd done was a selfless act of pleasure. And now he was... Cradling her close like she was a fragile thing.

As if he'd read her mind, he whispered against her temple. "I enjoyed that as much as you did. If not more."

That made her shiver. And then he tilted her chin upward and kissed her. Gently at first, then harder, deeper. Until the pleasure inside of her began to build again. Build to impossible levels. She shifted, and she felt him settle between her legs. And he was right. Now she just wanted him. Because she knew how wonderful it was to have something filling that void inside of her.

And she wanted it to be him.

He eased his way into her body slowly. And there was a moment, only a moment, where it felt painful. And then she just felt... Achingly warm. Deliciously filled. She clung to his shoulders, battling those same tears, because there was something gloriously brilliant about this moment that she hadn't even realized.

That she hadn't known at all.

And then he began to move.

He ramped up that arousal inside of her, pushing it to new heights, pushing her to levels she didn't know she could go. And then she broke. Shattered. And he followed behind, shouting her name.

And then she lay there, spent and broken.

It wasn't until she heard a piteous weeping sound that she realized there were tears on her face.

# CHAPTER THREE

WELL, HELL. He didn't know what to do with this.

He'd had a lot of compliments after he was done pleasuring a woman, but he'd never had one burst into tears. This was uncharted territory. And the fact of the matter was, it was Nelly. So, as much as she got under his skin, as much as he might pretend… He cared about her. He cared about her, dammit. She was… She was part of the Four Corners family, and he didn't want to see her hurting.

*Yeah. That's all it is. Just that general sense of responsibility you feel toward people who are part of this place. And nothing at all to do with her specifically.*

He gritted his teeth. "Nelly," he said, moving his thumb over her tearstained cheeks. "Honey, what's wrong?"

"I don't know," she said, sounding miserable.

"You don't know?"

"I just… Well, I've done it. I've done it and… It's really wonderful. It's really wonderful. And if I had been the seventeen-year-old girl, with a beautiful boyfriend, I think it's what I would've wanted to do all the time."

"Okay," he said.

"You don't understand."

"No," he said. "I don't understand. I fully don't understand. I'm sorry."

"It's just… It was Breanna."

The name slammed into his chest, a bad memory, a bad feeling, creeping up over his shoulders.

"What about her?"

"She was my best friend, Tag. And I think always kind of out of pity. And that I was so small and jealous when she and Wolf…"

"Did you like Wolf?"

No one spoke about Breanna, not ever. The shadow of her death hung over Wolf Garrett like a cloud, and as guilty as it made her feel sometimes… She hid in the shadow of his grief. Because she didn't want to think about what had happened. Didn't want to think about the last time she spoke to her, and the fact that no one at Four Corners ever spoke about it meant she rarely had to.

"No. I didn't. It wasn't about that. It was… She had a boyfriend. And she cared more about that than paying attention to me. In the last thing I said to her… I yelled at her. We had a horrible fight. I told her that she was… I told her she was stupid. Spending all her time having sex with Wolf. And I said I didn't even know her anymore. And she was going to go get herself pregnant, and everyone would know what they were doing. I said that…it was a pretty terrible friend who chose a boyfriend and silly things like sex over… Over their friendship. And… I just… I feel like I get it now, and it's too late. It's too late for me to get it. I was mean to her. And I felt isolated, and I passed that on to her. And it just… It would've been a stupid fight. It would've been. But then she died. She died and it wasn't fair. And she was… She was beautiful, and she had him. And I was… I was just small and mean."

"What happened to Breanna was damn tragic," Tag said. "And there wasn't a single one of us that wasn't devastated by it. You know that. And like you said, all that stuff… It was just a fight. I've said worse things than that to my own brothers. You get mad. You start fights. It's not the end of the world."

"Until it is. Until it's the end of somebody. Somebody that you cared for so much."

"I can't say anything to make that all better," he said. "I can't offer you any words to take away years of feeling… Of feeling guilty. Feeling sad. And hell, I'm not the person to do it. But Nelly, you can't feel guilty about what you didn't understand when you were sixteen."

"I want to," she said.

"Why?"

She let out a shuddering sigh. "I don't know. I guess because it's easier than… Because it's easier than grieving. Because it's easier than… You know, sometimes you just want to make tragedy mean something. Even if it's bad. I just… I wanted to take something from it. Because it doesn't feel fair or right that I'm still here. I grew up with her. And I couldn't imagine life without her. And then she was gone. And I'm just still here. I'm just still here, and I don't know quite what to do with that."

"Sometimes life sucks," he said. "Really. Sometimes it really does. And there's not a whole lot you can do about it. You know, my mother left, and my dad is—was—a dick. He was a drunken asshole. There's not a reason for it. It just is."

She sniffed, her shoulders shaking. "Well, I don't think that's true. He chooses to be."

That landed hard, sat there in his chest. He didn't know. Misery, when it came to the McCloud family, didn't seem to be much of a choice. It just seemed to be a fact. A fact of life. A fact of Four Corners. That was the thing. The ranch could be magical, but there were some tough home truths embedded in the dirt. Much like the Garrett family, the Mc-Clouds were unlucky in love. Generationally. The Sullivans had weathered tragedy, generations back, mostly, but they had. And then there were the Kings, who were the most separate—emotionally separated from everyone, and impossible to get close to. Whatever issues they had, they kept with their own.

And so he had figured that the alcohol, the meanness—all that was as inherited a trait as green eyes and dark hair. But the way she said it, as if the misery was a choice, as if they could choose something else... That struck something strange.

"It wasn't Breanna's choice to die. It was a terrible accident," Nelly said, her voice like stone. "I know that. But somewhere in there, I let myself get lost in my own grief with it. In my own guilt. And my guilt doesn't help anyone, does it?"

Her words felt far too close to scraping the tender spots on his heart, which he would've said that he didn't have. Not even a little. Not even at all. Because he was Taggart McCloud, who didn't give a shit about much of anything, who didn't get caught up in emotion. Who didn't worry about what anyone else thought.

Who didn't care what might happen tomorrow. The Taggart McCloud he was—or the Taggart McCloud he showed the world—only wanted to drink, get laid and have a good time. He wanted to work hard and play harder. But he didn't want anything permanent. He didn't want attachment. He didn't want anything other than to go to bed at night totally exhausted, so exhausted that he couldn't think, and wake up the next morning, stumble out of bed and do the same thing all over again.

But just thinking about that left a strange, gnawing ache in his heart. Looking at Nelly, looking at her right now, her sadness, her strength, it made him feel... Lacking. It made him feel like all the things that he did, all the defenses he'd put up around himself just weren't enough to make him...

The fact of the matter was, he never really thought about becoming a better man than his father. What he'd thought about was not dragging other people into this McCloud curse. All the things they were. He felt like that was a victory. Like that was better. His dad had gone ahead and had five sons and treated every single one of them like shit.

He had gotten married when he hadn't been able to handle such a thing, his wife had left him and no one could blame her. Except for the fact that she left her sons to take the beatings. Until Gus had gotten sick of it and decided it was time to get rid of the old man once and for all. Now the land was theirs... And rather than sell it, they figured they'd continue to work it, but what he knew for a fact was that none of his brothers had a vested interest in carrying on the line, that was for sure.

*It's his choice.*

"I think the guilt is sometimes unavoidable," he said.

"Well, I'm tired of it," she said, a tear rolling down her cheek. "I'm sick to death of it, honestly. I like being a librarian. I like my quiet life. I don't need more excitement than I have. What I have is excitement, whether that makes sense to anyone but me... It doesn't matter. I don't like drinking, I don't like going out every night. Those aren't the things that I regret. What I regret is how lonely I am. How lonely I feel. Because even though I have friends, I feel like I haven't let myself... I haven't ever really let myself connect fully with the people around me. Not since Breanna."

"It was a terrible thing," he said.

"I know," she said. "I know. And I feel... I'm so... I'm so sorry that it happened. And mostly, I'm just sorry that I can't go back and say something different to her the last time

I saw her. But I can't. I've been over and over it. I never go swimming anymore. Not because I'm scared, but because it just makes me think about her. What happened to her was a freak accident, and I get it. But I need to figure out all these… She haunts me. My grief haunts me. And my guilt. And I just want something different. I really do."

"Then let's go swimming."

"What?"

"It's a warm night. Let's go swimming. Full moon. We can go down to the swimming hole and get on the rope swing."

"Tag…"

"I'd say this is a night to banish some ghosts, wouldn't you?"

She blinked. "Okay. Okay. Then let's go."

# *CHAPTER FOUR*

SHE WAS SHIVERING, but not from the cold. Tag was right—it was warm outside. But much to her surprise, when he had taken her hand and led her outside, it had not been with clothes on. "No one's out at this hour," he said. Which was how she found herself walking naked through the woods with Tag McCloud.

"I'm going to step on something," she said.

And that was how she found herself being lifted off the ground into his strong arms. He carried her through the trees, and she looked up, at the way the moonlight filtered through the branches, at the twinkle of stars beyond. And it felt like a dream. Maybe it was. Maybe she would wake up and she would be at home in bed. She would still be a virgin, and Tag would never have kissed her or touched her.

Then she reached up and brushed her fingertips over his face. His stubble was prickly beneath her fingers, his skin warm. And she knew she wouldn't have imagined that. This exact feeling. The solid heat of his body, his chest hair. His muscles. Yeah, she couldn't have imagined all that.

Then they were there, down at the water. It wasn't the lake. The lake would've been a little bit too much. But the creek that was McCloud's Landing was just fine. He set her down on the sandy shore and tilted her chin up to look at his face. "You good?"

The sincere asking of that question, from Tag, who was so rarely sincere, made her heart flutter.

"I'm good," she said. "Tag… Whatever happens after this, I want you to know that tonight means so much to me. I wanted to find a way to start changing. To start healing, and I didn't know…" She cleared her throat. "I didn't expect to talk. I didn't expect…"

"You just expected to lose your virginity?"

"Yeah," she said.

"I guess that's fair enough. You and I haven't ever had all that much to talk about."

"I wonder if we did have a lot to talk about, and we just never… And we just never did. Because we didn't realize."

"Maybe," he said.

The air was balmy and wonderful, and he took her hand, leading her slowly into the water. Then he held her tight as she hissed, when the cold water got higher than her belly, covered her breasts. It was very cold. But he was right there, hot and perfect. Everything that she had never known she needed.

It made her heart feel like it was breaking open. She hadn't expected this. Not with him. But maybe… Maybe she should have. Because he had been part of her life; he had been someone she couldn't deny or avoid or stop thinking about, for so much time, and it had to be more than sex, because it had been since way before she knew what sex even was. There was something deep here. Something deep and connected that she didn't necessarily want to examine. Because she had a feeling that heartbreak would be on the other side of that examination.

Tag might have opened up to her a little bit tonight, but it was only a very little bit. And his having a conversation with her didn't mean that he wanted to change his entire life.

She liked her life. Hadn't she just said? How would the two of them ever make one together anyway? He liked to go out. He liked to drink. He didn't like to read. He had never even been to the library to see her.

And she ignored the little voice inside of her that whispered it didn't matter. That they would find a way to learn each other. To understand each other. That if the two of them could just spend their nights in that cozy little cabin, everything would have to be okay, because there was nothing quite like them. But that was fanciful, fairy-tale talk.

In the end, she'd have to walk away from this, because Tag wasn't the kind of man who would want more.

And would she change just because she had slept with a man, or was it about something deeper?

It was deeper, and she knew it. It wasn't about virginity, or the lack of it. It was just that she had lied to herself to get up here. Had lied to herself in order to work up the courage to be with him. "Rope swing?"

"I'm not that brave."

"You ran naked through a forest, and you're currently skinny-dipping with Four Corners' resident bad boy."

"I hate to break it to you," she said. "But at Four Corners bad boys are a dime a dozen. And if it didn't matter to me which one I was with… Well, I could've had an easier night with Landry or Denver or Wolf for that matter, or even Hunter…"

"Now, you talk one more time about being with one of my brothers, and there's going to be trouble."

"Trouble might be something I'm more interested in now than I was previously."

"I bet. Still, I think you're pretty brave. A hell of a lot braver than I am, Nelly Foster."

She couldn't read his expression in the light. She couldn't

tell if he was kidding or not. But she felt like he wasn't. Like nothing between them had been a joke since that first kiss. Not at all. Not the way he usually teased her.

She'd always known that fairy tales weren't real. Her mother had never told her stories of Prince Charming, had never let her believe in anything quite like that. Because for her, Prince Charming hadn't existed. For her, Prince Charming had turned out to be a nightmare. And Nelly had never been foolish enough to believe that she could dream past what her own mother had endured. And then there was Breanna, who'd found love. Who had found love and lost it, and it was just as terrible a thing as could ever exist in the world.

And how audacious would it be to believe that they could have something more?

Except what she'd said moments before about choice rang in her ears, and she had to wonder.

Because there were things you didn't choose—her mother being deceived by her father and being abused by him after she'd given him her trust. Breanna dying. And there were things you did choose—treating your family poorly. Using your fists on your sons.

And allowing the bad things that had come before you determine what you did ever after.

Yes, there were things that were choices.

She shivered, and Tag lowered his head and kissed her. And she just drank it in. Drank him in. Lived in this moment, because this moment was the most transcendent of her entire life.

Because this moment meant something deep. Something unending. Because it meant change.

"Trust me," he said, his voice husky, and she wanted to. So she clung to his shoulders and let him swim her over to the rope swing. He made sure that she was clinging to the jagged rocks that went up alongside the bank, and then began to climb up the side. He reached down and helped hoist her up onto the top of the rock with him. She clung to him, and he grabbed hold of the rope, which was looped over the branch of one of the trees.

"I won't drop you," he said. "Until I drop both of us."

The words made her shiver, as they resonated inside of her body. "I trust you," she said.

And then, they were airborne, his arms helping to hold them both up on the rope swing, his impossible strength a marvel. They were flying through the air, and then they both plunged down into the water. When they came back up, she took a deep breath. And she felt... Baptized. Reborn. She had come back up to the surface. Because she hadn't drowned. She had lived. But somewhere in there, she had forgotten. She had forgotten that living was more than breathing. She had forgotten that time had moved on. That it had marched on so vastly. So many, many years between now and that moment.

And that loss.

And it didn't make it less sad. It was tragic, no matter how much time passed. But it was simply that. Past. And no one could make it present, no one could rewind the clock and fix it.

She felt a deep sense of acceptance settle over her shoulders. Her last conversation with Breanna had been a fight. But it didn't erase the years of friendship they'd had before. She couldn't go back and change it. It would never be a good memory—there was nothing she could do about that. But it could at least be... It could be.

She didn't need to fight it. She didn't need to waste time regretting it.

Because there was nothing that could be done about it. Eighteen years on, there was nothing anyone could do.

There was nothing anyone could do but make the choice to live.

There was no sense to be made out of that tragedy. There was no magical place to put it so that people could marvel at all the good that had come of it.

There was no good that had come of it. A young girl had lost her life too soon. But they didn't need to compound the tragedy.

And it was fitting, somehow, that she was here with him. Though she didn't know why. But she sensed that he carried grief inside of him. Not over the same thing she did, no. But it was there. She had never seen it before, hiding behind the bluster, the smart-ass smile and all the swagger that he conducted himself with at all times. It was the same as her hiding her own trauma beneath the no-nonsense exterior.

He was hiding.

Her Tag.

She needed to not think of him that way. She needed to realize that this was one night. And maybe it was a night that was deeper than she had anticipated, a night for them to come to new realizations. At least a night for her to come to them. Change was possible here, deep change.

They stayed down in the water until they were both shivering, and then he carried her back to the cabin. He started a fire and wrapped them in blankets, and they both lay down on the floor wrapped in a fuzzy blanket. The fire crackled behind them, and she put her hand on his chest, looking up at his face. "What made you decide to be different than your father?"

He went stiff. "I don't know how to answer that."

"Something must have. Something must have made all

of you decide to be different. Because you are, and it's not an accident."

"Maybe it is. You know, we McClouds have a lot of charm that's accidental. I think the choice might be the other stuff."

"I don't know. When you're raised by that, and it's all that you see… Don't you think there's a better chance that you're going to turn out like the person who raised you than not?" She hesitated. "I know that my mother was afraid of that."

"Was afraid of what?"

She took a breath. "Well, I don't really want to talk about me. We've talked about me all night."

"You're the one who randomly showed up out of the blue to give me your virginity. You're entitled to the focus."

She swallowed. Hard.

"My father abused us. My mother changed her name and ran away to Four Corners to try and protect us." She looked at Tag, directly in the eyes. "She was afraid that if he found us, he would kill us."

# CHAPTER FIVE

TAG HELD ON more tightly to Nelly. The idea that a man had hit her, when she was a child, that he had then threatened her... It was beyond the pale. It enraged him. It was wrong, on every level. And if he could find the bastard that had done that to her, he would cheerfully kill him. And he wouldn't need alcohol to get mean and violent. No. Hell, the truth was, being a fighter was in his blood. It was just the alcohol that made him indiscriminate with it. And he might drink on occasion, but he made sure he only did it when he was in a good mood. He made sure he only did it when they went out for fun.

He never did it at home. He never did it alone. He never wanted it to toxify and turn into that thing his father did. That thing that seemed to rot him from the inside out. No. That, he had never wanted any part of.

He'd seen a lot of mean things, though, as a result of his father's behavior. And he'd accepted that the world was essentially a cold, hard place. But he was not immune to the idea of Nelly... Of Nelly being hurt. By a man who was supposed to care for her. He didn't put a lot of stock in fathers. His father had been terrible; his father's father had been terrible. On that score, he supposed Nelly was right. Learned cruelty passed down through generations seemed to be a family value for the McClouds.

And while he and his brothers had definitely broken the

cycle, none of them had married, either. None of the men had children. And he didn't think they ever would. Sometimes he wondered what that meant for the ranch. But at the end of the day, Four Corners would endure. There were so many people who worked the land, so many people involved in the day-to-day running of the place, it didn't really matter if it was a McCloud who kept things going at McCloud's Landing. It only mattered that the place endured.

And it would. Longer than their own flawed genetics, that was for sure and certain.

Because the land was honest. The land endured.

In spite of the frailties of men.

Yeah, he had a grim acceptance of those frailties. But not now. Not in this.

"The bastard who fathered you hurt you?"

"Not me as badly as my mother. I was very young. I barely remember it."

But he could tell from her voice that she did remember it. That it had lasting effects on her. And he knew well how true that was. Because his family was marred by violence, so how could he not know?

"Nelly," he said. "Why did you never tell me this before?"

"We don't talk," she said. "And plus… When we came here, when we started over—new last names, new clothes, new everything—my mom said we were best to leave it behind. She said that we had to remember the lessons. That you can't just trust men, even if they say nice things. Even if they say the right things, do the right things, you can't simply trust them. That you have to be wary. All the time."

"Nelly, have you ever thought that maybe that's why you were a virgin?"

She laughed. "Yes. But… The thing is, Tag, I've never been afraid of you. Ever."

And that hit him funny. Because he was descended from the kind of man who was just like her father. He was a cycle in repeat. And she knew it.

It also explained why her mother had been extra kind to the McCloud boys. She probably felt guilt. A lot of it. But then, at the time especially, there had been nothing anyone could do. The state trooper that patrolled the area that Four Corners was in was old friends with Seamus McCloud. There would be no help coming for the McCloud boys. They would be left to their own devices, left to police themselves.

"Why not?"

"Because you're a good man. Look, you've driven me crazy for years. But I could see, even in all of that, that you were… That you were good. And I wanted… I wanted to kiss you. When I was fifteen. And it terrified me. It terrified me because I thought that I was supposed to stay away from men. I mean, obviously that's not practical for forever. I don't really know what my plan was." She looked haunted all of a sudden. "I just haven't had a plan. I have been small and sad in the pursuit of safety and self-protection. Whether that was carving out a spot for my grief and guilt, or for the fear that I felt over my father. But here's what I can tell you— I've seen men like him. And it doesn't matter that I was little when we left. I remember. You're not that man. You're not just… In a battle to not become that man, and I feel like you think you are."

"I'll never be complacent," he said. "None of us will. It's pride that tells a man he's never going to become the kind of monster he's seen around him."

"How do you know? Did your father ever even try? Do you know?"

"No," he said. "I haven't had a conversation with my old

man in… Ever. We never had a conversation. And now he's gone."

"Did Gus kill him?"

He looked at her, then huffed out a laugh. "Is that what people think?"

"I don't know. I mean, I may have heard Alaina Sullivan say that she thought he might have. I didn't take it very seriously until now."

"Why now?"

"Because I realize how heavy it is for you. I wouldn't tell."

"No," he said. "Gus didn't kill him. He beat him up. Told him never to come back. Told him that… If he stayed, he might end up in an early grave, and who would convict him? Got the ranch signed over to us. That's the story Gus told, anyway. And I believe it. I believe him."

"That easy?"

He nodded slowly. "I don't know what made my father do anything he did. I think that's the worst part. I wish I knew. I wish I knew what made a person decide their whole life was going to be filled with alcohol and pain. They were going to just be a miserable cost to everyone around them. Run off their wife… He actually worshipped my mother. He would get drunk and he would say things, but he never laid a hand on her.

"*Never raise your fist to a lady*, he said. Just be a cruel ass, constantly. Of course, she left us to bear the brunt of it, so I don't know why that bothered her so much to be around it. She was okay with the idea of leaving us to it. To be honest, I think she believed he'd come after her, and I kind of think that's what she wanted. But he didn't. Instead… He took it out on us."

"Tag…" She laughed, but he knew it wasn't because anything was funny. "We're a lot more the same than it seems."

"Yeah," he said. "Not in ways anyone wants to be."

"Who would've thought?"

He didn't know why, but it got to him. Somewhere down much deeper than he wanted to admit. Deeper than he ever wanted to acknowledge. This woman.

And he had to wonder if there was something that he had recognized in her from the moment he'd first seen her. But that seemed crazy. Because what the hell could it even be?

She was strong. And she didn't wear all her hurts like armor. She was still soft. And she was still sweet. And she was still far more than a McCloud could ever hope to have. Could ever hope to hold. But maybe it was that very thing that made it all work. Maybe it was that very thing that called to him. Because he didn't have any sweetness of his own, that was for damn sure.

So he gathered her up in his arms and he took her back to bed, even though he knew he should let her have a break. Even though he knew they shouldn't do this again.

But he couldn't resist her, and the clock was ticking.

He had promised a night. And the night was all he had to give. A night was the kindest thing he could offer her.

Anything more and he risked tainting her with everything they were. The McClouds.

And she deserved better than that. She just damn well did.

But here in his bed, with his hands skimming over her curves, and her body underneath his, he could pretend. That the impulse to pull Nelly's pigtails was fate. That her being here was fate. That everything that had ever been together was fate. And that he was the kind of strong she was. That could still have softness and feelings and not just scarred over tissue that could never truly feel again.

Every sigh beneath him was a gift, every kiss against his lips was something extraordinary.

366 THE COWBOY SHE LOVES TO HATE

And when she found her pleasure and arched against him, he didn't think he'd ever seen anything more beautiful. He didn't think there ever had been anything more beautiful. His own pleasure didn't mean a damn thing. Not in the face of hers. In the face of what they shared.

Because in this moment, Tag McCloud didn't have to be a man of action. He didn't have to keep going. Didn't have to keep running. In this moment, he could just feel. With Nelly Foster.

And it was a gift that he had never known he needed. A gift that would expire with the sunrise.

A gift that he feared would leave him hollow with the loss of it for the rest of his life.

# CHAPTER SIX

NELLY WOKE UP on the floor. They were in front of the fireplace wrapped in a fur. It was the strangest thing. She remembered the lake, talking, going back to bed… But now here they were, tangled up in each other by the fire…

Her cheeks went red. She remembered. They had made love again in his bed, and then they had woken again and it was like he was possessed by an animal. It had been amazing and wonderful. Sharp and bright and verging on violent in a way that had made her feel powerful and strong, not small and scared.

He had pinned her arms above her head the better to kiss her entire body. He had growled like a beast, and thrust into her with a ferocity that had stolen her breath. With Tag hard and hot above her, and the furs cozy and soft at her back, she had felt thrilled, protected and invigorated all at once. It was truly a miracle. Being with him. A miracle in a way she had never thought it could be. But the sun was rising now, and she didn't know why, but she had the terrible feeling that everything had ended. They hadn't spoken about this. About it being a single night, but it was as if they both knew. Maybe that was what had driven him in the wee hours of the morning. The knowledge that it was over. The knowledge that it had to be over.

She felt scratchy. And tragic. And she wanted to hold all of her hurt hard to her chest so that she didn't have to look at it too closely. So that she could absorb it and pretend it was just part of the pain that had already been there. She looked at Tag, who was still sleeping, the hard cut of his jaw, the softer side to his mouth. She had read so many times that men looked younger in their sleep. Carefree. Not Tag. She could see the lines, the cares and the pain written across his face most particularly as he dreamed. As if the facade of carefree scoundrel had fallen away entirely, leaving in its place the truth of him.

The man that had been so badly hurt by his father.

They all had been. The McCloud boys. Tag, Brody and Hunter had gone rogue. Gotten wild. Lachlan and Gus more serious. But it was all the same. A mask for the hurt. A mask for the immense pain that they had endured.

And she wondered what he would do. If she said that she loved him.

Her insides shivered.

Did she love Tag McCloud? She had told herself that he drove her crazy, for all of her life. But she understood now that that had just been self-defense.

She had been bothered by him because he had been something that she couldn't be. Because he had been loud and brash and wild in the face of his particular trauma, and she had shrunken in on herself and gotten more and more afraid. The fear that she had taken on from the way her father had treated them, the fear that she had absorbed even deeper into her bones after Breanna had died. This sense of uncertainty and fragility.

But not Tag. The more the heart of the world pushed at him, the harder he pushed back. He refused to be small. And that had challenged her.

It had disrupted her.

It had damn near destroyed her.

But not now. Now she had followed this attraction all the way to its conclusion. Now she had followed it to the very brave end. And here she sat, her heart ringing with something that she was certain was love, and she was tempted to shrink yet again.

But no. She would be strong. Because that was what tonight had taught her. That the past was simply the past, and if you let it hobble you rather than teach you something, there wasn't much point to it.

What a terrible honor for her friend to have stopped her entire life because she couldn't get over that loss.

It was not right or fair. Breanna deserved more. More and better.

And so did Nelly.

And death and her father deserved no piece of who she was. No say over what she became and how far she went and how loud she lived.

"Tag," she whispered. She feathered kisses across his jaw, and she felt an echoing inside of her.

*Mine.*

Tag was hers. And he had been from the beginning, and it didn't matter how many women had touched him and kissed him, they didn't have a piece of his soul. And she did. She always had. They were fated. And they had been from the first moment they laid eyes on each other. It had never been irritation. It had always been a need that was too great for either of them to acknowledge. A desire that they had twisted into anger because it was so much easier to cope with. But wasn't that the smallest and meanest way to live your life? They knew that. It was the way her father had lived his life. Or perhaps was still doing it, she didn't know, and she hoped to God she never did.

He opened his eyes and looked at her. And in that moment

he looked younger. More carefree. In that moment she saw a light in him that she had never seen before. She brushed her fingertips over his lips. "I love you, Tag."

And then suddenly the light was gone.

"Nelly," he said, pulling away from her. And she knew, she knew full well exactly what was in his voice. That warning, that refusal.

And it broke her heart. It broke her heart, but she couldn't be angry. Because fierce, fearless Tag was afraid.

She understood, because she was too. Because she had committed to putting herself out there and confessing her love. But it had been like jumping off of a cliff. Not being able to see the bottom. Because everything in life was, in the end. Everything in life always would be. You had to take the risk. Take the leap. She had come to that conclusion because of him, but right now he wasn't ready to follow her. And it hurt. Because she didn't know when or if he would be. But she wasn't angry. She wasn't angry because this beautiful, wonderful man had pushed and goaded and dared her and loved her into a better version of herself. And for that she would always be grateful. For that she would always love him. Her Tag.

"Don't give me a speech, Taggart McCloud," she said. "I'm not a little girl."

"I didn't think you were."

"Then don't give me excuses. Don't patronize me. Don't pretend that this is another moment where you need to lecture me. Where you need to tell me how it is. Don't pretend that I'm so foolish I need you to educate me. That you need to let me down easy. Don't do that kind of a disservice to either of us. You're afraid. And I understand that. Let's not embarrass ourselves with excuses."

"I'm not afraid," he said. "Not for myself. Nelly, you're a sweet girl."

"A sweet girl. That is so patronizing."

"Maybe it is," he said. "Maybe it is, but you don't…"

"I don't understand? I don't understand what it's like to have a father who wants to hurt you? To have experienced loss? To have experienced fear? Because you know that isn't true."

"You don't know what it's like to feel afraid that you might be cut from the same cloth. Because I look at you and I see sweetness. Softness. And I look at myself and I see nothing but the hard, self-destructive recklessness that could easily be thought of as McCloud. And how do you think Gus feels? Sharing his name? What you went through taught you to be afraid of men. What we went through taught us to be afraid of ourselves."

"You are not your father."

"I know that. But I also don't know that I'm capable of giving you half of anything you deserve."

"So you won't try? You'll give me nothing?"

"I'm giving you the chance at having a life that doesn't include so much baggage." His voice was raw and painful. "I will always remember tonight. I will always remember this. And I'll… I will feel the fact that you loved me, even for a night, for…the rest of my damn life. I swear that to you."

"I don't want that. I don't want to be your tribute to feelings that you don't think you can accept. I want to be more than that. Because I'm more than that. I don't want to be the thing that you look back on with a beautiful, melodic tragedy in your heart, which is what we all know men like to do. Rather than heal. What you want to do is walk on being completely and utterly unknowable, and never having to change. You want to be wistful and sorry. I just want you to live. With everything that you could have. If that isn't me, Tag, then that's fine. If you don't love me, and that's because of me, then there's nothing I can do about that. But if you simply won't take the chance because of your fear... Well, then that is a tragedy."

She rolled out from beneath the furs, her heart feeling bruised.

"It doesn't matter whether you think I'm sad or not. The truth is, I probably am. We probably all are."

"Don't you think you should do something about it? Do something different? What if it were one of your brothers?"

"I'd tell him to do the right thing for the lady involved. That's all."

"And what about yourselves?"

"If people cared less about themselves, there would be fewer men like my father in the world. Fewer men like yours. If people cared more about the people they were with..."

"No," she said. "That's just not real. It isn't. You have to care enough about yourself to want to be better. You have to care enough about yourself to want more. To want everything. Don't discard yourself. That's what men like your father do. They treated people in their lives like garbage, and then you take that forward, don't you? You spend the rest of your life being afraid that they were right. Prove that he isn't. That's what you need to do. Prove that he isn't right. That you are worth something. That you're worth being happy."

But she wasn't going to stay, and she wasn't going to cry. She wasn't going to give him any more fuel to the fire that was propelling him forward now. This idea that he was the villain in the piece. He would like that. If she got upset. If she were hysterical. Because it would suit his narrative. Suit his narrative about how bad he was. How wrong. And she wouldn't allow it. She simply would not. So, with as much dignity as she could muster, and with as little softness as she could find inside of herself, she dressed. And she did not put her hair back in pigtails. Because she wasn't the same person she'd been when she first came. She was stronger. And more wounded all at once. She was tragic but perfectly fine. And she would find a way forward.

Because life was to be lived. And even if she wanted to live it with Tag, she could wait.

She had waited thirty years to lose her virginity. And she had waited thirty years to break through the realization that her antagonism for Tag was something deeper.

She had been waiting for him. Now she had to trust that in all the ways that counted, he had been waiting for her.

# CHAPTER SEVEN

IT REALLY WAS a shame that Tag had a policy against drinking his feelings away. As a matter of caution.

As the son of a raging, horrendous alcoholic, he did his very best to not lose himself in that way. A little bit of drinking when he went out, sure. But, when he was in this dangerous of a mood… No.

So instead, he shut himself up in the cabin, and didn't speak to anybody. Because there was just nothing to say.

So he hid in his cabin, licking his wounds, and he guessed he shouldn't have been super surprised when his brother Gus made the journey up and stood in his doorway looking as mean as he ever did.

Gus was huge and broad, his face horrifically scarred from a childhood accident he never spoke of. Tag barely remembered his brother's face another way, but that didn't make it less jarring sometimes.

Especially when he stood there with the harsh light making the valleys in those scars look deeper, and his whole posture indicated he had murder on his mind.

"So," he said, rocking back on his heels, looking at him in that authoritative way that he had. "What the hell?"

"What?" He stepped aside, because there was no way he was denying Gus entry. He wouldn't allow it.

You didn't go toe-to-toe with Gus McCloud.

"It's nothing."

"It's nothing, except you know I saw Nelly Foster leaving

your place the other morning. Bright and early. And unless she was giving your dumb ass a reading lesson…"

"Not," Tag said.

"Well. Look, Nelly doesn't have a father to come kick your ass, so… I'll do it if I need to." Gus had an overdeveloped sense of protectiveness when it came to…well everyone at Four Corners, but the women most especially.

"Nelly can defend herself."

"Yeah, but I might enjoy kicking your ass."

"She says she loves me," he said, not sure why he was telling his brother that. "Sit in that."

Gus blew out a breath. "Well, you really are a dumbass."

"I'm a dumbass?"

"Yeah."

"Well, Gus, I'd return the insult but it's tough to know if you're a dumbass or not when you basically live like a hermit. You seem smarter by default. But at least I'm living."

That was low. And he knew it. But maybe he wanted a fist to the face.

But Gus didn't punch him. Instead, he leaned back on his heels. "Is that what we're going to do? Just try to be as mean as possible? You gonna call me ugly? Hate to break it to you, but I don't care. But I'm starting to think you want me to punch you in the face, and then you can sit here in your self-loathing, drowning in it to your heart's content? We both know you like that."

"Fuck off, Gus."

"A woman loves you. A good woman. What about you? Do you love her?"

He laughed. "Are we capable of love?"

"Yeah," Gus said, his voice rough. "Deep and painful as a matter of fact."

Tag stared at Gus and tried to read what he meant by that. It wasn't that Gus didn't hook up with women—Tag

THE COWBOY SHE LOVES TO HATE

assumed. All the McCloud men had been gifted with good looks. It was what had made their dad such a dangerous tool. He'd been a handsome son of a bitch. And his sons were, too. Even more so.

Gus's looks had been ruined, and it wasn't just the scars. It had left behind an intensity that was almost too much to be around sometimes.

And the thing was, a lot of women enjoyed that. So while Gus wasn't a go out and party kind of guy, he got play when he wanted it.

But Tag hadn't ever considered his brother...had loved someone.

"The fact of the matter is," Gus continued, "you're being offered the thing that you actually want. We all know that you're obsessed with Nelly Foster. You have been from the moment you first laid eyes on her. You love her. Why the hell are you holding yourself back?"

"Because. Because of..."

"Dad? I handled his ass, Tag. And it wasn't so you could sit in your own bullshit for the rest of your life. Hell, half the town thinks I'm a murderer. And I'll wear it. I don't give a fuck. Because what I did is supposed to mean that we can all move on."

"I'm... I'm..."

"You're what? A mess? So is everybody."

"Yeah but..."

"You're scared. That's what you are. And I get it. There are a whole lot of things in this world that are beyond your control, though. The father that we have. The actions of other people who play games that could destroy everybody. But you don't need to hurt yourself. Not this way. What's the point of it?"

"I've gotta protect her."

"No. You're protecting yourself." Gus practically sneered. "Get over yourself, Tag."

"What? Just like that?" His chest felt bruised. His heart felt damaged. Because everything that Gus was saying was fair. And he hated that.

"She loves you. Figure out the rest."

Then Gus turned and walked out of the cabin, leaving Tag standing there alone.

He had a feeling he had to listen to his brother. But then… But then he was right. He could get hurt. He hadn't loved anyone other than his brothers in a long damn time. He was used to them. He took them for granted. And it was easy. He had wanted his father to love him. He had wanted his mother to love him. And they never had. Not really. Nelly's mother had brought her with her. Protected her. His own mother hadn't done that.

And at the end of the day, it was that… That feeling of not being quite certain if he deserved love that kept him from saying yes. That kept him from saying he loved her too. Because of course he did. Because how could he ever be sure?

*You can't.*

*Life is like that.*

*But you have to love anyway.*

*Or not,* he supposed. But then it would always be this. This cabin, alone. Wanting those pigtails—that woman—he would never let himself have.

And what was the purpose of protecting himself, if the person he was protecting was miserable, alone, even in a crowd of people.

Only Nelly Foster had ever really seen that. Seen him.

She'd asked him to be better.

She hadn't let him be the monster. She hadn't cried or wailed or begged.

She'd asked him to stand up and be a man.

And he was damn well going to do it.

## CHAPTER EIGHT

NELLY WAS JUST closing the library when she saw him. Standing in the parking lot, his cowboy hat drawn down low over his head.

*Tag.*

Her heart slammed against her breastbone, her whole body shaking. She opened the door quickly.

And her breath felt like it was sucked right from her lungs. She intended to say some sort of one-liner, but anything clever or casual was nowhere to be found.

So she just stood there. Staring.

"You're wearing pigtails."

She reached up and touched her hair. "Oh. Yes."

"Why do you do that?"

"I don't know."

"I think you do. I think it's because you know it drives me crazy."

She laughed, but tears filled her eyes. "Does it?"

He walked toward her, walked into the quiet, dark library. She had always felt calm and peaceful surrounded by books, but standing near Tag she didn't feel any of those things.

She felt bright and real and it was all so sharp it hurt.

"I'm sorry," he said. "I'm sorry I put us both through this, but I guess I had to...look at my life without you in it to understand that what I was doing didn't work anymore. It was easy, when I never had you, but once I did... Oh, Nelly, once I did… I can't go back to that. I can't go back to living without you."

And impossibly, against all odds, she felt a smile break out across her face. "I knew it."

"You knew what?"

"I knew you'd come for me."

She launched herself into his arms, and she kissed him. Deep and hard, with all the love inside her.

"I love you," he said.

"I know."

"What is this, now you're too cool to say it?"

"No it's just… I knew you did. I was miserable without you, but I knew you loved me. I knew you loved me and I knew I had to leave you to figure it out. Because you're just that hardheaded."

"This is your declaration of love?" he asked.

"No," she said. "It's yours. I made mine already."

"Well, in that case." He reached back and tugged on one pigtail, then another. "Oh, you have no idea how much I have wanted to do that…forever."

"Why?"

"I don't know," he said, his grin turning mystified and all the more adorable for it. "I just have. Just like how long I've loved you I think. It's just something I feel. Forever. Like part of me."

"Me too, Tag. Always."

Taggart McCloud had come for her. Just like she knew he would. And darned if he wasn't in a cowboy hat.

And the best part of all was it wasn't for a bet, it was just because he loved her.

* * * * *

*Welcome to Lone Rock—Oregon's Wild West—for the first book
in* **New York Times** *bestselling author Maisey Yates's
new series, The Carsons of Lone Rock.*

*No one infuriates Juniper Sohappy more than ranch owner
Chance Carson. But when Juniper finds him injured and amnesiac
on her property, she must help. She lets him believe he's her ranch
hand, and soon unexpected passion flares. But when the truth
comes to light, will everything fall apart?*

*Read on for a sneak peek at*
**Rancher's Forgotten Rival**.

Juniper felt hungry for more, but at the same time she didn't want to press
Chance. For so many reasons, but maybe the biggest one was her heart felt
really tender right now. For him.

That wasn't supposed to happen.

"All right," he said.

He stood up, and she stood at the same time, ready to take his bowl from
him.

"I can take the dishes."

"Oh, no, that's okay," he said, and she put her hand on the bowl, and her
fingertips brushed his, and their eyes locked.

And she felt a frisson of something magical go through her. Something
hot and delicious and sticky, like cayenne honey, flowing all the way through
her veins.

And she could hardly breathe around it. She could hardly think. All she
could do was stare. And feel the thundering rhythm of her heart, like a herd of
wild mustangs, the kind that you could find out here in Eastern Oregon, and
she was sure that he could hear it, too.

And then, gradually, that didn't worry her. Because she could see in the
look on his face that he was…hungry.

Hungry for her.

And she had to wonder if this was new, or if it had been there before.

Just like it was for her.

Maybe they felt the same.

She'd always thought she and Chance Carson felt absolutely different. About everything. But maybe not.

Maybe they felt the same.

Maybe they always had.

She opened her mouth to say something, but then he lowered his head and kissed her.

It was like an electric shock. His mouth was hot and firm, his lips certain and miraculous as they moved against hers.

She clung to him, instinctively, and it wasn't until she heard the bowl clatter to the ground that she realized she had let go of the metal vessel. And she was glad it wasn't glass.

But it was a metaphor. A metaphor for how precarious this was. Because she was forgetting. And she was letting herself get caught up in all the wrong things.

But she couldn't help but be caught up now. In his hold, in the searing kiss, the magical pressure of his mouth on hers. She'd had any number of kisses. But they had just been something to do.

Because when you thought a man was attractive, you might as well kiss him. Because even though she hadn't gone to bed with that many men, she had never found it to be that big of a deal, and if she was in a relationship, she was all right taking it to its natural conclusion.

A kiss had never scalded her like fire, searing her and leaving her feeling empty, a hollowed-out vessel forged by flame.

But his did.

*Don't miss what happens next in...*
Rancher's Forgotten Rival
*by* New York Times *bestselling author Maisey Yates,*
*the first book in her new Carsons of Lone Rock series!*

*Available February 2022 wherever*
*Harlequin Desire books and ebooks are sold.*

Harlequin.com

HDEXPO121MASSMAX